Dear Reader,

Welcome to Whitehorse, Montana. It is so nice for me to be back, since I live in a town so much like Whitehorse that locals think they see themselves in my books.

It's a Western town with lots of cowboys, pickup trucks, one grocery store and no stoplights. But most of us have everything we need here. If we feel adventurous we can drive five hundred miles round-trip to the closest Target store. Except in the winter when the roads are closed.

But I love the wild, open spaces where there are more cows than people and more dirt roads than paved ones. This is cowboy country and always has been. And that's why I set the Whitehorse series here.

Dark Horse, the first book in The McGraw Kidnapping series, introduces the McGraw family—and the tragedy that struck them twenty-five years ago when their two fraternal twins were kidnapped from their cribs and never returned.

Horse rancher Cull McGraw has closed himself off from the world, sick of all the publicity that had befallen his family. So he is furious when his father invites true-crime writer Nikki St. James to do a book on the kidnapping.

Nikki forces everyone to relive that night—especially Cull—exposing long-kept secrets and tearing down the walls Cull has built around himself.

As a bonus, you get *The Mystery Man* ██████████ an older Whitehorse book. I lov█████████████ healthy appetite, so it is n█████████████ and Laci Cavanaugh fall in ██████████ in the kitchen when these t████

I hope you enjoy these White███████████ ks as there are now twenty-seven ██████████ eries—and more to come next year!

B.J. Daniels

B.J. Daniels is a *New York Times* and *USA TODAY* bestselling author. She wrote her first book after a career as an award-winning newspaper journalist and author of thirty-seven published short stories. She lives in Montana with her husband, Parker, and three springer spaniels. When not writing, she quilts, boats and plays tennis. Contact her at bjdaniels.com, on Facebook or on Twitter, @bjdanielsauthor.

DARK HORSE

&

THE MYSTERY MAN OF WHITEHORSE

New York Times and USA TODAY Bestselling Author

B.J. DANIELS

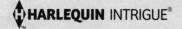

ISBN-13: 978-0-373-83903-2

Dark Horse & The Mystery Man of Whitehorse

Copyright © 2017 by Harlequin Books S.A.

The publisher acknowledges the copyright holder of the individual works as follows:

Dark Horse
Copyright © 2017 by Barbara Heinlein

The Mystery Man of Whitehorse
Copyright © 2007 by Barbara Heinlein

Recycling programs for this product may not exist in your area.

HARLEQUIN®
™ www.Harlequin.com

Printed in U.S.A.

CONTENTS

DARK HORSE

This Whitehorse, Montana book is for Sue Olsen,
who has brightened many a day for me
with her zest for life.
I just wish I had her energy.

CHAPTER ONE

THEIR FOOTFALLS ECHOED among the terrified screams
and woeful sobbing as they moved down the long hallway. The nurse's aide, a young woman named Tess,
stopped at a room in the criminally insane section of
the hospital and, with trembling fingers, pulled out a
key to unlock the door.

"I really shouldn't be doing this," Tess said, looking
around nervously. As the door swung open, she quickly
moved back. Nikki St. James felt a gust of air escape
the room like an exhaled breath. The light within the
interior was dim, but she could hear the sound of a chair
creaking rhythmically.

"I'm going to have to lock the door behind you,"
Tess whispered.

"Not yet." It took a moment for Nikki's eyes to adjust to the dim light within the room. She fought back
the chill that skittered over her skin like spider legs as
her gaze finally lit on the occupant.

"This is the wrong one," Nikki said, and tried to step
back into the hallway.

"That's her," the nurse's aide said, keeping her voice
down. "That's Marianne McGraw."

Nikki stared at the white-haired, slack-faced woman

rocking back and forth, back and forth, her gaze blank as if blind. "That woman is too old. Her hair—"

"Her hair turned white overnight after...well, after what happened. She's been like this ever since." Tess shuddered and hugged herself as if she felt the same chill Nikki did.

"She hasn't spoken in all that time?"

"Not a word. Her husband comes every day to visit her. She never responds."

Nikki was surprised that Travers McGraw would come to visit his former wife at all, given what she was suspected of doing. Maybe, like Nikki, he came hoping for answers. "What about her children?"

"They visit occasionally, the oldest son more than the others, but she doesn't react as if she knows any of them. That's all she does, rock like that for hours on end."

Cull McGraw, the oldest son, Nikki thought. He'd been seven, a few years older than her, at the time of the kidnapping. His brothers Boone and Ledger were probably too young to remember the kidnapping, maybe even too young to really remember their mother.

"If you're going in, you'd best hurry," Tess said, still looking around nervously.

Nikki took a step into the room, hating the thought of the nurse's aide locking the door behind her. As her eyes adjusted more to the lack of light, she saw that the woman had something clutched against her chest. A chill snaked up her spine as she made out two small glassy-eyed faces looking out at her from under matted heads of blond hair.

"What's that she's holding?" she whispered hoarsely as she hurriedly turned to Tess before the woman could close and lock the door.

"Her babies."

"Her *babies*?"

"They're just old dolls. They need to be thrown in the trash. We tried to switch them with new ones, but she had a fit. When we bathe or change her, we have to take them away. She screams and tears at her hair until we give them back. It was the doctor's idea, giving her the dolls. Before that, she was...violent. She had to be sedated or you couldn't get near her. Like I said, you go in there at your own risk. She's...unpredictable and if provoked, dangerous since she's a lot stronger than she looks. If I were you, I'd make it quick."

Nikki reached for her notebook as the door closed behind her. The tumblers in the lock sounded like a cannon going off as Tess locked the door.

At your own risk. Comforting words, Nikki thought as she took a tentative step deeper into the padded room. She'd read everything she could find on the McGraw kidnapping case. There'd been a lot of media coverage at the time—and a lot of speculation. Every anniversary for years, the same information had been repeated along with the same plea for anything about the two missing twins, Oakley Travers McGraw and Jesse Rose McGraw.

But no one had ever come forward. The ransom money had never been recovered nor the babies found. There'd been nothing new to report at the one-year anniversary, then the five, ten, fifteen and twenty year.

Now with the twenty-fifth one coming up, few people other than those around Whitehorse, Montana, would probably even remember the kidnapping.

"There is nothing worse than old news," her grandfather had told her when she'd dropped by his office at the large newspaper where he was publisher. Wendell St. James had been sitting behind his huge desk, his head of thick gray hair as wild as his eyebrows, his wire-rimmed glasses perched precariously on his patrician nose. "You're wasting your time with this one."

Actually he thought she was wasting her time writing true crime books. He'd hoped that she would follow him into the newspaper business instead. It didn't matter that out of the nine books she'd written, she'd solved seven of the crimes.

"*Someone* knows what happened that night," she'd argued.

"Well, if they do, it's a pretty safe bet they aren't going to suddenly talk after twenty-five years."

"Maybe they're getting old and they can't live with what they've done," she'd said. "It wouldn't be the first time."

He'd snorted and settled his steely gaze on her. "I wasn't for the other stories you chased, but this one…" He shook his head. "Don't you think I know what you're up to? I suspect this is your mother's fault. She just couldn't keep her mouth shut, could she?"

"She didn't tell me about my father," she'd corrected her grandfather. "I discovered it on my own." For years, she'd believed she was the daughter of a stranger her mother had fallen for one night. A mistake. "All these years, the two of you have lied to me, letting me believe I was an accident, a one-night stand and that explained why I had my mother's maiden name."

"We protected you, you mean. And now you've got some lamebrained idea of clearing your father's name." Wendell swore under his breath. "My daughter has proven that she is the worst possible judge of men, given her track record. But I thought you were smarter than this."

"There was no real proof my father was involved," Nikki had argued stubbornly. Her biological father had been working at the Sundown Stallion Station the summer of the kidnapping. His name had been linked with Marianne McGraw's, the mother of the twins. "Mother doesn't believe he had an affair with Marianne, nor does she believe he had any part in the kidnapping."

"What do you expect your mother to say?" he'd demanded.

"She knew him better than you."

Her grandfather mugged a disbelieving face. "What else did she tell you about the kidnapping?"

Her mother had actually known little. While Nikki would have demanded answers, her mother said she was just happy to visit with her husband, since he was locked up until his trial.

"She didn't ask him anything about the kidnapping because your mother wouldn't have wanted to hear the truth."

She'd realized then that her grandfather's journalistic instincts had clearly skipped a generation. Nikki would have had to know everything about that night, even if it meant finding out that her husband was involved.

"A jury of twelve found him guilty of not only the affair—but the kidnapping," her grandfather had said.

"On circumstantial evidence."

"On the testimony of the nanny who said that Marianne McGraw wasn't just unstable, she feared she might hurt the twins. The nanny also testified that she saw Marianne with your father numerous times in the barn and they seemed…close."

She'd realized that her grandfather knew more about this case than he'd originally let on. "Yes, the nanny, the woman who is now the new wife of Travers McGraw. That alone is suspicious. I would think you'd encourage me to get the real story of what happened that night. And what does...*close* mean anyway?"

Her grandfather had put down his pen with an impatient sigh. "The case is dead cold after twenty-five years. Dozens of very good reporters, not to mention FBI agents and local law enforcement, did their best to solve it, so what in hell's name makes you think that you can find something that they missed?"

She'd shrugged. "I have my grandfather's stubborn arrogance and the genes of one of the suspects. Why not me?"

He'd wagged his gray head again. "Because you're too personally involved, which means that whatever story you get won't be worth printing."

She'd dug her heels in. "I became a true crime writer because I wanted to know more than what I read in the newspapers."

"Bite your tongue," her grandfather said, only half joking. He sobered then, looking worried. "What if you don't like what you find out about your father, or your mother, for that matter? I know my daughter."

"What does that mean?"

He gave another shake of his gray head. "Clearly your mind is made up and since I can't sanction this..." With an air of dismissal, he picked up his pen again. "If that's all..."

She started toward the door but before she could exit, he called after her, "Watch your back, Punky." It had been his nickname for her since she was a baby. "Remember what I told you about family secrets."

People will kill to keep them, she thought now as she looked at Marianne McGraw.

The woman's rocking didn't change as Nikki stepped deeper into the room. "Mrs. McGraw?" She glanced behind her. The nurse's aide stood just outside the door, glancing at her watch.

Nikki knew she didn't have much time. It hadn't been easy getting in here. It had cost her fifty bucks after she'd found the nurse's aide was quitting soon to get married. She would have paid a lot more since so few people had laid eyes on Marianne McGraw in years.

She reached in her large purse for the camera she'd brought. No reporter had gotten in to see Marianne McGraw. Nikki had seen a photograph of Marianne McGraw taken twenty-five years ago, before her infant fraternal twins, a boy and girl, had been kidnapped. She'd been a beauty at thirty-two, a gorgeous dark-haired woman with huge green eyes and a contagious smile.

That woman held no resemblance to the one in the rocking chair. Marianne was a shell of her former self, appearing closer to eighty than fifty-seven.

"Mrs. McGraw, I'm Nikki St. James. I'm a true crime writer. How are you doing today?"

Nikki was close enough now that she could see nothing but blankness in the woman's green-eyed stare. It was as if Marianne McGraw had gone blind—and deaf, as well. The face beneath the wild mane of white hair was haggard, pale, lifeless. The mouth hung open, the lips cracked and dry.

"I want to ask you about your babies," Nikki said.

"Oakley and Jesse Rose?" Was it her imagination or did the woman clutch the dolls even harder to her thin chest?

"What happened the night they disappeared?" Did Nikki really expect an answer? She could hope, couldn't she? Mostly, she needed to hear the sound of her voice in this claustrophobic room. The rocking had a hypnotic effect, like being pulled down a rabbit hole.

"Everyone outside this room believes you had something to do with it. You and Nate Corwin." No response, no reaction to the name. "Was he your lover?"

She moved closer, catching the decaying scent that rose from the rocking chair as if the woman was already dead. "I don't believe it's true. But I think you might know who kidnapped your babies," she whispered.

The speculation at the time was that the kidnapping had been an inside job. Marianne had been suffering from postpartum depression. The nanny had said that Mrs. McGraw was having trouble bonding with the babies and that she'd been afraid to leave Marianne alone with them.

And, of course, there'd been Marianne's secret lover—the man who everyone believed had helped her kidnap her own children. He'd been implicated because of a shovel found in the stables with his bloody fingerprints on it—along with fresh soil—even though no fresh graves had been found.

"Was Nate Corwin involved, Marianne?" The court had decided that Marianne McGraw couldn't have acted alone. To get both babies out the second-story window, she would have needed an accomplice.

"Did my father help you?"

There was no sign that the woman even heard her,

let alone recognized her alleged lover's name. And if the woman *had* answered, Nikki knew she would have jumped out of her skin.

She checked to make sure Tess wasn't watching as she snapped a photo of the woman in the rocker. The flash lit the room for an instant and made a *snap* sound. As she started to take another, she thought she heard a low growling sound coming from the rocker.

She hurriedly took another photo, though hesitantly, as the growling sound seemed to grow louder. Her eye on the viewfinder, she was still focused on the woman in the rocker when Marianne McGraw seemed to rock forward as if lurching from her chair.

A shriek escaped her before she could pull down the camera. She had closed her eyes and thrown herself back, slamming into the wall. Pain raced up one shoulder. She stifled a scream as she waited for the feel of the woman's clawlike fingers on her throat.

But Marianne McGraw hadn't moved. It had only been a trick of the light. And yet, Nikki noticed something different about the woman.

Marianne was smiling.

CHAPTER TWO

WHEN A HAND touched her shoulder, Nikki jumped, unable to hold back the cry of fright.

"We have to go," Tess said, tugging on her shoulder. "They'll be coming around with meds soon."

Nikki hadn't heard the nurse's aide enter the room. Her gaze had been on Marianne McGraw—until Tess touched her shoulder.

Now she let her gaze go back to the woman. The white-haired patient was hunched in her chair, rocking back and forth, back and forth. The only sound in the room was that of the creaking rocking chair and the pounding of Nikki's pulse in her ears.

Marianne's face was slack again, her mouth open, the smile gone. If it had ever been there.

Nikki tried to swallow the lump in her throat. She'd let her imagination get the best of her, thinking that the woman had risen up from that rocker for a moment.

But she hadn't imagined the growling sound any more than she would forget that smile of amusement. Marianne McGraw was still inside that shriveled-up old white-haired woman.

And if she was right, she thought, looking down at

the camera in her hand, there would be proof in the photos she'd taken.

Tess pulled on her arm. "You have to go. *Now.* And put that camera away!"

Nikki nodded and let Tess leave the room ahead of her. All her instincts told her to get out now. She'd read that psychopaths were surprisingly strong and with only Tess to pull the woman off her...

She studied the white-haired woman in the rocker, trying to decide if Marianne McGraw was the monster everyone believed her to be.

"Did you let Nate Corwin die for a crime he didn't commit?" Nikki whispered. "Is your real accomplice still out there, spending the $250,000 without you? Or are you innocent in all this? As innocent as I believe my father was?"

For just an instant she thought she saw something flicker in Marianne McGraw's green eyes. The chill that climbed up her backbone froze her to her core. "You *know* what happened that night, don't you," Nikki whispered at the woman. In frustration, she realized that if her father and this woman were behind the kidnaping, Marianne might be the *only* person alive who knew the truth.

"Come on!" Tess whispered from the hallway.

Nikki was still staring at the woman in the rocker. "I'm going to find out." She turned to leave. Behind her, she heard the chilling low growling sound emanating from Marianne McGraw. It wasn't until the door was closed and locked behind her that she let out the breath she'd been holding.

TESS MOTIONED FOR Nikki to follow her. The hallway was long and full of shadows this late at night. Their footfalls sounded too loud on the linoleum floor. The air was choked with the smell of disinfectants that didn't quite cover the...other smells.

Someone cried out in a nearby room, making Nikki start. Behind them there were moans broken occasionally by bloodcurdling screams. She almost ran the last few feet to the back door.

Tess turned off the alarm, pushed open the door and, checking to make sure she had her keys, stepped out into the night air with her. They both breathed in the Montana night. Stars glittered in the midnight blue of the big sky overhead. In the distance, she could make out the dark outline of the Little Rockies.

"I told you she wouldn't be any help to your story," Tess said after a moment.

Nikki could tell that the nurse's aide couldn't wait until her last day at this job. She could see how a place like that would wear on you. Though she'd spent little time inside, she still was having trouble shaking it off.

"I still appreciate you letting me see her." She knew the only reason she'd gotten in was because the nurse's aide was getting married, had already given her two weeks' notice and was planning to move to Missoula with her future husband. Nikki had read it in the local newspaper under Engagements. It was why she'd made a point of finding out when Tess worked her last late-night shifts.

Nearby an owl hooted. Tess hugged herself even though the night wasn't that cold. Nikki longed for any sound other than the creak of a rocking chair. She feared she would hear it in her sleep.

"I heard you tell her that you were going to find out

what happened that night," Tess said. "Everyone around here already knows what happened."

Did they? Nikki thought of Marianne McGraw. Her hair had turned white overnight and now she was almost a corpse. The only man who might know whether the rumors were true, Nikki's own father, was dead.

"What does everyone believe happened?" she asked.

"She was having an affair with her horse trainer, so of course that's who she got to help her get rid of the babies," Tess said as she dug in her pocket for a cigarette. "I'm trying to quit. Before the wedding. But some nights…"

Nikki watched her light up and take a long drag. "Wait, why get rid of the babies? She still had three other sons."

"I guess she figured they'd be fine with their father. But babies… Also they needed the money. Easier to kidnap a couple of babies than one of the younger boys who'd make a fuss."

"Still, they didn't have to kill them."

"The horse trainer probably didn't want to be saddled with two babies. Not very romantic running away together with the money—and two squalling babies."

That was the story the prosecution had told that had gotten her father sent to prison. But was it true? "I thought he swore he didn't do it."

She scoffed. "That's what they all say."

Nate Corwin, according to what Nikki had been able to find, had said right up to the end when they were driving him to prison that he didn't do it. Maybe, if the van hadn't overturned and he wasn't killed, then maybe he could have fought his conviction, found proof… Or maybe he'd lied right up until his last breath.

"But I thought it was never proven that he was even Marianne's lover, let alone that he helped her kidnap her own children?" Nikki asked.

The nurse's aide made a disbelieving sound. "Who else was there?"

"I'd heard the nanny might have been involved."

"*Patty?* Well, I wouldn't put it past her."

This caught Nikki's attention. "You know her?"

The nurse's aide pursed her lips as if she shouldn't be talking about this, but fortunately that didn't stop her. Anyway, she'd already broken worse rules today by sneaking Nikki into the hospital.

"She accompanies her husband most of the time. You can tell *Patty* doesn't like him visiting his ex-wife," Tess said. Nikki got the impression that Patricia McGraw also didn't like being called Patty.

"She won't even step into Marianne's room," the nurse's aide was saying between puffs. "Not that I blame her, but instead she stands in the hallway and watches them like a hawk. Imagine being jealous of that poor woman in that room."

"I also heard that Travers McGraw himself might have been involved," Nikki threw out.

Tess shook her head emphatically. "No way. Mr. McGraw is the nicest, kindest man. He would never hurt a fly, let alone his own children." She lowered her voice conspiratorially even though they were alone at the back of the hospital and there was only open country behind them. "He hardly ever leaves the ranch except to come here to see his now ex-wife—that is until recently. I heard he's not feeling well."

Nikki had heard the same thing. Maybe that was

why he'd agreed to let her interview him and his family for the book.

When Nikki had first approached him, she had expected him to turn her down in a letter. The fact that she'd made a name for herself after solving the murders in so many of her books had helped, she was sure.

"You seem to have a talent for finding out the truth," Travers McGraw had said when he'd called her out of the blue. He'd been one of just three people she'd contacted about interviews and a book, but he'd been the one she wanted badly.

That was one reason she'd tried not to sound too eager when she'd talked to him. McGraw hadn't done any interviews other than the local press—not since a reporter had broken into his house and scared his family half to death.

"I work at finding the truth," she'd told him, surprised how nervous she was just to hear his voice.

"And you think you can find out the truth in our... case?"

"I want to." More than he could possibly know. "But I should warn you up front, I need access to everyone involved. It would require me basically moving in for a while. Are you sure you're agreeable to that?"

She'd held her breath. Long ago she'd found that making demands made her come off as more professional. It also shifted the power structure. She wasn't begging to do their story. She was doing them a favor.

The long silence on the other end of the line had made her close her eyes, tightening her hand around the phone. She had wanted this so badly. Probably too badly. Maybe she should have—

"When are you thinking of coming here?" Travers McGraw asked.

Her heart had been beating so hard she could barely speak. "I'm finishing up a project now."

"You do realize it's been twenty-five years?"

Not quite. She'd still had two weeks before the actual date that the two babies had been stolen out of the nursery and never seen again. She wanted to be in the house on anniversary night.

"I can be there in a week." She'd crossed her fingers even though she'd never been superstitious.

"I'll take care of everything. Will you be flying to Billings? I can have one of my sons—"

"That won't be necessary. I'll be driving." Though she was anxious to meet his sons. But the only other way, besides driving to Whitehorse, was to take the train that came right through town.

"I hope you can work your magic for us," McGraw said. "If there is anything I can do to help…"

"We'll talk when I get there. It would be best if no one knew I was coming. I'm sure in a small town like Whitehorse, word will get out soon enough."

"Yes, of course."

She'd left a few days before she'd told him she would be arriving. She'd wanted to see Marianne McGraw and get a feel for Whitehorse before she went out to the ranch. Once word got out about her, she would lose her anonymity.

Tess put out her cigarette in the dirt.

"If Travers McGraw is so devoted to the mother of his children, then why did he marry the nanny not long after his divorce?" Nikki asked, hoping to get more out of Tess before she went back inside.

"It was *nine* years after the kidnapping. I heard Patty showed up with a baby in her arms and a sob story. He's a nice man so I guess he was taken in by it." Tess definitely didn't like Patricia McGraw.

"A baby? *Was it his?*"

Again Tess shook her head stubbornly. "He adored his wife Marianne. He still does. Who knows whose baby Patty brought back with her."

"So what are the chances that nanny Patty had something to do with the kidnapping?"

Tess raised an eyebrow as she looked anxiously toward the back door of the hospital. "She got the husband, didn't she? Everyone says she married him for his money since there's a pretty big difference in their ages and she wouldn't have wanted Marianne's babies to raise. She has her hands full with her own child. Talk about a spoiled brat."

Nikki wondered what had brought the nanny back to the ranch after almost ten years. What if Patty Owens knew something about the kidnapping and Travers McGraw had married her to keep her quiet? But then why wait all those years?

"It certainly does make you wonder, huh," Tess said as she reached for the hospital keys. But she hesitated before she opened the door. "Something horrible had to have happened that night to turn her hair white. Something so horrible she can't speak."

"Something other than having her babies kidnapped?" Nikki asked.

Tess shuddered. "I try not to think about it. But if she was in love with the horse trainer..." She leaned toward Nikki and said conspiratorially, "What if she killed the babies before she dropped them out the window?"

Nikki felt a chill race through her. That was something she'd never considered. From what she'd read about the case, it was believed that someone—Marianne, according to the prosecutor—had given the babies cough syrup containing codeine so they would be quiet. Maybe she'd given them too much.

Her head ached. She'd thought of little else but this case since she'd stumbled across the old newspaper clippings in her mother's trunk and learned about her father, Nate Corwin—and the McGraw kidnapping.

At first she hadn't understood why her mother would have kept the stories. That was until she recognized the man in the photograph. The photo of him had been taken on the day Nate Corwin was convicted.

"I always wondered why if you loved my father, you didn't keep the Corwin name since you were legally married, right?" she'd asked her mother, and had seen horror cross her features.

"Why would you ask—" Her mother had never remarried but had gone back to her maiden name, St. James.

"You told me my father died."

"He *did* die."

"You just failed to mention he died on the way to prison for kidnapping and murder."

"He didn't do it. He swore he didn't do it," her mother had cried. She was convinced that her husband hadn't been involved with Marianne McGraw nor had anything to do with the kidnapping, let alone the double murder of two innocent babies.

But *someone* had. And if not her father, then someone had let him be convicted and die for a crime he hadn't committed.

Nikki was determined to get to the truth no matter what it took. She had just short of a week before the twenty-fifth anniversary of the kidnapping to get the real story. Travers desperately wanted her to do the book. It was the family she was worried about.

She'd been thinking about how to get close to at least one of the sons before she headed for Sundown Stallion Station and met the rest of the McGraws.

If there was one thing she believed it was that the people in that house had more information than they'd given the sheriff twenty-five years ago. They just might not realize the importance of what they'd seen or heard. Or they had their reasons for keeping it to themselves.

"So how did you get into writing crime books?" the nurse's aide asked as if putting off going back down that long hallway by herself.

"It's in my blood," Nikki said. "My grandfather was a Pulitzer Prize–winning newspaper reporter. From as far back as I can remember, I wanted to be just like him."

"He must be proud of you," Tess said almost wistfully.

Nikki nodded distractedly. Proving herself to her grandfather was another reason she would do whatever it took to get the real kidnapping story—or die trying.

CHAPTER THREE

Cull McGraw put down the windows on his pickup as he drove into Whitehorse. It was one of the big sky days where the deep blue ran from horizon to horizon without a cloud. In the distance, snow still capped the top of the Little Rockies, and everywhere he looked he saw spring as the land began to turn green.

Days like this, Cull felt like he could breathe. Part of it was getting out of the house. He just felt lucky that he'd intercepted the newspaper before Frieda, the family cook, had delivered it on the way to the kitchen.

He didn't need a calendar to know what time of the year it was. He had seen the approaching anniversary of the kidnapping in the pained look in his father's eyes. He could feel it take over the main house as if draping it in a black funeral shroud.

Every year, he just rode it out. The day would pass. Nothing would happen. No one would come forward with information about the missing twins. Another year would pass. Another year of watching his father get his hopes up only to be crushed under the weight of disappointment.

What always made it worse was the age-progression photographs in the newspaper of what Oakley and Jesse

Rose would look like now and his father's plea for any information on them.

Ahead, he could see the outskirts of the small Western town. Cull sighed. He should have known there would be a big write-up in the paper, since this would be the twenty-fifth anniversary. He glanced over at the newspaper lying on the seat next to him. He'd read just enough to set him off. When would his father realize that the twins were gone and would never be coming back? Knowing Travers McGraw the way he did, Cull knew his father would hold out hope until his last dying breath.

But this year, the publisher of the paper had talked his younger brother Ledger into an interview. As he drove down the main drag, he spotted Ledger's pickup right where he knew it would be—in front of the Whitehorse Café.

Just as Nikki had done for the past few days, she watched Ledger McGraw enter the Whitehorse Café. He had arrived at the same time each morning, pulled up out front in a Sundown Stallion Station pickup and adjusted his Stetson before climbing out.

Across the street in the park, Nikki observed him from behind the latest weekly newspaper as he hesitated just inside the café door. She saw him looking around, and after watching him for three mornings, she knew exactly what he was looking for. *Who* he was looking for.

He tipped his hat to the young redheaded waitress, just as he had the past three mornings, before he took a seat at a booth in her section. He had been three when the twins were kidnapped, which now made him about twenty-eight. There was an innocence about him and an old-fashioned chivalrous politeness. She'd seen it in the way he wiped his boots on the mat just outside the café door. In the way he always removed his hat the moment he stepped in. In the way he waited to be offered a seat as if he had all day.

She'd keyed in on Ledger when she'd realized that no one else in the McGraw family had such a predictable routine. That wasn't the only reason she'd chosen him. In the days she'd been in town watching him each morning, she had seen his trusting nature and hoped he would be the son she might get to help her.

Nikki didn't kid herself that this was going to be easy. She'd heard from other journalists that the family hated reporters and all of them except Travers had refused to talk about the kidnapping. She desperately needed someone on that ranch who would be agreeable to help her. Ledger might be the one.

Nikki wished she had more time before making her move. But the clock was ticking. The twenty-fifth anniversary of the kidnapping was approaching rapidly. It still gave her a chill when she looked at the photographs she'd taken of Marianne McGraw. It hadn't been her imagination. The woman had risen up from her chair, eyes wild, hands clenched around the "babies" in her arms.

If Nikki had had any doubt that the woman was still in that shell of a body, she no longer did. Now she had to find out if the rumors were true about Marianne and Nate Corwin.

From across the street, she watched Ledger take a seat in his usual booth. A moment later, the redhead put a cup of coffee, a menu and the folded edition of what Nikki assumed was the *Milk River Courier* on his table.

The local weekly had just come out this morning. Ledger had been interviewed, which surprised her, since it was the first time she knew of that he'd spoken to the press, but it also made her even more convinced that Ledger was her way into the family.

Inside the café, she watched Ledger looking bashful as he picked up the menu, but he didn't look at it. Instead, he secretly watched the redheaded waitress as she walked away.

Nikki saw something in his expression that touched her heart. A vulnerability that made her turn away for a moment. There was a yearning that was all too evident to anyone watching.

But no one else *was* watching. Clearly this young man was besotted with this redhead. Today, though, Nikki noticed something she'd missed the days before.

As she watched the waitress return to the table to take his order, she saw *why* she'd missed it. Along with the obvious sexual tension between them, there was the glint of a gold band on the young woman's left-hand ring finger.

Her heart ached all the more for Ledger because this was clearly a case of unrequited love. Add to that an obvious shared history and Nikki knew she was witnessing heartbreak at its rawest. The redhead had moved on, but Ledger apparently hadn't.

High school sweethearts? But if so, what had torn them apart? she wondered, then quickly brushed her curiosity aside. Her grandfather had often warned her about getting emotionally involved with the people she wrote about.

She knew in this case, she had to be especially careful.

"Care, and you lose your objectivity," he'd said when, as a girl, she'd asked how he could write about the pain and suffering of people the way he did. "The best stories are about another person's pain. It's the nature of the business because people who've lost something make good human-interest stories. Everyone can relate because we have all lost something dear to us."

"What have *you* lost?" she'd asked her grandfather, since she'd never seen vulnerability in him ever.

"Nothing."

She'd always assumed that was true. Nothing stopped her grandfather from getting what he wanted. He'd go to any extreme to get a story and later to run the newspaper he bought, even if it meant risking his life or his business. But then again, that was one of the reasons Nikki suspected her grandmother had left him to marry another man. Not that her grandfather had seemed to notice. Or maybe he hid his pain well.

Ledger McGraw was in pain and it couldn't help but touch her heart. Nikki knew her grandfather would encourage her to use this new information to her advantage.

"Keep your eye on the goal," he'd always said. "The goal is getting the best story you possibly can. You aren't there to try to make things better or bond with these people."

That had sounded cold to her.

"It's all about emotional distance. Pretend you're a fly on the wall," he'd said. "A fly that sometimes has to buzz around and get things going if you hope to get anything worth writing about."

Nikki now felt anxious. She had to make her move

today. Ledger would be finishing his breakfast soon. She couldn't put this off any longer. Just as she decided it was time, she saw Ledger grab the redhead's wrist as she started to step past his table.

Nikki saw those too shallowly buried emotions arc between them as the waitress reacted to whatever he was saying to her. The waitress jerked free of his hold and looked as if she might cry. But Nikki's gaze was on Ledger's face. His pain was so naked that she couldn't help feeling it at heart level.

Ledger McGraw was incredibly young, his protectiveness for this woman touching. *He's still a boy*, Nikki thought, and felt guilty for what she was about to do.

LEDGER IMMEDIATELY REGRETTED grabbing Abby's wrist. Without looking at her, he said, "He's hurt you again."

"Don't, Ledger."

As she jerked free of his hold, he raised his gaze to meet hers again. "Abby." The word came out a plea. "Any man who would hurt you—"

"Stay out of it, please," she whispered, tears in her eyes. *"Please."* Her lowered voice cracked with emotion. "You don't understand."

He shook his head. He understood only too well. "A man who hurts you doesn't love you."

Her throat worked as she hastily brushed at her tears. "You don't know anything about it," she snapped before rushing toward the kitchen and away from him. "He just grabbed my wrist too hard. It's nothing."

He swore under his breath, realizing he didn't know anything about it. He'd never understood what she saw in Wade Pierce. He especially didn't understand why Abby stayed with the man.

Ledger finished what he could eat of his breakfast. Digging out the cost of his meal and tip from his jeans' pocket, he dropped the money on the table, grabbed his hat and left.

Once outside, he stopped in the bright sunlight as he tried to control the emotions roiling inside him. It wasn't the first time he'd seen the bruises, even though Abby had done her best to hide them. The bastard was mistreating her—he was sure of it.

He wanted to kill Wade with his bare hands. It was all he could do not to drive over to the feedlot and call the man out. But he knew that the only thing that would accomplish was more pain for Abby.

When was she going to see Wade for what he really was—a bully and a blowhard and... With a curse, he realized that Abby might never come to her senses. She was convinced he couldn't live without her.

"Ledger?"

He turned at the sound of a woman's voice.

Marta, the other waitress and a friend of Abby's, held out the newspaper to him. "You forgot this," she said, sympathy in her expression.

That was the trouble with a small town. Everyone knew your business, including watching your heart break. He hadn't looked at the newspaper, wasn't sure he wanted to. He hadn't been thinking when the publisher had cornered him.

He took the paper from Marta and mumbled, "Thanks," before the door closed. Gripping the newsprint, he turned toward his ranch pickup. He felt light-headed with fury and frustration and that constant ache in his heart. Not to mention he was worried about what would happen when the rest of the family saw the story in the paper.

And yet, all he could think about was driving over to the feedlot and dragging Wade out and kicking his butt all the way from Whitehorse to the North Dakota border.

But even as he thought it, he knew he was to blame for this. He'd let Abby get away. He'd practically propelled her into Wade's arms. He hadn't been ready for marriage. As much as he loved her, he'd wanted to wait until he had the money for a place of his own. He couldn't bring Abby into the house at Sundown Stallion Station. He could barely stand living on the ranch himself. He'd told himself he couldn't do that to her. Then Wade had come along, seeming to offer everything Ledger couldn't.

Head down, he was almost to his pickup when he heard someone call his name.

THE COWBOY WHO got out of the second Sundown Stallion Station pickup made Nikki catch her breath. She'd seen photos of Cull McGraw, usually candid paparazzi shots over the years, but none of them captured the raw power of the man in person.

From his broad shoulders to the long denim-clad legs now striding toward his brother, he looked like a man to be reckoned with. The one thing he had in common with all the photos she'd ever seen of him was the scowl.

"Ledger!" Cull looked like he wanted to tear up the pavement as he closed in on his brother. "Have you seen this?" he demanded, waving what appeared to be a newspaper clutched in his big fist.

Ledger stared at him as if confused, as if he was still

thinking of the waitress back in the café. Clearly, he hadn't bothered to look at the newspaper he was now gripping in his own hand.

"Why in the hell did you talk to the press? Not to mention, why you didn't tell me that Dad had raised the reward. *Again!*" Cull slapped the paper against his muscular thigh. "Patricia is going to lose her mind over this. All hell is going to break loose."

"We probably shouldn't talk about this out here," she heard Ledger say. "Enough of our lives is open to public consumption, don't you think?"

Cull swore and looked toward the café. Two waitresses stood looking out the large plate-glass window along with several patrons.

"Fine. We'll take this up at home," Cull said through gritted teeth as he turned on his boot heel and headed back toward his pickup.

With an expression of resignation, Ledger turned toward the café window. The redheaded waitress was no longer at the window. He stood for a moment, looking as if he had the weight of the world on his shoulders before he headed for his truck and climbed behind the wheel. The engine revved and he roared past, sending up dust from Whitehorse's main street.

Nikki shifted her gaze to Cull, realizing her plan had just taken a turn she hadn't expected. She hesitated, no longer sure.

Cull had reached his truck, but hadn't gotten in. He was watching Ledger leave, still looking angry.

If Cull was this upset about the article in the newspaper and new reward, wait until he found out that she would be doing a book about the family and the kidnapping case.

She almost changed her mind about the truly dangerous part of her plan. Almost.

JERKING THE DOOR of his pickup open, Cull climbed in, angry with himself for coming here this morning to confront his brother. He should have waited, but he'd been so angry with his brother... He knew Ledger hadn't meant any harm.

Tossing the newspaper on the pickup seat, he reached for the key in the ignition. Like most people in Whitehorse, he'd left his keys in his rig while he'd confronted his brother. Had it been winter instead of a warm spring day, he would have left the truck running so it would be warm when he came back.

The newspaper fell open to the front-page story. A bold two-deck headline ran across the top of the page. Twenty-Five Years After Kidnapping: Where Are the McGraw Twins?

The damned anniversary of the kidnapping was something he dreaded, he thought with a shake of his head. Like clockwork, the paper did a story, longer ones on some years like this one. He hadn't seen anything but the first few quotes, one from his brother Ledger and the other from their father, when he'd grabbed up the paper and headed for his truck.

It was just like the publisher to talk to Ledger. His brother was too nice, too polite. If the publisher had approached *him*, the man would have gotten one hell of a quote. Instead, Ledger had said that the loss of the twins was "killing" his father after twenty-five years of torture.

How could their father still be convinced that Oakley and Jesse Rose were alive? Travers McGraw had this crazy fantasy that the twins had been sold to a couple who, not realizing the babies were stolen, had raised them as their own.

Cull and his brothers had tried to reason with him. "How could this couple not have heard about the kidnapping? It was in all the newspapers across the country—not to mention on the television news nationally."

His father had no answer, just that he knew the twins were alive and that they would be coming home one day soon.

He knew his father had to believe that. The alternative—that his wife and her alleged lover had kidnapped and killed the twins for money—was too horrible to contemplate.

Under the newspaper fold were the photographs of the babies that his father had provided. Both had the McGraw dark hair, the big blue eyes like their other siblings. Both looked angelic with their bow-shaped mouths and chubby cheeks. They looked like the kind of babies that a person would kill for.

When he'd seen that this year his father was doubling the reward for information, Cull had lost it.

With a curse, he could well imagine what his stepmother was going to say about this. Worse, a reward that size would bring every crank and con man out of the woodwork—just as it had over the years. What had his father been thinking? He was desperate, Cull realized, and the thought scared him.

His father had been sick and didn't seem to be getting any better. Was this a last-ditch effort to find the twins because he was dying? Cull felt rattled as the idea sunk in. Was their father keeping the truth from them?

Accompanying the story were also photos of Oakley and Jesse Rose digitally age-progressed to show what the twins could look like now. Cull shuddered. How could his father bear to look at these? It was heartbreaking to see what they would have looked like had they lived.

The rest of the story was just a rehash of the kidnapping that summer night twenty-five years ago. What wasn't in the story was that Travers McGraw had sold his most prized quarter horse to raise the ransom demand, and that even after horse trainer Nate Corwin's arrest, the $250,000 ransom had never been recovered.

Nor was there anything about what Travers and Marianne had lost. Not to mention the children left behind. Their mother was in a mental institution and their father had fallen into a debilitating grief and held on to a crazy hope that might be killing him.

Cull wadded up the newspaper and threw it onto the passenger-side floorboard. Had he really thought he could keep this from his family? It was only a matter of time before everyone back at the ranch saw this. His stepmother, Patricia, had long ago tired of this yearly search for the twins. This latest story would set her off royally.

The local weekly paper was only the beginning, he thought with a curse. With the twenty-fifth anniversary of the kidnapping mere days away, other papers would pick up the story and run it, including television news shows.

A part of him wanted to leave town until things died back down again. But as upset as he was with his father, he knew he couldn't run away. His father needed his sons, maybe now more than ever before. Because he might be sicker than they thought. Because once the story was out about the huge reward...

He backed out of his space, wanting to get home and put out as many fires as he could. He'd just thrown the pickup into first gear and gone only a few feet when a young woman stepped off the curb right in front of his truck.

Cull stomped on the brakes, but too late. He heard the truck make contact and saw her fall, disappearing from view before he could leap out, his heart in his throat, to find her sprawled on the pavement.

CHAPTER FOUR

CULL KNELT BESIDE the dark-haired woman on the pavement, terrified that he might have killed her. He heard people come running out of the café. Someone was calling 9-1-1 as he touched the young woman's shoulder. She didn't stir.

"Is she alive?" someone cried from in front of the café. "The 9-1-1 operator needs to know if she's breathing and how badly she's injured."

Cull took the young woman's slim wrist and felt for a pulse. But his own heart was pounding so hard, he couldn't tell if she had one. He leaned closer to put his cheek against her full lips and prayed.

With a relief that left him weak, he felt her warm breath against his skin. As he drew back, her eyes opened. They were big and a startling blue as bright as the Montana day. A collective sigh of relief moved through the crowd as the woman tried to sit up.

"Don't move," Cull ordered. "An ambulance is on the way."

She shook her head. "An ambulance?" She seemed to see the people around her. "What happened?"

"You stepped out into the street," he said. "I didn't see you until it was too late."

"Please let me up. I'm fine."

"But I hit you with my truck."

She sat up, insistent that she was fine. "Just help me to my feet." She glanced around on the ground next to her. "Where is my purse?"

Just then Sheriff McCall Crawford pushed her way through the crowd. "What happened?" she asked as she knelt beside the woman.

"She stepped into the street," Cull said. "I hit my brakes but—" He'd had so much on his mind. He hadn't even seen her until she'd stepped off the curb.

"I told you," the woman said. "You didn't *hit* me. You might have bumped into me and then… I must have fainted." She looked around her. "If you would just hand me my purse…"

The sheriff glanced around as well, spied her large shoulder bag and handed it to her. "Are you sure you're all right, Miss…?"

"St. James. Nikki St. James."

"Still I'd like the EMTs to have a look at you," the sheriff insisted.

"That really isn't necessary. I feel so silly. If I had been paying attention…"

"No," Cull said. "I was the one not paying attention."

The ambulance arrived and two EMTs jumped out. Cull stepped back to let them get to the woman. Nikki St. James. He frowned. He'd seen that name somewhere recently.

The sheriff pulled him aside. "I'm going to have to write up a report on this. I suggest you call your insurance agent."

"She said she was fine."

"It doesn't appear that you actually *hit* her," the sheriff said. "More than likely she just stepped off the curb and fainted when she realized she'd stepped in front of your truck. But as a precaution, let your insurance office know. They might want you to get her to sign something."

In front of his pickup, the EMTs were helping the woman to her feet. Cull heard her say she needed to go to her rental car. She was late for an appointment.

"I'm not sure you should be driving," one of the EMTs said.

"I can take you wherever you need to go," Cull said, stepping forward. "I agree. You shouldn't drive."

Tears welled in her eyes. "Actually, I would appreciate that," she said. "I'm not familiar with this area. As shaken as I am, I would probably get lost."

"Where are you headed?"

"A ranch outside of town. The Sundown Stallion Station—are you familiar with it?"

Cull stared at her, feeling all the blood drain from his face. He remembered now where he'd seen her name before. On a scratch pad on his father's desk.

SHERIFF MCCALL CRAWFORD watched Cull help the woman into the passenger side of his pickup. He looked more shaken than Nikki St. James did.

She tried to still the bad feeling that had settled in her stomach as she watched Cull slip behind the wheel. She'd seen his face when the woman had told him where she'd been headed—to his ranch.

McCall could no more help her suspicious nature than she could flap her arms and fly. She'd heard about scams involving people who appeared to have been hit by vehicles. It usually involved a payoff of some kind.

As she watched Cull start his truck and pull away, she couldn't help wondering who Nikki St. James was and, more to the point, what she was after. Did she really have an appointment at the ranch? Or was she a reporter trying to get a foot in the door?

Travers McGraw had been forced to get a locked gate for the ranch entrance because of the publicity about the kidnapping. With the twenty-fifth anniversary coming up next week, McCall worried that Cull had just been scammed.

She looked toward the café, suspecting someone in there had witnessed the accident. Wouldn't hurt to ask and still that tiny voice inside her that told her there was something wrong about this. Also she could use a cup of coffee.

As Cull drove past, she saw him glance at the woman in the passenger seat of his pickup. He looked worried. McCall thought he should be.

Nikki St. James was looking out the side window as they passed. She seemed to be interested in someone inside the café.

McCall turned to see redheaded waitress Abby Pierce standing in the window.

NIKKI TRIED TO RELAX, but she could feel Cull's gaze on her periodically as he drove. That had been more than risky back there. He could very well have killed her.

Her original plan was for Ledger. She'd seen how kindhearted he was. It was one thing to have Travers on her side, but she needed at least one family member she could count on. She'd hoped her stunt would make him more amenable to helping her once he knew who she was.

With Cull, she wasn't sure. At first, he'd been so scared that he would have done anything for her. But then she'd seen his shock when she'd told him where her appointment was.

As he drove south, she said, "Thank you for doing this. I hate to have you going out of your way for me."

"It's not out of my way. Your appointment is with Travers McGraw?"

"Yes."

His gaze was like a laser. "He's my father. I'm Cull McGraw, his oldest son."

She'd feigned surprise. "I knew Whitehorse was a small town, but…"

Nikki saw suspicion in his eyes as they met hers. He would have been a fool not to be suspicious and Cull was no fool. She could see that right away.

She recalled the change in him she'd seen after she'd mentioned her name—and where her appointment was. Had the sheriff said something to him to make him question the accident?

He'd said little since they'd left the small Western town behind them. This part of Montana was rolling prairie where thousands of bison had once ranged. In the distance she could make out the Little Rockies, the only mountains on the horizon.

Wild country, she thought, watching the cowboy out of the corner of her eye. It took a special breed to live in a place where the temperature could change in a heartbeat from fifty above to fifty below zero.

Nikki tried to relax but it was hard. There was an all-male aura about Cull that seemed to fill the pickup cab. She would have had to be in a coma not to be aware of the handsome cowboy, even with his scowling. Did he suspect that what happened back there had been a stunt? She should have stayed with her original plan and waited for Ledger.

Too late to worry about that now. With relief, she saw the sign for the turnoff ahead. Her pulse jumped when she saw the Sundown Stallion Station horse ranch come into view. It reminded her of every horse movie she'd ever seen as a girl. Miles of brilliant green grass fenced in by sparkling white-painted wooden fence that made the place look as if it should be in Kentucky—not the backwoods of Montana.

Cull McGraw hit the remote control on the massive white gate that she knew had been erected not long after the kidnapping to keep out the media and morbidly curious. People not so unlike herself.

The gate swung open without a sound, and after he drove the truck through, it closed behind them.

She was really doing this. Her grandfather had taught her that nothing was out of line to get a story. She would get this one. Her head ached and she was regretting her stunt back in town. It almost got her killed and it hadn't worked. Cull seemed even more distrusting of her.

Out of the corner of her eye, she saw him glance over at her. "How are you feeling?" he asked.

Nervous, scared, excited, terrified. "I have a little headache," she said. She'd hit the pavement harder than she'd planned.

He looked worried and guilty. She felt a sharp stab of her own guilt. But she quickly brushed it away. She had to know the truth about her father. Even as she thought it, a lump formed in her throat.

What if her grandfather was right and she couldn't handle the truth?

This case was definitely more than just a book for her; she could admit that now. She'd come here to prove that Nate Corwin had been innocent.

"Nate Corwin was a philanderer," her grandfather told her the day before she'd left for Whitehorse, Montana. "Of course, he was having an affair with Marianne McGraw. He loved women with money. It's why he married your mother."

"I don't believe that."

"Too bad you can't ask your mother, but she's off on some shopping spree in Paris, I hear. But then again, she'd just defend him like she always did," Wendell St. James had said. "Don't come crying to me when you find out the worst."

"I've never come crying to you," she'd pointed out.

"Smart girl," he'd said.

When she'd first confronted her mother about what she'd found out, Georgia had told her that her father had never liked Nate.

"It was because Nate was his own man," her mother had told her. "Daddy tried to hire him right after we got married. But your father flat out refused. 'I'm a horse trainer, not some flunky who sits behind a desk, especially a newspaper one.'" She'd chuckled. "You can imagine how that went over."

Nikki could. "So there is no truth in the newspaper accounts that he was cheating on you?"

Her mother had smiled. "Your father loved me and adored you. He couldn't wait to finish his work at the ranch and get back to us."

"Why would he leave us if that were true?" she'd asked.

"Because his true love was his work and horses. Yes,

he was away a lot because of his job, but he wouldn't have cheated," her mother had said simply.

Cheated? Or done much worse?

"I'll get you some aspirin when we reach the house," Cull said now as he drove along the tree-lined drive. "If you feel too ill, I'm sure you could get your appointment changed to another day."

She shook her head. "Aspirin would be greatly appreciated. I really can't put this off."

The sun flickered through the dark green of the leaves. Ahead, the big white two-story house loomed.

Nikki looked over at him, torn between apprehension and excitement. She was finally going to get into the McGraw house. "I'm a little anxious about my appointment."

"Yes, your appointment."

She didn't like the way he said it and decided to hit him with the worst of it and get it over with. "I'm nervous about meeting your father. I'd thought maybe he would have told you. I'm a true crime writer. I'm going to write a book on the kidnapping."

Cull swore as he brought the pickup to a dust-boiling stop in front of the house. He seemed at a loss for words as he stared at her and she stared right back as if unable to understand the problem. A muscle jumped in his jaw, his hands gripping the steering wheel so tightly she thought it might snap. Those blue eyes had turned to ice and peered out just as cold and hard.

Fortunately, they were both saved. The front door of the house opened; a woman appeared. Nikki knew at once that she was the notorious Patricia "Patty" Owens McGraw.

She'd been able to learn little about Patricia Owens,

the nanny, or Patty Owens McGraw, the second Mrs. McGraw, other than the fact that she was from a neighboring town and had gotten Ted to divorce Marianne so he could marry her sixteen years ago.

The only photo she'd seen of Patty the nanny had been a blurry black and white that had run in the newspaper at the time of the kidnapping. It showed a teenager with straight brown hair, thick glasses and a timid look in her pale eyes.

That's why Nikki was surprised to see the woman who came out to the edge of the porch. Patty was now winter-wheat blonde, sans the ugly eyeglasses, and any sign of timidity was long gone. She wore a large rock on her ring finger and several nice-sized diamonds on each earlobe—all catching the sunlight and glittering wildly. The dress she wore looked straight from some swank New York City boutique, as did her high heels and the rest of her tasteful adornments.

Patty had been nineteen the summer when she'd gone to work as a nanny at the ranch, which would make her about forty-four now. Her husband, Travers McGraw, was sixty.

Frowning, Patricia spun on one high heel and marched back into the house, leaving the front door standing open. She didn't look happy to see that Cull had a woman with him. Had Travers told his wife about Nikki?

She stared at the rambling, infamous house she'd only seen in grainy newspaper photographs—and always from a distance. Was she really going to pull this off? Her heart was a low thunder in her chest as she opened her door and stepped out of the pickup.

She tried to wrangle in her fears. The clock was ticking. She'd done this all before. Once she showed up, anyone with a secret started getting nervous. It usually didn't take long before the mystery began to unravel.

Nikki had only days to discover the truth before the anniversary, which was usually plenty of time to make progress on a book. But from the look on Patricia's face before she'd disappeared back inside the house, and Cull's cursing inside his pickup, it was going to be an uphill battle.

CULL KNEW HE'D acted impulsively. He should have listened to Sheriff Crawford. Instead he'd offered the woman a ride only to realize she was going to the same place he was—and for a reason he would never have imagined.

"True crime writer?" he repeated as he climbed out of the pickup after her. Had his father lost his mind?

He'd looked up to see his stepmother appear in the open doorway looking like she'd sucked on a lemon before she'd gone back inside in a snit. Did she already know about this? If not, when she found out, she would go ballistic. He felt the same way himself.

Cull wanted to storm into the house and demand to know what the hell his father had been thinking. Not that it would do any good, he thought, remembering the newspaper story.

He saw Nikki St. James rub her temple where she'd hit the pavement. Even if she'd stepped in front of his pickup on purpose, he grimaced at the thought that he could have killed her. He reminded himself that he'd promised her aspirin, while a part of him wished he'd almost hit the gas harder back in town.

Mostly, he was just anxious to see his father. The

only one more anxious, he noticed, was Nikki St. James. His father had no idea what he'd done.

Raised voices came from the house. Had Patricia seen the newspaper article and the increased reward her husband was offering? If so, she was already on the warpath. Even after twenty-five years, there was too much curiosity about their family. So much so that they seldom had guests out to the house. They'd isolated themselves from the world and now his father had invited the worst kind of reporter into their home.

What did his father even know about this Nikki St. James? Had he checked out her credentials? One thing was obvious, Cull thought as he walked with her toward the house. All Hades was about to be unleashed.

He hesitated at the porch steps, noticing something he hadn't before. Clearly this woman wasn't from around here, given the way she was dressed—in slacks, a white blouse, pale coral tank and high heels—and the faint accent he hadn't been able to place. It definitely wasn't Montanan.

"Hold up," Cull said to her backside as she continued up the steps.

She stopped midway but didn't turn until he joined her. She looked pale and for a moment he worried that she was more hurt that she'd let on. She touched her temple. He could see that it was red, a bruise forming, and his heart ached at the sight. No matter who she was or what she was doing here, he hadn't meant to hurt her. If only he'd been paying attention…

"Maybe you should sit down for a minute," he suggested.

"I'm fine. Really."

She didn't look fine and he felt guilty in spite of how

he felt about her being here. He actually felt sorry for her. She had no idea what she was getting into.

"Look, I'm not sure whose idea this was, but it was a bad one. What you're about to walk into... My family—"

He didn't get the chance to warn her further, let alone try to talk her out of this before it was too late. His stepsister, Kitten, stormed out of the house and across the wide porch to block their path. Kitten was sixteen and at the age that she thought everything was about her. He could see from the scowl on her face that she'd been arguing with her mother—as usual.

"My mother is impossible," the teen said around a wad of gum. She was dressed in a crop top and a very short skirt and strappy sandals, as if headed for town, a big expensive leather purse slung over one shoulder. "Can I borrow your truck?"

"No, Kitten," he said, and started to push past her.

"One of these days you'll regret being so mean to me," the girl said, then seemed to see Nikki. "Who's this?" she demanded, narrowing her eyes suspiciously as she took in the woman next to him. "You finally get a girlfriend, Cull?"

CHAPTER FIVE

NIKKI GUESSED THIS teenager blocking their way must be Patty's child, the one she'd brought back with her to the ranch when the girl was just a baby. That would have been about sixteen years ago, making the young woman standing in front of her sixteen, if Nikki's math was correct.

The nanny, Patricia "Patty" Owens, had left the ranch after the kidnapping only to return nine years later with a baby. The father of the child had never been revealed. Was it possible this teen was Travers's?

"Back off, Kitten," Cull said as he and Nikki ascended the rest of the steps. "I'm not in the mood."

"Why is everyone in such a bad mood today?" the teen demanded, clearly taking it personally.

Nikki stepped through the front door, followed by Cull, then stopped, wanting to take it all in. But she wasn't given a chance.

"Cull? Is that Ms. St. James with you?" a deep male voice called from an open doorway off to her right. "Please have her come in."

"I'll get you those aspirin," Cull said as Nikki turned toward the open doorway.

Travers McGraw seemed preoccupied, one hand on

his forehead, his elbow resting on the large oak desk in front of him.

Nikki stopped in the open doorway, studying him for a moment. She'd seen dozens of photographs of Travers McGraw, most taken right after the kidnapping. He'd been a big, strong, handsome man, dark-haired with the same pale blue eyes as the two sons she'd seen.

The past twenty-five years had not been kind to him. While his hair hadn't turned as white as his ex-wife Marianne's, it was shot with gray and there were deep lines etched around his eyes. He seemed to have shrunk in size, his body thin, his shoulders stooped.

But as he looked up, his smile was welcoming.

"Mr. McGraw, I'm Nikki St. James," she said, stepping forward to extend her hand. "The crime writer."

He seemed to come alive as he got to his feet. Hope burned bright in his eyes with such intensity that the weight of it hit her hard. He was depending on her to solve the case.

"Please, call me Travers," he said as he shook her hand, clasping it with both of his. "I'm so glad you're here. I didn't hear you come in." He glanced toward the open doorway. "I thought you were going to call for directions to the ranch."

"Actually, I ran into your son Cull in town—" literally, she thought "—and he brought me out."

"Wonderful," Travers said a little distractedly. "All that matters is that you're here and you're going to find out what happened to the twins." He rubbed his temples as if he had a headache, too.

She hoped she didn't make it worse. She started to reiterate that she couldn't make any promises, but she didn't get the words out before Patty burst into the room.

"Tell me I'm misinformed," Patricia said, looking from Nikki to her husband, her blue eyes wild with anger. "Tell me you haven't brought this…this…woman into our home."

"Patricia." He sighed, looking defeated again. "This is not the place to—"

"*Not the place?* This has to stop. I thought we decided—"

"*You* decided," he said, looking a little less beat down. "I will never stop looking for them."

His words fanned the flames of the woman's fury, but seemed to leave her speechless for a moment.

"We need to talk," Patricia said to her husband between gritted teeth.

"I'm sure we will," he agreed as he sat back down behind his desk and motioned for Nikki to take a seat. "But right now I need you to leave and close the door behind you."

All color drained from the woman's face. Clearly appalled, she stormed out, slamming the door behind her.

"I apologize for my wife's behavior," he said after a moment. "I hope this doesn't change your mind."

Nikki shook her head. "Not at all." It wasn't the first time she'd run into a relative who didn't want anyone digging into the past. It wouldn't be the last.

She hadn't expected to get much out of Patty Owens McGraw anyway. But if the answers were on this ranch, she told herself she would find them even without the woman's help.

"You said that I would be allowed the run of the ranch," Nikki reminded him. "I hope you haven't changed your mind."

He shook his head. "If there is even the slightest chance that you might find out the truth… Just let me know what you need from me. I should warn you. My wife isn't the only one who might be opposed to this."

"Your sons."

He nodded. "Also my lawyer and a close family friend who was in the house that night. They both are quite adamant that this is a mistake. I completely disagree with them, understand. But you might find getting information from them difficult, and I'm sorry about that."

"I've worked with families before that were...skeptical," she said.

He smiled at her understatement of the current situation and raked a hand through his graying hair, looking apologetic. "I had hoped that once you were here it might be easier. Please don't think I'm a coward for not telling my sons. They don't want me to be disappointed again and I really wasn't up to arguing before you got here. With so much time having passed and no new evidence..."

"I hate to get your hopes up as well, but I can promise you that I will do everything I can to find out the truth. I'd like to take a look around the house and the ranch," Nikki said, getting to her feet. "But first if someone can show me to my room. I'm afraid my car and luggage are still in town."

"Not a problem. I'll have someone pick it up for you," he said as he rose from behind his desk.

There was a tap at the door before it swung in. She turned to see Cull silhouetted in the doorway. He stepped forward, holding out a glass of water and two aspirin. She took them as she listened to Travers asking his son to see that Nikki's car was brought out to the ranch.

"But first if you wouldn't mind showing her to the guest room," the older man finished.

"I'll show her to her room," came a voice from the open doorway. It was the teenager who'd accosted her earlier on the porch steps. It was clear that Kitten had been close by, eavesdropping.

The insincere smile had an almost demented quality to it. Nikki wondered again about Patricia's daughter, the mystery child she'd brought back to the ranch years ago.

"Kitten, this is Nikki St. James," Travers said, introducing them. "She will be staying with us while she works on a book about the kidnapping."

The girl raised one brow. "Fascinating." She sounded like her mother, the word just snide enough.

"I want you to be nice to her," he said.

"Of course, Daddy," Kitten said, almost purring. "Later, can I borrow your car to go into town? I'm meeting some friends."

"You just got your license. I'm not sure that's a good idea. What did your mother say?"

"She said she didn't care if I went after dinner, but…" She mugged a face. "She's afraid I'm going to wreck her precious car."

"You can take mine," he said, sounding tired. "Just promise me that you'll be careful and come home whatever time your mother tells you."

The teen rushed to him and kissed his cheek. "Thank you, Daddy." As she turned, she mugged a face at Nikki.

Travers turned to Nikki. "Leave me your keys. Cull will see that everything is taken care of."

She thanked him as she handed them over, only to find Cull standing behind her. He scooped the keys up from the desk and pocketed them, then left without a word. She figured he'd been too surprised earlier to voice his displeasure, but his swearing had given her a clue as to how he felt about her being here.

"We can talk after dinner, Ms. St. James," Travers said as she and Kitten started out of the room.

"Nikki, please," she said, stopping in the doorway.

He smiled. "I can't tell you how glad I am that you're here, Nikki. Dinner is at six. It's informal."

She nodded and followed Kitten out the door. "Can you point out the wing where the twins' nursery was?" Nikki asked the girl.

Kitten smiled. "Of course."

They'd barely left the room before Patricia, who'd clearly been waiting only yards away, rushed into her husband's office, slamming the door behind her. Nikki could hear her raised voice as Kitten led her up the wide stairway.

CULL COULD HAVE handed off the job of retrieving Nikki St. James's car and luggage from town to a couple of the hired hands. After all, he was as unhappy about this turn of events as his stepmother. He was also anxious to talk to his father.

But right now Patricia was chewing Travers's ear, and the best place to be was far from the house until some of the dust settled.

Also, he wanted to know more about Nikki St. James before he confronted his father.

"I could use your help," he said when he found his younger brother in the barn. "Can you drive me into town?"

"Can't Boone do it?" Ledger asked as he rubbed a hand down the long neck of the newest horse.

"He's gone to pick up that stallion Dad bought last week."

Ledger sighed. "Fine. What's going on in the house, or do I even have to guess?" he asked as they walked along the path next to the house.

Even from here, Cull could hear Patricia's voice raised in fury. He and his brother usually escaped to the horse barns when their father and Patricia were arguing. That's how he'd known where he would find Ledger, especially today after the newspaper article.

"We have a surprise guest."

Ledger blinked. *"Guest?"* He perked up so much that Cull realized for some unknown reason his brother had hoped it was Abby Pierce, the waitress at the Whitehorse Café and his brother's former love. For some reason, Ledger thought that Abby was going to come back to him.

"Dad has hired a crime writer to do a book on the kidnapping," he said before Ledger's unrealistic hopes could be raised further.

"What?"

"I'll tell you all about it on the way into town."

True to his word, he told his brother everything he knew, which wasn't that much.

"Dad has lost his mind," Ledger said when he'd finished.

"Seems that way. She's going to be staying at the house. That's why I need to pick up her car for her. According to what it says on the key, it's a blue compact with Billings plates. We should find it parked near the café where I found you this morning."

"Wait, how did she get to the ranch?"

"I drove her. It's a long story. But suffice it to say, we're apparently stuck with her for a while," Cull said.

"So what does she look like?" his brother asked, turning toward him as they reached town.

He hesitated a little too long.

Ledger laughed. "I've never seen you at a loss for words when it comes to describing a woman."

"It's not like that with this one. She's all right to look at, but I don't trust her."

"Well, once she realizes there is nothing new to write about, she'll leave."

"Let's hope so. I'm just worried about how much damage she'll do before that. Dad—"

"He looks bad, doesn't he?"

Cull nodded around the sudden lump in his throat as he pulled up behind the rental car parked on the main drag of Whitehorse. "I'm going to do what I have to to protect him. Starting by finding out everything I can about Nikki St. James."

NIKKI AND KITTEN were almost to the top of the stairs when Kitten turned abruptly. Swinging around, her large purse hit Nikki, throwing her off balance. Her gaze shot up to Kitten's.

The teen looked surprised for a moment, then a small smile curled her lips as Nikki teetered on her high heels. She grabbed wildly for the handrail. The tips of her fingers glossed over it, but she couldn't find purchase. She could feel herself going over backward.

At the last minute, Kitten grabbed her hand, the two of them almost tumbling down the stairs as Nikki fought to get her feet back under her.

"That was a close call," the teen said in a mocking tone. "You really should be more careful. People in town say this house is cursed. Terrible things have happened here." She blinked wide blue eyes. "We should get you to your room. You don't look well."

With that she turned and started up the stairs. It was all Nikki could do not to grab the back of her shirt and fling her down the stairs. She was shaking from the near fall and still a little unsteady on her feet. It didn't help that the two aspirin Cull had given her hadn't started to work yet on her headache.

Nikki had faced opposition before. She'd also put herself in dangerous situations. It went with the territory. But as she stared after Kitten, she realized that she'd glimpsed something in the teen that frightened her more than the near accident.

She would have to watch her back in this house— just as her grandfather had warned her. Except it wasn't the kidnapper she apparently had to worry about. But it could be the spawn of one of the kidnappers, she thought, reminded of the look in Kitten's eyes moments ago.

While Nikki thought the purse incident had been an accident, the girl hadn't been that sorry it had happened.

CHAPTER SIX

WHEN MCCALL WANTED information about Whitehorse, she went to her grandmother. Even though Pepper lived on Winchester Ranch miles from town, she had always known what was going on in the county sooner than most.

McCall hadn't doubted that she would remember the McGraw kidnapping.

"Remember it?" Pepper exclaimed after the two of them were seated in the living room. For most of her life, McCall had never laid eyes on Winchester Ranch—or her grandmother. Pepper had denied that McCall was her granddaughter until events had thrown them together. Now they had a mutual respect for each other that verged on love.

"I dug this out after you called," Pepper said, and handed her a file stuffed with newspaper and magazine articles.

"All this is about the kidnapping?"

Her grandmother nodded.

McCall glanced at a couple of articles, but this wasn't what she was looking for. She turned to her grandmother. "I need the dirt. The rumors. The things your old cook used to bring you."

Pepper laughed. "I'd almost forgotten about her." The woman had drugged her grandmother to keep her from demanding too much. McCall had never understood the relationship between the two women, since her grandmother knew what was going on and did nothing about it. Apparently Pepper had some affection for the woman to put up with it for so long.

"There were lots of rumors, if that's what you want. Marianne McGraw and the horse trainer, Nate Corwin. Travers McGraw and the nanny, Patricia Owens. Then there were disgruntled ranch hands looking to make a buck. There is the former ranch manager and close friend Blake Ryan. But I always suspected the lawyer. He was one sleazy bastard, that one."

"Jim Waters? But he's still the McGraw lawyer."

Pepper raised a brow. "That should tell you something."

"That he's trusted?"

"That Travers lives in a houseful of vipers and doesn't realize it," her grandmother said. "The man married Patricia Owens." She raised a brow as if that said everything.

"I suppose you heard—"

"About the true crime writer?" Pepper laughed at her granddaughter's surprise. "Also heard that Patty threw a fit."

"Nikki St. James is writing a book about the kidnapping," McCall said.

Her grandmother lifted another finely tuned eyebrow. "You don't trust her?"

"Something happened in town—"

"That little *accident* in front of the Whitehorse Café?"

McCall laughed. "You must have thought the same thing I did."

"The young woman staged it."

She nodded. "I'm just not sure what she thought it would get her. Cull McGraw was driving the pickup. He's the oldest. He was upset and gave her a ride out to the ranch. But when he found out who she was, I'm sure he was suspicious."

"Probably," Pepper agreed. "Those McGraw sons are smart as well as good-looking."

"I've heard there is no love lost between them and Patricia."

"What do you expect? No one in town can stand her," Pepper said. "The question you should be asking yourself is why Travers married her to begin with."

"He's a nice guy. She was young, had a baby, needed his help," the sheriff suggested.

"Or she had something on him," her grandmother suggested. "Guilt is a huge motivator—if not blackmail."

NIKKI PAUSED AT the top of the stairs for a moment to look back at the house. She felt she needed to catch her breath—and not just from her near fall. She still couldn't believe she was in this house—her father had once walked some of these halls. From what she'd gathered in her research, Nate Corwin had been a frequent guest.

But she wondered if it had been at Travers's request—or his wife's.

Pushing that thought away, she turned to look back down the stairs.

She'd wanted to see the inside of this house from the

moment she'd found the newspaper clippings and discovered how her father had really died.

Now she looked around at all the grandeur, not surprised how beautiful it was. She'd read that Travers McGraw had built the house for his first wife as an anniversary gift. The two had started out relatively poor, living in a small house some distance away. But when he'd begun siring prize-winning quarter horses, he'd had the house built for Marianne. By that time, she had already given him three sons—Cull, Boone and Ledger.

He'd spared no expense on the house and it had no doubt become the talk of the town as well as the county. Was that what had given the kidnapper the idea of taking her two youngest children?

After meeting him, Nikki had hated to get Travers McGraw's hopes up. He seemed a fragile man who'd been through too much. She wondered if another disappointment might kill him.

But she had hoped that there was something here to find—someone who had something to hide. She thought of Patricia. The former nanny had ended up with Travers, and if she played her cards right, she could end up with the ranch, since he didn't seem long for this world.

Except for the fact that Travers still had three grown sons. Did she plan to get rid of them, too? So why would she have kidnapped the twins all those years ago? What would have been her motive?

True, she'd implicated Marianne McGraw. But even if she wanted to be rid of both the wife and the babies, it seemed a little too desperate as a means to an end. Especially if that end was getting Travers McGraw.

Kidnappings usually were about money. But as far as Nikki knew, the ransom money had never been spent.

Because the kidnappers had accidentally killed the twins and had gotten too scared? She thought of the broken rung halfway down the ladder. Had the kidnapper fallen? Had he dropped one of the babies or both of them?

For all the research she'd done, Nikki had too many questions still. All her instincts, though, told her that the answers were here in this house. Someone in this house knew at least a piece of the truth. Once she had all those pieces...

"Are you coming?" Kitten demanded from down the hall.

Nikki sighed and turned to follow the teen. She couldn't help looking into each room they passed, feeling a tingle of excitement. The house was beautifully decorated. Had that been Marianne's doing? Or the new Mrs. McGraw?

Kitten had stopped at the end of the hall. Nikki knew the layout of the house. Downstairs was the large living room, Travers's office, the master bedroom and a huge farm kitchen and dining room.

Upstairs at the back part of the house were the bedrooms for the children and nanny. They were arranged down a long hallway that ran north to south, with the nanny's larger room and the playroom at the south end.

When Nikki joined Kitten, she turned north down a short hallway. Nikki recalled that the twins' nursery had been on the south wing—next to Patricia's. She glanced in that direction. The hallway was dark. A heavy silence seemed to hunker in its shadowy depths.

"This way," Kitten said, and walked to the end of the hall, where she opened a door into a room decorated in shades of blue. "This was Cull's room growing up." She smiled at Nikki's surprise.

She shot Kitten a look. "This is the room I'm staying in?" She'd distinctly heard Travers tell her the guest room.

The teen gave her an innocent smile. "You want to be in this wing, right? Otherwise, they're going to stick you away somewhere since no one stays on these wings anymore."

Nikki looked out the window and saw the addition to the house that had been added after the kidnapping so Travers would be closer to his remaining children. Past it, she saw what appeared to be a pool and pool house.

While what the girl said made sense, Nikki knew what Kitten was up to. The one person who would be most upset about her staying in his room would be Cull. But she decided she would play along and deal with Cull when the time came.

"It's a lovely room." She glanced around, chilled a little at the thought that he hadn't stayed in this room since the kidnapping. This entire wing had been left exactly as it had been. What had he heard that night? Or was it true that he, like the others, had slept right through the kidnapping?

She realized she was rubbing her bare arms as if to warm them. It wasn't cold in the room. On the contrary, the air felt heavy. It was being in Cull's childhood room, being in this house, being this close to the room where the twins had been taken from, she told herself.

"Creepy, huh," Kitten said, no doubt seeing her reaction. Kitten didn't miss much.

"Yes," Nikki agreed. Something horrible had happened in this house. A kidnapping that had probably led to the murder of two innocent babies. And Nate Corwin had been in this house. Possibly climbed the same stairs she had, maybe even walked down this very hallway. What if her grandfather was right? What if she found out that her father had been part of the kidnapping? Part of something even worse?

She thought of Marianne McGraw's snow-white hair and blank, empty eyes, and shuddered inwardly.

Kitten moved to the window and pulled back the drapes, blinding her for a moment. Past the teen, Nikki could see the barn and corrals where her father had worked. Beyond them was the bunkhouse where he'd lived. She'd seen the layout of the ranch from an aerial photo that had been shot after the kidnapping. Since then, some cabins had been added at the back of the property. Was that where Travers's sons lived?

Turning, she watched Kitten pick up a toy cowboy on a plastic horse from a shelf near the bed. "No one comes up here but Tilly to clean. So," she said as she put the horse back on the shelf and met Nikki's gaze, "you'll have it all to yourself. Good luck. Tilly swears she's seen ghosts up here and heard babies crying."

Kitten was trying to scare her *again*, not realizing that what scared her most would be the truth about that night.

"Thank you for showing me to the room, Kitten."

"It's Katherine. Only my family calls me Kitten."

"Duly noted." Her head throbbed. She couldn't wait for this young woman to leave. "I might lie down for a while before dinner."

"Yes, dinner," Kitten said, and smiled. "All the family and my father's attorney will be there. I can't wait for everyone to meet you."

As he returned from town with Nikki's rental car, Cull heard Kitten's and her mother's raised voices. He quickly stepped into the office, hoping to find his father and avoid the latest upset.

The room was empty. A small fire burned in the fireplace and the latest edition of the *Milk River Courier* was spread on his father's desk. He stepped closer. One glance at the headline about the kidnapping and he let out a curse. Getting rid of the other newspaper before the cook brought it into the house hadn't done any good. Wadding up this newspaper, he angrily tossed it into the fire as his father came into the room.

Travers spotted the burning newspaper and gave Cull a sympathetic shake of his head. "I appreciate you trying to spare me, but I've already read it." He joined him in front of the fire and laid a hand on his shoulder. "Even if I hadn't, you can't burn every newspaper in town."

"I hate for you to have to go through this again," Cull said.

His father smiled wearily. "*I* was the one who contacted the newspaper, son. Anyway, it isn't something I can ever forget."

"We should talk about this woman—"

"Nikki St. James. Thank you for bringing her out to the ranch. You and Ledger, I understand, went in and brought back her car. Please see that her luggage is taken upstairs."

"I intend to take it up myself," Cull said. "But I have to ask you. Are you sure about this?" He'd gotten on his phone after Ledger had dropped him off and done some research on the woman. He'd hoped to find something that would dissuade his father from going through with this.

Unfortunately, what he found was a professional website, heartwarming reviews and a pretty astounding track record for unearthing new information on true crimes. He could see how his father might have been impressed that she wanted to do a book on the kidnapping.

Travers McGraw didn't answer right away. He lowered himself into his chair before meeting Cull's gaze. "It's been twenty-five years. Your stepmother is right about one thing—I can't keep doing this to myself or to all of you. This is it, Cull. If nothing comes of this book, then I'm done."

Cull let out a sigh of relief. "I know how much this means to you, but I'm glad to hear you feel that way. I'm worried it's going to kill you otherwise."

His father nodded. "So please, help this woman with anything she needs and ask your brothers to do the same. I'll appeal to Patty and Kitten, though I don't hold out much hope for their cooperation." His smile was sad. "I can't help but hope."

Cull wanted to change his father's mind, to argue that he didn't know anything about this woman and that bringing her into the house could lead to disastrous consequences.

He put a hand on his father's shoulder and quickly swallowed back the words, surprised how thin the shoulder felt, how weak his father looked. "I best get her luggage to her."

As he left his father's office, his stepmother came flying in, slamming the door behind her. Cull picked up Nikki St. James's designer suitcase and, taking the stairs three at a time, was at the top when he heard his stepsister call to him from the ground floor below.

"I put her in your old room," Kitten said. He stopped, nearly losing his balance as he turned to look back at her. She stood smiling that impish smile at him.

"Why would you put her in my old room?" he demanded through gritted teeth.

"Because that's the one that Tilly says is haunted the worst." She laughed and took off out the front door.

He almost forgot himself. That girl had needed a good tanning for years. Although he doubted it would do any good. She was just like her mother, spoiled and impossible, he thought as he heard the raised voices coming from the office. Maybe it wasn't his father's loss that was killing him. Maybe it was Patricia and her…daughter.

He often wondered why his father put up with the two of them. Travers had raised Kitten as his own. According to the scuttlebutt in town, she *was* his own. The story was that they'd been lovers all along and that—on top of the kidnapping of her babies—their affair pushed Marianne McGraw over the edge.

For the story to be true, then Patty and his father had renewed their relationship in secret. He and Ledger would have been in high school when Kitten was conceived.

Cull shook his head as he topped the stairs. He didn't have time to speculate on the past. Right now, he was headed for his childhood bedroom in the wing of the house that he hadn't entered in years.

After the kidnapping, he and his brother had been moved to other rooms, closer to his parents. That was back before they took his mother away one day, never to return.

As he walked down the hallway, he couldn't help being furious with Nikki St. James for bringing up bad memories already—and she hadn't even begun writing the darned book.

Who knew what she might discover?

That thought turned his blood to slush. He'd buried so many memories of that night and the days after. And now she would be poking around, forcing him to relive them. Worse, reminding him of the secret he'd sworn he'd keep until his dying day.

NIKKI FRESHENED UP, waiting to make sure that Kitten had left. Cull's childhood bedroom was all boy, from the blue decor to the many male toys. He'd just turned seven at the time of the kidnapping, so he must not have spent much time in this beautifully decorated room before this wing was abandoned. Which explained why the room looked as if a little boy might return at any moment.

Hoping the coast was clear, she went to the door, opened it and peered out into the hallway. It was empty. Hearing nothing, she stepped out, easing the door closed behind her, and started down the hall. All of the doors to the rooms were closed.

Where the other hallway she and Kitten had come down intersected, she stopped and peered around the corner. Seeing no one, she headed for the south wing of the sprawling house. This was where the nursery was located, along with a playroom and nanny quarters. This was where Patty Owens had lived before the kidnapping.

The twins' bedroom room was at the end of the hall-way across from the nanny's room next to a back stairway.

As Nikki neared the end of the hall, she slowed and glanced over her shoulder. That same uneasy feeling she'd felt earlier in Cull's former room now washed over her. While immaculately clean and cared for, the wing still had an abandoned feel. No wonder the housekeeper, Tilly, thought she felt ghosts up here. That is, if Kitten hadn't just been trying to scare Nikki with the story.

Though it wasn't necessary, she found herself tip-toeing the rest of the way. The door to the twins' room was closed. She took hold of the doorknob and jerked her hand back as if she'd been burned. It wasn't until she touched it again that she realized it wasn't hot—it was ice-cold. The heat must be turned off in this wing.

She turned the knob.

CHAPTER SEVEN

As THE DOOR swung into the former nursery, Nikki was hit with a draft of freezing cold air. Movement. Her heart slammed against her ribs. It took a moment for her eyes to adjust to the dim light. A curtain billowed in the wind. It snapped, then fell silent for a moment before another gust raised it like a ghost coming through the window.

She let her heart rate drop back to normal before she stepped into the room. The wall by the window was painted in alternating blue-and-pink stripes. Someone had started a pastoral mural on the wall opposite the cribs. It had faded. This room, like Cull's, gave her a feeling of being transported back to another more innocent time.

Two cribs were positioned side by side on the opposite wall. She could see the horse patterns on the matching mattress sets. One with a blue background, the other pink. Nikki moved closer, stopping when she saw the tiny covers pulled back. Was that how the kidnapper had left them?

She thought she caught the scent of baby powder, a sick sweetness that turned her stomach. She fought her revulsion and moved to the window, careful not to touch anything. The room still felt like a crime scene.

At the window, she saw the faint dark residue where fingerprints had been lifted off the windowsill and frame. Nikki wondered if the window had been left open by the housekeeper or if the kidnapper had left it like this.

The breeze stirred the cute pink-and-blue curtains and the white sheers under them. On closer inspection she saw that the fabric had faded pink-and-blue prints of tiny ducks. Something about that brought a lump to her throat.

As often as she'd thought of the twins since she'd found the newspaper clippings and discovered her father's involvement with the McGraws, this was the first time she'd felt the full weight of what had happened here.

The cold draft of air seemed to move through the room. She shivered as it curled around her neck. She couldn't imagine anything worse than losing a child— let alone two.

She rubbed her bare arms to chase away the chill as she considered the nursery. Whoever had prepared this room for the twins must have been excited for their arrival.

Had it been their mother, Marianne? Or had they paid someone to get it ready? Nanny Patty Owens had been here several weeks before the twins were born. Nikki couldn't imagine the woman she'd met downstairs taking such pains to prepare for another woman's infants. But maybe Patty had been as unthreatening as she'd appeared back then.

Nikki moved closer so she could look out the window

to the ground below. The FBI had found boot prints in the soft earth where a ladder had been placed against the side of the house—just like in the Lindbergh case.

"What are you doing in here?"

Nikki jumped, startled by the low husky male voice directly behind her. She hadn't heard anyone come down the hall, let alone enter the room. She suspected the tall, broad-shouldered, slim-hipped cowboy now standing only inches away had planned it that way as she met Cull's blue-eyed glare with one of her own.

"Your father gave me the run of the house, including this room," she said defiantly. He'd scared her and she could tell he was glad of it. She'd scared him earlier. Did he think that made them even?

He looked toward the open window. "There's nothing here to find."

"Thank you, but I'll be the judge of that."

His hair was long and dark, in stark contrast to the pale blue of his eyes. The resemblance between the McGraw men made her think of Kitten, with her long dark hair and intense blue eyes. She could have been a McGraw.

"Is the window always left open like that?" she asked, looking past him. She could see part of the horse barn where her father had worked as the window parted the curtains.

"Tilly closes it, but when my father comes up, especially this time of year, he opens it so it's as it was that night when the twins were found missing." His gaze, which had been on the window for a moment, moved to hers. There was a primal maleness to Cull that resonated in those eyes. It was as if he could see his effect on her. That, too, seemed to please him.

"You really have no idea what you've gotten yourself into," he said with a shake of his head.

"I've done other books that involved murders and—"

His laugh cut her off. "You feel it, don't you?" She started to ask what he was talking about, but he didn't give her a chance. "This house, this…" He waved his arms, his gaze boring into hers. "Evil that an open window will never blow from this house."

"If you're going to tell me about the ghosts—"

"That Tilly has seen?" He smiled as he shook his head. "No, I'm talking about a place where something horrible has happened. The evil stays. Like a residue. Like a bad feeling. Like part of the furnishings. You can never get rid of it."

"So why do *you* stay here?"

"Because raising horses is in my blood. But I don't live in the house. I have a cabin on the ranch. You couldn't get me to spend a night on this wing or even under this roof. You don't believe in ghosts? You will."

She thought of how Travers McGraw looked ghost-like. He didn't appear to have fared much better than his former wife. He was thin to the point of gaunt, his face ashen, making her fear he hadn't been well. More than ever, she thought that was why he'd allowed her the opportunity to write the book on the kidnapping.

"What is wrong with your father?"

The abrupt change of subject caught Cull off guard for a moment. "What do you think? All this has taken a toll on him."

"Has he seen a doctor?"

"You seriously can't see what has caused his decline?"

"It has to be more than the kidnapping. He really doesn't look well."

Cull sighed. "I've been trying to get him to see a doctor. He's stubborn."

"Like his son."

He shot her a warning look. "Let's say you are as good as your book publicist claims. What you uncover about the case could kill him."

"Is that what you're afraid of? Or is there a reason you don't want the truth to come out? Maybe some secret of your own?"

Something flickered in those deep blue eyes, but he quickly hid it. "I had just turned seven years old."

"Plenty old enough to remember that night. Maybe remember more than you've ever told anyone."

She thought she saw him flinch as if she'd hit too close to the truth. "I've found that often family members know more than they want to tell. They're covering for someone or they're worried what will happen if they tell."

Cull shook his head. "I'm just worried about my family and what you're about to do to it."

"You could help me."

He shook his head. "Have you not heard a word I've said?"

"Your father needs to know what happened that night. Can't you see that?"

Cull let out a low curse. "He already knows what happened."

"No, I don't think so. I don't believe your mother had anything to do with the kidnapping. Nor do I believe Nate Corwin did."

He looked surprised. "Then who?"

She cocked a brow at him. "That's what I'm going to find out. With your help."

"Sorry, but there isn't anything to find. You're wasting your time. Worse, you're giving my father false hope."

"What if hope is the only thing keeping him alive?"

"I almost feel sorry for you," Cull said. "You start digging in the past and all you're going to do is stir up more trouble than even you can handle."

"That almost sounds like a threat."

He shrugged. "Just remember. I tried to warn you." He turned toward the door. Over his shoulder he said, "Dinner's ready."

"I'm going to find out the truth with or without your help," she called to his retreating backside.

He stopped in the doorway to look back at her. "Let me know when you have it solved because I've spent years trying to figure out what happened that night and I was actually in the house. I heard Patty's screams. I still hear them."

NIKKI STARED AT HIM. The man threw her off balance. She would have to be very careful around him, she thought just an instant before the sound of high heels could be heard making a noisy, angry tattoo in the hallway as they approached.

They both looked toward the doorway as Patty McGraw appeared. Nikki heard Cull curse under his breath.

"What are the two of you doing in here?" Patricia demanded. She looked from her stepson to Nikki and back. "You brought her in here, Cull? What is wrong with you and the rest of this family?"

"She found her way on her own," he said, his hooded gaze taking in Nikki again. "I dropped her suitcase in my room where Kitten put her."

"You have no business in here," Patricia chided her as if Nikki were a child in a china cabinet. "If Travers caught you in here…"

"He gave me permission to—"

"He shouldn't have done that." Patricia motioned frantically for Nikki to leave. "This room, this entire wing, is off-limits. I've had your things moved downstairs to the pool house."

"The pool house?" Cull said with an arch of one eyebrow.

Nikki shot him a puzzled look as she tried to understand why he seemed amused by this.

Cull shook his head in disapproval at his stepmother. "The pool house will allow her to have the run of the entire ranch while the rest of us are asleep in our beds."

"Well, what did you expect me to do with her?" Patricia demanded. "Your father wouldn't hear of putting her up in a motel in town or better yet sending her back where she came from."

Nikki wanted to remind them that she was still in the room. "I'm sorry. I didn't mean to cause any trouble."

"Oh, please," Patricia said, spinning on her heels. "*Everyone* knows what you're really about. You aren't the first one who's come here wanting to satisfy your morbid curiosity."

"I hope to help."

The woman's laugh could have shattered crystal. *"Help?"* She seemed to be choking on laughter. "You've thrown the entire house into turmoil. You call this helping?"

Nikki could feel Cull's keen gaze on her. She rubbed at the painful spot on her temple, still surprised she'd hit as hard as she had. She really was lucky she hadn't been hurt worse or killed.

"Cull will show you to the pool house after dinner." With that, Patricia made a rude sound and stormed away.

Her leaving the room, though, didn't cool the heated anger in it. Nikki could feel it coming off Cull in waves.

"This must give you great pleasure, this front-row seat into our family drama," Cull said through clenched teeth.

"The kidnapping has been a lot of stress on your family for twenty-five years," she pointed out.

He smiled at that. "You think?" His intense blue gaze seemed to drill into her skull as he locked eyes with her. "You know all about us, though, don't you? I suspect you knew who I was when you stepped in front of my pickup. That you've known everything about this family for some time."

She lifted her chin a little higher. There was no reason to deny it. He'd seen through her stunt. She could have mentally kicked herself. Hadn't she known that Cull was the wrong person to cross?

"You know so much about us and yet we know so little about you," he was saying. "It makes me wonder why you chose our…tragedy for a book." When she didn't respond, he continued. "Well, seems you're going to be our guest for a while. Until you get what you need." His deep, soft voice reverberated through her. While Ledger had seemed impossibly young and innocent, Cull was anything but. This was a man not to be fooled with.

"But I have to wonder what a woman like you needs," he finished, his voice so low and so seductive that it felt like a deep, dark well drawing her in. "I have to wonder just how far you will go."

Nikki swallowed and asked, "Has anyone been staying in the pool house? I don't want to put them out of their lodgings."

Cull's smile filled her with dread. "The pool house has been empty since the night of the kidnapping. It's where an item from one of the twins' beds was found. Apparently, the kidnapper and accomplice met there before at least one of them disappeared with the twins."

A chill rattled through her. Nikki hugged herself. That information hadn't been in *any* of the research she'd done on the case. It was the kind of thing that the FBI held back. What item had been found in the place where she would be staying? That meant that at least one of the kidnappers had been in that building that night. Her father? Marianne? Or someone in this house right now?

"You should be quite comfortable there since the place has its own set of ghosts," Cull assured her. "It's far enough away from the house that you won't be able to hear my father and stepmother arguing and yet no one will hear you should you run into trouble and need help. I'll try not to be too far away though. For your own sake. Wouldn't want you to have another...*accident*. How is your head by the way?"

She ignored the sarcasm laced with accusation. "The aspirin helped, thank you." Picking Cull had definitely been a mistake. Why had she thought he would be more helpful to her if he thought he'd almost killed her? From the look in his eye, he was wishing he hadn't braked.

"So you and your brothers live…"

"I would imagine you saw our cabins from the twins' window."

She had seen what looked like cabins set back in the trees some distance from the house. "You really are afraid of the ghosts," she only half joked.

His handsome face grew serious. "You think I'm joking? We'll see how you feel in a few days."

CHAPTER EIGHT

As NIKKI AND Cull descended the stairs, Ledger came out of his father's office.

"I don't believe you've met our houseguest," Cull said to his brother. "This is Ms. Nikki St. James, the famous true crime writer."

Ledger had clearly already heard about her, Nikki thought. He shook her hand warily.

"Patty has decided our guest would be more comfortable in the pool house," Cull said.

Ledger looked surprised, but added, "Whatever makes Patty happy."

"I need to make a quick call. Why don't you show Nikki to the dining room," Cull said.

"I'm glad we finally get to meet," she told the young man.

"You realize we're all shocked that our father would hire you."

"He didn't hire me. He's just giving me access to the ranch and the family so I can write about the kidnapping and hopefully uncover what really happened that night. I hope you'll help me."

Ledger let out a nervous laugh. "Me? I can't imagine how I could help. I was three."

"You might be surprised what you remember," she said, making him appear even more nervous. She quickly changed the subject. "I'm afraid I've upset your step-mother."

"Don't worry about it," he said as they walked toward the back of the house. "She's often upset over something."

"She caught me in the nursery."

He slowed so he studied her. "Oh. No one is allowed in that wing except the housekeeper, and even Tilly hates to go in there. The nursery is exactly as it was twenty-five years ago. My father insisted it be left that way. At first so that no evidence was lost. He was convinced that the FBI and local law enforcement would find the twins. Later it was left because he couldn't bear to change it."

"How awful for your family."

"Yes," he agreed as they reached the dining room. "Not to mention the glare of the media over the years. You can't believe the extremes some reporters will go to in an attempt to get a story."

She felt her face heat at his words.

"That's why I'm surprised my father opened the doors to you. Here we are," he said.

Stepping through the dining room doorway ahead of Ledger, she saw that Patricia and Travers were having a muted discussion in the far corner. At the center of the room was a huge cherrywood table and chairs that seemed to dwarf the large room. Kitten was already seated, and so were two men she didn't recognize.

Nikki felt a draft move across the back of her neck and shivered as it quilled the tiny hairs. She turned, expecting... Not sure what she expected to see. One of the ghosts?

THAT NIGHT AT DINNER, the sheriff told her husband about the woman who Cull McGraw had nearly run down. "I think it was staged. Too much of a coincidence that she steps in front of a McGraw pickup when she's on her way to the house anyway. But unfortunately, no one in the café saw anything."

"You have a very suspicious mind," Luke said, looking up from his meal. "What do you think she's after?"

"Supposedly, she's there to write a book about the McGraw kidnapping for the twenty-fifth anniversary."

"That sounds reasonable. I'm sure you checked her out."

McCall nodded. "She was born Nikki Ann Corwin."

"Corwin—why does that name ring a bell?"

"Because her father was Nate Corwin, the man who was convicted of the kidnapping," she said. "I can't help but wonder if Travers McGraw knows that."

"No wonder you're suspicious." He reached over onto Tracey's high chair to drop more finely chopped beef roast. She'd named her daughter after her father, Trace Winchester.

Tracey beat the high-chair tray with her spoon for a moment before laughing, then, ignoring the spoon, began eating the beef with the fingers of her free hand.

McCall smiled at her daughter. She never got tired of watching her, fascinated by the simple things the child did. She'd been so afraid of motherhood and hadn't admitted it until she was nine months pregnant.

Luke had talked her into taking a three-month leave while she decided if she wanted to be a stay-at-home mother or keep her job as sheriff.

"It's whatever you want," he'd told her. "I know you can do both. It's up to you."

McCall was glad she'd taken the time off. She loved being with her baby, but she also loved her job. She'd been afraid he was wrong and she really couldn't have both.

"I think I might drive out to the Sundown Stallion Station in the morning," she said as she straightened her daughter's bib and was rewarded with a huge toothy smile.

Being a game warden with the Fish, Wildlife and Parks Department, Luke was trained and served as an officer of the law. She didn't have to tell him why this year in particular, the McGraw kidnapping was on her mind.

"I have the day off tomorrow," he said. "Pepper's invited us out for lunch. Ruby's going, too."

McCall lifted a brow in surprise. "My mother and grandmother at lunch together? We need to get Tracey a bulletproof vest."

He chuckled as he rose to pull their daughter out of her high chair. "Probably a good idea."

The sheriff had to smile. That her mother and grandmother could be in the same room together and not kill each other was nothing short of amazing. For years Pepper Winchester hadn't acknowledged that McCall was even her granddaughter because of her dislike for Ruby.

Ruby had married Pepper's favorite son. Pepper had believed that Ruby had trapped Trace by getting pregnant and had wanted nothing to do with her—or the baby she had been carrying. Until a few years ago, McCall hadn't known anything about that side of her family, since her father had disappeared before she was born.

She'd never even laid eyes on her grandmother who'd

become a recluse after Trace's disappearance. Nor had she known why Pepper Winchester wanted nothing to do with her. Her mother, Ruby, certainly hadn't been a wealth of information.

Then McCall, who'd been working as a deputy back then, had stumbled onto an old shallow grave. In the grave was proof of her father's identity. Everyone had thought that he'd left town, run out on her and her mother. Finding his remains had brought more than his murder to light.

It had opened up a world to her that had always been a mystery. McCall would never forget the first time she'd seen the Winchester Ranch—let alone met her grandmother Pepper. It had changed all of their lives.

"Give my regards to Pepper tomorrow," she said now. "I'm sure she understands why I can't make lunch."

"Your grandmother loves that you're sheriff. You know she would have been disappointed if you had quit."

McCall did know that. She just hoped her grandmother didn't have an ulterior motive for inviting them to lunch. It wouldn't be the first time Pepper had something going on that she didn't want the law involved in.

As her husband began to get their daughter ready for bed, McCall felt a shiver. Just the thought of the kidnapping sent a spike of cold terror through her. She couldn't imagine losing her daughter. It was no wonder Marianne McGraw had lost her mind and was now locked away in the mental hospital.

McCall had been a child herself at the time of the kidnapping, but she'd heard stories about it and read both the newspaper accounts as well as the police file on it.

The FBI had been called in almost at once and taken over the case, but from what she'd read about the investigation, there had been several suspects, including the babies' own mother, Marianne. But it had always seemed that the dalliance between the stable manager, Nate Corwin, and Marianne McGraw had been conjecture without any solid evidence.

The person who'd testified about the affair had been the nanny, Patricia Owens—now Travers McGraw's second wife.

It was speculated that Nate and Marianne had come up with the kidnapping of the twins for the ransom money. Nate Corwin was a mere horse trainer. Marianne had no money of her own. What they'd planned to do with the twins after they collected the ransom was unknown since neither had confessed. Marianne had gone into shock. Nate had denied his involvement right up until his death.

McCall knew what it was like to fall so deeply in love that you could lose all perspective. But she shuddered at the thought that a mother would jeopardize the lives of her babies for money and a man. Any man.

TRAVERS SAW NIKKI as she entered the dining room, and said something quietly to his wife before greeting her. "I don't believe you've met our attorney. Jim Waters, this is the woman I told you about," Travers said.

The attorney was fiftysomething with thinning brown hair and small brown eyes. He turned awkwardly, a deep frown burrowing between his brows, and held out his hand. His handshake was limp and slightly damp, and his eyes didn't meet hers.

"And this is Blake Ryan, our former ranch manager and a close friend."

Blake was about the same age as the other man, but unlike Waters, he was distinguished and cover-model handsome. His dark hair had grayed at the temples, bringing out the steel of his gray eyes. His handshake was strong and he met her gaze with both suspicion and wariness.

"Why don't you sit over here by me," Travers said to her after making the introductions. He didn't need to tell her that both men had some concerns about her being here.

She'd just sat down when she heard the sound of boot soles on the wood floor. She sensed rather than saw Cull enter the dining room because she kept her gaze averted. She didn't glance over at him as he took a chair next to his father, directly across from her.

Suddenly the room felt too small. She took a shallow breath and dared to look at him. His gaze was on her, those blue eyes drilling her to her chair.

Ledger had taken a seat down the table next to Kitten, who looked far too happy, all things considered, since she hadn't gotten to go into town yet.

Nikki tried to relax but the tension in the dining room was dense enough to smother her. Patricia had lowered herself into her chair at the end of the table with a sullen dignity, only to glare down the length of it at her husband.

Boone was the last brother to come in. She hadn't met him yet because he'd been out of town picking up a horse, she'd heard. He stopped in the doorway. He could have been Cull's twin. He had the same thick dark hair, the same intense blue eyes, the same broad shoulders, the same scowl.

"What's going on?" Boone asked as if feeling the tension in the air before his gaze lit on her.

Travers got to his feet. "Please sit down, son." He waited for Boone to take a chair before he said, "This is Nikki St. James. She's a true crime writer and will be investigating the kidnapping for a book. I want you all to cooperate with her."

"Like hell." Boone shoved back his chair and stood, towering over the table. "I'm sorry, Dad, but this was a huge mistake. I'm not having anything to do with this…book or—" he turned his gaze on Nikki "—or this woman." With that he stomped out.

"I apologize for my son," Travers said wearily.

"You don't have to do that," she said as she heard the front door slam and the sound of an engine rev after it. "I know how hard this is on your family." She glanced around the table. She could feel Cull's gaze on her. Like Boone, he didn't want her here.

Kitten was giving her that snotty look she'd apparently perfected. Her mother's steely blue gaze could have burned through sheet metal. Ledger was the only one who gave her a slight smile as if he felt sorry for her.

"I will try to make it as painless as I can, but I need all of your help if I have any chance of solving this," she finished.

"Solving it?" Patricia said with a snort, but quickly reverted her gaze to her plate as her husband gave her an impatient look.

"I'll speak to Boone," Travers said. "I should have told him about this. He doesn't do well with surprises."

Though Boone had been only five when the twins were kidnapped, he might still have memories of that night.

"I should help Frieda." Patricia got up and went into the kitchen. A few moments later, she returned with the cook, who was carrying a large tray full of small bowls of soup. Patricia put a bowl in front of Travers and another in front of Cull before she sat down. Frieda placed soup in front of Patricia, then worked her way around the table until she came to Nikki. For a moment, she looked confused. "I guess I left yours in the kitchen," the cook said.

"Let me," Kitten said, jumping up and hurrying after her.

The two returned moments later. Kitten, all smiles, put a bowl of soup in front of Nikki before sitting down again.

"Thank you, Kitten," Travers said, smiling at the teen, though looking surprised she would get up to help.

Cook placed two large plates of sandwiches in the center of the table and left.

Nikki picked up her spoon. Steam rose from the soup. She caught a scent she didn't recognize. Kitten leaned behind Waters to whisper, "Aren't you afraid it might be poisoned?"

Normally she had a good appetite. Even without Kitten taunting her, she wasn't that hungry. She started to dip her spoon into the soup, when Cull reached across the table and switched bowls with her. He gave his stepsister a challenging look. Kitten rolled her eyes and waited for him to take a bite.

"What is going on?" Patricia demanded.

"It seems Kitten thinks Nikki's soup may be poisoned," Cull said. The man had remarkably good hearing. Or he knew Kitten too well.

"What?" Patricia seemed beside herself.

Kitten gave her a shrug as if she had no idea what Cull was talking about.

"This is ridiculous," Patricia said, and started to get up. But before she could, Travers reached over and switched bowls with Cull.

"Kitten, I will speak with you later," he said. He picked up his spoon and took a sip of the soup.

"I didn't do anything," the teen whined, and glared over at her brother who hadn't touched his soup.

Travers started to take a second spoonful, when he suddenly dropped his spoon. It hit the edge of the bowl. The sound was startling in the silent room. Everyone looked in his direction as he clutched his chest, his eyes wide and terrified before he toppled to the floor.

CHAPTER NINE

CULL STUDIED THE toes of his boots. Anything to keep him from looking at Nikki St. James sitting a seat away from the family in the hospital waiting room.

If his fool stepsister had tried to poison the woman... He glanced at Kitten. She was sulking in the corner. On the way to the hospital, all of them piled in Patricia's Suburban, Kitten had continued to protest that she hadn't poisoned Nikki's soup, that she'd just been teasing and that maybe the cook had done it.

Finally, Cull had told her to keep quiet, at which point Patricia had gone off on all of them for mistreating Kitten. "She's as upset as the rest of you and she's just a child!"

Cull had concentrated on the road ahead, determined not to get into it with any of them. They'd followed the ambulance to the hospital and were told to wait.

Earlier Ledger had gotten everyone coffee. Cull had watched him ask Nikki if she wanted some. She'd volunteered to go with him to the machine. After hearing how it was that Cull had brought her to the ranch, Ledger had accused him of "literally running her down on Main Street."

Since then Ledger had been especially nice to the

crime writer in spite of Cull telling him that he didn't trust the woman. He could see what Nikki was up to and he planned to put an end to it once they were alone.

At the sound of footfalls, Cull looked up—as did the rest of them—and saw Boone storming in. *"What happened?"* he demanded. He had beer on his breath, which answered the question as to where he'd gone after he'd stomped out earlier.

"We don't know for sure—" Cull didn't get to finish.

"Someone poisoned Dad," Ledger said. "At least that's what we think happened."

"Poisoned him?"

"We don't know for sure," Cull said.

Patricia jumped to her feet. "This is all her fault," she accused, pointing a finger at Nikki. "It was her bowl of soup—"

Boone shot a look at Nikki.

"Hold on, everyone," Cull said, raising his hands as they all started talking at once. "Nikki was the intended *victim.* Perhaps, Patricia, you should be talking to your daughter. She was the one who brought the bowl of soup out of the kitchen."

Patricia sputtered as if unable to get the words out fast enough. *"Kitten?* Kitten wouldn't… How can you possibly think…"

"I was just teasing." Kitten burst into tears and ran from the waiting room.

"Now see what you've done?" Patricia demanded before she went after her daughter.

"Let's all just calm down," Cull said. "I called the sheriff when we got here. I'm sure McCall will be able to—" He stopped as he saw the doctor and the sheriff coming down the hall toward him. Heart in his throat, he waited, fearing what the news was going to be.

NIKKI WATCHED THE two come down the hall. She couldn't tell from their somber faces what they'd discovered. If Travers had been poisoned… Her stomach knotted at the thought. Was there someone in this family *that* determined to keep her from learning the truth? What if because of her, Travers McGraw lost his life? She couldn't bear the thought.

Boone started to speak, but the sheriff cut him off. "Your father wasn't poisoned."

Nikki felt a wave of relief wash over her. She'd been so afraid that Kitten had done something stupid in an attempt to get rid of her.

"He's had a heart attack," the doctor said. "He's in stable condition, but not out of the woods yet. Were any of you aware of your father's heart problems?"

The attorney, who'd been sitting at the edge of the group, spoke for the first time. "Travers knew he had a bad ticker?" Jim Waters asked.

The doctor nodded. "I've warned him how important it was for him to relieve stress and eat healthy and slow down. I had hoped he might have shared that information with his family."

Cull groaned. "It was just like him not to."

"I want to see him," Boone said.

"If anyone should get to see him, it should be me," Patricia said as she came down the hall.

The doctor held up his hands. "None of you are going to see him. Right now the last thing he needs is more… stress." As Patricia started to argue, the doctor said, "You will be able to see him possibly in the morning, but only one at a time. And I won't have *any* of you upsetting him."

They all fell silent for a moment before Cull said, "You heard him. Dad's in stable condition. Let's all go home."

Nikki's head ached. She couldn't wait to get back to the ranch and take a couple of aspirin.

"I'm not riding with *you*," Kitten announced to Cull. "I'm riding with Boone."

Patricia took her daughter's hand. "No one's leaving until you all apologize to my daughter."

Cull let out a curse. "An apology? Have you forgotten that no one would have thought that Dad had been poisoned if it wasn't for Kitten? Fortunately the doctor recognized his condition as a heart attack, otherwise they would have been pumping his stomach while he was dying of heart failure."

"All that matters is that Dad is going to be all right. But this constant bickering has to stop," Ledger said.

"Then get rid of *her*!" Patricia said, pointing again at Nikki. "Now with Travers in the hospital, the whole idea of a book on the kidnapping should be scrapped."

"Patricia's right," Boone said, speaking up. "You just heard what the doctor said. Dad doesn't need the stress of having someone digging up the past, and for no reason, since we all know who kidnapped the twins."

Cull shook his head. "This isn't the time or the place to discuss this, and if any one of you dare bring this up when you see Dad…" He saw from their faces that they got the message. "In the meantime, Nikki stays and does whatever it is she does. If Dad changes his mind, *he'll* send her packing—but not us and not before Dad is well enough to make that call. Boone, I'm going to take your pickup. You can ride in Patricia's Suburban since you've obviously been drinking. Nikki, you come with me. The rest of you can go with Patricia or walk, I don't care." He reached for Nikki. "Let's go."

CULL GRIPPED THE steering wheel so hard he was white-knuckled as they left the hospital.

"Thank you for sticking up for me back at the hospital," Nikki said once they were on the road headed toward the ranch.

"I didn't do it for you," Cull said through gritted teeth without looking at her. "I did it for my father."

Out of the corner of his eye, he saw her turn away to look out her side window. Open prairie ran for miles, broken only occasionally by farmland all the way to the Little Rockies. He loved this country. Where some people saw nothing, he saw the beauty of the wild grasses, the rolling landscape, the huge sky overhead that ran from horizon to horizon, living up to the name Big Sky Country.

The night was clear and cool. Stars glittered in a canopy of navy velvet. He rolled down his window as they left town behind. The smell of sage and dust and wild grasses filled his nostrils. He breathed it in and tried to calm down. This was home. The prairie soothed him in a way no other landscape ever had. He loved this part of Montana the way others loved the mountains and pine trees.

For a moment, he wondered what Nikki saw when she looked out there. Or did she yearn for towering mountains studded with pine trees? He'd found few women who appreciated his part of the state. It was one reason he'd never settled down.

"I feel responsible for what's happened," she said. "I'm so glad your father is going to be all right."

He glanced over at her, his expression softening when he saw the tears in her eyes. "It's not your fault. Dad hasn't been well. You heard what the doctor said. The anniversary of the kidnapping is just one more weight piled onto all the stress he's normally under."

"I'm sorry," she said. "I wish there was some way I could help. If my leaving would help…"

He slowed for the turn into the ranch. "You would give up that easily? I thought you were determined to find out the truth about the kidnapping?"

"I am, but I can't promise—"

Cull laughed. "*Now* you play coy?" He shook his head. "Sorry, I'm not buying it. I think you'd do anything to get this particular story and that makes me wonder about you."

"What you see is what you get," she said, then added quickly, "You know what I mean."

He smiled. "You would have eaten that soup, wouldn't you?"

"Yes. Why does that bother you?" she asked.

Cull scoffed. "Because it shows me the kind of woman you are. You don't back down."

"I'm going to take that as a compliment."

"Suit yourself." He could feel her gaze on him as he pulled up in front of the house and parked.

"You know what I think? I think the reason you and the others are frightened of my digging into the kidnapping is because you have something to hide. There's something you held back all those years ago. Maybe it's just a memory that has haunted you. A sound, something that was said, something that you saw but didn't understand at the time."

He wanted to tell her how crazy she was, but she'd gotten too close to the truth. But some secrets were best kept silent, since they wouldn't change the kidnapping. Nor would they change who'd been behind it. "That's what you're counting on to solve this? Good luck."

"I was hoping that all of you would want this solved as much as your father does," she said.

Cull turned off the engine and turned to face her. "You just don't get it. We've been living with this for twenty-five years. Do you have any idea how painful all this is for us to have to relive every year? Can't you now see that it's killing my father?"

"That's why he needs to know what really happened."

Cull shook his head as he took off his Stetson and raked a hand through his hair. A dark lock fell over his eyes before he shoved the hat back on. For a moment, he simply studied her, wanting to look deeper, clear to her soul. If she hadn't already sold it for a story.

"I swear this tops it all. A *true crime writer*? And I thought the psychic he hired was bad enough."

"The sooner I can get to work, the sooner I will be gone."

He cocked his head, narrowing his eyes. "Gone, but not forgotten."

She seemed to ignore that and met his gaze with a steely one of her own.

"Why? What does it matter to you? I'm sure there are other tragic stories for you to delve into out there. So what is it about our particular story?"

Nikki looked away, giving him the impression that

for some reason this time it was more than finding out the truth for a bestseller. Again he found himself wondering, *Who is this woman?*

All his instincts told him that she was hiding something but he couldn't for the life of him figure out what it was. She was already a *New York Times* bestselling author. From what he could tell, she didn't need the money or the attention. She'd already made a name for herself. Writing another book about some horrendous crime wasn't going to get her anything she didn't already have.

Or would it?

"I'm not sure what you're after," he said carefully. "But I saw the way you were with my brother. You're not using Ledger to get whatever it is you're really after. Right now because of another woman who took him for a ride, he doesn't know his ass from a teakettle. You stay away from him. He was too young to remember anything about the kidnapping. I won't have you using him."

"I'm not using your brother."

Cull scoffed. "And you just happened to be in Whitehorse today sitting across from the café where my brother has breakfast on the days his ex-girlfriend waitresses there."

He caught her moment of surprise before she carefully hid it. "That's right," he said with a bitter chuckle. "For whatever reason, you will do whatever you have to, use whoever you have to, tear this family apart to get what you want." He frowned as he studied her. "For a book? I don't think so. Just know that while you're digging into every dark corner of our lives, I'm going to be digging into yours. I can't wait to find out what your real story is, Nikki St. James."

With that he opened his door and climbed out. He heard her open her door and exit, as well. A set of headlights washed over him as Patricia pulled the Suburban up in the yard.

Cull was in no mood for any of them. He didn't bother going inside, but instead took the path beside the house and headed for the stables. He was breathing hard, sucking in the cold night air as he tried to cool his anger. Chill down the heat that filled him whenever he got around that woman. Nikki St. James rattled him more than he wanted to admit. No good could come of this for any of them. He had to find a way to get rid of her and soon.

NIKKI STOOD NEXT to the ranch pickup feeling as if she'd just gone three rounds in the ring. Cull suspected there was more to her story for being here. He hadn't found it. Not yet, but he suspected enough that he wouldn't stop until he discovered the truth about her.

She let out a humorless chuckle. He said she wouldn't stop at anything? He was just like her. She watched him take off and realized he'd left her not so she could deal with his family, but so he could escape all of them.

"He's not usually so…rude."

Nikki spun around to find Ledger standing right behind her. "You startled me."

"Sorry." Ledger glanced toward the rest of his family entering the house. Patricia was arguing with Kitten about something as they started up the porch steps. Nikki was reminded of earlier when the teen almost knocked her down the stairs.

Jim Waters and Blake Ryan both walked past without looking at her. Patricia stopped on the porch and called down, "I'll get cook to put sandwiches out. I don't know about the rest of you, but I'm starved." Her gaze lit on Nikki. She turned quickly and went into the house.

"I heard that Patricia moved you out of the wing upstairs and put your belongings in the pool house," Ledger said. "Why don't I go with you to make sure everything is ready for you?"

"Thank you. That would be nice," she said, happy to have some time alone with Ledger. She was reminded, though, of what Cull said about not using his brother. "But Cull might not approve. He's worried that I'll take advantage of you."

Ledger chuckled. "Cull's the oldest so he always thinks he has to protect us all. His heart is in the right place, though."

"Why do you think he feels he needs to protect you from me?" she asked innocently enough as they walked down a path that led around the house.

"He thinks I'm a fool."

"Because of the woman at the café," she said as they left the house behind and walked through a stand of aspens. "I was sitting across the street this morning. I couldn't help but notice."

His smile was sad. "Abby."

The darkness felt good. So did being around Ledger. There was a quiet confidence about him that was nice, especially after the intensity of his older brother. "You're in love with her."

"It's that obvious, huh?" He laughed. "I guess Cull's right. I'm pretty transparent. He thinks I should forget her." He shrugged. "Can't."

"You're worried about her."

"With good reason. Her husband is…" He waved his hand through the air as if he couldn't come up with a name that was appropriate in front of her.

"But she won't leave him."

"Nope," he said with a shake of his head. She could hear the frustration in his words. "She says he needs her. I don't get it."

Nikki said nothing. There was nothing she could say. Women often stayed with controlling men for their own reasons. Who knew what Abby's real reason was.

"What do you remember about the night of the kidnapping?"

He glanced over at her, clearly a little taken aback by the quick change of subject. But she also noticed that his guard had gone up.

"I told you, I was three."

"Oh, I thought you might be able to help, especially given your father's health. I want to find out the truth for him more than ever now."

He nodded, looking guilty. "I think I remember… little things. Waking up to hear Patty screaming. The sound of people running down the hallway toward the nursery. My father on the phone to the sheriff. But I've heard my brothers say the same thing over the years, so maybe they are actually their memories and not even mine. There is one memory that I think is mine because when I think about that night I see myself standing at the end of the hall until someone noticed me."

"Who noticed you?"

"Patty. She was our nanny then."

"Did she say anything?"

"I'm sure I asked her what was going on." He

shrugged. "I have a faint memory of her saying something about making pancakes in the morning. See, I really have nothing that could help."

Pancakes? That sounded like a very strange conversation, if that's what it had been.

Ledger stopped in front of a small building. Next to it was a large swimming pool. The breeze ruffled the surface of the water, making it lap at the edges. He looked back at the house. Golden light spilled from most of the windows as if all the lights had been turned on.

"What if you find out who kidnapped Oakley and Jesse Rose only to discover that they're dead?"

"I think not knowing is worse for your father. Maybe if the truth came out, it would let everyone heal."

He shook his head. "Dad lives with hope. If you take that away…"

In the silence that fell between them, she heard voices coming from the back porch. Two figures were silhouetted there against the lights coming from the house. One was clearly Patricia. The other was a man, but she couldn't be sure who.

She turned, trying to catch their words on the breeze. Behind her, she heard Ledger open the door to the pool house. A moment later, a bright light came on.

"There you go," Ledger said in a voice loud enough that it would carry to the back of the house. "If you need anything, just holler."

The voices silenced. She turned to look at Ledger, surprised to realize that he'd signaled Patricia and whoever she'd been in an intense conversation with that they weren't alone. When Nikki looked back, the two figures had bled into the shadows and were gone.

Cull was so sure that she had Ledger wrapped around

her little finger. That he would do anything she asked. That he would let her use him.

As Ledger met her gaze, she saw something in his eyes before they darted away that gave her a start. Ledger was just as protective of the McGraw secrets as his brother Cull.

They were definitely hiding something, but she couldn't be sure it had anything to do with the kidnapping. What had the boys seen or heard that night that they were afraid she was going to uncover? Was there a secret they'd been keeping all these years? But if true, *who* were they protecting?

Glancing toward the stables, she thought she saw a figure standing just inside out of the light. Cull? Over her shoulder, she said to Ledger, "I know there is something you're all keeping from me. What I don't understand is why."

There was no answer. When she looked back, she saw that he was headed for the house. He appeared to be in a hurry.

Seeing her suitcase waiting for her just inside, she pushed open the door to the pool house. The place was beautifully furnished. As it hadn't been used since the kidnapping, she had to assume that Marianne was the one who'd decorated not only the pool house but the main house, as well.

She would be quite comfortable here instead of Cull's former room on the haunted wing, she thought, even though this small building might have even more persistent ghosts. Why, though, did Patricia want her out of the house so badly?

Before she walked through the door, she glanced again toward the house.

Her pulse jumped, her heart taking off like the wild stallion Boone had brought home earlier. Someone was standing at a second-story window. Her chest constricted as she realized that the window was at the end of the south wing. Someone had been watching her and Ledger from the nursery.

A shock wave moved through her as she saw the figure was a woman dressed in all white. Even her hair appeared to be white. For just a heartbeat, she thought it was Marianne.

The breeze billowed the curtains. Nikki blinked and the figure was gone as if she'd only imagined it—unlike the chill that moved through her, turning her blood to ice.

CHAPTER TEN

PATRICIA CALLED FROM the back porch saying cook had set out the sandwiches as Nikki started to close the pool house door. She felt her stomach growl. They'd missed lunch and now it was way past dinner.

"I can bring you a sandwich if you'd rather not go back to the house tonight."

She saw Cull come out of the darkness on the path from the barn. "I'm not that hun—" Her stomach growled again. By then, he'd reached her. He grinned, clearly having heard her stomach, and turned toward the house. "I'll be right back."

"Thank you, but I hate to have you go if you aren't hungry."

Cull stopped to look back at her. "If you want to eat by the pool, I'll bring back enough for both of us. Then we can talk."

She nodded, although she wasn't sure she liked the sound of that. Had Travers called and told him to send her packing? Or was Cull willing to help her with the book?

Nikki had yet to step inside the pool house, where she would be staying. She did so now, then picked up her suitcase and carried it into the bedroom.

It had been a long day. All she could think about was climbing into the bed and sleeping. But even as she thought it, she wondered how much sleep she would be able to get. So much had happened today and her list of suspects just seemed to continue to grow.

Not to mention the fact that she was starving.

Hearing a tap at the open door a few minutes later, she looked up to find Cull standing there. He had a tray with sandwiches, glasses of milk and cake. Chocolate cake. Her stomach growled loudly.

"Let's get you fed," he said, motioning toward the pool rather than coming inside. She'd been surprised that the McGraws had a pool since it was so seasonal in Montana. She said as much as she joined him at the outdoor table.

"My mother loved to swim. Now Kitten enjoys it. I take a dip occasionally." He handed her a plate with several sandwich options.

"But no one uses the pool house?"

"My mother used to come down here and read when she needed a break from all of us," Cull said. "It was her...sanctuary." He seemed to remember that the kidnappers had possibly met here that night before the twins were whisked off, never to be seen again. His expression soured.

Nikki wanted to ask him questions about his mother but right now seemed the wrong time. She took a bite of one of the quartered sandwiches. Chicken salad. It tasted wonderful.

"How is your father?" she asked after she'd swallowed.

He didn't seem surprised that she would know he'd

call the hospital after they got back. "Resting comfortably, the doctor said."

Nikki took another bite and noticed that Cull hadn't touched his yet. He was watching her.

"What?" she asked as she finished and picked up another.

"You. I'm used to women who don't eat carbs. Hell, don't eat anything, from what I can tell." For a moment, she wanted to defend her eating habits and her rounded though slim figure. He didn't give her a chance. "I like women who have curves."

Cull seemed to realize what he'd said. "I mean—" He laughed softly and picked up a sandwich. "I should just shut up and eat, huh."

They ate in a companionable silence for a while. He'd turned on the pool lights. The water shimmered invitingly.

"You're welcome to go in," he said, clearly having noticed the longing in her expression.

"I didn't bring a suit."

"I wouldn't let that stop you."

She laughed at that. "I've already caused a stir around here. I can well imagine what your stepmother would say."

"Yes, Patty." He shook his head. "Life is strange, isn't it?"

"Do you remember her when she was your nanny?"

He nodded thoughtfully. "Quiet, shy, mousy, I think is how the press described her. I've often wondered about the change in her." He eyed her closely. "I'm sure you do, too."

She met his gaze for a moment before she lowered hers and hesitated as she looked at the chocolate cake.

Cull picked up a piece and put it in front of her. "Enjoy—you deserve it after the day you've had."

"I could say the same to you."

He nodded and looked toward the pool. "I'm sorry I gave you such a hard time earlier."

"Speaking of earlier, I heard Patty talking to someone behind the house. It sounded rather heated."

"I think it was Blake. He's been with Dad from as far back as I can remember. They were probably arguing over Dad's health. Blake thinks Patty could be more…agreeable."

Nikki wondered if Cull really expected her to believe that's what they were arguing about. She hadn't been able to make out much of the argument but it hadn't been about Travers's health. And she suspected Cull knew that, since the barn was closer to the house—and the argument.

"I really doubt that was what they were arguing about and you know it," she said, calling him on it. "Why lie about it? What is it you're all trying so hard to keep from me?"

He looked up at her in surprise, his gaze suddenly calculating. "You don't miss much."

"It's my job," she said defensively.

"For the book."

There was that suspicion again. She felt her heart quicken—from his look, from his words. "I know it's hard. A stranger coming in who might uncover your most intimate secrets. It's hard for me, too. I often get emotionally involved with the family. I'm human. But I'm not here to hurt any of you. I just want—"

"The truth." He nodded as if he still had his doubts about her real reasons as he rose from his chair. "You look as if you are going to fall asleep right out here by the pool." He removed the other piece of chocolate cake from the tray and picked up the dirty dishes. "I'll take these up to the house. The cake…well, you might wake up in the middle of the night and need something."

It was such a sweet gesture, bringing down the sandwiches, eating with her out here by the pool, leaving the cake and taking the dirty dishes. She couldn't help but be touched. "Thank you."

"I'm sure I'll see you in the morning. Breakfast is at seven but if that is too early for you, Frieda will see that you get whatever you need." He seemed to hesitate for a moment as if there was more he wanted to say. But then he smiled almost sadly and said, "Good night, Nikki. Sleep well."

"So THAT'S WHAT'S going on," Patricia said the moment Cull pushed open the door to the kitchen and put down the tray. "Conspiring with the enemy."

He shook his head. It was late and he was too exhausted from the day he'd had to argue with her. "Let's not get into it." He started to turn away, but she grabbed his arm.

"Your father is lying in a hospital bed and it is all that woman's fault!"

He turned to face her. "*No, it's not.* If anyone is to blame, it's you. You harp and harp at him until I'm amazed he doesn't just tell you to shut the hell up."

Her eyes widened in shock. "How dare you—"

"Oh, I dare," he said, taking a step toward her. "I have been wanting to tell you how I feel for a very long time. My father took you in, married you and has helped raise your daughter and neither of you have ever said thank-you. You both just demand and demand. Nothing is ever enough."

She was shaking her head furiously. "You can't blame me for his heart attack. It's this stupid kidnapping. He just won't leave it alone."

Cull took a step back giving her an incredulous look. "*Stupid* kidnapping? Patty, his children were taken. For all he knows they're dead. Are you that self-centered that you can't understand that?"

She looked chastised for a moment, but quickly recovered. "Well, it's been twenty-five years. How long do you expect me to put up with this?"

"He is *never* going to forget. If you can't accept that, then there's the door. No one is forcing you and Kitten to stay here."

"You'd love to see that, wouldn't you?"

He said nothing, his earlier anger receding, leaving him feeling sorry for his harsh words, no matter how heartfelt. "Can't you just be happy?" He opened his arms to encompass not just the kitchen but the entire ranch. "Look where you live, look how you live. Can't you just embrace that?"

She sniffed and looked as if she might cry.

"And leave Nikki alone. Let her do what she came here to do."

"She's not going to find out anything more than the FBI and the sheriff did all those years ago." Something in her voice gave away her hope that that was the case. He'd often wondered if Patty had something to hide about the night of the kidnapping. If so, was she worried that Nikki would be able to uncover it? That could explain why she'd been so upset about the crime writer's appearance here.

"Only time will tell, I guess. I figure she'll be gone soon enough." He started to turn away again but this time it was her words that stopped him.

"Are you sure that's what you want?" There was accusation as well as mocking in her tone.

He stopped at the door, but didn't turn. "It's what we all want." And he was betting that each of them had their own reasons for wanting Nikki gone.

AFTER CULL LEFT, Nikki went inside the pool house, locking the doors before heading to the bedroom. She was so tired that she quickly brushed her teeth, stumbled into her pajamas and fell onto the bed.

She'd been so sure she wouldn't be able to sleep with everything that was going on. Everything including Cull. She thought of his intense blue eyes. He saw too much. But that meant he always had—even as a child. There was no doubt in her mind that he knew more about the kidnapping than he'd told anyone.

He was her last thought before she dropped into the deep, dark hole of sleep. That was why it took more than a few minutes for her to drag her way up and out of the dream.

She sat up in bed, rubbing her hands over her face as she tried to let go of what had started as a nice dream and had turned into a nightmare. Even as she thought it, she could feel the dream slipping away, leaving only that heavy, suffocating feeling of doom.

Nikki tried to hang on to the thread of her nightmare. Something to do with Cull and the horses in the barn and her father. She shook her head. Clearly not one of those dreams that made a lot of sense. She'd never even known her father. But he was in the dream. He was in the stables. And something horrible was happening.

That's when she woke up. She sat listening to the night sounds. An owl hooted in the distance. Closer she heard a horse whinny. Then another horse, then another.

She frowned as she got out of bed and padded barefoot into the living area of the pool house to look out toward the stables. A light was on. She caught movement. Someone was in the horse barn.

Remnants of her nightmare made her heart beat faster. Maybe it hadn't been a dream. Maybe she'd heard something…

She opened the door. The Montana night was clear, the stars glittering overhead, only a slit of silver moon dangling over the barn. She made her way along the path, hugging herself against the slight chill in the air.

As she drew closer, she could hear the horses, restless in their stalls. A shadow moved along the edge of the horse barn. A moment later she heard raised voices. Male voices.

Her bare feet were beginning to ache from the cold of the stones along the path. She shivered, debating turning back. But curiosity won out. Her showing up at the ranch had caused a stir. If whoever was arguing in the barn this late at night had something to do with the kidnapping…

She moved to the edge of the barn door so she could hear better over the whinnying and stomping of the horses inside.

"You're making a terrible mistake. If you're wrong…" She didn't recognize the male voice and wondered if it could be the former ranch manager who'd apparently been arguing with Patricia earlier.

"I know what I'm doing. I'll do whatever I have to." Her heart slammed against her rib cage. This voice she recognized. *Cull.*

"You said you don't want anyone to get hurt. I don't see how that can be avoided under the circumstances. This crime writer—"

"Don't worry. I'll take care of her myself if this all goes south."

Nikki felt the air rush from her lungs. She stumbled back, her shoulder hitting the gate. The metal latch rattled.

"Did you hear that?" the unfamiliar male voice asked a second before Nikki heard someone moving in her direction.

She flattened herself against the side of the barn but quickly realized she would be seen by whoever came out. Her only hope of getting away unseen was to go around the side of the building. But that meant climbing into the corral.

Nikki hurriedly climbed over the corral railing, dropping down to the soft hoof-turned earth. Her bare feet sunk into the dirt, slowing her escape. Just a few more yards and—

Suddenly out of the corner of her eye, she saw a horse come galloping out of the barn and into the corral. It headed right for her, ears back, hooves throwing up dirt clods as it barreled forward.

Nikki lunged for the corral fence as the huge horse bore down on her. Her hands brushed the railing and missed. Not that she would have been able to climb out before the horse reached her anyway.

Two strong, large hands grabbed her from around the waist and swung her up and over the railing. She felt the horse's breath at her neck. Before she knew what was happening, she slammed into a very solid male chest. Behind her, the horse stomped and snorted just feet away past the corral railing. She realized it must be the stallion that Boone had delivered to the ranch earlier.

The arms that had wrapped around her now set her down hard at the edge of the corral. *"What the hell do you think you're doing?"* Cull demanded as he held her at arm's length. "You could have been killed. What were you thinking getting into the corral?"

She couldn't speak and realized she was trembling all over from the close call. Worse, as she glanced toward the barn, she began trembling harder when she realized that someone had set that horse free in the corral. Cull? Then why save her?

"What are *you* doing out here?" she demanded.

"Checking the horses. I heard something."

She nodded. "So did I." She'd heard enough, that was for sure.

His gaze never left Nikki's face. He was studying her in the dim light from the barn as if he was trying to understand her. "You have no business in the corral. That's a wild horse in there."

She nodded and tried to swallow down the lump in her throat. Tears stung her eyes as she realized how close she'd come to being trampled. Worse, that she couldn't trust Cull.

He shook his head. She couldn't tell if he thought her silly and stupid. "Come on. I'll walk you back to the pool house."

She glanced toward the barn. The horses had settled back down. She saw no movement deep in the stalls. Whoever Cull had been talking to, he was gone. Which left the question of who had let the stallion out and why. Had he hoped to scare her? Or kill her?

She could smell Cull's very masculine scent intermingled with saddle leather and fresh air. If the purpose had been to scare her, then the stallion had done his job. She would have to be more careful, given what she'd overhead. Especially more careful when it came to Cull McGraw.

CHAPTER ELEVEN

NIKKI DROVE INTO Whitehorse as the sun arced over the prairie. The day was beautiful, sunny and warm, the big sky blue and dotted with white fluffy clouds. She'd awoken before dawn with a suspicion that had felt like a douse of ice water.

She'd hurriedly done research on her phone before giving the sheriff a call and asking if she could come by and see her.

Sheriff McCall Crawford looked up from her desk as Nikki came in. She was a slim, pretty woman who Nikki had heard was a no-nonsense law officer. Mostly she'd heard that McCall could be trusted.

"Thanks for seeing me," she said, and closed the door behind her.

The sheriff raised a brow. "You sounded so cryptic on the phone." She motioned to a chair and Nikki sat down. "I was planning to drive out this morning to the ranch and see how you were doing."

"I'm sorry we met the way we did yesterday," Nikki said honestly. "Now I am hesitant to even voice my suspicions, but I hope you will take what I have to tell you seriously."

"Your suspicions after only one day at the Sundown Stallion Station? You really do work fast. I'm intrigued."

"Were you aware of Travers McGraw's health before his heart attack?"

"I'll admit I hadn't seen him in a good while," the sheriff said as she leaned back in her chair. "I was taken aback by his condition."

Nikki nodded. "His family seems to think the cause is his obsession with finding out what happened to the twins."

"But you don't think that's it?"

She shook her head. "I think he really *is* being poisoned." She pulled out her phone. "I've seen this once before. His symptoms are consistent with those of people who are being slowly exposed to small amounts of arsenic over time. Headaches, loss of weight, confusion, depression. In his case, finally cardiac arrest."

The sheriff looked skeptical. "I'm assuming you have no proof of this?"

"No, and I had the same reaction at first that you are. But then I remembered that his wife Marianne had the same symptoms."

"Twenty-five years ago?" The sheriff sat up, leaning her elbows on her desk, definitely interested now.

"But in the same house. The same house *and* the same people living there," she said. "If I'm right, that would seem like too much of a coincidence, don't you think?"

"Marianne's depression was blamed on postpartum. Her other symptoms on possibly an illicit love affair."

Nikki nodded.

"No one else is experiencing these symptoms at the house?" the sheriff asked slowly, studying her.

"No, so I doubt it's tainted water or any other factor in the house causing it other than the obvious. Someone is intentionally poisoning him."

The sheriff said, "He's in the hospital. If he was being poisoned, it probably wouldn't still be in his system, except possibly in a strand of hair from his head."

Nikki nodded. It was one way to find out if there was any basis for her suspicion.

"Speaking of suspicion," the sheriff said, "how are you since your accident in front of the Whitehorse Café?"

"Fortunately, I wasn't hurt other than a knock on my head."

"Fortunately," the sheriff said, smiling.

Nikki got to her feet. "I won't keep you, but I was hoping you might see if my suspicions are valid. Given Travers McGraw's condition, I didn't think it was something that could wait."

"I suppose you have a suspect to go along with your suspicions?"

"It's a short list," Nikki said. "But I'm sure you can guess who's on it. The person who has the most to profit if Mr. McGraw should die. The same person who had reason to want to get rid of Marianne McGraw twenty-five years ago."

CULL FELT THE full responsibility of keeping peace at home along with running the ranch, with his father in the hospital. Blake Ryan had handled that job for years. But a couple of years ago he had stepped down, and Cull, as oldest son, had moved into the position alongside his father.

Running the ranch, he could do. It was keeping peace

in the house that was the problem. Patricia had been on a rampage since yesterday. He'd heard her yelling at Frieda, their elderly family cook, this morning. He'd broken that up only to find that Nikki St. James had taken off before breakfast and no one knew where she'd gone.

Had she seen how useless this was and left? He could only hope, but even as he thought it, he knew better. Nikki wasn't a quitter. Wherever she'd gone, she'd be back.

As crazy as things had been, he hoped that his father's heart attack would be a wake-up call for him. Something had to change.

"How is he?" Cull asked the nurse when he reached his father's hospital floor after driving in from the ranch.

"He's doing well," she said. "You can see him. Just keep your visit short and don't upset him."

That meant not mentioning Nikki or the twins or Patty or Kitten or the ranch, Cull thought as he walked down the hall. He hesitated at his father's door. He'd watched the man get sicker and sicker and hadn't been able to do anything. Travers McGraw was stubborn; Cull knew that only too well. But maybe now he was ready to face things.

As he walked into the room, he saw that his father's eyes were closed and he was breathing steadily. He stood for a moment, simply relieved. He was glad to see his father's color was better. Stepping to the bed, he touched his hand.

His father's eyes opened and he smiled. "Hope I didn't give you a scare."

Cull chuckled. "Naw, we all just finished our meals before rushing you to the hospital," he joked.

"I'm fine," his father assured him. "The doctor said it was a minor heart attack and he's already lectured me, so you don't have to."

He nodded. Travers McGraw was anything but fine. He needed to make some changes in his life. If he didn't realize that now...

"Is Ms. St. James still at the house?"

Technically, she'd spent last night in the pool house, where Patricia had exiled her, and was gone before he'd gotten up. But he said, "She is," hoping his father would ask him to send her away.

"Good. I still want her to do the book, no matter how it turns out."

He wanted to argue with his father, but he bit his tongue. "Okay."

"I'd appreciate it if you would help her, do whatever she needs."

His father was asking too much, but he nodded, thinking of working closely with Ms. St. James. He had a sudden vision of her swimming half-naked in the pool on a moonlit night— Where had that come from? He smothered the thought, but it took a while for the heat in his belly to go away.

"Is Kitten all right? I hope I didn't scare her."

Cull chuckled at that. "Little scares Kitten."

"So you'll see to it that Ms. St. James gets everything she needs."

He'd love to see to her...needs. "I will."

"Good." His father seemed to relax. He closed his eyes and for a moment, Cull thought he'd dropped back to sleep.

"I can't tell you how much it means to me to have you for a son, Cull." His father opened his eyes again and reached for his hand. "I know I can depend on you and your brothers."

The nurse came in then and shooed Cull out. He promised to come back later and left the hospital.

On the way back to the ranch, he spent most of the time grumbling to himself. By the time he reached the front door of the house, he'd made up his mind.

He would do exactly what his father asked him to do. He'd help Nikki in every way possible. And once she realized there was nothing new to write, she would leave. His father would be disappointed, but he was going to be disappointed anyway.

As he parked in front of the house, he saw that Nikki wasn't back. He wondered where she'd gotten off to so early in the morning and if she'd tell him if he asked. He headed for the pool house only to cross paths with Kitten.

"She's not there," the teen said. "I heard her tell Frieda that she was going into town to do some research." Kitten made it sound like Nikki had lied. "I bet she's meeting a man." Her eyes glinted with mischief. "Which means you got dumped. Looks like you'll never get a girlfriend, even one you had to run over with your truck."

He had wondered how long it would take for that little tidbit to get around. Now he knew. "Kitten, there is a big, black spider on your shoulder."

The girl screamed and began running around swatting at her shoulders.

"Sorry, it wasn't a spider. It was that chip you have on your shoulder."

She mugged a face at him. "I'm going to tell Mother."

"Be my guest." He headed for the stables, wondering what kind of research Nikki was doing in town. Or if Kitten was right and Nikki had lied.

ALL THE WAY back to the ranch, Nikki told herself she'd done the right thing going to the sheriff. If nothing came of it or if she was dead wrong, then at least she'd shared her suspicions.

Now she had to get on with her work. As soon as she reached the ranch, she went looking for Patricia. As a true crime writer, she'd learned that where she found the truth was in the inconsistencies. Not just slight changes in a person's story, but new information that they hadn't remembered before. It always surprised her. Small tidbits were often drawn up from some well of memory to surprise both her and her interviewee.

While she also looked for changes in the stories, she found that those who had the most to hide had almost memorized their statements. They would provide an almost word-for-word account even as many as twenty-five years later.

After something horrible happened, of course people often changed. How much or how little was also often a clue. In Patricia's case, the change had been huge.

Nikki had read Travers's testimony as well as Patricia's from the sheriff's reports along with hundreds of newspaper articles. Travers had awakened to find his wife gone and had rushed out into the hallway on hearing Patty's screams. He raced down the hall to find the window near the twins' cribs wide-open, the cribs empty and a ladder leaning against the side of the house.

He saw no one, but had raced outside only to find

footprints in the soft dirt under the window. He'd immediately called the sheriff.

It wasn't until later that he saw Marianne. She'd apparently gone for a swim in the middle of the night because she was coming from the pool house.

Nikki had a pretty good idea that Patty's story would be the same one she had told dozens and dozens of times after the kidnapping. But still she needed to hear it herself.

As she entered the house, she heard voices coming from the kitchen. Patty's voice carried well and while Nikki couldn't make out her words, she could hear the tone. Patty was unhappy with someone.

She found her at the breakfast bar in front of a muffin. From the tension in the room, Patricia had been having a heated discussion with the cook, Frieda Holmes. Clearly Nikki had just interrupted it.

The cook turned her back to the stove, but not before Nikki had seen her blotched red face and her tears.

"I hope this is a good time," she said, knowing full well that it wasn't. What had the two been discussing that had them both so upset? "Mrs. McGraw, I need to ask you some questions."

"You can't be serious," Patricia said, shoving away her crumb-filled plate. "My husband is in the hospital possibly dying and you're intent on—"

"Doing what he asked me to do. I know you told the authorities what happened that night, but I need to hear it from you. The sooner I get everything I need, the sooner I will be gone."

Patricia sighed. "Not here," she said, glancing at the cook's back. Frieda didn't seem to hear. Or at least didn't react. "Let's go into Travers's office."

Nikki followed her, thinking about yesterday and the first time she'd seen Travers. She was glad to hear he was doing better and would be allowed to have visitors later today.

As if thinking the same thing Nikki was, Patricia said, "When I see my husband this afternoon, I'm going to convince him to put an end to this book of yours."

"You do realize I can write the book without his permission."

Patricia huffed as she sat down at her husband's desk. "Well, I have nothing to add."

Maybe. Maybe not. "I wanted to ask you about Marianne. You were living in the house. You would know if there were problems between her and her husband. If there was another man." She looked down at her notes and turned on her digital recorder. "In other interviews, you've said she'd been acting...strangely."

Clearly Patricia had expected to simply tell the same old story she'd been telling about that night. Her dislike of Marianne became quickly evident. "*Strangely* was putting it mildly. She would wander around the backyard as if lost. I thought for sure she'd lost her mind and as it turns out..."

"What about her relationship with her husband?" Nikki purposely avoided saying Travers's name.

Patricia rolled her eyes and seemed to relax a little. Gossip was clearly something she could get her teeth into. "I knew the minute I was hired that there was trouble in that marriage. I'd seen the signs. It wasn't my first rodeo. Marianne was miserable and not just because of this unexpected pregnancy. That's right, the twins were an accident." She nodded enthusiastically as she leaned closer. "From the start I could tell that she didn't want them."

"Was there another man?"

With a sigh, Patricia sat back. "You should have seen the way she was with that horse trainer. She made a fuss over him. It was so obvious."

"I'm sure her husband must have noticed."

Patricia shook her head in disgust. "He was blind to anything she did. Sure he noticed, but he thought she was just being nice to him since he was away from his wife and child and clearly lonely."

"Maybe that's all it was."

"Then why would the two of them cook up this kidnapping scheme?" Patricia demanded.

"Maybe they didn't. When the horse trainer was arrested, he didn't have the money. Neither did Marianne. So what happened to the ransom money?"

Patricia shrugged. "Maybe he hid it, waiting until the two of them could run away together."

"Strange, though, that it hasn't been found. I know the authorities searched the ranch for any sign of the money—and the twins."

"You mean searched for graves."

"But they found nothing."

"Have you taken a look at this country around the ranch? It's Missouri Breaks, miles and miles of nothing but gullies and cliffs and pines, millions of places to hide anything you want."

Nikki couldn't argue that. "Let's talk about that night."

Patricia proceeded to tell her story almost verbatim from her other accounts. Just as Nikki had assumed, she got the same old, same old.

Patricia claimed she'd been awakened by a noise and gotten up to check the twins. As she'd crossed the hall, she'd been surprised to feel the breeze coming in— convinced she'd left their window closed.

On entering the room, she'd gone to close it when she noticed that one of the cribs was empty. She'd quickly checked the other and panicked.

"I stepped to the window, saw the ladder and the footprints below and started screaming."

"Tell me where everyone else was at that point."

She frowned. "It's really a blur. Everyone came running down the hallway toward the nursery. Travers got there first and then the kids. Travers told me to take the children to my room and stay there to wait for the sheriff. That's about the time Marianne showed up, her hair wet. I didn't realize until later that she'd been for a swim—in the middle of the night." She rolled her eyes, making it clear she thought the woman had been crazy even back then.

"Let's not forget that Jesse Rose's blanket was found in the pool house after the kidnapping," Patricia said and raised an eyebrow.

Jesse Rose's blanket. So that's what the kidnapper had left behind? She tried not to give away her surprise in her expression. "And you had all three boys with you?"

The woman started to nod, but stopped. "No, Ledger was always the one lagging behind. I saw him down the hall and called to him."

"Had he come from his room?"

"No." She frowned, seeming surprised by her answer. "His bare feet were all muddy. I had to wash them in my tub in my room before I let him get into my bed.

But that was nothing unusual. Ledger often went out at night and wandered around. Like Marianne."

"Did he say anything to you that night about where he'd been or what he might have seen?"

"Seen?" She scoffed at the idea. "He was a child. Three years old. Cull was only seven and Boone, he was barely five. None of them said a word. I put them all into my bed. Like me, they were wide-eyed with terror and listening to what was going on outside my room."

AFTER TALKING TO PATTY, Nikki went looking for Ledger. But when she reached the barn, it was Cull who she found feeding the horses.

"Have you seen Ledger?" she asked.

"He's gone into town for breakfast," Cull said without looking at her.

Abby, she thought, and her heart went out to him.

"Well, since I have you…" she said.

He stopped what he was doing to give her his full attention. "So you think you have me, huh? You think you have the entire family now." He shook his head.

She ignored him. Patricia had proven Nikki's theory this morning. There'd been a slight change in her story, giving Nikki new information that Patricia hadn't remembered before. It was something small, something that even Nikki wasn't sure mattered.

"What part of 'it's not safe for you to be here' don't you get?" he demanded.

"I've been around horses before—just not unbroken stallions let out into a corral I happen to be in."

He ignored the accusation. "Not *here* in the stables. On this ranch. Didn't dinner last night teach you anything?"

"The soup *wasn't* poisoned," she said as she stepped closer to rub a horse's neck.

"The point is in this house it could have been," he said without looking at her. "You have no idea. The past twenty-five years…" He shook his head as if he couldn't go on. "Everyone is sick of hearing about the kidnapping let alone talking about it."

"Everyone but your father."

A muscle in his jaw jumped. "My father is the kind of man who just doesn't give up."

"What kind of man are you?"

He shifted those blue eyes to her, welding her to the spot. "The kind who knows a lost cause when he sees one."

"We've already had this argument. I'm not leaving and I'm guessing your father isn't giving up. He still wants me to do the book." She narrowed her eyes at him. "And unless I'm wrong, which I don't believe I am, he asked you to help me."

He chuckled as he shook his head again. "All you're doing is making things worse for everyone, including yourself."

"Don't you want to know the kind of woman I am?" When he said nothing, she continued. "I'm like your father. When I start something I finish it."

Cull seemed to consider that before he turned toward her, his lips quirking into a grin as his eyes blazed with challenge. "Is that right?"

Before she could react, he grabbed her and dragged her to him. His mouth dropped to hers in a demanding kiss as he pushed her back against the barn wall.

Fleetingly she wondered how far he would go. He

was angry, frustrated with what was happening to his family, scared. She knew those emotions only too well.

But she thought she also knew Cull McGraw. No matter what her grandfather said, she thought she was a pretty good judge of character. Cull wasn't the kind of man who would force a woman. He didn't have to. He was trying to scare her—just as he had with his talk of evil here on the ranch.

She did her best not to react to the kiss. It was a fine one even though she hadn't asked for it and his heart wasn't really in it. But she'd felt his fire, his passion fueled by the well of emotions surging through him.

The kiss made her want a real one from him, which was more dangerous for her than a wild stallion. The kiss ended as abruptly as it had started. Cull shoved off the barn wall and took two steps back. If anything, he looked more upset than he had before.

"You should be afraid of me," he said, his voice rough with emotion as he jerked off his straw cowboy hat and raked a hand through his thick dark hair. "I even scare myself."

"You don't scare me."

"Then you are more foolish than I thought. What happened here changed us all. If you can't feel the malice…" His gaze shifted toward the open barn door. She could see the house in the distance.

Nikki looked toward the nursery window. The curtain moved but it could have merely been the breeze stirring it.

When she looked at Cull again, all she saw was his backside headed out to pasture. She watched him go, aware of the lingering taste and scent of him, both more disturbing than she'd wanted to admit earlier.

Now she found herself alone in the barn where her father had worked all those years ago. An eerie quiet seemed to fall over it in Cull's absence.

She moved to the horse she'd petted earlier and again rubbed its neck, needing to feel the warmth. Cull was right. She could feel malice here, but unlike him, she didn't believe in dark spirits.

Instead, she believed that evil lived in the heart of man—and woman. She thought of Sheriff McCall Crawford and wondered if she'd do anything about her suspicions. Nikki was anxious to find out if she'd been right, if her instincts hadn't let her down.

Meanwhile, those instincts told her that someone in this house knew what had happened to the twins. She'd never felt it more strongly.

A breeze rustled the nearby pines, making the boughs groan softly. A hinge creaked somewhere deep in the barn. The hair quilled on the back of her neck, a gust of cold air rushing over her skin to raise goose bumps.

Suddenly she had the feeling she was no longer alone. She shuddered at what felt like breath on the back of her neck. As she rushed toward the barn door, she told herself she didn't believe in evil ghosts. Whatever she'd just felt in the barn was only her overactive imagination, nothing more.

And yet the feeling hung with her all the way to the pool house.

CHAPTER TWELVE

NIKKI CLOSED THE pool house door behind her, shaken by whatever that had been in the barn. She told herself it was a reaction to Cull. Every run-in with him left her off-kilter. He was angry and afraid—she could understand that. But kissing her? That had scared him more than it had her.

At least that's what she thought. He wanted her gone. Well, it couldn't be soon enough for Nikki, she thought, surprised she felt that way. She wasn't safe here from herself. She didn't scare easily, but Cull was right. There was something on the wind that turned her blood to ice.

Not that she could leave before she was done. Which reminded her that she needed to take advantage of whatever time she had here. She glanced through the window toward the house. Earlier she'd heard just enough of what Patricia had been saying to the cook this morning, to make her anxious to talk to Frieda.

At the main house, Nikki entered the kitchen to find Frieda Holmes sitting in a chair in the corner. The cook had a threaded needle in her hand and a quilt lay over her lap. Nikki had seen her elderly neighbor sew on a quilt binding enough times that she knew at once what the woman was doing.

"What a beautiful quilt," she said. "Did you sew it yourself?"

Frieda nodded almost shyly. She was a small, almost homely woman with dark hair shot with gray. She was in her early sixties, by Nikki's calculations, and had been the cook for years.That was back before they could afford a full-time nanny. Back before the twins.

Nikki moved closer. "I love the colors, and your quilting is amazing. My goodness, it's all done by hand." This surprised her, since her neighbor quilted with a sewing machine and only hand sewed the binding.

"It relaxes me," Frieda said proudly as she ran a hand over the tiny, closely spaced stitches.

At the sound of footfalls behind her, Nikki turned as Patricia came into the kitchen. "What's going on?" she demanded.

Frieda stuck her finger with the needle as she hurriedly tried to put the quilt away. She tucked the needle in the fabric and shoved the quilt into a bag next to the chair. She wiped the blood from her stuck finger on a corner of her apron and rushed to her feet.

"I was waiting on the pies in the oven," the cook said as if feeling guilty for getting off her feet for even a break.

"And I was just admiring Frieda's quilt," Nikki said.

Patricia dismissed that with a flip of her hand. "I've never understood why anyone would want to cut up perfectly good fabric and then sew it back together. It makes no sense."

"It makes beautiful quilts," Nikki said, seeing how Patricia's remark had hurt Frieda's feelings. "My neighbor quilts. Unfortunately, I've never taken the time to learn."

"Well, if you like quilts that much, you should drive out to Old Town and visit the Whitehorse Sewing Circle." Patricia turned to Frieda. "Don't you still meet in the community center down there? It's not that far from here. There are always a bunch of old ladies in the back working on a quilt. Isn't that right, Frieda?"

Frieda looked even more upset. Was it the crack about old ladies? Or something else? "I would love to do that," Nikki said. "Is there a certain day I could go?"

But it was her boss who answered for the cook. "Frieda goes on her day off, Wednesday. I'm sure she'd be happy to take you." There was something in Patricia's tone, an underlying menace, that made no sense to Nikki.

The timer on the oven went off and Frieda quickly picked up two hot pads and opened the oven without saying a word.

"I'm going into town to the hospital to see my husband," Patricia announced as she looked at Nikki. "You might not be here by Wednesday if Travers has decided to stop this ridiculous book." She waved a hand through the air, not giving Nikki a chance to remind the woman that she could do the book without Travers's permission, before she turned to Frieda.

"There are fresh vegetables from the garden that need to be washed and refrigerated right away," the woman said to the cook. "Please don't keep Frieda from her work," she said to Nikki. "I believe Cull has a horse saddled and waiting for you. He told me to tell you to have Frieda provide you with a picnic lunch. Apparently, he's taking you for a horseback ride." Her gaze took in what Nikki was wearing. "You might want to change."

With that she spun on her heel and stormed out in a cloud of expensive perfume.

Cull was taking her on a horseback ride? That was news to her. Frieda still seemed upset even with Patricia gone as she took out four beautiful apple pies from the oven. Nikki noticed that the woman's hands were shaking. Patricia had upset her and it was unclear to Nikki how exactly other than the woman's demanding and demeaning tone. So why was Frieda still working for her? Surely she could get a job elsewhere.

"I'll put together a picnic lunch for you while you change," the cook said, clearly wanting Nikki out of her kitchen.

"Thank you." She left to go change and when she returned, Frieda handed her an insulated bag heavy with food. As she thanked her again, Frieda busied herself washing the vegetables as per her boss's orders.

On the way to the barn, Nikki wondered if this horseback picnic ride was Cull's idea—or Patricia's. Either way, it would give her time alone with him away from a lot of the drama.

CULL WATCHED THROUGH the open doorway as Nikki made her way down to the barn. She'd changed from the slacks, blouse and high heels she'd been wearing earlier. Now she was in a pair of jeans, a T-shirt and tennis shoes. He should have realized she wouldn't own any cowboy boots.

Still, she looked good. She had a bag in one hand, no doubt their picnic lunch. He smiled to himself. The horseback ride had been Patricia's idea when she'd found him in the barn.

"Get her out of here for a while," the woman had

said, and he hadn't needed to ask whom she was re-
ferring to. "Take her for a horseback ride. Even better, leave her out there in the wilds. Or…" A look had
come over his stepmother. "Or cut her cinch so she has
an accident. Just joking," she added quickly at his mock
shocked expression.

Patricia had caught him at just the right time. He felt
antsy and knew exactly what he needed, and it was to
get on the back of a horse and ride out of here. "I'll take
her for a ride," he said, making Patricia smile.

As Nikki approached the barn, he said, "I should
have asked you if you rode."

"Or if I wanted to go on a picnic with you," she said
but was smiling. "I have ridden before. Once at a fair
when I was a child."

Great, he thought. Green. Just what he needed. "I
have a mild-mannered horse you'll like." He could see
that she was trying to think of a good reason to say no.
Who could blame her after earlier in the barn? That had
been stupid kissing her. What had he been thinking?

And then springing this horseback ride and picnic
on her. If he was her, he'd be suspicious.

"You should see the ranch," he said, determined that
she would go with him. "Consider it research. Also I
know you're dying to get me alone so you can…grill
me."

She was looking skeptically at the horse he'd saddled
for her. "I'm not sure about this." It had been too long
since she'd been on the back of a horse, but he didn't
like leaving her here alone with almost everyone gone.

"Where is that woman who will stop at nothing to
get what she wants?" he asked her.

She smiled and looked resigned.

"Hey, it's going to be fun. Trust me. You're in good hands with me."

Clearly, she wasn't so sure about that. But he'd promised his father he would help her. And wasn't that what he was doing? But how long before she realized there was nothing new to write about? How long before she realized that she'd wasted her time coming here?

Soon, he hoped. She didn't want to believe it, but she'd put herself in danger. She had a reputation for getting to the truth. What if there was someone on the ranch who had more to hide than he did?

He hadn't been trying to scare her. There was something evil in that house. He'd felt it too many times. But unlike Nikki, he couldn't leave here. His father needed him. So did his mother.

He thought of Marianne. He needed to go visit her and tell her about his father's heart attack. Not that she might hear him, let alone understand. But he felt he owed her that. She had the right to know. He often told her about things going on at the ranch.

She would rock, holding those horrible dolls, and he would tell her about the horses they'd bought and sold. His mother had always loved horses, loved to ride. It was something she had shared with her husband. Unlike Patricia, who didn't ride and complained that horses smelled. Kitten was just as bad. Which was fine with Cull. It meant that they never came down to the barns.

Cull shoved away any thoughts of Patricia as he led the horses out of the barn. Soon he and Nikki would be lost in the wilds of the Missouri Breaks. Just the thought stirred an unexpected desire. Nikki St. James was more dangerous than she realized.

Fortunately she wouldn't be with them long.

CHAPTER THIRTEEN

NIKKI'S MIND WAS still racing with what had happened in the kitchen. The relationship between Frieda and Patricia perplexed her. Why wouldn't Patricia want her talking to Frieda? What was she worried the cook would tell her? And yet she'd suggested Frieda take her to her quilt group?

Just her showing up at a crime scene like this was often a catalyst that brought secrets to the surface. Nikki thought of the other books she'd researched and the times she'd uncovered so much that it had almost cost her her life. While that should have been a warning, she knew she had to get Frieda alone so she'd have a chance to talk to her without Patricia being around.

But right now she had something more troublesome to occupy her thoughts. Getting on a horse and riding off into the wilds with Cull. He took the picnic lunch, stuffed it into a saddlebag on his horse, then grabbed a straw cowboy hat hanging on the wall and dropped it on her head.

"You'll be glad you have it, trust me," he said as he cupped his hands to hoist her up into the saddle. She hadn't been completely truthful about her experience with horses. Her mother had been deathly afraid of them and had passed that fear on to her. Which was strange, since Nikki's father had trained horses.

Sitting high in the saddle, she watched Cull swing gracefully up onto his horse. He gave it a nudge with his boot heels and started out of the corral. For a moment, she thought her horse wasn't going to move. She gave it a nudge with the heels of her tennis shoes. Nothing. Cull looked back over his shoulder at her. Grinning, he let out a whistle and her horse began to follow him.

Nikki clung to the saddlehorn, feeling as if she might fall off the horse at any moment.

"You'll get use to the rhythm," Cull said, still grinning as her horse trotted up next to his. "Just relax."

"Easy for you to say. You've probably been riding since you were born."

"Not quite. I must have been close to a year old the first time."

They rode out of the corral, past the stand of trees behind the house and into the pasture. Ahead, the land opened into rolling prairie that stretched to the Little Rockies. She could see steep cliffs of rock shining in the sunshine and huge stands of pines.

"You're doing fine," Cull said, his voice gentle. She looked over at him and tried to relax. She had a stray thought. Cull was the kind of man a woman could fall hard for. She watched him run one of his big, sunbrowned hands over his horse's neck, an affectionate caress. She imagined his hand touching her like that and had to look away.

"It's beautiful out here," she said. The afternoon light had an intensity that made the landscape glow. She sat up in the saddle a little straighter, feeling a little more confident. The horse hadn't taken off at a dead run, hadn't bucked, hadn't lain down and tried to roll over, hadn't ditched her the first chance it got.

All in all, she thought things were going pretty well—if she didn't think about the fact that soon she would be entirely alone with the man next to her. The same one she'd heard say he would "take care" of her.

CULL FELT AT HOME in the saddle. He felt the strain of the last twenty-four hours drain from him as they rode toward the Missouri Breaks. What he loved most about this country was the wild openness and the lack of people. He'd read that the population was only .03 persons per square mile out here. He didn't need anyone to tell him that there were more cattle than humans.

He glanced over at Nikki. She seemed comfortable in the saddle. He'd chosen a gentle horse for her, one of his favorites. His gaze shifted to the country ahead of them. It dropped toward the Missouri River in rolling prairie, becoming wilder with each mile as they skirted the Little Rockies.

They didn't talk as they rode, the sun lounging overhead in a brilliant blue sky filled with cumulous clouds. A faint breeze bent the deep grasses and kept the day cool.

"What an amazing day," Nikki said when they stopped near an outcropping of rocks in a stand of pine trees. There was plenty of shade, so Cull thought they could have some lunch here.

They hadn't talked on the ride. He had gotten the impression that like him Nikki was enjoying the peace and quiet, something sorely missing on the ranch. But he was smart enough to know it was temporary. He hadn't forgotten why she was here.

He watched her push back the straw cowboy hat and squint at him. Even though he knew what was coming, he didn't care. The warm afternoon sun glowed on her face. She really was stunning in a not-so-classical way.

Sure she was attractive, but he liked to think he wasn't the kind of man who could be taken in by looks alone. A part of him admired the hell out of her. The woman had fortitude—that was for sure. He thought of all the journalists who had tried to get stories over the years. Where they'd failed to get a foot in the door, Nikki St. James had the run of the house—and the ranch.

They ate, both seemingly lost in their own thoughts. He was curious about her childhood, but didn't want to break the peaceful quiet between them to ask.

As he was putting away the last of the picnic, she finally brought up the kidnapping. He'd been waiting, knowing she couldn't possibly not take advantage of the two of them being alone.

"I need to ask you about that night and even the days leading up to it," she said almost apologetically. "I'd rather do it out here than back at the house, if you don't mind."

To his surprise, he realized he didn't. His father had asked him to cooperate, so he would. He'd rather get it over with out here than back at the ranch anyway. He lay back against one of the smooth rocks and looked out toward the Breaks, dark with pine trees and deep gullies.

"You were seven," she continued. "I'm guessing the sheriff and FBI didn't question you at any length."

He shook his head. "Because I didn't know anything."

NIKKI HAD HOPED after the horseback ride that Cull would be more forthcoming. She wasn't going to let him put her off. She moved so she could look into his blue eyes, determined to find out what he was hiding.

"You've had years to think about that night. I think you know more than you've ever told anyone. I think you're protecting someone. Your mother?"

Cull looked away for a moment. "My mother had nothing to do with this."

"You know why the sheriff and the FBI believe it was an inside job and that your mother might have been involved," she said carefully. "A bottle of codeine cough syrup that had been prescribed to your mother was found in the twins' room. That's why they speculated that the twins had been drugged to keep them quiet during the kidnapping."

"It wasn't my mother," Cull said with more force than he'd obviously intended as he turned back to her.

Nikki heard something in his voice. Fear. "The cough syrup wasn't just her prescription. Her fingerprints were the only ones on the bottle, but," she said quickly before he could argue, "maybe the twins weren't drugged with the cough syrup. Maybe it was left there to frame your mother."

He stared at her for a long moment. "Why are you giving her the benefit of doubt?"

"Because I've often found that things aren't what they seem. If I'm good at anything, it's realizing that."

She saw him waver. "Still, there had to be someone inside the house who had access to the cough syrup and helped get the twins out of their cribs and to the window and the person on the ladder," he said.

"Patricia had access to the cough syrup. Maybe she'd given one of you older kids some. Do you remember having a cold or cough?"

He shook his head. "Are you saying Patty—"

"Not necessarily. That wing is isolated from the rest of the house and has an entrance and exit just down the stairs from the twins' room—anyone could have been let in. Someone inside the house could have taken the cough syrup before the kidnapping to frame her."

"Exactly. Which brings us back to the same spot. Someone in the house was in on it. Someone let the kidnapper in. Someone got hold of my mother's cough syrup."

"Which is why I need to know what you remember."

"I told you—"

"I know you're holding something back, Cull."

He sat up and for a moment she thought he might get up to leave. But instead, he settled again, then snapped, "You're a mind reader now?"

"No, I just know that often when people are afraid, it's because they know something that they fear will hurt someone they love. You and your mother were close, weren't you?" Cull still visited his mother. She knew that from her visit with Tess at the mental hospital. "Isn't it time that you told someone what you saw that night?"

He looked away. A muscle jumped along his strong jawline.

"What is it that you're so terrified I'm going to find out?" Nikki demanded.

Cull didn't move. "Why did you have to come here?"

She heard such anguish in his voice that it broke her heart, but she said nothing, waiting.

"I saw my mother."

Relief flooded her. "That night?"

He nodded as he returned his gaze to her. He looked

resigned and she wondered if a huge weight hadn't come off his shoulders. She knew only too well what secrets could do to a person.

"It was earlier that I saw her. She'd just come out of the twins' room," he said as if seeing it all again. "She looked right through me. It was as if she didn't see me until I spoke."

"Is it possible she was sleepwalking?"

He seemed surprised by the question. "She did walk in her sleep and had since she was a child, which according to the doctor implied a neurological problem that had gone undiagnosed. But to me, she seemed completely out of it. Now I wonder if she wasn't in shock."

"You think she'd already been to the nursery and found the twins missing?"

"I don't know." Cull shook his head before leaning back against the rocks where they were sitting. "I saw her walk down the hallway. I followed her, afraid she might hurt herself. I didn't think to check on the twins."

She heard the naked guilt strain his voice. "You were a child. It wasn't your place—"

As if he'd said all this to himself already and not believed it, he said, "If my mother was in on the kidnapping, then maybe the twins were already gone. Or maybe that's when she gave the twins the cough syrup. It wasn't much later that the twins were found missing. If I had told someone, they might have caught the kidnapper before he could get away with them."

Nikki considered that for a few moments, her heart aching at the guilt she saw in his face. "You said you followed your mother that night?"

"She must have heard me behind her, because she stopped and told me to go back to bed. That everything was going to be all right. She said she was going for a swim." His blue eyes shone with unshed tears. "Do you see why I have kept that to myself all these years? It only makes her look more guilty since we know the kidnapper was in the pool house that night after the twins were taken."

She knew that the FBI agents were convinced that Marianne had met her co-kidnapper in the pool house that night and that the swim had just been a ruse.

Nikki gave him a few moments before she asked, "What were you doing in the hallway that night?"

He frowned as if he'd never asked himself that question. "I was looking for Ledger. When I woke I looked into this room and saw that he wasn't in his bed. He had a habit of wandering around the ranch at night. I had gone looking for him."

"Did you go outside?"

He shook his head. "That's when I heard Patty screaming. She was standing outside the twins' room screaming that they were gone. My first thought was that my mother had taken them somewhere, which was terrifying enough given the way she was acting. The way she had been acting since their births."

"It was speculated that she was suffering from postpartum depression."

He nodded. "She kept saying she was fine but something was definitely wrong. She seemed confused a lot of the time and complained of not feeling well, but when my father took her to the doctor, he couldn't find anything wrong with her."

Nikki knew that he'd just described his father's recent condition. They'd all just assumed it was over the anniversary of the kidnapping just as they'd assumed Marianne's was postpartum depression.

"Did you see anyone else in the hallway that night?" Nikki asked.

"Everyone came out of their rooms after they heard Patty screaming and ran down to the nursery. I just remember Dad going past."

She stared at him. "But you didn't go." She saw it on his handsome face, the anguish, the fear, the regret.

He shook his head. "Somehow, I knew the twins were gone and something horrible had happened. I was terrified that my mother had done something to them."

"What about your brothers Ledger and Boone? When did you see them?"

Cull frowned again as if picturing it in his mind. "Boone came out of his room, but I don't remember seeing Ledger until later."

From what Patty had told her, there was a good chance that Ledger had been out roaming the ranch that night. Three was old enough to remember in some instances. Nikki herself could remember things that had happened at that age. Maybe Ledger remembered something. But hadn't been old enough to realize that what he'd seen at the time had been the kidnapper.

"ENJOY YOUR RIDE?" Patricia demanded when Cull came into the house, Nikki at his side. "Your father is being released from the hospital. Ledger and Boone have gone in to pick him up. I wanted to go, but you know how they can be."

The woman picked nervously at the suit jacket she was wearing. "I want everything to be perfect when he gets here." Her gaze shifted to Nikki. "I think it would be better if she wasn't here."

"Patricia—"

"I don't care what your father wants at this point. He could have died. All this is too upsetting for him. He needs his rest."

Cull shook his head. "I talked to the doctor this morning. Dad is doing well. In fact, his health has improved since he's been in the hospital or the doctor wouldn't be releasing him."

"I just don't want him upset," she said, holding her ground.

"Well, sending Nikki away would upset him, since he was very specific about that."

The woman let out a sigh. "Fine, but if she kills him, don't blame me." With that, she turned and stormed off toward the kitchen.

Cull cursed under his breath. "That woman is going to be the death of all of us."

Nikki watched her go, thinking again of the symptoms that both Marianne and Travers shared—although twenty-five years apart. The common denominator was that both had been living in this house at the time.

Well, she'd done what she could by going to the sheriff. Now it was in McCall Crawford's hands.

"I think I'm going to go rest for a while," she said, looking at the time.

Cull nodded as if he thought it was a good idea for her to be away when his father arrived back at the house.

The horseback ride had been wonderful, but she felt sunburned and tired. While glad Travers was being released, she worried about what he was coming home to, given her suspicions.

Surely, if she was right, no one would try to harm him now. Nikki had been afraid that Travers would change his mind about letting her stay here for the book. Fortunately he apparently hadn't. She couldn't help feeling bad for him. When she'd seen him collapse, it brought home just how serious this was. She didn't want to inflict any more pain on this family than it had already been through.

She'd seen Cull's pain earlier when he'd told her what he'd seen that night. Like what Patricia had remembered and told her, it was another piece of the intricate puzzle. There were still so many pieces missing, though. Worse, she hated what the final picture would reveal. Maybe her grandfather was right and she was too emotionally involved in this one.

She walked toward the pool house. The wind had come up. It whipped the branches of the cottonwood trees, lashing the new green leaves against the glass. Past the trees, she saw the horses running, their manes and tails blowing back as they cavorted in the deep green of the pasture. She thought about Cull and his brothers and their obvious love for the horses they raised. The reminder of Cull's hand gently stroking the mare's neck sent a shiver through her.

Nikki told herself that her reaction to Cull was normal. She hadn't met anyone like him and was now thrown together with him in a household where she had few to no allies. What worried her was that the man seemed able to see into her soul. That made him more than a little dangerous. Not to mention he already suspected that her motives for being here had to do with more than just the book. What was he going do when he found out that Nate Corwin was her father?

As she entered the pool house, she walked directly to her bedroom. She would have a shower before dinner, but right now, she just wanted to lie down for a while.

At a sound behind her, she turned to look back into the living room. Had someone been there? A movement near the door caught her eye. She stared as a single sheet of paper slid under the door and was caught by the wind from the window. The paper whirled up off the floor.

Hurriedly stepping to it, Nikki chased the sheet of paper down until she could catch it, then rushed to look out to see who had shoved it under her door.

She saw no one. Wind shook the nearby trees, sending dust and dirt into the air. She cupped a hand over her eyes as she looked in the direction of the house. The curtain moved on the second-floor window of the nursery and then fell silent.

With a shiver, she turned back inside, closing and locking the door behind her before she looked at what she held in her hand.

With a start she saw what appeared to be a page torn from a diary.

CHAPTER FOURTEEN

NIKKI LEANED AGAINST the pool house door, her heart pounding as she looked at the sheet of paper in her hand. It appeared to have been torn from a diary or journal, but there were no dates on the page. She began to read it as she walked over to the window, closed it and dropped into a chair.

I heard the screaming last night. Travers said it was just the wind, but I've never heard wind like that ever.

I got up and went up to check the children. I hate having them on a separate floor even knowing that the nanny is close by. But Travers insisted that we move to the lower floor master bedroom as soon as it was finished. He says I need my rest. I feel like all I do it rest. Sometimes I feel like I am going crazy.

In the nursery, the twins looked like sleeping angels. I call them the twins because their names seem too large for such small babies. They scare me they are so small, so fragile.

Just looking at them makes me cry. I feel such anguish, such guilt. When I found out I was pregnant with them, I was upset. I didn't want them. Still don't feel a connection to them. I want to love them, but they are so needy, so demanding. Even when I help Patty with them, I don't feel like I'm their mother. I can tell that she knows, that she's judging me and finding me wanting. I asked Travers to fire her and let me take care of them, but he refused. I'm sure Patty heard us arguing about it.

As I started to leave the twins' room, I saw the light in the stables. I thought about waking Travers, but I have awakened him too many times terrified only to be told there is nothing out in the darkness. Nothing that wants to hurt me, let alone destroy me. So why do I feel this way?

I know I shouldn't go out there alone, but I won't be able to sleep until I know that the horses are all right. That there is nothing out there to fear. Maybe it is only Nate working late. He is such a kind, caring man. I can talk to him. He seems to understand. He doesn't judge me. He lets me cry without looking at me as if I'm crazy. I'll go for a swim after I check the stables. That seems to help me sleep.

On the back, the text continued.

The light was on again tonight. I am trying to ignore it. Just as I am trying to sleep after my swim. But I'm restless. I know I should stay in the house and not go out there. But I need to see Nate. He is the only—

The words ended abruptly. Nikki turned the page over, forgetting that it was only one diary page. So where was the rest? Her heart was in her throat at the mention

of her father. Was this how it had started? Marianne
afraid at night and going out to the barn to talk to Nate.
He is such a kind, caring man. Her father. What had
this kind, caring man done to help Marianne McGraw?

She stared at the paper. Who had left this and why?
Had they wanted her to believe that her father and Marianne had been lovers? Had the two of them made a
plan to get rid of the twins—and have enough money
to run away?

More to the point, why had she never heard that Marianne kept a diary? Who had known about it? Not the
FBI or sheriff, or Nikki would have found the information during her research. The diary would also have
been mentioned in the court transcripts—even if the
judge had excluded it.

And where was the rest of it? Clearly someone on
this ranch had the diary.

But why hadn't they turned it over to the FBI at the
time of the kidnapping? Because it incriminated Marianne? Or incriminated the person who now had it in
their possession?

They wanted her to believe Marianne and Nate had
been lovers, had been the kidnappers. But in their attempt to convince her, they'd now made her aware of
the diary.

Instead of convincing her, they'd only managed to
make her more convinced her father was innocent on
all counts.

So who had put it under her door?

NIKKI FOUND CULL in the pasture inspecting one of the
horses' hooves.

"Your mother kept a diary?" Nikki demanded.

He looked up in surprise. "I beg your pardon?"

"Why is it that this is the first time I've heard that your mother kept a diary?"

Cull rose slowly to his feet, stretching out his long legs and then his back, before he said, "Because I didn't know she did—if she did."

Cull and his mother had been close, but it was clear he hadn't known. He looked as surprised as she'd been. "Well, someone knew she did," she said, waving the page she held in her hand.

He caught her wrist with warm strong fingers and slowly pried her fingers open to take the sheet from her.

"Is that your mother's handwriting?" she asked, half afraid he would say it wasn't and that someone was playing an elaborate joke on her.

"It looks like her handwriting." Stepping out of the horse's shadow, he held the page up to the waning sunlight. "Where did you get this?" he demanded after reading it.

"Someone slipped it under my door."

He looked angry as if he wanted to crush it in his big hand, but she snatched it from him before he could. "Whoever gave you that wants you to think my mother had an affair with the horse trainer."

"If true, then why not produce the entire diary?" She shook her head. "Whoever put this under my door wants me to believe that. But if this is the most incriminating part, it doesn't prove your mother had an affair." Nikki prayed she was right. If her father hadn't fallen in love with Marianne, then he had no motive for being involved in the kidnapping.

Cull pulled off his Stetson and raked his fingers

through his thick dark hair. "I can't imagine who would have known about the diary."

"And kept it from the FBI and sheriff all these years."

He nodded, frowning.

"You must have seen her with Nate," she said quietly, hating that she couldn't let the subject go.

"No more than I saw her with anyone else. Nate was a nice guy. He gave me a pocket knife and taught me how to whittle so I didn't cut myself."

"You don't think he was involved in the kidnapping."

Cull looked away for a moment before he shrugged. "How well do we really know another person?" His gaze locked with hers just long enough for her to wonder if he knew the truth about her.

HIS MOTHER HAD kept a diary. Cull hated to think what might be in the rest of it. Something even more incriminating in the rest? If so, then why did whoever had it wait so long to share even this much of it?

Nikki didn't think whatever was in there would be more incriminating. He hoped she was right. For years he'd believed in his mother's innocence. The last thing he wanted was to know that he'd been wrong.

But who in this house had it?

There were times he'd certainly wanted to be anyone but a McGraw. All the media attention had been horrible over the years, not to mention the suspicion that had fallen on every member of the household.

Nikki seemed surprised when he showed up at the pool house door, insisting that she come to dinner that night. "Wouldn't it be better if it was just family?"

"Probably, but Patricia invited my father's attorney

and friend Blake. I'm sure she thinks they can convince him what a mistake it is having you here."

"I would think everyone would be happy if I was gone, you included," she said.

He met her gaze. "Don't presume to know how I feel."

She looked at him as if surprised by that. "So you don't want to get rid of me?"

"Maybe I just want to see an end to this. My father promised that if nothing comes of your...book, then he will quit searching for the twins."

So that was it. "Is there a reason the attorney and former ranch manager wouldn't want the truth about the kidnapping to come out?" she asked, recalling what he said about Patricia using them at dinner tonight.

"They're both protective of my father—and Patty, for that matter. Blake knows my father will always take care of him because of the years he put in here. As for the family attorney, Jim Waters is pretty happy the way things are now with my father continuing to pay him to look into claims by those believing they either know something about the kidnapping or are one of the twins. If Jim didn't have a gambling problem, he'd be quite wealthy by now."

"So if I find out what really happened to the twins, it will put Waters out of business?"

Cull smiled. "Not completely, but it would hurt because he would have to go back to just being the family lawyer. We should get on up to the house. You're sure you're up to this?"

She was sore from her horseback ride and it was clear that he knew it. "I'm fine."

He smiled. "Yes, you are."

Everyone had already gathered outside the dining room when she and Cull came in from outside.

Travers McGraw saw her from his wheelchair and turned toward her, extending his hand. She took it in both of hers. "The wheelchair was doctor's orders. He wants me to rest, but I assure you I'm fine. Better than ever."

He did look better, she admitted. "I'm so glad. I was worried."

"No need. I'm just glad you're still here. Are you making progress?"

Before she could answer, Patricia interrupted to say that dinner was served. They filed into the dining room, Travers insisting they all go ahead of him. All Nikki could think about was the last time they were all in here.

A hush fell over the group after they were all seated at their places. Patricia stood and clinked her butter knife against her empty wineglass. "I just want to say how happy I am to have my husband home." She beamed down the table at him. "I'm glad you are all here to celebrate." Her gaze lit on Nikki, but quickly moved to attorney Jim Waters. She gave him a meaningful look before she sat down and Frieda began to pour the wine.

Nikki noticed that everyone but Travers was subdued. She could feel the tension. This was not a welcome-home celebration. It was exactly what Cull had suspected—a bushwhacking. Patricia wanted the lawyer and former ranch manager to talk Travers into forgetting about the kidnapping book.

She noticed that even Kitten wasn't her usual self. She fidgeted until the first course was brought out and then barely touched her food.

It wasn't until right before dessert that Jim Waters cleared his voice and said, "Travers, we're all glad you're all right. But I think we need to talk about the future."

Travers cut him off at once. "If this is about the book Nikki is researching here, please save your breath, Jim. I hope my heart attack will only make her that much more determined to find out the truth about that night."

Nikki smiled at him.

"I think you should hear them out," Patricia said, and smiled sweetly.

"We know what this means to you," Waters continued. "But at what cost? You have three sons, a wife and a stepdaughter to think about. If you were to—"

"I'm sorry, Jim, but I've made myself perfectly clear on this," Travers said, putting down his fork. "I won't hear any more about this subject from any of you." He looked pointedly at his wife.

"Then you need to know who this woman really is," Waters said, getting to his feet to point an accusing finger at Nikki.

She felt her heart drop as she saw the satisfaction in his gaze. He knew and now he was about to destroy her credibility with Travers and there was nothing she could do about it.

"She isn't here just to write a book about the kidnapping. She's—"

"We already know," Cull said, cutting Waters off.

"You *don't* know." Jim Waters looked furious that he'd been interrupted. "Nate Corwin—"

"Was her father," Cull said, finishing his sentence.

"What?" Patricia demanded, and looked to her hus-

band as if this was the first time she was hearing about it. No one at the table bought her act.

All the air rushed out of the attorney in a gush as he looked at Travers for confirmation. He'd been so sure he was about to drop a bombshell.

Nikki couldn't breathe. Her gaze was on Cull. How long had he known? She looked toward Travers. Did he know?

"Your *father* was Nate Corwin, the man who…?" Patricia acted as if it was so horrible she couldn't even finish.

Travers smiled at Nikki and reached over to pat her hand. "Cull told me everything."

"Well, it would have been nice if someone had bothered to tell me," Patricia said, her face flushed with anger. This hadn't gone at all as she'd planned. "So this was her plan from the beginning. She's writing a book that will make her father look innocent."

Cull didn't bother to respond to her accusation. "Nikki didn't know Nate was her father until recently," he said, still without looking at her. "I'm sure it's one reason she became interested in the case. But not the only reason."

She stared at him, speechless. How did he know that? *Her grandfather.* He'd talked to her grandfather, which meant he'd been investigating *her.* The irony of it didn't escape her. He'd warned that he would be digging into her life, but she'd thought it was an empty threat.

"Still you have to question her motives," Jim Waters said as he started to sit back down.

"Actually, it's your motives I'm more concerned about, Jim." Travers pushed his wheelchair away from the table. "Why don't we talk about that in my office?"

The attorney had just sat. Now he pushed back up and, looking like a hangdog, followed Travers out of the dining room.

"Why is it that I'm not allowed to mention anything distasteful and he gets to say things like that?" Kitten demanded, getting to her feet and leaving.

"I can't believe you and your father kept this from me," Patricia said to Cull as he tossed down his napkin and turned to Nikki.

"I would imagine you'll have to take that up with my father, Patty. You usually do," he said as he reached for Nikki's hand. "There's something I need to show you in the horse barn."

She stood on rubbery legs. His large hand was warm as it wrapped around hers. She felt that electric thrill at his touch even as she let him lead her out of the dining room. He was angry with her—she could feel it in the no-nonsense way he held her hand all the way to the back door.

"Cull, let me explain," she said as he opened the back door and waited for her to walk through it.

"Not here," was all he said in a low gruff voice.

She swallowed back whatever explanation she'd been about to give and went out the door. She could feel him behind her, hear his boots on the stone path, could almost feel the heat of his anger against her back.

CULL RUED THE day that Patricia had entered their lives for a second time. Their father had remained married to their mother even though she no longer seemed to know him—or her children. Then sixteen years ago, Patty had shown up at the ranch, a baby in her arms and no doubt a sad story to go with it.

Travers McGraw had not just taken her in, he'd divorced his wife and married her. She'd never been a mother to any of them, except Kitten. Admittedly, Cull and his brothers hadn't made it easy for her. He'd resented her intrusion into their lives—and still did.

He reached the barn and turned to find Nikki had followed him as far as the door. She stood silhouetted against it. In the dim light, he couldn't make out her expression, but something about the way she stood made him want to pull her into his arms and hold her.

"I know you're angry," she said quietly.

"Not at you. I knew Patricia had something planned at dinner. All my warnings about not upsetting Dad…" He shook his head.

"How long have you known about my father?" she asked.

"Did you really think I wouldn't check up on you? I made a few calls that first day when I went back into town to get your car."

She took a step toward him. "You talked to my grandfather."

He nodded.

"Why didn't you out me right away?"

Why hadn't he? He'd told his father, who'd taken the news even better than Cull had. "Then she is motivated to solve this even more, isn't she," his father had said. "Don't mention to her that you know. We'll keep it as our little secret for the time being."

"My father asked me not to say anything, but I wouldn't have anyway." He took a step toward her. "If my father had been Nate Corwin, I would try to clear his name, too. It's funny," he said, closing the distance between them. "You seemed…familiar the first time I saw you. There was just something about you. Now I realize what it is. You remind me of your father." He saw that his words pleased her.

"Then you understand why I don't want to believe that your mother and my father…" Her voice broke and she sounded close to tears.

"They were just friends." He brushed a lock of her hair back from her face, his fingertips grazing the soft smooth skin of her cheek. "I'm going to help you find out the truth."

Her eyes widened. "Why?" she asked on a breath.

"Because I liked your father—because I like you." His gaze dropped to her mouth and then his mouth was on hers. He dragged her to him, deepening the kiss as she came willingly into his arms.

CHAPTER FIFTEEN

NIKKI WOKE THE next morning to a knock on the pool house door. She quickly dressed and went to answer it, hoping it was Cull. She'd had a hard time getting to sleep after The Kiss. Unlike their first kiss, they'd both been into this one. It had sparked a fire to life inside them both. She shuddered to think what they might have done right there in the barn if they hadn't been interrupted.

The memory of that kiss sent a wave of need through her. She'd wanted Cull desperately, but they'd been interrupted by one of the ranch hands who'd apparently needed him more than she did. She hadn't seen him again last night.

Cull had unleashed a desire in her that she hadn't known existed. This morning she had to remind herself that she never mixed business and pleasure. But who was she kidding? She hadn't met anyone who made her interested in dating, let alone losing herself in pleasure.

She opened the door, a smile already on her lips, only to find it wasn't Cull on her doorstep looking worried.

"Ledger?" she said, unable to hide her surprise.

"My father sent me." From his expression, it was clear he wouldn't have been here on his own. "He was surprised you hadn't talked to me yet about the kidnapping."

"I was looking for you yesterday before Cull and I went for a horseback ride."

He nodded as if he'd made himself scarce knowing it was just a matter of time. "Is now a bad time?"

"No." She could see that he wanted to get it over with. "Let's go sit by the pool."

Once they were seated, Nikki put the recorder on the small end table between them. "Let's talk about that night."

"That's just it, I don't remember anything. I was only three."

Nikki nodded, then smiled. "I heard you loved to go outside at night after everyone was asleep." He said nothing. "In fact, when I spoke with Patricia, she told me that you had been outside that night."

His eyes widened in alarm. "Why would she say that? I was in bed asleep."

"I thought you didn't remember?"

"I'm just saying, I must have been in bed asleep." He looked flustered.

"I've already spoken with Cull. He said he awakened that night to find you weren't in your bed. He'd gotten up to go find you when he heard Patricia start screaming." It wasn't exactly what Cull had said, but it was close enough to the truth to hopefully jog Ledger's memory of that night.

He had a faraway, scared look in his eyes. "I told you, I don't remember. But it that's what Cull said…"

"Patricia also told me that when you showed up your bare feet were dirty. She had to wash them before she put you and your brothers into her bed." She let that sink in for a moment. "Does any of this bring back memories?"

He shook his head.

"You'd been outside that night. I think you saw something. Someone. Maybe the kidnapper. Maybe someone carrying away the twins."

He shook his head again and looked away as he shifted in his chair. "I told you—"

"But you saw someone, someone you recognized."

She watched him swallow and look toward the woods. Her heart began to pound. "Who did you see?"

He started to shake his head. The next words out of his mouth were so soft that she had to lean toward him to hear them. "I saw the bogeyman." He looked up at her, clearly embarrassed. "You see now why I never said anything. I was *three*. Who knows what I saw."

"You saw a man who scared you?"

He nodded. "He came out of the dark pines. He was big and scary."

"Did he see you?"

"No, I hid."

"Where did he go?" she asked, her voice cracking a little.

"Toward the house."

Toward the house. Nikki said nothing for a moment before she asked, "Was he carrying anything when you saw him?"

"No, not that I saw."

"Did you see him again?"

"Not that night," he said, and met her gaze. "I never told. I was too scared. I thought he would come back for me." That long-ago fear made his eyes shine with the terror he'd felt as that three-year-old.

"But you saw him some other time?"

He swallowed and avoided her gaze. "A few days before the kidnapping. He was standing on a street corner in town talking to our cook, Frieda. They seemed to be arguing. He looked up right at me." Ledger shivered. "It was the way he looked at me. But it might not even have been the same man. Another reason I never said anything."

"Did you ever see him again after the kidnapping?"

"No. Only in my nightmares."

"Did you say anything to Frieda?"

He shook his head. "Do you think he was the man who took the twins?"

"I don't know. He didn't have them when you saw him, so probably not," she said, realizing that she wanted to reassure him.

But her heart was pounding. She feared that Ledger's bogeyman had been the kidnapper—before he'd taken the twins.

NIKKI FOUND PATRICIA coming out of the kitchen.

"Whatever it is, I don't have time for it," the woman said in greeting.

As Nikki had come into the house, she'd heard mother and daughter arguing about shopping. Apparently, Patricia was going shopping and wasn't waiting until Kitten got out of school so she could go with her.

"I just need to ask you a few quick questions," she said. "I'm sure your shopping can wait that long."

Patricia gave her a haughty, irritated look, but then glanced toward Travers's office. He was behind his desk and he was watching their discussion. The woman's expression sweetened like saccharine. "I guess I could spare a few minutes."

"Use my office," her husband said and wheeled out from behind his desk. "I'll go see if I can make Kitten feel better."

Patricia let out a low growl as her husband passed, but kept a smile plastered on her face. She sighed as her husband disappeared into the back of the house. "I really don't have time for this."

From what Nikki had seen, all Patricia had was time. She was overdressed for a shopping trip into Whitehorse. Was that really why she was going into town, or was she headed somewhere else? Nikki wondered, catching the sweet scent of the woman's perfume.

"I'll make it quick," Nikki promised as Patty glanced at her watch in clear irritation. She walked behind her husband's desk, but didn't sit.

Nikki took a chair facing her and turned on the recorder and said, "After twenty-five years, maybe there are things you remember that you didn't that night."

"Well, there aren't. We already did this. And I don't want to relive all of it again. I'm sure you also have my testimony that I gave the FBI and sheriff at the time. That should be sufficient. It isn't going to change. Anyway, I don't understand what the point is since we already know what happened that night."

Nikki ignored that. "I can imagine how hard all this has been on you, living under the suspicion and the mystery of what happened to the twins," she said, trying another approach.

"You have no idea what it is has been like for me," Patricia said, her voice breaking. "It isn't just the suspicion. I live in *Marianne's* shadow." She put a world of contempt into that one word as she dropped her voice. "You think it doesn't bother me that Travers goes to see her every day? She's completely loony-bin nuts, doesn't speak, doesn't do anything but rock. Does it make any difference to him? No. He still loves her. He still misses her." She sniffed and looked away toward the window as she folded her arms over her chest. "There are days when I just want to get in my car and drive as far away from here as I can. But where would I go? What would I do? I have Kitten to think about."

Nikki had listened without interrupting, but now she asked, "Why *did* you come back?"

Patricia turned to look at her as if for a few minutes, she'd forgotten she was there. "I had nowhere to go and Travers had always been kind to me. When I'd left, he told me that I always had a home at Sundown Stallion Station."

"And now you're his wife."

"I didn't come back to marry him, if that's what you're thinking. I was…desperate, if you must know. I'd lost my job and with a baby to support… He was lonely."

"What about Kitten's father?"

"*Travers* is her father."

"Her *biological* father?"

"Of course not," Patricia snapped. "Her biological father was never involved."

Nikki could have argued that point since he was the one who got her pregnant. "You left here soon after the kidnapping."

"It wasn't like I could stay!" Her voice rose to shrill. "Even after Marianne went crazy and Nate Corwin was arrested, everyone still blamed me. I was the *nanny*. How had I let this happen?"

"It must have been hard to come back," Nikki said.

"I guess I thought after almost ten years that things would be different."

"And you had Kitten to think about."

Patricia narrowed her gaze. "You think I came back for Travers's money?"

"You're a lot younger than your husband."

The woman actually smiled. "You and the rest of the county can think whatever you want." She stretched to her full height. "I really don't care. But you'd better not write anything bad about me. If you defame me, I will sue you for everything you have."

"Yes, your husband employs his own lawyer. You must have known Jim Waters when you were the nanny, back when you were nineteen. You also knew Blake Ryan, the ranch manager and close family friend."

Patricia narrowed her eyes. "I don't know what you're getting at," she said, but Nikki was sure she did. "You should be careful making accusations. If I had my way, you wouldn't have gotten near my house, near me or my daughter. I personally am not going to do this anymore, no matter what my husband says." With that, she stalked out. A few moments later, Nikki heard her raising her voice in the kitchen, arguing with her husband and berating Frieda.

But Nikki was going to find out once and for all why Frieda put up with it.

AFTER THE KITCHEN cleared out, with Patricia storming off to town, Kitten taking Travers's car to school and Travers locking himself in his office, Nikki went into the kitchen.

Frieda was hard at work, but she seemed more beaten down than ever this morning.

"I thought Wednesday was your day off?" Nikki asked.

Frieda turned from what she'd been doing. "Patricia had a few things she wanted me to do before I left."

"One of the problems of living under the same roof," Nikki commented. "Well, I really want to go with you to your quilting group. If that's all right." She could see by Frieda's anxious look that it wasn't.

The woman glanced around as if frantically trying to come up with a way out of it. "I wasn't planning to quilt today."

Nikki took a step toward her. "Frieda, I thought it would be nice to get us both out of here. I'd love to see what everyone is working on. We can make it a quick trip."

Frieda looked resigned. "I can finish up here and leave in about thirty minutes then."

"Great, we can take my rental. You can just relax and enjoy the ride."

But even as she said it, Frieda looked anything but relaxed.

She'd just returned to the pool house when there was a knock at her door. She feared it might be Frieda with a better excuse for not going today, but when she opened the door, she found Cull standing there. One look at him and she could tell he was upset.

"You went to the sheriff without mentioning it to me?" he demanded as he pushed his way in, forcing her to step back.

"I'm worried about your father. I would think you would be, too. I didn't want to say anything to anyone else since it was just a suspicion and I knew you'd get upset."

He pulled off his Stetson to rake a hand through his

thick hair. All the fight seemed to go out of him. "My father just told me about the sheriff coming by the hospital before he was released to take a hair sample. You can't think that she's poisoning him."

Of course that was exactly what she thought. "It can't be much of a reach for you since you didn't even ask who I suspected—and neither did the sheriff."

"If true, Patty can't possibly think she can get away with it," he said.

"Why not, if she got away with it before?" Nikki said as she walked into the small pool house kitchen. "Coffee? I made a pot this morning."

He nodded and joined her in the small space. "What are you talking about—she did it before?"

"I don't just suspect she is poisoning your father. I think she did the same thing to your mother in the weeks leading up to the kidnapping."

He stared at her as she poured him a cup.

"Think about it. Your mother was acting…strangely. What if it wasn't postpartum depression at all? What if she was acting the way she was because she was being poisoned? I know it seems like a stretch but when I saw your father and how he looked…" She handed him his cup of coffee and poured one for herself.

"If what you're saying is true…"

"It's just a suspicion at this point. That's why I went to the sheriff. Hopefully when the lab test comes back, it will prove that I'm wrong."

"Or right."

Motioning to a chair, she sat down and Cull did the same.

He seemed lost in thought. "You do realize that if you're right, I'm going to kill her."

"No, you're not. You're not a killer."

He met her gaze. "You sure about that?"

"Yes." Was she basing that on the kiss? Or something more?

Cull swore under his breath. "You're right, but I'm going to want to."

"Did the sheriff say when they'd have lab results?"

"She said she'd marked them a priority and would get back to us."

"What did your father say?" Nikki had to ask.

"He was upset, of course. He defended her, but not very strongly. It made me wonder if he suspected something. What man wants to admit, though, that his spouse is poisoning him?"

"We don't know that's the case."

"Yet," Cull said. "McCall told me the symptoms of long-term arsenic poisoning. I can understand why you thought of it. I'm sorry I didn't."

"I have a suspicious mind, and murder is kind of my business."

He met her gaze. "I've noticed that. What now?"

"I continue gathering information. I still have to talk to Tilly and Frieda. They both were live-in staff at the time of the kidnapping." She didn't tell him that she especially wanted to talk to Frieda after what Ledger had told her about his "bogeyman."

THE SHERIFF HAD asked the lab to put a rush on the hair samples. She'd never been good at waiting. She especially wasn't now.

Her husband had called from Winchester Ranch to tell her that her grandmother and mother weren't at each other's throats and that their daughter was enjoying being around the grandmas.

"How are *you* doing?" she asked him.

"I forget how pretty it is out here. And lunch was good."

Luke always tried to see the good in everything. It was incredibly annoying. But she smiled in spite of herself.

"I'm waiting for the lab to bring me results. A case of a husband possibly being poisoned by his wife."

"Yikes. I'd better check your mother. I wouldn't put it past your grandmother to put something in her food."

She knew he was kidding, but still it worried her. Her grandmother wasn't the most patient person and the bad blood between her and McCall's mother, Ruby, ran blood-spilling deep.

"I'm kidding," her husband said. "You sound too serious on your end of the phone."

"You can hear that?"

"Because I know you so well," he said. "I love you."

"I love you."

"Hope you get the lab tests soon. What will you do if they come back positive for poison?" he asked. "Do you have enough for an arrest?"

"Not yet. The next step will be to get a warrant to search the house."

"Sounds like that's what you're expecting."

McCall realized it was. "If true, it gets complicated. This might not be the first time this woman has systematically poisoned someone to get rid of them."

CHAPTER SIXTEEN

UNABLE TO SIT still after Cull left, Nikki found Tilly running the vacuum in the off-limits wing. She called her name, but the older woman didn't hear her. Matilda "Tilly" Marks had been twenty-five, married and in debt the year the twins were kidnapped.

Now at fifty, she was divorced and still in debt. Nikki knew that the sheriff and FBI had done a thorough investigation of everyone in the house that night—including Tilly and her husband. They'd found nothing.

"Tilly?" Nikki raised her voice over the whine of the vacuum as she approached the woman. *"Tilly!"*

The sunlight coming in the window seemed to turn the woman's bleached blond hair white. With a start, she realized that it was this white-haired woman she'd seen at this window.

"Tilly?" When she still didn't hear her, she touched the housekeeper's arm.

The poor woman jumped a foot, making Nikki feel terrible.

"I'm sorry," she mouthed as Tilly fumbled to turn off the vacuum. In the silence that fell, she repeated, "I'm sorry. I didn't mean to scare you."

Tilly held her hand over her heart as if to still it. She

was a short thin nondescript woman with bottle blond hair and manicured nails. She moved through the house like a ghost, paying little attention to anyone and vice versa, from what Nikki had seen.

"I need to ask you about the night of the kidnapping. Could you take a break for a few minutes?"

Tilly nodded. "I could use a cigarette. Can we step outside?"

Nikki followed the woman to the end of the hall and down the stairs. If the kidnapper wasn't already in the house that night, he could have come in through this entrance. The stairs led down to a small patio next to the woods. Anyone coming in this way wouldn't have been seen.

But in order to get in, someone would have had to leave the door unlocked.

Nikki let the woman light her cigarette and take a drag before she asked, "What can you tell me about that night?"

"Not much. I had a cold and had taken some medicine so I could sleep. Plus I wear earplugs. I didn't hear a thing until I was awakened by someone pounding on my door. It was a sheriff's deputy. That's when I found out what had happened."

"Where was your room?"

"At the other end of the wing from where the twins were taken," she said, and tilted her head back as she blew out smoke.

"So you were in the room next to Frieda's."

Something in the way Tilly nodded caught her attention. "You would have been able to hear her leave her room."

"Under normal circumstances, but like I said, I took cold medicine that night."

"But you'd heard her come and go other nights," Nikki said, fishing for whatever it was Tilly wasn't saying.

"Sure. I heard her and whoever else come and go."

She took a not-so-wild guess. "A man?"

Tilly shrugged.

"Who was he?"

"A no 'count. I tried to warn her, but she didn't listen. I knew him. I told her he was going to break her heart."

Nikki was still reeling from the fact that Tilly was telling her that Frieda had a man visitor in her room. "Was it all right for her to have a man in her room?"

"Not hardly. Mrs. McGraw, the first Mrs., was very strict about that. Frieda could have been fired, but I wasn't about to tell on her. I got the impression that it was the first man she'd ever…dated, if you know what I mean. She was thirty-nine and never been kissed until him. So, of course, she fell hard."

"Was he a big man? Kind of scary looking?"

Tilly laughed. "Not exactly handsome or bright either."

"So Frieda snuck him in? Did you tell the sheriff and FBI about this?"

The housekeeper put out her cigarette in the dirt, pocketed the stub and lit another with trembling fingers. "He wasn't in her room that night, so why mention it?"

Nikki stared at her. "How do you know that if you were knocked out with cold medicine?"

Tilly sighed. "Because I had a talk with him. Like I said, I knew him. I knew he was using her. I didn't like him in the house at night. He was a bum. I thought he might steal something."

"Like the McGraws twins?"

"No, he wasn't that ambitious or that smart to pull something like that off. I was trying to protect Frieda. So I told him I was going to tell Mr. McGraw and the next time he snuck into the house, he'd be facing a shotgun. That did the trick. Never saw him again."

"Still you had taken the cold medicine—"

"Before I went to bed, before I took the medicine, I heard Frieda in her room pacing. It was late. He hadn't shown up. I knew she'd be disappointed, but it was for the best."

"He could have entered the house after you went to bed."

She shook her head as she took a drag on her cigarette and blew out smoke. "I made sure the door was locked. As I came back up, I saw that her light was out. I could hear her crying. She knew he wasn't going to come by."

Nikki took in this information. "What is this man's name?"

"Harold Cline, but like I said, I never saw him again and neither did Frieda. He left town."

"You don't think it's strange that he disappeared about the same time as the kidnapping?"

"He probably thought he'd be blamed for it once Frieda told the sheriff that she'd been letting him in at night."

"But Frieda must not have told, otherwise wouldn't she have been let go?"

Tilly seemed to consider that. "I suppose you're right."

"And that's the same reason *you* never told."

The housekeeper suddenly looked worried. "You aren't going to tell Mr. McGraw. At my age it's impossible to find another job." Was that what Frieda thought, as well?

"No." If there was something to this lead, then it could come out when the book did. In the meantime...

Tilly seemed to relax. "Like I said, Harold wasn't smart enough to pull off the kidnapping and if he had, he would have spent the money. The ransom money never turned up, right?"

"Right." Still, Nikki wanted to know more about Harold Cline.

CULL FOUND HIS father in his office. "I hope you aren't working."

Travers smiled up at him. "I'm not. I've always liked this room. I feel comfortable in here." The phone rang. He motioned to Cull to give him a minute and answered.

"No, Patricia, I can't tell Frieda that. It's her day off. She told me that she and Nikki are going to visit her quilting group. You have to stop making her work on her day off. Fine. Whatever." He hung up and sighed.

Cull saw that his father was upset. He wanted to wring Patricia's neck.

"I'm going to see Mother. I thought you might like to go with me."

"I can't. Jim Waters will be stopping by. I need to talk to him."

Cull studied his father. "Tell me you're going to fire him."

His father chuckled. "He's been with me a long time." Travers believed in rewarding loyalty. "Maybe too long." He turned toward the door. "I'll tell Mother hello for you."

"Thank you. Tell her…tell her I still love her."

Cull nodded and left, his thoughts veering from one to the next and always coming back to Nikki. He'd fought his attraction to her, but it was so much more than that. The woman fascinated him. He'd never met anyone like her. If only they had met under other circumstances.

AT THE HOSPITAL, he let a nurse lead him down to his mother's room. Marianne McGraw was right where he expected her to be—in her rocking chair holding the two worn dolls. She didn't react when he pulled up a chair and sat down in front of her. The blank eyes stared straight ahead, unseeing.

"Hello, Mother," he said. "It's Cull. Dad wanted me to tell you that he still loves you. Also I thought you'd want to know that he had a heart attack." Did her rocking change? "He's okay though. Weak, but recovering."

He listened to the steady creak of the rocker for a few moments. "I met someone." He let out a chuckle. "After all this time I meet someone who interests me and she ends up being a true crime writer doing a book on the kidnapping. But I guess we can't help the people we fall for, huh."

The admission surprised him, but had no effect on his mother.

He talked for another ten minutes, telling her about the ranch, the new stallion, her other children.

"Ledger is still in love with Abby," he said with a sigh. "I can't see any way that can have a happy ending." Just like his own situation, he thought. "Boone, well, he's ornery enough that it will take a special woman to turn his head."

He watched his mother's blank expression as she rocked back and forth, the rocker creaking with her movement. "This woman who's staying at the ranch, the true crime writer, she thinks she can find out what really happened that night. A part of me hopes it's true. But another part of me…" He swallowed, surprised at the fear that filled him. "What if she finds out that it was you? You and Nate? I don't believe it. But if it turns out I'm wrong… I can't let that happen, Mother. But I'm not sure I can stop her. I don't think anyone can."

THE SHERIFF HAD just gotten back from a meeting when she saw that she had a message from the lab. She quickly dialed the number and was handed off to the lab tech who'd taken the test.

"You have the results?" she said in the phone. McCall wasn't sure what she expected to hear. That Nikki St. James was wrong. Or that it was true and there was someone in that house systematically poisoning Travers McGraw. She'd been in law enforcement long enough that nothing should surprise her.

"We found arsenic in the hair follicles," the lab tech said.

McCall let out the breath she'd been holding. So it was true. "Thank you. Please have those results sent to my office." She started to hang up, but instead disconnected and dialed a judge she had a good working relationship with.

"I'm going to need a warrant," she told him and quickly informed him of the lab test. Poison had always been a woman's weapon throughout history.

"I'll have your warrant within the hour," the judge promised. "I'm assuming you have a suspect?"

Everyone in the county knew Patricia Owens Mc-Graw. She could count the number of people who she'd befriended on one hand. "Let's just hope she doesn't know we're on to her. I'd like to wrap this one up quickly. The media is going to have a field day."

"Yes," the judge agreed. "Especially with the anniversary of the kidnapping only days away."

She hung up, thinking about Nikki St. James. The woman was sharp. She just might have saved Travers McGraw's life. But the irony didn't escape McCall. If Nikki discovered through her investigation for her book that the twins were dead, it might kill him given his condition.

NIKKI HAD FOUND out what she could about Harold Cline before she returned to the kitchen to find Frieda finishing her chores.

Just as Tilly had told her, Harold had been a ne'er-do-well with a sketchy background. He'd done poorly in school, had trouble holding jobs, had been married and divorced, but had never had a run-in with the law.

She had to agree with Tilly that he didn't look like someone who could engineer one of the most famous kidnappings in Montana history and get away with it. But whoever had taken the twins had help, and that person could have been the mastermind behind the kidnapping. Harold Cline could have just been the muscle.

The fact that Harold Cline seemed to have dropped off the face of the earth right after the kidnapping also made Nikki suspicious. She couldn't find anywhere in the information she'd gotten on the case that the sheriff or FBI had talked to Harold. Either they hadn't known about him or didn't consider him a suspect. She was betting it was the former.

Which was why she was anxious to talk to Frieda away from Patricia's prying eyes and ears.

The cook took off her apron and still seemed to hesitate. "I'm not staying at the Whitehorse Sewing Circle today. I'm just dropping off some fabric for future quilts. We make quilts for new babies in the area." She stopped short as if she hadn't meant to say that much.

"Great, I'll get my car. You can tell me where to go."

Frieda looked resigned as she climbed into the passenger side of the rental car a few minutes later, hugging the bag of fabric.

"I thought this would give us a chance to talk without any interruptions," Nikki said once they were on the road.

The cook said nothing as she looked out the side window.

She drove south, away from Whitehorse, deeper into the Missouri Breaks, following Frieda's directions. "I'm surprised they meet this far from Whitehorse."

"The first settlement of Whitehorse was actually nearer the Missouri River," Frieda said. "But when the railroad came through, the town migrated five miles to the north, taking the name with it. So now, it's called Old Town. It's little more than a ghost town, though some families have remained." Again she stopped abruptly.

Nikki drove through rolling prairie, the purple outline of the Little Rockies off to their right, before she dropped over a hill and slowed at a rusted sign warning there were children at play. A tumbleweed cartwheeled across the road in front of the rental. Frieda was right about Old Town being a ghost town. There were a few buildings still standing, including what appeared to have once been a country schoolhouse.

"It's that large building on the right," Frieda said as they passed the old school yard and she saw a weathered sign on the next building that read Old Town White-horse Community Center.

There were three pickups parked out front. Nikki pulled in next to the one on the end and shut off the engine.

"Looks like the whole group is here," Frieda said. She suddenly seemed even more nervous.

"If you prefer I not come in…" Nikki said.

"I just need to drop this fabric off." The cook looked conflicted. "You might as well come in and see what they're working on today."

As they stepped inside, Nikki was hit with a scent that reminded her of the old trunk in her mother's attic where she'd found the newspaper clippings about Nate Corwin.

It took a moment for her eyes to adjust to the cool dimness inside. Three older women sat around a quilting hoop. They all turned, their hands holding the needles and thread hovering above the fabric.

"I brought a guest," Frieda announced into the deathly silence.

The women quickly welcomed Nikki, though they seemed to watch her with interest.

"This is Nikki St. James. She's a true crime writer. She's doing a story on the McGraw kidnapping," Frieda blurted and took a breath.

"So we heard," said a small gray-haired woman with bright blue eyes. "It's a small town. Do you quilt?"

"No," Nikki said as she watched the woman make tiny perfect stitches in what appeared to be a baby quilt. "My neighbor does. I have one of her quilts. I love it."

"Did Frieda tell you that we have been quilting he __ for years? Used to make a quilt for every newborn in the area. Now not so much," the woman said almost wistfully. "Our numbers have dropped considerably."

Nikki had done her homework and found out that along with quilting the women of the Whitehorse Sewing Circle had also placed babies out for adoption illegally since the 1930s. No one had seen any jail time since most of the "leaders" behind the illegal adoptions were dead now.

"So tell us about your book," a large white-haired woman inquired.

"Not much to tell," Nikki admitted. "I've just begun my interviews."

Frieda hugged the bag of fabric she'd brought. "Has she interviewed you?" a sour-face dyed redhead asked Frieda.

"Why would she? I have nothing to add," Frieda said without looking at Nikki.

"I'm sure Frieda will help if she can. We all want to know what happened to the twins," Nikki said, hoping it was true.

"Well, most of us already know," the sour-faced one said. "One look at Marianne McGraw tells the whole story."

The three women who'd been at the table when Nikki had entered all shook their heads as if in condolence to poor Marianne. "Imagine the nightmares that woman has," the sweet little gray-haired woman said in sympathy.

"Of course there's a chance she wasn't involved," Nikki said.

Sour-face scoffed.

"There is always a chance that new information will surface," Nikki said and all the women gave her a look of pity.

"That good-looking horse trainer turned Marianne McGraw's head. It happens all the time and look how it ended," said the bottle redhead. "They both got what they had coming."

"But what about those sweet babies?" the little gray-haired woman said.

"They're long dead," sour-face snapped. "Someone will stumble onto their graves one of these days, you'll see. Lucky the kidnappers are dead or locked up. Otherwise, it would be dangerous digging around in the past for your book."

Next to Nikki, Frieda dropped the bag of fabric she'd been holding. "I'm so clumsy," she said, sounding close to tears.

They all turned to look at her as she quickly retrieved it from the floor and put it on a nearby table. All the color had washed from her face. For a moment Nikki was afraid the cook might faint. What had the women said that had upset her?

"WE SHOULD GO and let you ladies get back to work," Frieda said. She had regained some composure, but clearly didn't look well as they said their goodbyes and left.

Nikki thought about what Patricia had said to Frieda

about the quilt group, how the cook had gotten upset that day, as well. But what was it about this group of older women quilting?

"Are you all right?" Nikki had asked as she started the car.

"I just remembered something I promised Mrs. Mc-Graw I would do today."

"I thought it was your day off," Nikki reminded her.

"Since I started living on the ranch, Mrs. McGraw gets confused about what days I'm actually off," Frieda said, turning away to look out the side window.

Nikki backed out onto the dirt road. "Whose idea was it for you to move in?"

"The first Mrs. McGraw thought it would save me time driving back and forth from Whitehorse and save me money on a rental when I spent most of my time at the ranch anyway. It was a kind gesture on her part since my husband, George, is a truck driver who spends a lot of time on the road."

Unlike Patricia, who treated her like her private servant, Nikki thought. "I'm surprised you've stayed with the McGraws all these years," she said carefully as she drove away from Old Town.

She couldn't shake the feeling that Patricia was holding something over Frieda. Why else would the cook put up with the way the woman treated her?

Frieda remained quiet.

"Patricia must be a hard woman to work for." Still nothing. Nikki looked over at her. "Frieda, either you are working on sainthood or Patty is holding something over you. Which is it?"

All the color drained from Frieda's face again. "I don't know what…you're talking about," she stammered.

"Given the way she treats you and how wonderfully you cook, why haven't you quit? I know there are other ranches that would snatch you up in a heartbeat." Nikki looked over at the woman in her passenger seat.

"I can't leave Mr. McGraw. Or the boys," she mumbled, and looked embarrassed.

Nikki thought that might have something to do with it, but not everything. "You know what I think? I think the woman is holding something over your head. I think it might have something to do with a man. Wouldn't you feel better to get it off your chest? To get her off your back?"

She let out a bitter chuckle. "You have no idea."

"Let me help you," Nikki said.

Frieda merely stared out the side window.

Nikki's attention was drawn away from the woman as she caught movement in the rearview mirror. She'd been driving down the dirt road through the wild country and hadn't seen another car the whole way.

Now, though, an old rusty truck had come roaring up behind her. Nikki looked for a place to pull off, but there was nothing but a ditch on both sides of the road. She sped up a little since she had been going slow.

The truck stayed right with her, riding her bumper. She couldn't see the driver because of the glare off the cracked windshield of the truck.

Frieda had noticed something was wrong. She sat up and was watching in her side mirror. "I was afraid this would happen," she said, her voice breaking with fear. "He's going to kill us."

Nikki shot her a surprised look. What was she talking about? "No one's going to kill us."

"You have no idea what you've done by coming here,

asking all these questions, digging up the past," Frieda said, sounding close to tears.

"What have I done?" she asked, speeding up as she looked ahead for a place to pull over so the truck could pass.

The woman shook her head. She looked like a woman of seventy, her blonde hair appearing gray, worry making her face look haggard.

"Frieda, I've known something was wrong since I got here. You can tell me."

The woman turned to look at her, eyes shimmering with tears. "I knew it would come out one day. It isn't like I ever thought…" Her voice broke.

Nikki couldn't see a place to pull over and the truck driver seemed determined to get past even though there was only the one lane and no shoulder to pull off on.

"This has something to do with Harold Cline, doesn't it? The reason you let Patricia treat you so badly."

Frieda let out a cry and covered her face with both hands as the pickup slammed into the back of the rental car. "I told you he was going to kill us."

Fighting to keep the rental car on the narrow road, Nikki demanded, "Who is that driving the truck?"

Frieda said nothing and hunkered on her side of the car as the truck came up fast and crashed into them again.

The back of the rental fishtailed and for a moment Nikki feared she would lose control. "Get your cell phone out. Call the sheriff!" Frieda didn't move. "Frieda!"

They were coming to one of the rolling hills and a curve. Nikki hated to go any faster but she had no choice. She pushed down on the accelerator, hoping to outrun the truck. But the driver must have anticipated her plan.

The truck came up with so much speed that when it hit the back of the rental there was no controlling it any longer. The car tires caught a rut and the next thing Nikki knew they were sideways in the road. But not for long.

The tires caught another rut and she felt the car tilt.

"Hang on!" she cried as the rental car went off the road and over the edge of the hillside. It rolled once, then again and again until it came to rest at the bottom of the hill in a gully.

CHAPTER SEVENTEEN

"Is THERE A PROBLEM?" Cull asked as he glanced to where Patricia was slamming pots and pans around in the kitchen, before he took a stool at the breakfast bar. Kitten had her head in the refrigerator.

"Frieda isn't back to make dinner. I'm going to fire her. I've put up with that woman long enough."

"It's her day off," Cull said, but Patricia didn't seem to hear. She appeared nervous and overly upset over something that happened once a week. Usually, though, Frieda gave in and cooked.

"Do we have any celery?" Kitten was asking. "You think it's true that it takes more calories to eat celery than it has in it?"

Cull didn't bother to respond. "Have you seen Nikki?" he asked even though he knew that would be a sore subject and the woman was already in a foul mood.

"She took off with Frieda," Kitten said, coming out from behind the refrigerator door with a stalk of celery in her hand.

Patricia slammed down a pot. "Who knows what that fool woman might tell her about all of us."

"I hope you aren't planning to cook or we are all

going to starve," Cull said. "Or wish we did," he added under his breath. "So where did Nikki go with Frieda?"

"To that old lady quilt group," Kitten said between bites of celery.

Patricia cussed under her breath and looked at her watch. "Shouldn't they be back by now?"

Having enough of this, Cull headed toward the living room. Looking up, he saw the sheriff and two deputies coming down the stairs. They headed toward his father's office. Travers McGraw was behind his desk. He looked as if he'd aged in the last few minutes.

"What's happened?" Cull demanded, his heart in his throat. Had there been an accident? Was it one of his brothers? Was it their mother? Was it... His pulse began to pound. Nikki? With a start he saw that one of the deputies was carrying what appeared to be an evidence bag. Cull realized that the lab tests must have come back—and that Nikki had been right.

"Where is your stepmother?" Travers asked as he came out of his office. McCall gave him a nod, and Cull saw the pain in his father's expression before he answered.

"She's in the kitchen with Kitten. I don't believe she heard you arrive." The sheriff and deputies started in that direction. "Please don't handcuff her. Not in front of her daughter," Travers said.

Cull turned to his father. "It's *true*? She's been poisoning you?"

He nodded. "Just as we suspect she did your mother twenty-five years ago."

"Patricia McGraw?" he heard the sheriff ask.

From his vantage point, Cull watched as Patty

turned. Her eyes widened as she looked from the sheriff to the deputies and past them to her husband.

"If you could step out into the living room," the sheriff said to her.

Patty looked as if she wanted to make a run for it. "What is this about?"

"If you could please ask your daughter to stay in here," the sheriff said as she took Patty's arm and led her out of the kitchen.

Kitten started to follow, but Travers wheeled past the deputy to keep her in the kitchen. "What is going on with Mother?" the teen demanded.

The sheriff was saying, "Patricia Owens McGraw, you're under arrest for attempted murder. You have the right to remain silent..." McCall continued reading the Miranda rights as Patty argued that she didn't know what the sheriff was talking about.

One of the deputies showed her something they'd found upstairs. Arsenic? Cull hoped they put her *under* the jail. If all of Nikki's suspicions were true... He fisted his hands at his side.

"Call my lawyer!" she barked at Cull as she was handcuffed, a lawman holding each of her elbows as they steered her toward the front door. "Call Jim. It's all a mistake. That poison was planted in my room."

"No one said we found it in your room," the sheriff said.

"It's all lies! I'm being framed! It's that writer. She did this!" Patricia looked over her shoulder at Cull. "Why would I poison your father? I love him."

"Where are they taking my mother?" Kitten cried as she tried to get past her stepfather's wheelchair. A moment later, the front door closed, car engines revved and Travers rolled out of the kitchen with a crying Kitten.

Ledger and Boone both came in then, both looking worried. No doubt they'd seen the sheriff's patrol cars out front and Patricia being led away.

"I'll explain everything," Travers said as he asked them all to sit down. Cull listened as his father explained that lab tests had been taken of his hair. Patricia had been poisoning him for some time, which no doubt was why he'd been so sick.

"Not just sick. She almost killed you!" Boone cried. "How did you figure it out?"

"Nikki St. James suspected it and went to the sheriff," their father said.

Cull glanced at his watch, worry burrowing in his belly. "Kitten said that Nikki and Frieda had gone out to Old Town." His father nodded. "Shouldn't they have been back by now? I'm going to drive down there. Let me know if you hear from Nikki," he said and he was out the door and driving toward Old Town Whitehorse.

NIKKI CAME TO SLOWLY, as if she'd either been stunned or knocked unconscious. For a moment, she didn't know where she was or what had happened. It came back to her in a rush. To her surprise, the car had landed right side up in a gully.

She looked over at Frieda, who thankfully appeared to be shaken but not injured. "Are you all right?"

The woman nodded. "You're bleeding."

Nikki touched her temple, her fingers coming away wet with blood. "I'm all right," she said, more to assure herself than Frieda as she dug out her cell phone. She prayed there would be enough coverage out here to get the sheriff. She looked back up the hillside they had rolled down, half expecting to see the pickup truck idling there.

The road above them appeared to be empty.

Nikki was glad to see she had a few bars on her phone and quickly tapped in 9-1-1. When the dispatcher answered, she told her what had happened. "I'm not sure exactly where we are."

"Near Alkali Creek," Frieda said.

She gave this information to the dispatcher. "No, I don't think we need an ambulance. But please hurry." She disconnected and tried to open her door. It was jammed. She thought she smelled gas. "Can you get your door open?"

Frieda didn't seem to hear her. She'd begun to cry.

Nikki reached across her to open the passenger-side door. "We need to get out of the car, Frieda."

As if in a fugue state, the cook climbed out, staggering against the hillside before sitting down hard. Nikki climbed out the passenger side and reached for Frieda's hand.

"We need to get away from the car. Gas is leaking out. I don't think it is going to blow, but it could catch fire. Do you hear me?" She stared at the woman, worried that maybe she was injured more than she'd first thought.

When she looked up at Nikki, there were tears in her eyes. "I told you he would kill us."

She took Frieda's hand and pulled her up, leading her away from the car to an outcropping of rock before letting her sit down again.

"He'll come back," Frieda said. "He can't let us live. He thinks we know too much."

"Who?"

The cook shook her head. She could see that the woman was terrified. Nikki had been so focused on making sure Frieda was all right and getting them away from the car that she hadn't let the full weight of what had happened register.

"Frieda, if you know who that was who ran us off the road, you need to tell me. Does this have something to do with the kidnapping? Frieda, talk to me. I can help you. Whatever is going on, you can't keep it to yourself anymore. This is serious."

"It's all my fault," the cook said and began to sob.

Nikki was trying to imagine Frieda being part of the kidnapping. The woman *had* been living in the house at the time of the kidnapping and could have drugged the babies and then handed them out the window to her boyfriend, Harold Cline. But that would mean that Frieda had been the mastermind behind the plot. That seemed doubtful.

"Frieda, please tell me. Whatever it is—"

"I was thirty-nine. *Thirty-nine!* Old enough to know better."

Nikki guessed at once that she was talking about Harold Cline. She felt her skin prickle. She tried to keep her voice calm, consoling. "You fell in love?"

She seemed surprised that Nikki had guessed. "He was funny, made me laugh, and he really seemed to like me."

Nikki feared what was coming. "You thought you'd found the man for you," she said instead of asking what the man had conned her into doing.

"I would have done anything for him."

And did, Nikki feared. She wanted to ask but waited

as patiently as she could for the rest of the story to come out. She could still smell gas leaking from the car nearby and wondered if they should move farther away, but didn't want to interrupt Frieda now that she had her talking.

"I would sneak him into the house at night," Frieda said between tearful jags. "He'd come to my room and..." She looked away. "He wasn't the only one sneaking in at night."

Nikki thought of her father.

"Patty had her own boyfriend."

She felt another wave of relief wash over her as she thought about the argument she'd witnessed the first night. "Jim Waters? Or Blake Ryan."

"Blake."

"Is it still going on?" she had to ask.

The older woman merely gave her a look.

"So you left the door open on the night of the kidnapping," Nikki guessed, still not sure yet where this was going.

Frieda began to cry again. "He didn't show up. I was so stupid. I really thought he was the one."

"Did you see him again after that night?" Nikki asked.

The woman only cried harder.

She took a breath, warning herself to tread softly. "Patty found out you'd been letting him in." It wasn't a question. It had to be what Patricia was now holding over the cook's head. Unless it had something to do with the kidnapping. "Did she tell the sheriff and FBI about your boyfriend?"

Another look that said she hadn't.

Nikki's heart began to pound. "I don't understand

why Patty didn't tell the sheriff and FBI. Unless she was already using it against you." She glanced over at Frieda and saw that was exactly what Patty had been doing.

Patty had known the man was sneaking in and was using it against Frieda even twenty-five years ago. But if the sheriff and FBI found out that Patty had known all this before the kidnapping, then she would be under even more suspicion than she had been at the time, so she'd kept her mouth shut and used it to keep Frieda under her thumb.

"She said she was protecting me and that I owed her," Frieda said between sobs.

Nikki had thought she couldn't dislike Patricia more, but she'd been wrong. How could Patricia keep something like that quiet all these years? Even now, it would be Frieda's word against the new Mrs. McGraw's.

"Was this man ever questioned by the authorities?" Nikki had to ask even though she knew the answer already, if indeed Frieda's lover had been Harold Cline, as Tilly had told her.

Frieda shook her head as she wiped at her tears. "I don't care what the sheriff does to me. I deserve it, but do you have to put it in your book?"

"I won't put in anything until I have the whole story."

That seemed to relieve Frieda. "I never told. Marianne was already locked up and so was the horse trainer. I figured they had the kidnappers and that it wasn't my…lover."

"I'm going to need to know the name of the man, Frieda."

She hesitated but only a moment. "Harold Cline."

Her mind was racing as she tried to understand what it was Frieda was telling her—and wasn't telling her.

"You'd want to know why he hadn't shown that night. Maybe he'd seen the horse trainer stealing the babies," Nikki said. "You would have gone to see him."

Frieda looked away again.

Nikki felt her heart sink. Tilly was wrong about one thing. Harold Cline had kidnapped the twins and Frieda knew it. Knew it because she'd seen him with the babies?

She was frantically trying to put the pieces together. Frieda had said it was all her fault. "Was there any reason to fear for the twins' safety in that house twenty-five years ago?"

"You don't know what the first Mrs. McGraw was like then. She was confused all the time. Often she couldn't remember the names of her children. I overheard her say that she didn't want the twins, wanted nothing to do with them and wished they would disappear."

A piece of the puzzle dropped into place. "You shared this information with your boyfriend."

Frieda let out a sob. "I had no idea he would kidnap the twins."

There it was. Harold Cline had taken the twins. "That's why you feel so guilty." But when she saw Frieda's expression, she knew that telling him about Marianne's state of mind wasn't the only reason Frieda felt guilty. Her heart dropped.

"Your boyfriend must have thought he was saving them," Nikki said, hoping to keep the cook talking. "That they would get better homes." But why not take the kidnapping ransom money and let the twins be found alive and well? Why make them disappear?

She thought about the broken rung on the ladder and

the concern that the kidnapper had fallen, injuring one or both of the babies.

What other reason would the kidnapper have for not returning the babies?

"He did plan to find them good homes, right?"

Frieda's eyes filled with tears again.

She heard the sound of a vehicle. Shouldn't the sheriff be here by now? What if Frieda was right and the man who'd tried to run them off the road had come back?

She looked around for a place they might hide and saw nothing but short scrub pine and sagebrush.

"Maybe I should call the sheriff again," she said to Frieda, but the woman didn't seem to hear her. Nikki realized that the key pieces of the puzzle were still missing.

"Where is Harold Cline now?" she asked as she started to dig her cell phone out of her pocket. Frieda had said that "he" would kill them. "Is Harold Cline the man who ran us off the road?"

"No," Frieda said her voice cold and hard. "He's dead. I killed him."

CULL TOOK A shortcut to Old Town and arrived at the Whitehorse Community Center as several older women were coming out.

He looked around for Nikki's rental car, but didn't see it. "Was Frieda here?" he asked a small gray-haired woman.

"Earlier, she and the writer. They left a long time ago, though."

He thanked her and headed down the main road thinking he must have missed them by taking the short-

cut. Patricia's arrest had thrown him. He was still trying to process the fact that she'd been systematically
poisoning his father—and might have done the same
thing twenty-five years ago to his mother.

A feeling of doom had come over him when he'd realized that Frieda and Nikki should have been back to
the ranch a good hour ago.

Maybe it was seeing his mother this morning, but he
kept thinking that Nikki was right. If Patty had been
poisoning his mother twenty-five years ago, it would
explain her behavior more than postpartum depression.
It could also explain her breakdown and how quickly
she'd gone downhill. Losing the twins must have been
the last straw.

But if it was true, would the sheriff be able to prove
that Marianne was a victim of Patty's, and so was her
husband? He wished he could get his hands around Patty's throat. He would choke the truth out of her.

The arrest had happened so quickly that he hadn't
had time to think—let alone react. Now he was furious.
Patty could have killed his father. Travers had taken it
better than Cull would have. What wife poisoned her
husband?

His cell phone rang. He answered, surprised he could
get service this far out. "Hello?"

"A call just came in over the scanner," his brother
Ledger told him. "A car was run off the road near Alkali Creek. Isn't that on the way to Old Town?"

"Who put in the call to the sheriff?" Cull asked and
held his breath.

"Nikki St. James. She said she and Frieda weren't
hurt. Deputies are on the way. They got held up because
of Patricia's arrest. Where are you?"

"On my way to Alkali Creek," he said, and disconnected.

Cull hadn't gone far when he saw the tracks. He slowed. There was broken glass from a headlight at the edge of the road. Ahead he saw more tracks and in the distance, a dark green pickup parked off the road.

He had his window down as he drove toward the tracks. He hadn't gone far when he heard the gunshot.

NIKKI WAS STUNNED by Frieda's confession. So stunned that it took a moment to realize what was happening. There was a sound like something hard hitting stone. At the same time, Frieda flinched and let out a soft cry.

When she looked over at the woman sitting with her back against a large rock, Nikki saw that Frieda was holding a hand over her stomach. It took her a wild moment to realize that blood was oozing out from between her fingers.

The second rifle shot pinged off the rock above Nikki's head. She scrambled up, grabbed hold of Frieda and dragged her around the rock outcropping. Again she heard the sound of a vehicle engine.

She fumbled out her cell phone and quickly punched in 9-1-1 again, telling the dispatcher what had happened.

"An ambulance is on the way," she told Frieda as she disconnected.

The woman was still breathing, but her breaths were shallow and she was clearly in a lot of pain. Nikki had stanched the bleeding as much as she could with her jacket.

Her mind was racing.

"I can't die yet. I can't die with this on my conscience."

"You're not going to die."

A crooked smile curled her lips. "When I heard that someone had taken the twins, I knew."

"Frieda, you shouldn't try to talk."

The woman didn't seem to hear her. "I prayed it wasn't him. But when I couldn't reach him… There was an old cabin in the Little Rockies that Harold used during hunting season. I knew the ransom had been paid, but the babies still hadn't been returned." She grimaced in pain, her voice choked with tears as she said, "He was digging a hole to bury them when I found him."

Nikki felt her heart drop like a stone. She couldn't breathe, couldn't speak.

"He said it was my fault. I'm the one who said the twins weren't safe and he was just doing what I wanted him to do. The babies were in a burlap bag on the ground next to the hole he'd been digging. I begged him to take them back."

Hope soared at her words. "Take them back? They were still alive?"

Still Frieda didn't seem to hear her. She was lost in the past, lost in telling a secret hard kept all these years. "He said, 'Have you lost your mind? The place is crawling with cops. And what would I say? Yes, I took the little snots, but I've decided to return them because Frieda has changed her mind? You're in this as deep as I am. You'll go to prison with me. You think they will believe that I did this on my own?'"

She felt her blood run cold at Frieda's words. "Who did help him?"

Frieda shook her head. She took a ragged breath. "He never told me." Nikki could tell that she was in terrible pain. "All I cared about was the babies. I told him I was taking them and going to the authorities."

"'You're not doin' nothin' but goin' back to the ranch and keepin' your trap shut.' I told him I couldn't go back, not without the babies. 'You don't go back and you'll look guilty and I will be long gone and you can rot in prison.'"

Nikki couldn't bear to hear this and yet she hung on every word as she prayed for the sound of the ambulance and sheriff.

"I knew he was right. No one would believe me," Frieda said, her voice getting weaker. "He walked over to the babies. He was going to put them into that grave he'd dug. Put them in there still alive. I picked up the shovel." She began to cry again. "I dug the hole larger and buried him and the ransom money."

"What did you do with the babies, Frieda?" Nikki asked, her voice breaking.

The woman's eyes met hers. "I took them to the Whitehorse Sewing Circle. Pearl Cavanaugh was the only one there that night after everyone else had gone. I told her the same story I told Harold about Marianne. I begged her to find them good homes."

Relief rushed through her. "And did she?"

Frieda didn't answer. When Nikki looked into her eyes again, she saw that the woman was gone.

CHAPTER EIGHTEEN

ACROSS THE RAVINE, Cull saw a man with a rifle run to his pickup. Something flashed in the sunlight as the man jumped behind the wheel. A moment later he took off in a cloud of dust. Was he going for help? What had he been doing with a rifle?

Cull pulled over to the side of the road and jumped out to look down into the ravine. In the distance he could hear the sound of sirens as he looked down to the bottom and saw the wrecked rental car. His heart dropped.

"Nikki!" he called. *"Nikki!"* He had already started down the hillside at a run when she came out from behind the rocks. His mouth went dry. He hadn't realized how terrified he'd been until he saw her—saw her injured and covered in blood.

He ran to her, weak with relief. "How badly are you hurt?" He could see that she had a scrape on the side of her face and there was dried blood on her temple, but it was the blood on the front of her shirt that had him shaking inside.

"It's not me. It's Frieda." She burst into tears. "She's been shot. She's dead."

He pulled her into his arms, the sound of sirens

growing closer. She felt so good in his arms that he never wanted to let her go. Relief gave way to realization. He'd seen the shooter leave in that old truck. "Did you get a look at the shooter?"

Nikki shook her head against his chest. "He ran us off the road, then came back..."

A sheriff's department patrol SUV stopped at the top of the hill followed by an ambulance, sirens blaring.

"Let's get you up to the road," he told Nikki.

She pulled back to wipe her eyes. "I can't leave Frieda."

"Let the EMTs take care of Frieda."

"But I'm the one who got her killed."

CHAPTER NINETEEN

IT RAINED THE day of Frieda Holmes's funeral, but all of the McGraws were there standing under black umbrellas, listening to the preacher put her to rest. Frieda had no family except for the McGraws. But members of her quilting group had come to pay their respects.

Nikki stood next to Cull, the rain making a soft patter on the umbrella he held over them. Her heart still ached for Frieda. She'd paid a high price for what she'd done and the secret she'd kept all these years.

Still shaken by what had happened, Nikki questioned why she'd become a true crime writer. What drove this need of hers for the truth? Whatever it was, she'd gotten the woman killed. Her relentless need to dig in other people's tragedies had caused this. She would have to take that to her own grave.

As she looked around the cemetery, she thought of her father. She knew now that he had nothing to do with the kidnapping, but it would take more than that to clear his name. She had to find out who inside that house had helped Harold Cline. She would never believe it was Frieda.

The preacher was winding up his sermon. She looked to Travers McGraw, wondering how he was holding up given everything that had happened. He stood tall and erect beside the cook's grave, insisting he didn't need the wheelchair. In the days since Patricia's arrest, he'd improved. No doubt because he wasn't being poisoned, but it would take time for him to recover—if he ever fully did.

Cull had been afraid that the news about the twins would be the straw that finally broke him. But Nikki saw that he was filled with even more hope now. He was also stronger now that he knew why his health had deteriorated like it had. He would never be the man he'd been, but he was more determined than ever to find the twins.

The family gathered back at the ranch after the funeral. Tilly had made them all lunch, but no one was hungry. There were still so many questions, but now at least they knew that the babies had been saved. Unfortunately, Pearl Cavanaugh, the member of the Whitehorse Sewing Circle who Frieda had given the twins to, was dead. She'd died some years ago after having several strokes.

Travers had asked Nikki to tell them all what Frieda had confessed before she died. When she finished, the room fell silent.

"You believe Patty was poisoning our mother twenty-five years ago?" Ledger asked.

"It would explain your mother's behavior," Nikki said. "I'm not sure the sheriff will be able to prove it, though."

"We still don't know who helped this Harold Cline take the twins," Boone pointed out.

"But we do know that Frieda got them to Pearl Cavanaugh and that she probably found them good homes," Nikki said.

"But she is the only one who knows where they went and she's dead," Boone pointed out. "It's just another dead end."

"I have to wonder about the adoptive parents," Cull added. "They had to know about the McGraw kidnapping. It was on national news. Wouldn't they have questioned where their babies came from?"

Nikki had thought of that. "I'm sure Pearl had a story prepared. Remember, Frieda told her that Marianne wasn't stable, that the babies weren't safe here. I'm sure the new parents thought they were saving them."

"They were," Travers said.

"Which means they aren't together. Oakley and Jesse Rose had to have been adopted separately," Ledger said.

The room fell silent for a few moments.

"What now?" Boone asked, looking at Nikki, then his father.

"I'm sure Nikki is still planning to do the book," Travers said, and Nikki nodded. "I got a call from the sheriff earlier. They found the hunting cabin in the Little Rockies that Harold Cline used. They found his grave and the ransom money." His voice broke as he added, "The sheriff found a burlap bag in the cabin that had both Oakley's and Jesse Rose's DNA on it."

He turned to Nikki. "One of the things that was never released to the media was that when the twins were taken, so were their favorite animals that slept with them at night—and their blankets. Jesse Rose's blanket was found in the pool house. But Oakley's was never found. The small stuffed animals were horses with ribbons around their necks. Each twin had a different-colored ribbon."

Cull frowned. "So there is one blanket and two stuffed horses still missing. Let me guess. You're planning to release this information in hopes that the twins will see it."

Travers smiled at his son and nodded. "Just the information about the toy horses."

Boone got to his feet. "You're going to bring every nutcase out of the woodwork. Isn't it bad enough with all the publicity about Patricia?"

"The twins are alive," Travers said. "I've felt it soul deep since they were taken. What Nikki found out from Frieda only proves it. This is a chance I have to take. With Nikki's help, we'll put out the information and pray that the twins will find *us*."

Boone shook his head. "I have work to do. We are still a horse ranch, aren't we?" He walked out, mumbling, "This family is cursed."

"He's right. I still can't believe what Patty did," Cull said, looking over at his father.

"I suspect she got the idea from when she slowly poisoned your mother over twenty-five years ago and made her think she was crazy," Travers said.

Cull shook his head in disbelief. "She would have killed you and none of us would have suspected what she was doing. If Jim Waters gets her out of jail…"

"He won't," Travers said. "Patricia has no money of her own. She won't be able to make bail. Not only that, but also the judge thinks she is a flight risk and so do I."

"You're sure Waters isn't defending her?" Cull asked with disgust.

"He might have, before he realized she didn't have

any money to pay him. Before we got married, I made Patricia sign a prenuptial agreement. I worried that if we divorced she could force me to sell the ranch that I've built for my children."

"But she would get something. What happened if you died?" Nikki asked.

"She would have gotten a few acres so she could build a place for herself, if she so desired, and a large amount of money to live on the rest of her life. I'm sure she would have sold the land," Travers said. "Now we know that she couldn't wait for me to die." There was pain in his tone. He wasn't used to being betrayed.

"Nikki tells me that your mother kept a diary," Travers said to his sons. "One of the pages has turned up. Do you know anything about it?" he asked his family. There was a general shake of heads.

"The first I heard of it was when Nikki brought me the page someone had shoved under her door," Cull said. "Isn't it possible Patricia was involved? She seems to have been involved in everything else, including blackmailing Frieda."

"I'm going to go by the sheriff's office and see if Patty will talk to me," Nikki said. "If she has the diary hidden somewhere, I doubt she will give it up, though. But all I can do is try."

"Good luck with that," Cull piped up.

"Did the sheriff say if they've had any luck finding the person who ran us off the road and shot Frieda?" Nikki asked.

Travers shook his head. "They're looking for the pickup that both you and Cull provided a description for, but they've had no luck so far. There are so many old barns around here, not to mention thousands of ravines and ponds where it could have been dumped. That's what the sheriff thinks Frieda did with Harold Cline's old car he drove. She suspects it is rusting out in one of the ponds near the Little Rockies. It wouldn't be the first time a vehicle was hidden in one."

"Are you sure Patty wasn't in on the kidnapping?" Ledger asked.

Nikki shook her head. "Frieda didn't know who Harold Cline had helping him in the house. It could have been Patty, but I have my doubts. Yes, she wanted your mother's life, always did. The kidnapping I believe messed up her plans and forced her to leave. Also because of the large ransom demand, your father didn't have any money for a long while after that." Nikki shrugged. "It wasn't until she had her daughter and your father had recouped his losses that she doubled back."

"We still don't know who fathered her baby?" Ledger asked.

His father shook his head. "I never asked. Kitten has gone to stay with an aunt. Patricia insisted." He sounded sad. Travers had raised the child as his own and now she, too, had been taken from him.

Cull swore. "That coldhearted—"

"Patricia will get what's coming to her," Travers said as he got to his feet. "Boone's right. We have a horse ranch to run. Nikki will take care of releasing the information to the media. She tells me she can do that from back home while she's writing the book, so she'll be leaving tomorrow. Thank you again. If you hadn't come here…" He smiled at her, his eyes filling with tears.

"She can't finish her book until we find the twins," Ledger said. "So I hope that means you'll be back."

"We'll see what releasing the information about the

twins' stuffed animals turns up." She glanced over at Cull. He seemed to be studying the toes of his worn boots.

Ledger rose to his feet.

"Tell me you aren't going into town to the White-horse Café," Cull said, finally glancing up.

His younger brother shrugged. "You've never been in love, so you couldn't possibly understand."

"Uh-huh," Cull said. "Just watch your back. I hope I don't have to warn you about Wade Pierce."

"There is nothing you can tell me about him that I don't already know," Ledger said, and headed for the door.

"You're worried about him," Nikki said when she and Cull were alone. She shared his concern.

"With good reason. My brother is in love with another man's wife. No good can come out of that." He settled his gaze on her. "So you're leaving."

"I'll go home and start the book. I can do what your father needs me to do from there. No reason for me to stay now."

"I guess not." He lumbered to his feet. "Well, if I don't see you before you leave, have a safe trip back home."

Nikki had two things she had to do before she left town tomorrow. She had to see Marianne McGraw again and then she would pay a visit to Patricia in jail.

This time she went through proper channels, and having Travers's permission, she was taken down the long hallway to the woman's room. Nothing had changed since the last time she'd been here.

Marianne was in her rocker, the dolls clutched in her

arms, her slippered feet propelling her back and forth as she stared off into space.

Nikki dragged up the extra chair in the room and sat down in front of the woman. "You probably don't remember me. I came here to find out who kidnapped your children. I promised I would come back when I knew."

There was no change in expression or in the rocking motion.

"It was your cook Frieda Holmes's boyfriend. She wasn't involved. But the news I have to tell you is that her boyfriend is dead. She killed him and saved your babies. We suspect they went to good homes and eventually we will find them. So we believe that Oakley and Jesse Rose are alive."

Still nothing.

"You should also know that twenty-five years ago when you thought you were losing your mind? You were being *poisoned*. That's why you were confused. It's why you were having trouble bonding with the twins. Patty, your nanny, was poisoning you. She wanted your husband—and she finally got him. She's in jail for attempted murder because once she had Travers, she decided to get rid of him. Apparently what she really wanted was the ranch and you out of the way."

Marianne seemed to hug the dolls tighter as she rocked.

Nikki couldn't be sure any of this was getting through the walled-up dark place where the woman's mind had holed up all these years.

"Now everyone knows you had nothing to do with the kidnapping. Your name is cleared and soon, God willing, your twins will be found alive and well and Patty will be in her prison."

She looked into the woman's face for a moment, remembering the last time she was here. She'd gotten a reaction out of Marianne, but this time there was nothing.

Standing, Nikki pushed the chair back. "I'm so sorry you can't hear what I'm saying. I'd hoped it might free you." She turned and walked to the door to tap on it. A moment later, the door opened.

As she started to step out, she looked back, realizing that the rocking had stopped. Marianne was looking at her. Her arms opened and the tattered dolls tumbled to the floor. The woman let out a bloodcurdling cry that Nikki knew she would hear in her dreams the rest of her life.

"I CAN'T BELIEVE you'd have the nerve to come here," Patricia snapped as Nikki took the phone in the visitors' room and sat down on the safe side of the Plexiglas. "Your lies got me in here. But I'll get out. I have friends."

"I think lover more than friend," Nikki interrupted. "So which one of them were you arguing with the first night I arrived? Was it Blake Ryan or Jim Waters? I can see Kitten in either of them. I bet a DNA test would prove which one was her father. I'm also betting that whichever one it was, it was his idea for you to come back to Whitehorse and the McGraw ranch."

Patricia narrowed her eyes. "You think you know so much, don't you? Prove any of it."

"A simple DNA test will do that."

"Like I'm going to allow my daughter to be tested."

"You do realize that once the sheriff starts questioning Blake Ryan and Jim Waters, your…lover will turn on you and make a deal. Once the sheriff finds the old truck one of them used to force me and Frieda off the road… Once they find the man's DNA inside… I know he shot her to shut her up. If Travers had found out that you'd withheld information on the kidnapping… Well, he might have changed his will—before you killed him—and cut you off without a cent."

"You don't know what you're talking about."

"I know you don't want the twins to be found. You don't need two more McGraws turning up when you already have three stepsons watching you. But a little more poison and Travers's next heart attack would have probably killed him. You would have had some land to sell and money to do whatever you wanted. What did you plan to do, Patty?"

"Are you sure you aren't a fiction writer? It seems to me you just make things up as you go," the woman said. "What do you want?"

"To say goodbye. I'm leaving."

"Finally. Too bad you ever came here."

Nikki stared at her. She'd met others who lacked true compassion. Psychopaths who took pleasure in hurting others. People like Patty only felt pain when it was their own. She thought of the mousy nanny. No wonder no one had suspected what she was doing to poor Marianne. Not that the sheriff would ever be able to prove it.

"Did you ever have a dog?" Nikki asked.

"*What?* A dog? What does that have—"

"Just curious. I've found that people who can't love an animal are missing a part of their souls."

"I have no idea what you're trying to say," she said, looking away.

"I told Marianne that you were systematically poisoning her twenty-five years ago and that was why she thought she was losing her mind."

Patty laughed. "Marianne? She's a vegetable. You really can't believe she understood anything you said."

"You might be surprised." Nikki stood, still holding the phone. "By the way, what did you do with her diary?"

Was that surprise in her eyes? "Her life was so boring. Why would she bother to keep a diary?"

"Have it your way. I would imagine you'll produce it if you can find a way for it to help save you. But ultimately, you're going away for a very long time. I bet Blake is making a deal right now with the prosecuting attorney."

Patty looked scared. Nikki felt bad that she took pleasure in seeing the woman squirm. She thought of what Patty had done to Marianne, Frieda and Travers, and didn't feel so bad.

As she hung up the phone, she saw Patricia signal the guard that she was done.

CHAPTER TWENTY

NIKKI DIDN'T SEE Cull when she went up to the house to say goodbye to Travers and tell him about both Marianne's and Patty's reactions to her visits.

"I'm sorry to see you go," the older man said. "You saved my life. I'll never forget that. Are sure you can't work from here?"

"This is best."

He nodded slowly. "My boys...well, they're gun-shy of relationships. Rightly so, given what they've been through. But you and Cull..."

She smiled. "There was a lot going on. I think we all need time."

"Maybe." He walked her out to her new rental car, which had been delivered that morning. "We'll talk soon."

Nikki held back the tears until she reached the ranch gate. She made the mistake of looking back. A half-dozen of the horses stood at the fence watching her leave. She thought of her father. He'd been innocent just as her mother had known, just as Nikki had prayed.

But what brought tears to her eyes was the pain in her heart. Cull had unlocked something in her. She could just hear what her grandfather would have said—if she was crazy enough to tell him.

She'd gotten too emotionally involved. With the family. With the story. With the oldest son. She and Cull had connected in a way that had scared them both. They were too young to feel this way, weren't they?

Look at Ledger. He'd fallen in love with Abby at the Whitehorse Café when they were teenagers—and nothing had changed even when she'd foolishly married another man. Nikki hoped they found their way back to each other. Ledger deserved a happy ending. So did Cull, but she figured it would be with some local girl now that the truth had come out about the kidnapping.

She drove away from the ranch, telling herself she'd be back but wondering if she ever would. Could she bear seeing Cull again? Bear seeing him with another woman? She thought not.

Tears blurred her eyes. She made a swipe at them as she drove, forcing her to slow down.

CULL WAS SADDLING his horse when his brothers found him. "What's up?" he asked, half-afraid something else had happened.

"We need to talk to you," Boone said. "What's going on between you and the writer?"

Cull almost laughed. This was it? "None of your damned business." He turned back to saddling the horse. He needed this ride more than either of them could imagine. Nikki was the only thing on his mind and he had to do something about that. He did his best thinking on the back of a horse.

"Are you serious about her?" Ledger asked.

Cull sighed and turned back to them. "Maybe I didn't make myself clear—" He frowned. "I thought you went into town?"

"Boone needed my help to make you see reason. We like Nikki. We think she's good for you," Ledger said, taking him by surprise. "She...challenges you. You need that."

Boone sighed. "You do realize that once she gets what she needs for her book she has no excuse to come back."

"I'm aware of that."

"Personally, I don't care what you do, but Ledger is convinced you're in love with her and too stupid to do anything about it."

"Thanks," he said to his youngest brother.

"Well, what *are* you going to do about it?" Ledger asked. "You going to let her get away?"

"She isn't some horse I can lasso and haul back to the corral," Cull said, annoyed that they were butting into his love life. His love life? Had he just thought that? "The woman has a mind of her own."

"So if you could lasso her and haul her back to the corral, you would?" Ledger demanded.

In a heartbeat. "I'm not discussing this with the two of you. Not one lovesick brother who lost his woman or a brother who's too ornery to ever lasso a woman."

"I don't want to see you make the mistake I did," Ledger said, obviously not taking offense at Cull's description of him.

"I could lasso any woman I want. I just haven't found one worth bringing back to the corral," Boone protested.

Cull shook his head. "What do you want from me?"

"If you love her, then go after her. Tell her how you feel," Ledger said.

"And if she leaves anyway?" he asked, hating how vulnerable he sounded.

"Then at least you tried," Boone said, surprising him even more. "We already have one brother moping around here over a woman. I can't bear two. Fix it." With that his brother turned and stalked away.

"He's right," Ledger said. "Fix it or you'll regret it the rest of your life."

"She's already gone," he said.

"You might be able to catch her if you take the short-cut across the ranch," Ledger suggested. "Since you were going on a horseback ride anyway." He smiled.

Cull cuffed his brother on the shoulder as he swung up in the saddle. "I'll think about it."

CULL RODE HARD toward the cutoff road. It felt good, the wind in his face, the power of the horse under him, the freedom of escape that filled him.

He couldn't believe that his brothers had ganged up on him. Go after Nikki and what? Tell her he didn't want her to go? Even with Patricia out of the house, things were still too up in the air.

Not only that; he also told himself that he barely knew the woman. It wasn't like he could have fallen in love with her that quickly. It wasn't like it had been love at first sight. He thought of her lying on the street in front of his pickup and groaned.

She'd never admitted that she'd done that on purpose. What kind of woman would risk her life for…for what? To make him more sympathetic to the book she planned to write?

Pretty daring thing to do. He hated the admiration he felt. It had been a stupid thing to do. Too risky. She could have been killed. A woman like that...well, who knew what she'd do next.

He smiled to himself at the thought. He'd never met anyone like her. He could see her fitting in just fine on the ranch now that Patricia was gone. He could see her just fine as his wife.

That thought hit him like a low limb.

He'd almost reached the road. In the distance he could make out her rental car. A tail of dust trailed behind it.

Cull brought his horse up short at the fence. Why had he let his brothers talk him into this? He had no idea what he was going to say to her. For all he knew she didn't feel the same way. She might even have a boyfriend back home.

Not the way she kissed you. He smiled to himself, remembering those kisses and hating the thought of never getting another one. He'd never told any woman that he loved her. He'd had crushes, even dated the same girl a couple of years in high school. He'd loved her, but he hadn't *loved* her. Not the kind of love that lasts a lifetime.

Nikki was getting closer. He could almost make out her face through the windshield.

Ride away now! You're just going to make a fool of yourself.

NIKKI COULDN'T BELIEVE what she was seeing. She squinted through the sun-dappled windshield. Was that Cull on a horse waiting for her by the ranch fence?

She touched the brakes, wondering what he wanted

as she slowed and hurriedly wiped away the rest of her tears. Maybe she'd forgotten something. But he didn't seem to have anything in his hands. Or maybe Travers had sent him with a message.

Bringing the car to a stop next to him and his horse, she lowered the passenger-side window. "Is something wrong?"

Cull nodded. She watched him slide out of the saddle. He hesitated for a moment, his gaze meeting hers before he vaulted over the fence. As he walked toward her new rental car, her heart lodged in her throat. She'd fallen so desperately in love with this man. How had she let that happen?

He leaned in the passenger-side window she'd lowered.

"I've been thinking," he said, and cleared his throat. "You're going to have to get over your fear of horses."

She frowned. Surely he hadn't ridden all this way to tell her that. "Really? I suppose you have something in mind?"

Cull's blue gaze locked with hers. "I have all kinds of things in mind." He let out a curse and drew back only to walk around to her side of the car. Opening the door, he reached for her hand.

Still mystified, she let him take it and pull her from behind the wheel. "Cull, what—"

"I don't want you to go."

"I'll be back to do more work on the book." It was a lie. She couldn't bear being this close to him and not being in his arms. She wouldn't be back.

"No," he said as if struggling to find the right words. Again his gaze met hers and held it. "I... I know it sounds crazy. It *is* crazy. I come riding out here like some kind of a fool being chased by the devil to tell you…" He faltered.

"To tell me…? Has something happened to your father?"

He shook his head. "I love you." He let out a breath and laughed. "I. *Love*. You."

She was so surprised that she didn't know what to say. She hadn't let herself admit her feelings until today. She'd blamed whatever it was between them on simple chemistry. She and Cull had been like fire and ice. But when they were fire…

"I just had to tell you how I feel." He took a step back from her. "I feel…better getting it out, how about that?" He grinned. "I think I've been wanting to say that for a while now." His blue eyes shone as they locked with hers. "I still can't believe it. I love you."

Nikki laughed. "That's it?"

He looked taken aback. "Hell, woman, you have no idea how hard that was to say. I've never told anyone… and you…you—" He blew out air as he stepped to her again. "*You* make me crazy." His fingers caught her hair at the nape of her neck and buried themselves in the long strands. "All I think about is kissing you. I want to make love to you slow and easy. I want to wake up every morning with you in my arms. I can't stop thinking about you. I don't think I can live without you."

She couldn't breathe at his words, at the look in his eyes. "Oh, Cull. From the moment I laid eyes on you… I felt…" She shook her head. "I've never felt like this before. I love you too."

He pulled her to him in a sizzling kiss that left her teetering on her high heels. As he drew back, he said,

"The first thing we're going to do is buy you a pair of cowboy boots, woman."

She laughed. "*That's* the first thing?"

Cull dragged her into another kiss, this one hotter than the last. "Maybe not the first thing."

* * * * *

THE MYSTERY MAN
OF WHITEHORSE

This one is for good friend Al Knauber.
Hope you're loving Alaska.
We're missing you down here.

CHAPTER ONE

LACI CAVANAUGH BLAMED the champagne. Normally she didn't drink anything stronger than coffee, so of course the champagne had gone right to her head.

Her best friend's wedding called for champagne, though. Laci and Alyson Banning had been friends since birth. Like Laci, Alyson had ended up being raised by her grandparents south of Whitehorse, Montana, just down the county road from each other. And while both had left for college and careers, both were now back.

Unfortunately, Alyson's return had been bittersweet. Just weeks before her wedding, her grandfather had died. With the invitations already sent, she had stuck to her plans, knowing that's what her grandfather would have wanted. The wedding reception now had the community center jam-packed, the large room shimmering with candles and silver streamers, the air alive with laughter and happy voices.

Laci had never seen her friend so blissful, and the best news of all was that Alyson and Spencer might be staying around Whitehorse after their honeymoon. All Alyson had to do was convince Spencer, and Laci didn't think that was going to be a problem given that the man clearly idolized his new bride. Laci loved the prospect of having her best friend here. She was already fantasizing about their children growing up together.

Assuming, of course, that Laci's Prince Charming came riding up soon and swept her off her feet, as Alyson's had. It had all sounded so romantic—and, of course, being best friends, Alyson had told Laci *everything*. Love at first sight, Alyson had said. Not two weeks into the relationship she'd brought him home to meet her grandfather.

Laci had been in Billings with her cousin Maddie, so she hadn't gotten to meet Spencer that time. She'd only really got to spend any time around him at the rehearsal dinner. But she'd seen at once why Alyson had fallen for the man. He was charming and incredibly handsome, not to mention attentive and clearly crazy about Alyson.

Laci had felt a twinge of envy. Unfortunately, men like Spencer didn't come along every day. At least they hadn't for her.

As she took a sip of her champagne and watched the bride and groom dance, she was overwhelmed with happiness for her friend. The two looked so perfect together: Alyson beautiful with her long, flowing auburn hair and slender body, Spencer tall, dark and handsome as any movie star. The perfect couple.

As the dance ended, Alyson turned to say something to one of the guests. Laci found herself looking at Spencer, thinking how adorable the couple's children would be.

Spencer was smiling, his eyes on his bride as he watched her converse with the guest.

And that's when it happened.

His expression changed so quickly that Laci told herself she'd only imagined the look he gave his bride. It lasted all of a split second. Just a flicker of something dark and disturbing.

Just long enough for Laci's blood to turn to ice. Her champagne glass slipped from her fingers, shattering as loudly as a gunshot as it hit the floor. Laci didn't hear it. Nor did she see anything but the groom. It was as if only she and Spencer were in the room.

He turned his head. Maybe at the sound of the glass breaking. Or maybe he'd felt her gaze on him. His eyes locked with hers. Time stopped.

He blinked, then smiled as if he thought he could hide the fact that he was visibly shaken and upset. He *knew* she'd seen him. Laci gasped, not realizing until then that she'd been holding her breath. Music and laughter filled the space again. One of the caterer's crew rushed to clean up her broken glass and the spilled champagne.

She stumbled back, feeling weak and sick to her stomach as she watched her best friend turn back to Spencer and whisper something in his ear. They both laughed, then Spencer swept Alyson into his arms and whirled her across the dance floor.

"They make a beautiful couple, don't they?" said a tall brunette woman Laci didn't know but whose too-sweet perfume was making her sicker.

Laci could only nod, her heart beating so hard it hurt. She fought her way through the crowd to the back door, feeling suddenly faint as she told herself that she hadn't seen anything.

It was just the champagne. That and her overactive imagination. Or maybe she'd misread his look. She couldn't even be sure he'd been looking at Alyson.

Her mind raced. All she knew for sure was that the look she'd seen had been hateful and dangerous. And now her best friend was married to the man. Not just married to him, head over heels in love with him.

It made no sense. Why would Spencer marry Alyson if he didn't love her? Unless her friend was pregnant and he'd felt forced into the marriage?

But Alyson would have confided in Laci if that had been the case. Aly told her everything, didn't she?

Outside, Laci took deep, gasping breaths, tears burning her eyes as she rushed around the side of the building to the darkness and leaned her palms against the wall of the community center and retched.

"Weddings have the same effect on me," said a deep male voice behind her.

She started, fearful that Spencer had followed her. But the voice had come from the playground of the one-room schoolhouse next door.

A man in a tuxedo rose from where he'd been sitting on the merry-go-round and walked toward her. He handed her the napkin that had been wrapped around the stem of his champagne glass. The paper cloth was cold and damp. Just what she needed.

She wiped her face, the chilly night air slowly bringing her back to her senses. "Must have been something I ate."

"Sure," he said. "Couldn't have been anything you drank." His sarcasm was at odds with the deep timbre of his voice. He was tall and solid-looking and vaguely familiar.

She took a step back and bumped into the wall.

"You really should sit down," he said.

"I need to get back inside." It was the last thing she

wanted to do. Just the thought of seeing Spencer with Alyson made her feel sick again.

"Here," the man said, taking her arm. "Just sit down for a minute." He drew her over to the merry-go-round, his grip strong and sure.

"I'm fine," she protested, but she grabbed the railing and sat as her legs gave way under her.

"Yeah, you're great," he said. "If you were any better, you'd be flat on the ground."

She put her head between her knees, afraid he was right. She'd never fainted in her life, but tonight could be a first.

She told herself she'd sit for just a minute, then she had to go warn Alyson. Even as she thought it, Laci questioned the sanity of that idea. She'd spent the last twenty-nine years going off half-cocked. Never one to look before she leaped, she'd suffered the consequences of her actions, especially when it came to relationships.

Was she seriously thinking of telling Alyson about the "look" she'd seen? Aly would never believe her, especially based on some brief, questionable glance. Laci would only come off as jealous or spiteful or both.

"You all right?" he asked as he took a seat next to her.

Out of the corner of her eye she saw him finish off his champagne and set the glass down on the ground. She mumbled, "Uh-huh."

He didn't say anything after that, just leaned back against the railing and stretched out his long legs. He wore cowboy boots with his tux. Something about that made her feel a little safer in his company.

Laci concentrated on breathing and convincing herself she was losing her mind. A better alternative than thinking that her best friend had just married not only the wrong man, but also a man who was…what? Dangerous?

After a few minutes, she sat up, feeling a little better, and glanced over at the man beside her. He was staring up at the stars, both hands behind his head, his profile serene.

"Better?" he asked, not looking at her.

"Yes. Thank you." As she heard the front door of the community center open and the crowd rush out, she pushed to her feet, still feeling a bit wobbly.

"Looks like the bride and groom are about to make their departure," her merry-go-round companion said without moving.

Laci hurried toward the excited guests. She could hear the sound of a motor. Exhaust rose into the darkness as a car was pulled around to the front of the center. Within moments Alyson and Spencer would drive away.

As Laci pushed her way through the crowd, she spotted the bride and groom. Spencer had his arm around Alyson and seemed to be searching the crowd for someone.

When he spotted Laci, he said, "There she is."

"Laci!" Alyson rushed to her and threw her arms around her. "I told Spencer I couldn't possibly leave without saying goodbye to you," she said, sounding both breathless and blissful.

"Aly," Laci said, hugging her friend tightly. "I don't want you to go."

Alyson laughed. "I'll be back in a week."

"No, listen—"

"Come on, sweetheart," Spencer said beside them. Laci felt his hand on her arm. "Let me give Laci a hug, and then we really have to get moving if we hope to make our connections tonight."

"No," Laci said, fighting the feeling that this might be the last time she saw her friend. "Aly, listen, I have to tell you—"

Spencer pulled her into a breath-stealing hug that stifled the rest of her words. Her skin crawled as he bent his head, his lips brushing her ear, and whispered, "Goodbye, Laci."

"No," she cried as she pulled back from him and tried to see her friend. "Aly!"

But Spencer had already turned and swept Alyson up as he rushed to the waiting car, the guests surging around the pair, cutting Laci off.

Laci could only watch through tears as her friend waved from the back window, the car speeding off down the road, the lights dying away in the darkness of the November night.

CHAPTER TWO

LACI CAVANAUGH WOKE the next morning dizzy, head-achy and sick to her stomach.

"How much did you drink last night?" she asked her image in the bathroom mirror and groaned. It was so unlike her to overindulge. She didn't even sample the wine when she was cooking, although most chefs did.

After the bride and groom had taken off, the brides-maids had insisted Laci go into town with them to one of the bars. She'd been in a daze. She vaguely remem-bered the bartender having to ask them to leave at clos-ing time. No wonder she felt so horrible.

But as she stared into the mirror she knew it wasn't just the drinks that had made her sick this morning. It was that niggling worry that she had tried to kill last night with alcohol. Alyson. Her best friend was in trouble.

Or was she?

This morning, in the light of day, Laci had to ques-tion everything that had happened last night at the re-ception. What had she *really* seen? A split second of something dark and disturbing on Spencer Donovan's face. She couldn't even be sure it had been directed at Alyson.

True, Laci had thought a second later that when he'd looked at her he'd been upset—as if he'd realized she'd seen him. She remembered how rattled she'd felt, how convinced he meant Alyson harm.

This morning, though, she admitted it was probably the champagne. Or her imagination—which, as her older sister Laney often pointed out, was more often than not out of control.

Even the way Spencer had said goodbye to Laci could have been innocent enough. Only *she* could read something into "Goodbye, Laci." Just as she could have imagined that he'd rushed Alyson off in such a hurry because he was afraid of what Laci would say.

She sighed. As if there had been anything she could have said to Alyson to keep her from going. She cringed at the thought of what she *might* have said. *I saw your new husband look at you funny. Like he hated you. I think he wants you dead.* Great thing to tell someone right before they take off on their honeymoon.

Wandering into the kitchen, she poured herself a large glass of orange juice. To make matters worse, she recalled her behaviour in front of the man in the school playground. He'd looked so familiar, but she couldn't place him now any more than she could last night. Not that it mattered.

Taking a sip of orange juice, she eyed the phone. Even if she could have called Alyson—who would now be on a flight to Hawaii for her honeymoon—she wouldn't have, she assured herself.

Besides, what would she say to her friend? By all appearances, Spencer seemed to be the perfect husband. Attentive, handsome, obviously educated, successful and well-off financially. Plus, Alyson adored him.

"You're wrong about him," Laci said with false conviction as she picked up the phone and dialed her sister's cell. Laney was the sensible one. That's why Laci always used her as a sounding board. And right now she needed sensible—even if her sister was on her own honeymoon.

BRIDGER DUVALL STOOD in the middle of the musty building in downtown Whitehorse, telling himself he should have gone with his first instinct and left town.

"What do you think?" the young Realtor asked. She was a cute blonde with a husband and at least one young son and was so green that he suspected this could be her first sale.

What did he *think*? He thought he should have his head examined. He looked around the building. The structure had been sitting empty for a couple of years at least. Which should have told him that opening *any* business in this town was more than a little risky, but a restaurant was crazy.

The building needed to be completely remodeled. Fortunately, he could do a lot of the work himself.

As he stood there, he could imagine the brick walls with art on them, cloth-covered tables along both sides with candles glowing, low music playing in the background and some alluring scents coming out of the kitchen at the back.

If he closed his eyes, he could almost smell his marinara sauce and hear the clatter of dishes, the murmur of voices and, of course, the comforting ding of the cash register.

"It would need a lot of work," the Realtor said.

An understatement. "It would need a *whole* lot of

work." But even as he said it he knew he was going to take the place. There was plenty of light, the building was more than adequate for what he wanted to do and the price was right. With luck, he could be open before Christmas.

It wouldn't be the restaurant of his dreams. Not in this isolated part of the state. But since he couldn't leave here, he might as well do something while he was waiting.

"Let's write up an offer," he said and saw the Realtor's surprise.

"Really?"

He laughed. "You talked me out of every other place in town."

"Maybe I should try to talk you out of this one."

"Don't waste your breath." He looked around him, seeing again the dust and dirt and peeling paint. Still... "There is something about this place."

She followed his gaze, clearly not seeing it. "Well, if you're sure this is the building you want..."

He smiled at her. "It is." Wait until the residents of Old Town Whitehorse heard he was opening a restaurant. It would be a clear message to them: he was staying until he got what he wanted. Or until he went broke, he thought with a wry smile.

"Do YOU HAVE any idea what time it is out here?" Laney Cavanaugh Giovanni asked, sounding half-asleep as she answered the phone.

Laci hadn't thought about the time difference between Whitehorse, Montana, and Honolulu. "Sorry. I needed someone to talk to."

"You should get a pet. Or just talk to yourself."

"I *am* talking to myself. I just don't like the answers I'm getting." Laci could hear her sister get up, then the sound of glass doors opening and closing as Laney took the phone outside. She could imagine the view of the ocean, the smell of salty sea air, the lull of the surf below the balcony and the cries of the gulls. Every woman she knew was on her honeymoon.

"How was Alyson's wedding?" Laney asked after a big yawn. But she sounded more awake. And it wasn't as though Laci would have let her go back to sleep— and she would know that.

"It was…nice."

"Nice?" Laney asked. "Okay, what happened? You didn't do anything you shouldn't have, did you?"

Now that she had her sister on the phone, Laci wasn't sure she wanted to tell her. It sounded too nuts, even for her. "Of course not. Look, it's nothing. Really. Sorry I woke you up. I should let you go."

"Oh, no, you don't. What is it?" her sister demanded.

Laci groaned. "You're going to think I've lost my mind."

"I already think you're nuttier than peanut brittle," Laney said, repeating something their grandmother Pearl always used to say before a stroke had left her incapacitated in a nursing home.

"Okay, something *did* happen. At least I think it did. It was probably just my imagination. I'm sure it was."

"Laci!"

"It's Alyson's husband, Spencer."

"Do not tell me he made a pass at you at the reception."

"No," Laci said. It was much worse than that. "I caught him looking at Alyson strangely."

"How strangely?" Laney asked, sounding as if she was taking this seriously.

Laci realized she'd hoped that her sister would tell her what a fool she was and relieve her mind. "He looked as if he couldn't stand the sight of her. As if he hated her. As if he wanted to harm her." The words were out and she wished she could call them back. She felt as if she was being disloyal to her best friend. "I know it sounds round the bend—"

"How was he acting right before that?"

"That's just it. He was laughing and smiling and dancing with her as if he couldn't believe how lucky he was to have married her. I'm sure I must be mistaken."

She groaned, remembering the look Spencer had given her when he'd felt her watching him. He'd been upset, hadn't he?

"That is really odd," Laney said. "You're sure he was looking at Alyson?"

"No. But since he doesn't know anyone else in town, who else *could* he have been looking at? Like I said, it was just for an instant. I'm probably wrong."

She waited for her sister to agree, but instead Laney asked, "Have you seen Alyson since?"

"No. Right after that they left on their honeymoon." She recalled the way Spencer had hustled Aly off. "Just tell me that I'm silly to be worried about her."

Her sister seemed to hesitate. "You're silly to worry about her."

The words lacked conviction but Laci felt better. "Speaking of honeymoons..."

"Yes, I probably should get back to mine," Laney said, a smile in her voice.

"You know that I will always suspect that you eloped

so you wouldn't have to ask me to cater your reception," Laci said.

Laney laughed. "I eloped because I've decided to become more impulsive, like you."

"I don't think that's a good idea," Laci said in all seriousness. "One of us has to be the stable one. I like it when it's you."

"Eloping was the first impulsive thing I've ever done. You're the one who always told me to go with my feelings instead of being so analytical."

"I don't know why you would take advice from me."

"Maybe we'll have a reception when we get back," Laney said. "And you can cater it."

"Okay," Laci said but without her usual enthusiasm. Her mind was back on Alyson.

"We can talk more when I get home. It won't be that long, which is why I'm resuming my honeymoon *now*," Laney said, and Laci could tell by her sister's tone that Nick had joined her on the balcony. Nick was gorgeous and crazy in love with her big sister. "'Bye, sis."

"Oh, Laney, I forgot to tell you. Alyson and Spencer are spending their honeymoon in Hawaii, too. Maybe you'll run into them." But Laci realized her sister had already hung up.

AFTER WRITING UP an offer for the building, Bridger Duvall spent the rest of the day digging through old newspaper archives, looking for any mention of Dr. Holloway, the Whitehorse Sewing Circle or Pearl Cavanaugh.

As he searched, he thought of Pearl's granddaughter Laci and their chance meeting at the wedding. Fate? Not likely given the size of Whitehorse, Montana. Laci lived five miles south of town in what was locally known as Old Town. The now near ghost town had once been Whitehorse. That was, until the railroad came through in the 1800s and the town moved north to the rails, taking the name with it.

He recalled the first time he'd seen Old Town. If a tumbleweed hadn't rolled across the dirt street in front of his car, he wouldn't have slowed and would have missed the place entirely.

Little was left of the small ranching community. At one time there'd been a gas station, but that building was sitting empty, the pumps long gone. There was a community center, which was still called Whitehorse Community Center. Every small community in this part of Montana had one of those. And there was the one-room schoolhouse next to it.

There were a few houses, one large one that was boarded up, a Condemned sign nailed to the door, an old shutter banging in the wind.

For years the community had been run by Titus and Pearl Cavanaugh, both descendants of early homesteaders and just as strong and determined as the first settlers.

Titus was as close to a mayor as Old Town had. He provided a church service every Sunday morning at the community center and saw to the hiring of a schoolteacher when needed.

Pearl's mother Abigail had started the Whitehorse Sewing Circle. The women of the community got together a few times a week to make quilts for every new baby and every newlywed in the area.

The old cemetery on the hill had also kept the Whitehorse name. The iron on the sign that hung over the arched entrance was rusted but readable: Whitehorse Cemetery.

Bridger had learned a lot about the area just stopping at a café in Whitehorse proper, five miles to the north and the last real town for miles. All he'd had to do was ask about Old Town Whitehorse and he got an earful. The people were clannish and stuck to themselves. The old-timers still resented the town moving and taking the name. And, like Whitehorse proper, both communities were dying.

A lack of jobs was sending the younger residents to more prosperous parts of the state or the country. The population in the entire county was dropping each year. People joked about who would be around to turn the lights out when Whitehorse completely died.

While Bridger had learned a lot, he hadn't gotten what he'd come here to find. Not yet, anyway.

And now he'd made the acquaintance of Pearl's granddaughter, Laci. She was a cute thing, fair skinned, slender, with short curly blond hair and blue eyes.

Life was strange, he thought as he continued to search the old newspapers. In a way, his life had started here. And now here he was, thirty-two years old and back here in hopes of finding himself.

The one thing he'd learned quickly was that being an outsider was a disadvantage in a small Montana town. Not that he'd expected to be accepted immediately just because he lived here and was now opening a restaurant.

But he'd found it was going to take time. Fortunately, time was the one thing he had plenty of.

His eye caught on a notice in one of the old newspapers he'd been thumbing through. A city permit for a fence at a house owned by the late Dr. Holloway.

Bridger felt a rush of excitement. For months he'd been trying to track down his birth mother after finding out that he was adopted.

Not just adopted—illegally adopted. The story his adoptive mother told him on her deathbed involved a group of women called the Whitehorse Sewing Circle.

Thirty-two years ago, his parents, both too old to adopt through the usual channels, had gotten a call in the middle of the night telling them to come to the Whitehorse Cemetery.

There an elderly woman gave them a baby and a birth certificate. No money exchanged hands. Nor names. Bridger had surmised over his time here that the woman in the cemetery that night was none other than Pearl Cavanaugh.

How a group of women had decided to get into the illegal adoption business was still beyond him. Nor did he know how many babies had been placed over the years.

He'd come to town months ago, rented an old farmhouse just outside of Old Town and begun his search.

Unfortunately, his quest had come at a high price. Most of the people involved were now dead. The doctor who Bridger believed had handled the adoptions—Dr. Holloway—had been murdered by one of his coconspirators, his office building burned to the ground, all records apparently lost.

The woman he believed to be the ringleader, Pearl Cavanaugh, had suffered a stroke. Another key player, an elderly women named Nina Mae Cross, had Alzheimer's. Both women were in the nursing home now. Neither was able to tell him anything.

But Bridger was convinced Holloway was too smart to keep records of his illegal adoption activities with his patients' medical records at the office. So he held out hope that the records would be found elsewhere.

But where would the doctor have hidden them to make sure they never surfaced? Maybe in this house Bridger had discovered.

Or maybe no records had been kept. Certainly no charges had been filed against anyone involved, for lack of evidence.

But even if Bridger found proof, not one of the women in the original Whitehorse Sewing Circle was less than seventy now. None would ever see prison. The only thing he could hope for was learning his true identity.

"Even if you had proof that would stand up in court," the sheriff had said, "you sure you want these women thrown in jail? If they hadn't gotten you and your twin sister good homes, neither of you might be alive today."

Bridger knew he probably owed his life to the Whitehorse Sewing Circle. The women had taken babies who needed homes and placed them with loving couples who either couldn't conceive or were ineligible to adopt because of their age.

Also, something good had come out of his quest: he'd found his twin sister, Eve Bailey. Eve had grown up in Old Town and suspected from an early age that she was adopted. She'd come back here also looking for answers and, like him, had ended up staying.

As he copied down the address of the house that Dr. Holloway had owned, he felt a surge of hope. The doctor had lived in an apartment over his office. So what had he used the house for?

Bridger tried not to get his hopes up, telling himself

that if he didn't find anything at the house, there was always Pearl Cavanaugh's granddaughter.

One way or the other, maybe he'd finally get lucky.

LACI JUMPED WHEN the phone rang and picked it up before even checking caller ID. She'd been thinking about Alyson, so she'd just assumed it would be her.

"Laci?"

"Maddie?" She realized she hadn't heard from her cousin in weeks, not since Maddie Cavanaugh had moved to Bozeman to attend Montana State University. "How are you?"

"Great. Really great," Maddie said, sounding like her old self again.

Laci couldn't have been more relieved. Maddie had been through so much, not the least being suspected of murder. But probably the hardest was her breakup with her fiancé, Bo Evans.

The hold Bo had on Maddie was still a concern. Laci feared that Maddie might weaken and go back to that destructive relationship.

"So tell me about your classes," Laci said, and Maddie launched into an enthusiastic rundown. She sounded so happy that Laci began to relax a little.

Counseling and college seemed to have helped Maddie put Bo Evans and a need to punish herself behind her.

Maddie asked about Laci's catering business, and Laci quickly changed the subject. Her lack of business was the least of her worries right now, but she didn't want to get into the Alyson and Spencer situation with her cousin.

"I have a test first thing in the morning, so I'd better go," Maddie said after they'd talked for a while. "I wanted to let you know that my roommate has invited me home for Christmas. She's from Kalispell, so…"

Laci tried to hide her disappointment. Maddie had planned to spend Christmas with her. Laney and Nick had already made plans to have Christmas with his family in California. "Oh, you'll have a great time. What a nice invitation."

"You don't mind?" Maddie asked, sounding relieved.

"Of course I will miss you, but I'm so glad you're enjoying college and making friends." Laci knew that Laney would now insist she come to California—the last thing she wanted to do. Christmas required snow. Christmas was Montana. Also, she couldn't leave her grandfather alone for the holidays.

"I'm really proud of you," Laci said. "You've been through a lot."

"You know us Cavanaugh women," Maddie said with a laugh. "I'm excited about the future." Her cousin sounded surprised by that. After everything she'd been through, it was no wonder.

Laci hung up, relieved that Maddie hadn't asked about Bo Evans. Maybe she was finally over him. Laci would rather believe that than believe Maddie hadn't wanted to come home for Christmas because she was afraid to see Bo again. Either because she feared she might be tempted or because she was scared of the Evans family. Laci could understand being afraid of *that* family.

ARLENE EVANS COULDN'T believe the mental hospital wouldn't let her see her daughter Violet.

"I told you they wouldn't let us in," Charlotte said as she inspected the ends of her long blond hair.

Arlene glanced over at her younger daughter as she put the car into gear. More and more, Charlotte was starting to annoy her. The whiny voice. The obsession with her split ends. The way she'd put on weight since the "incidents."

Arlene insisted the family all refer to the attempts on her life as "those unfortunate *incidents*" if they had to refer to them at all. She would just as soon forget the whole thing. But that was a little difficult since the entire country had heard about her three children trying to kill her.

It had almost cost Arlene the farm in lawyer fees to get her two youngest off. It *had* cost her her husband. Floyd divorced her and ran off with some grain seed saleswoman. Good riddance. She'd leased out the land and would be just fine now that her Rural Meet-A-Mate internet dating service was doing so well. Being on national TV hadn't hurt.

Whatever the cost, it had been worth it to get Charlotte and Bo cleared. In her own mind, Arlene knew where the blame for the whole mess lay: her old-maid daughter Violet. Violet had always been the problem child. Charlotte, barely eighteen, and Bo, now twenty, would never have even contemplated the terrible things they'd done without Violet as the ringleader.

Alice Miller, that old busybody who lived down the road, had suggested the children were fed too much sugar. The woman really needed to turn off the talk-show television and take care of her own business.

Fortunately, Arlene had been able to hire a good lawyer for Charlotte and Bo and got them probation. The judge had insisted they come home and live with her so they could begin to heal. Arlene wasn't sure that's what had been going on at the house, though.

Bo stayed in his room listening to that horrible music and barely had a civil word for her, except late at night when he went out doing who knew what. Charlotte, restricted from going into town on Saturday nights because of those other unfortunate *incidents* involving strange men, hung around the house and ate.

Half the time, Arlene couldn't stand the sight of her own children. Now *there* was an episode for the talk shows.

The only way she'd been able to stay sane was to concentrate on her business. Her internet rural dating business had taken off after she'd been interviewed on one of the national morning TV shows. But many locals were still wary of the internet. She'd been forced to remove some people's profiles who hadn't asked to be put on her Web page. The ingratitude of people still amazed her.

Like the Cavanaughs. The whole bunch of them blamed Bo for Maddie's problems. All Arlene could say was good riddance to that one, too. She hated to think what Bo's life would have been like if he'd married that girl.

Arlene couldn't believe the injustice in the world. That's probably why, when she got to the point that she found herself finding fault with Charlotte and Bo, she would turn all her anger and frustration on the one person who really deserved it—her oldest daughter, Violet. On the fast track to thirty-five and insane, Violet had little chance of ever getting married now. And wasn't it just like everyone to blame the mother for it.

"I'd love to give Violet a piece of my mind," Arlene said as she left the mental hospital, tires spitting gravel. She'd even hired a lawyer, but the hospital hadn't budged, saying that it would not be in Violet's best interest to see her mother. As if Arlene gave a fig about Violet's best interest.

Did Violet appreciate all the years Arlene had labored tirelessly to try to get her married off? No. How did Violet pay her back? She'd tried to kill her own mother and had drawn in her younger sister and brother as accomplices.

"Sometimes I just don't know why I try," Arlene said and sighed as she drove toward Old Town Whitehorse. Beside her, Charlotte pulled a candy bar from her jacket pocket, at least her third this morning.

"Watch where you're going!" Charlotte yelled as the car almost went off the road. "What is your *problem*?"

Arlene got the car back on the road and looked over at her daughter again. She'd never noticed before how much Charlotte was beginning to resemble her sister Violet.

BACK AT THE HOSPITAL, Violet Evans felt the drool run down her chin but didn't move a muscle to stop it.

"Violet?"

She stared into nothingness, her eyes glazed over, her mind miles away. Miles away in Old Town Whitehorse.

"Violet, can you hear me?"

The doctors called her condition a "semicatatonic state." She'd been like this ever since she'd been brought to the mental hospital after admitting to trying to kill her mother. It was a textbook-classic case, she'd heard the doctors say and had to suppress the urge to laugh.

It *should* be textbook-classic; that's where she'd found the symptoms for the condition. Lately, though, the doctors had noticed that she was starting to come out of it.

Violet loved fooling with them. One day soon she would come out of it, all right. She wouldn't remember anything. When they told her about her crimes, she would be shocked, feel incredible remorse for the misery she'd caused and find it almost unbearable.

There would be suspicion with her apparent confusion about where she'd been, what she'd done. There would be more psychiatric tests, but finally they would have to release her back into society. They would have to since she'd clearly been sick when she'd tried to kill her own mother. And soon she would be well.

But for now, Violet Evans saw nothing, felt nothing, was nothing. At least on the surface. Her mind worked 24-7, planning and plotting for the day when she would walk out the front door of the hospital a free woman.

Inside, she smiled to herself. It wouldn't be long now. Soon she would be free. Only this time she would be much smarter. This time she wouldn't get caught. Nor was she just going to finish the job she'd started. That was the problem with too much time to think—it made you realize there were a lot of people you wouldn't mind seeing dead.

THE PHONE RANG the minute Laci hung up from talking with her cousin. She smiled as she picked up the receiver, sure it was Maddie calling her back.

"What did you forget to tell me?" she said without bothering to say hello.

Silence.

"Maddie?"

No answer.

She checked the caller ID. Blocked. Her heart began to pound as she recognized the faint sound of someone breathing on the other end of the line.

She told herself there was nothing to be frightened about. It was just a bad connection. Then why could she hear the breathing just fine? "Hello?"

Still no answer.

"What do you want?" she demanded into the phone.

The caller hung up with a click.

Her heart drummed in her chest as she tried to convince herself it was just a wrong number. She hung up and hit star-6-9.

The recording confirmed that the phone number could not be accessed.

She hung up, telling herself she was overreacting. As usual. But now she was spooked, the call feeling like an omen.

CHAPTER THREE

AT THE SOUND of a car, Laci wandered into the living room, still feeling under the weather. And while she was relieved about Maddie, she couldn't get Alyson out of her mind. Or the strange phone call.

One of Alyson's bridesmaids, a younger friend they'd both grown up with, trotted up the front steps.

Laci opened the door, glad to see McKenna Bailey. McKenna, all cowgirl, was dressed in jeans, Western shirt, boots and a straw Western hat pulled down over her blond hair.

"I guess I don't need to ask how *you're* feeling," McKenna said with a laugh. "I couldn't believe you last night. I've never seen you drink that much."

Which could partly explain why she felt so horrible. But she knew the perfect cure of whatever ailed her.

"Pancakes," Laci said drawing McKenna into the kitchen.

"*Pancakes?* You can't be serious," McKenna said as she took off her cowboy hat and set it on the stool next to her at the breakfast bar.

"Pumpkin pancakes." As Laci whipped up the batter, she began to feel better. Cooking always did that for her. McKenna talked about the wedding ceremony, the food at the reception—the town women had insisted on doing a potluck, almost as if there were a plot against Laci and her catering company.

Ever since she'd decided to start Cavanaugh Catering, nothing had gone right. True, her first catered party had ended with a woman being poisoned to death—not Laci's fault, though.

Since then, she hadn't had any business and was starting to wonder if her sister had been right about it being a mistake to run a catering business here in the middle of nowhere.

Laci spooned some of the golden batter into a sizzling-hot skillet. The smell alone made her feel better.

"Spencer is really something, huh?" McKenna said.

Laci shot a look over her shoulder at McKenna. "He's handsome enough," she said noncommittally.

McKenna laughed. "Arlene Evans is positive she's seen him in one of her movie magazines." She lowered her voice. "But you should have heard what Harvey Alderson said."

Laci could well imagine, knowing Harvey.

"He said the guy looked like a porn star to him," McKenna said and laughed again. "Makes you wonder what Harvey knows about porn stars, doesn't it?"

Laci laughed and turned back to her cooking. The pancakes had bubbled up nicely. She flipped each one, then brought out the apple-cinnamon syrup and fresh creamery butter and put them on the counter in front of McKenna, happy her friend had stopped by. She wished McKenna was home for more than the weekend.

"The thing about men as good-looking as Spencer Donovan—you'd have to keep him corralled at home," McKenna said, only half joking. "Every woman in the county would be after him. Speaking of men...I did something really stupid last night."

Laci couldn't imagine McKenna Bailey doing anything stupid in her life. She hadn't even had that much to drink last night. "What?"

"I signed up on Arlene Evans's rural dating internet site," McKenna said and grimaced. "I'm never going to find my handsome cowboy helping Eve with the ranch. Or at vet school. I figured, what would it hurt, you know?"

"I know," Laci said with a laugh as she slid a plateful of silver-dollar pancakes in front of McKenna and watched her slather them with butter before making another skilletful for herself.

Was that all it had been last night? A splash of champagne and a shot of envy, stirred not shaken, with a healthy dose of vivid imagination? She sure hoped so because she really didn't want her friend to be in trouble. She glanced at the kitchen clock over the stove as she sat down, not even hungry for her favorite pancakes. Alyson would be in Honolulu soon.

"Laci, these pancakes are to die for," McKenna said between bites. And the conversation turned to Laci's catering business—and lack of clients. And for a while Laci stopped worrying about Alyson and worried instead about how to get Cavanaugh Catering cooking.

BRIDGER DUVALL SNAPPED on his flashlight as he descended the rickety basement stairs of Dr. Holloway's former house. It was dusty and dark down here, the overhead light dim. The place, he'd learned, had been sitting empty for years. He doubted anyone had been down here in all that time.

"Can't be much of interest down there, but you're welcome to look, I guess," the elderly neighbor said from the top of the stairs.

"Thanks," Bridger called over his shoulder as he descended deeper. He'd managed to talk the neighbor into letting him into the house after discovering it was empty, and the man thought he knew where there might be a key.

In a town like Whitehorse, neighbors were often given a spare key to the house next door. Bridger loved that about this part of Montana. As it turned out, the door hadn't even been locked.

A house that the doc owned—but apparently had never lived in—seemed like the perfect place to store records you didn't want anyone to ever see.

The basement smelled of dampness and mildew. He stopped on the bottom stair. He heard something scurry across one dark corner and shot his flashlight beam in that direction quick enough to catch the shape of a mouse before it disappeared into a hole in the concrete.

Great. Who knew what else lived down here.

Bridger shone the flashlight around the small, damp basement. It was little more than a root cellar. He brushed aside the cobwebs to peer into a hole that ran back under the house. There was a lot of junk down here, most of it looking as if it had been there since the house was originally built a hundred years before.

One box held what appeared to be women's clothing. He held up one of the dresses. Dated. Had the clothes belonged to the doctor's wife before her death? Or had the doctor had a mistress who'd lived here?

Bridger dug through several of the boxes, finding more old clothing but no files. No records.

He couldn't help his disappointment. He'd hit one dead end after another. In the last box he opened he found an old photo album. He flipped it open. Most of the pages were empty except for a few colored photographs of two little girls. Children who'd been part of the adoption ring?

Tucking the album under his jacket, Bridger climbed up out of the basement, anxious for some fresh air.

The helpful neighbor was waiting in the living room. "Find anything?" he asked.

"Nothing much." He'd told the old man that he was looking for his mother's medical records. No lie there. He feared the man wouldn't let him take the photo album if he told him about it, so he kept it hidden under his jacket.

Bridger handed him back the key, thanked him and took one last look at the inside of the house, wondering why Dr. Holloway had kept it and whose clothing that was downstairs. The dresses had been in different sizes, so that seemed to rule out a mistress.

A thought struck him, giving him a chill. Was it possible the birth mothers had stayed here in this house until they'd given birth? Maybe even Bridger's own mother?

The used furniture appeared to be a good thirty years old and was now covered in dust. If his mother had stayed here, there was no sign of her after all this time.

He followed the old man out the front door, glancing back only once. For just a split second he imagined a woman standing at the front window, her belly swollen with the fraternal twins she carried, her face lost behind the dirty window.

To keep from calling Alyson and ruining her honeymoon, Laci tried to stay busy. She cooked everything she could think to make, then had to find a home for all the food.

She dropped off a week's meals at her grandfather Titus's apartment—the one he'd taken in town so he could spend more time at his wife's bedside at the nursing home.

Gramma Pearl's condition hadn't changed since her stroke. Her eyes were open, but she wasn't able to respond, even though Laci liked to believe she knew her and understood what Laci said to her. Once, Laci would have sworn her grandmother squeezed her hand. Laney said it must have been her imagination.

Laci's imagination was legendary.

The treats Laci had baked she took to the staff at the rest home when she went to visit her grandmother. They all seemed to love her cookies and cakes.

As she came out of the nursing home, Laci was debating what to do with the batch of her famous spicy meatballs she had in her car. They were too spicy for— She collided with what felt like a brick wall, emitting an "ufft" as strong arms grabbed her to keep her from toppling over backward.

"We really have to quit meeting like this," said a teasing male voice.

She looked up as she recognized the voice from the wedding reception. Actually, from the merry-go-round in the schoolyard next to the community center, where he'd come to her assistance.

"Oh, it's you," she said, embarrassed.

"Nice to see you, too," he said and grinned. "Glad to see you've recovered from the wedding. Still having trouble staying on your feet, though, I see."

He was even better looking in broad daylight. He

wore a Western shirt, jeans and boots. His dark hair curled at the nape of his neck beneath his gray Stetson. She noted that his clothing was worn and dusty as if he'd been working.

She hadn't taken him for a working cowboy last night—even though he'd been wearing boots with his tux. Apparently he was the real thing. Having grown up in old Whitehorse, she had a soft spot for cowboys. Especially ones as gallant as this one.

"Still rescuing damsels in distress, I see," she said, cringing inside at the memory of what happened at the wedding.

He smiled and held out his hand. "I don't think we were ever officially introduced. Bridger Duvall."

Bridger Duvall? The mystery man of Old Town Whitehorse? Now she remembered why he'd seemed vaguely familiar. While their paths had never crossed, she'd certainly heard about him.

"Laci Cavanaugh," she said, taking his hand. It was wonderfully large and warm and comforting. There was something so chivalrous about him. She recalled how he'd given her his napkin outside the community center. Also how he'd given her peace and quiet. She'd appreciated both.

"Nice to meet you," he said, looking into her eyes before letting go of her hand.

"So you're Bridger Duvall," she said, feeling more than a little off-kilter considering the way their paths had crossed both times.

"The scurrilous rumors about me are highly exaggerated," he said with a twinkle in his dark eyes.

She cocked her head at him, curious and maybe flirting just a little. He did have a great handshake, and that voice of his was so wonderfully deep and soft. Like being bathed in silk.

"Which rumors are those?" she asked.

"That I only come out at night, that I'm fabulously wealthy and that I'm doing weird experiments in the barn out on the ranch."

She liked his sense of humor. "And how are they exaggerated?"

Grinning, he leaned toward her conspiratorially. "I do the weird experiments in the basement."

"That house doesn't have a *basement*."

Bridger laughed as they walked toward their vehicles. "Caught me."

Laci Cavanaugh. Granddaughter of Pearl Cavanaugh. He felt only a twinge of guilt. It had been no accident running into her today. He hadn't meant the run-in to be so literal, though. But whatever worked.

"Well, at least now I know which rumors *are* true," she said as she moved to her car and started to open the door.

"It was nice seeing you again," he said, surprised he meant it—and not because of his ulterior motive.

She smiled. "I'm sure we'll run into each other again."

As she opened her car door, he was hit with a tantalizing aroma that took his breath away. "What is that wonderful scent?" he asked stepping over to lean past her into the open car door to take a whiff.

She laughed. "Meatballs and spaghetti. I was planning to drop the dish off at the senior center, but I'm afraid it's too spicy for their tastes."

Bridger cocked a brow at her. "Well, it *is* almost dinnertime, and I just happen to know the perfect place to take it. I can assure you it would be greatly appreciated. Just follow me. It's only a few blocks from here."

He saw her hesitate, as if worried that the rumors about him might be true, before accepting. If she only knew.

Laci followed his pickup, surprised when he turned into a spot in front of one of the old empty buildings on the main street, and wondered if she hadn't made a mistake in coming here with him.

"I don't understand," she said, looking from him to the building, which apparently was being remodeled.

"You will." He opened her car door and took out the casserole dish. "Right this way."

He led her through the front of the restaurant, which was filled with sawhorses, tools, dust and paint supplies, through two swinging doors that led to the new stainless-steel commercial kitchen. Everything but a small table and two chairs was covered with plastic until the painting was finished.

Clearly this was where he'd been working. He put the casserole on the round table and dug under the plastic to open a cabinet and bring out dishes.

"I have some leftover bread and a salad I'd planned to eat for supper," he said, setting both on the table.

"What is this place?" she asked, looking back toward the front of the building as he began to cut thick slices of the bread.

"It's a restaurant. Well, that is, it will be once it's finished," he said with obvious pride, and she realized he worked here.

"Opening a new restaurant in Whitehorse?" She hadn't meant to sound so disbelieving.

"I know it's risky—"

"*Risky* is one way of putting it." She wondered who'd take such a risk, since the last restaurant in this building hadn't lasted six months.

She lifted the lid on the casserole, and he groaned and breathed in the rich scent with obvious pleasure. She couldn't help but smile with pleasure of her own.

"If that tastes half as good as it smells…"

She laughed as she dished him up some of the meatballs and spaghetti hiding beneath the sauce and waited as he sat down and picked up his fork.

He took a bite, closing his eyes and savoring the wonderful flavors. His eyes flew open. "Who made this?"

"I bought it from some woman cooking beside the road," she joked, thinking he must be doing the same, as she filled her plate and took a bite of his salad. "This salad is wonderful. Did the restaurant's cook make it?"

He grinned. "Yeah, you like?"

She nodded, looking surprised as she took a bite of the bread. "Yum. Homemade bread. Maybe this restaurant will do all right after all."

"Maybe, if it has these meatballs on the menu," he said and took another bite. "I'm serious," he said between bites. "I'm hiring whoever made this."

"Hiring them to do what?" Laci asked.

"*Cook*, what else?"

She glanced toward all the stainless steel in the kitchen. "This is *your* restaurant?"

It hadn't dawned on her. For some reason, she'd just assumed he was doing the construction on the place—not that he owned it—given how he was dressed.

About then she noticed that he was looking at her oddly. "*You* made this?" he asked, sounding as surprised as she'd been about him.

She bristled. "Don't I look like someone who could have made this?" She realized her skin was a little thin since her catering business had gone nowhere fast.

He still looked stunned, and she realized he had to be regretting saying he wanted to hire whoever had made the meatballs now that he'd found out it was her. "Is this about the job offer? Because if it is, I'm definitely not looking for a job."

"Sorry, it's just that…" He shook his head. "Can you cook anything else?"

She bristled again. "Of course. I can cook *anything*."

"That's big talk," he said, his tone challenging. "I assume you're willing to back it up?"

She glared across the table at him. "Name your terms."

He grinned. "I can have the kitchen ready tomorrow. Say 9:00 a.m.? You don't mind a little friendly competition?"

"You mean from your chef?"

He nodded, looking pleased with himself.

Not that she had to prove anything with her cooking. But damn if she wasn't going to show him. She smiled across the table at him, wanting to cook something that would knock this cowboy and his chef on their ears.

They ate in a strangely companionable silence. She couldn't remember a meal she'd enjoyed as much. After they'd finished, she started to pick up her casserole dish, but he put a hand over hers. There were only two meatballs and just a little sauce and spaghetti left.

"Mind if I finish that off later? I'd be happy to get your dish back to you tomorrow."

She looked into his dark eyes, surprised that she hadn't noticed before the tiny flecks of gold in all that warm-brownie chocolate. What was she thinking taking a cooking dare from this man?

She didn't want a job in a restaurant. She was determined to make Cavanaugh Catering a success.

But she couldn't let him think that she was a one-dish cook. No way. Her pride was at stake here.

And not just that, Laci realized as she left and headed home. Bridger Duvall had taken her mind off worrying about Alyson for a while. And for that she was thankful.

But when she reached home, she knew that she couldn't put off calling her friend any longer. She dialed the number Alyson had given her for the hotel where they would be staying in Hawaii.

"I'm sorry, we have no one by that name registered here," the desk clerk informed her.

"But that's not possible," Laci said. "Mrs. Spencer Donovan gave me this number."

"When were they to arrive?" the clerk asked.

Laci told him and waited while he checked.

"Apparently Mr. Donovan canceled those reservations."

Laci stood holding the phone, dumbstruck, her fear spiking. Spencer had canceled the hotel reservations? Why?

So Laci couldn't warn Alyson.

As BRIDGER HEADED out of town toward the ranch he rented outside of Old Town Whitehorse, he spotted the nursing home marquee announcing one of the resident's birthdays. It was later than usual, but still he turned into the lot.

It had become a ritual, stopping by every day to pay Pearl Cavanaugh and the other elderly Whitehorse Sewing Circle women a visit. He'd been told by the nurses that Pearl had been quite the woman before her stroke.

While her mother may have started the quilting group and possibly the adoptions, there was little doubt that Pearl Cavanaugh had been the ringleader during the time that he and Eve were adopted.

He stuck his head in Pearl's room. Her husband Titus visited every morning and early in the afternoon. Bridger made a point of making sure their paths didn't cross. He'd attempted to ask Titus about the adoption ring but had been quickly rebuked and threatened with slander. If Titus knew anything, he wasn't talking. Just like the rest of them.

Pearl was lying in bed, her blue eyes open and fixed on the ceiling.

"How are you doing today, Pearl?"

No response. But then, he hadn't expected one.

He pulled up a chair beside her bed and looked into her soft-skinned wrinkled face. It reflected years of living, and yet there was a gentle strength about her. He wished he had known her before the stroke. Guilt consumed him since he felt he was partly to blame for putting her here. If he hadn't come to Whitehorse looking for answers, maybe she wouldn't have had the stroke.

He took her frail hand. The skin was thin and pale, lifeless. Her eyes moved to him. "Remember me? Bridger Duvall. I'm one of your babies."

Did something change in her expression? He could never be sure as he told her—as he always did—about his adoptive parents, about growing up on a ranch outside of Roundup, Montana.

"I loved my parents and miss them terribly, but I still want to know who my birth mother is. From what everyone has told me about you," he continued, "you have to have known that some of the children you adopted out would come looking for their birth parents. You would have kept a record."

He thought he saw something flicker in her pale blue eyes—eyes the same exact color as her granddaughter Laci's. He was more convinced than ever that Pearl was in there, just unable to respond.

"You know who she is, don't you?" He looked down at her hand. It was cool to the touch, the skin silken and thinly lined with veins. He stroked it gently.

"How to get that information out is the problem, huh? Don't worry, I'll be here every day to see you, and one of these days you'll be able to tell me." He smiled at her. "You're going to get better."

Tears welled in her eyes, and for a moment he thought she'd squeezed his hand just a little as he placed it carefully back on the bed.

As he rose, he saw that she was no longer looking at him but behind him. He spun around expecting to see Titus in the doorway, but it was another elderly lady he'd seen around the nursing home.

The woman was tall with cropped gray hair and a permanent scowl on her face. She quickly turned and took off down the hall.

As he started after her, a nurse appeared in the doorway. "Everything all right in here? I just saw Bertie Cavanaugh take off like a shot. She wasn't bothering you, was she?"

Bridger shook his head. The nursing staff had been very kind to him. At first they'd been suspicious, but after a while seemed thankful for his visits to the patients.

"Bertie *Cavanaugh*?" he said. "Any relation to Pearl?"

"Everyone from Old Town Whitehorse is related one way or another," the nurse said with a laugh. "I think they might be second cousins through marriage."

Another elderly woman from Old Town. Had she belonged to the sewing circle? He'd have to find out. He tried not to get his hopes up. One of his first leads was a woman who was deeply involved in the illegal adoption ring, Nina Mae Cross. Unfortunately Nina Mae had Alzheimer's and was of no help at all to him, even though he continued to visit her, as well.

"See you tomorrow, Pearl," he said as he left. She was staring up at the ceiling again, but he had the strangest feeling that seeing Bertie Cavanaugh had upset her.

Or did she fear that Bertie had overheard what they'd been talking about? His adoption.

CHAPTER FOUR

LACI TRIED TO stem her panic as she questioned the hotel clerk about the last-minute change. "Do you have any idea where Mr. and Mrs. Donovan went?" She heard the slight hesitation in the young man's tone. "It's urgent that I contact my friend. It really could be a matter of life and death."

"We're not supposed to give out that information," the clerk said, dropping his voice. "But I did overhear the conversation. He asked our manager about a hotel more out of the way. More *secluded*."

Her heart lodged in her throat. More secluded?

"I heard our manager tell him to try the Pacific Cove."

"Thank you so much. You may have saved a life. You don't happen to have that number, do you?"

The clerk at the Pacific Cove Inn rang Mrs. Spencer Donovan's room. The phone rang three times, and Laci was debating whether she should leave a message or not when Alyson came on the line giggling.

"Aly?"

"Laci!" her friend cried in surprise. "I was so worried you wouldn't get the message."

"Message? Why? Has something happened?" Laci

asked, heart pounding. Her friend sounded fine, but still Laci couldn't help the fear she heard in her own voice.

"Happened? No, silly. The message that Spencer left you about the change of lodging. He is so thoughtful. He insisted we upgrade to a place that was more romantic."

More romantic? Or just more isolated? Laci thought, barely able to breathe. She hadn't gotten any message from Spencer. Or had that been him calling earlier today? "So it's just the two of you there?"

Alyson laughed. "Of course not. It's just a little smaller hotel with a private beach."

"Then everything is all right?"

"It's amazing. Laci, I'm having the time of my life. Spencer is so wonderful. I keep pinching myself. I can't believe any of this—Hawaii, marriage, Spencer… Just a minute, he wants to say hello."

Laci swore under her breath as Alyson handed off the phone before Laci could stop her.

"Laci, hi. I wasn't sure you got my message about the hotel change. The line sounded funny. I didn't think you could hear me."

She'd heard breathing. She knew he'd been able to hear her. Or had he?

"I just wanted to thank you for everything," Spencer was saying. "Alyson and I were just talking about what a great friend you are. So great, in fact, we've made a decision." He sounded excited.

Laci held her breath.

"We're going to settle on the ranch in Old Town Whitehorse," Spencer said with a flourish. "It's definite. With my business, I can work from anywhere, and Aly's heart is set on being near you."

"I'm so glad," Laci managed to get out. He was calling Alyson *Aly*? That's what Laci called her.

"Great, she'd hoped you would be. I'll tell her. I'm looking forward to getting to know you better. Listen, we were just heading out for some early sightseeing, but thanks again for everything. Aly says she'll talk to you soon." The line went dead.

Laci stood holding the phone, her hand shaking, her emotions running wild. Had Spencer really tried to leave her a message? Had she been wrong about hearing breathing on the line? He'd sounded so sincere on the phone. And Alyson... Aly was apparently safe, happy and having the time of her life. Not only that, the two planned to settle here.

Laci still couldn't believe it. Was it possible she'd been wrong?

She breathed a shaky sigh of relief, telling herself that everything was going to be fine. It had been the champagne mixed with a huge dose of overactive imagination. Or maybe she really was losing her mind.

After all, she'd agreed to this cook-off at Bridger Duvall's new restaurant. Clearly she couldn't trust her instincts.

She went out on the porch, needing fresh air to clear her head. She knew she should be going through her recipes for the cooking contest with Bridger's head chef tomorrow. Who had he got? Probably someone out of Bozeman. She'd eaten at several of the more elite restaurants there and knew they had some excellent chefs.

As she started to sit down in the porch swing, she noticed a square of white paper under it on the floor. Bending, she picked up a white envelope and turned it over to see in small, boxy print the words *Laci Cherry*.

Cherry? That had been her father's name, but after his death and her mother's desertion, her grandparents had adopted her and her sister Laney and given them the family name Cavanaugh.

She stared down at the envelope. No one knew her as Laci Cherry. Except maybe one person who might not know that her name had changed, she thought, her pulse pounding in her ears. That person had left Old Town Whitehorse twenty-eight years ago, when Laci was barely a year old, and had never been heard from again.

Laci's mother, Geneva Cavanaugh Cherry.

She stared down at the envelope, her fingers trembling. There was no return address, no stamp. Nothing but her former name.

She wasn't sure what frightened her more: what was inside the envelope or why someone would just leave it on her porch. Carefully she turned the small white envelope over in her fingers. How long had it been under the swing and she just hadn't noticed? She had no way of telling.

If the envelope hadn't been addressed to Laci *Cherry*, she wouldn't have thought anything about it. But this reminder from the past scared her.

If only Laney were here. Her sister would have opened it by now.

Laci looked up the road as if she might see a vehicle. There was nothing but open prairie and rolling hills for miles, no sign of life. No clue as to who might have left it.

Feeling vulnerable, as if her home had been violated, she stepped inside and sniffed the air to see if she could tell whether the person had done more than just leave the note on her porch.

She never locked her door. Few people around here ever did. She walked through the house. Nothing that she could tell had been disturbed. But that didn't mean that someone hadn't been inside.

At the small desk in the kitchen, she took out the letter opener. Making a nice clean slice, she cut open the envelope and peered inside. A single sheet of matching white paper.

You're going to feel so foolish when you read what's inside. Nothing scary. No ghosts from the past. Just someone caught in a time warp. Like Alice Miller. She often got the names of residents confused, but she was almost ninety.

Carefully, as if lifting out something fragile, Laci took the sheet of paper from the envelope and unfolded it.

She'd been hoping the paper would contain a nice note from someone in the community. A note telling her how elegant she'd looked at Alyson's wedding. Or even a thank-you for the goodies she'd been baking and taking to the nursing home.

But, of course, it was neither. Normal people mailed their letters. They didn't leave them on your porch, where you may or may not find them.

All the writing was in the center of the note. Small and boxy, just like the writing on the envelope.

I know what really happened to your mother.

A dagger of ice ran through her. She stared at the words, telling herself it was just somebody's idea of a prank. If the person really knew something, then why not come forward? And why wait nearly thirty years to do so?

She debated just tossing the note in the trash, but instead carefully put it back into the envelope, checking to make sure she hadn't missed an address or other identifying mark before putting it into the kitchen desk drawer, all the time wondering if this had something to do with that mysterious call she'd gotten before. Had someone been trying to tell her something then but decided to send her a note instead?

The one thing she wasn't going to do was call Laney again on her honeymoon and upset her, even though Laci was sure her sister would have told her it was nothing. But then, Laney didn't like talking about their mother.

From the time Laci was small she'd always heard that her mother had packed up a few things and left town shortly after her husband had been killed in a car accident north of Old Town Whitehorse.

Apparently her mother had been so deeply in love with Russell Cherry that she hadn't been able to live with any reminders of him. Those reminders, Laci assumed, being Old Town Whitehorse and the house her parents had built for her and her husband and her children, Laney and Laci.

Laci had never understood how any mother could leave two small children, just walk out the door with little more than a photo album, a suitcase and a few dollars in her purse and never look back.

Laci had been so young that she didn't even remember her mother. While she knew now that her mother had never been back, she'd once pretended that her mother hadn't really left. That Geneva watched over her and Laney.

Like the first day of school, both sisters scrubbed clean and wearing their best dresses. What mother could miss that? Laci had walked with her head up, wanting to make her mother proud as she entered the one-room schoolhouse, positive that Geneva was hiding in the trees nearby watching her and Laney.

Other major events Laci had been sure her mother had witnessed, as well. Her daughters' birthdays, Christmas, Easter Sunday service and egg hunts, elementary, high school and college graduations.

Laci had often searched the crowd, hoping to see her mother's face, although she believed her mother was too good at hiding to ever be seen.

And while struggling with why her mother had left, why she had never shown herself, Laci had held on to her fantasy that her mother cared.

That was, until she'd returned to the house in Old Town Whitehorse. At twenty-nine, she no longer kidded herself that Geneva Cherry was hiding behind the old barn in the distance or behind the big trees by the schoolhouse, watching over her daughters.

Geneva Cherry had left and never come back. Not for Laci's first day of school, not for her home run in Little League, not for her culinary school graduation or even Gramma Pearl's stroke.

Or had she?

BRIDGER DUVALL WASN'T altogether sure Laci would show up. She'd been pretty adamant about not wanting the job. He was counting on her love of cooking.

Not just to get her to show up for their cook-off but to make her accept his job offer.

True, he had an ulterior motive. Several, in fact. He really did need a chef. Also, he liked her. And then there was the fact that she was Pearl Cavanaugh's granddaughter. It was a long shot that she'd know anything about the Whitehorse Sewing Circle's adoptions. She wasn't even born the night his parents rendezvoused with her grandmother in the Whitehorse Cemetery.

Either way, he was looking forward to seeing her again. He'd asked around and found out that Laci had started a catering business but hadn't had the best of results since someone was poisoned at her very first event.

While the case had been solved and Laci cleared, he doubted it had helped business.

He looked up at the sound of the front door opening. She came in with a large box of supplies and a look of determination on her face, both making him grin. She'd shown up. He breathed a sigh of relief, happier to see her than he probably should have been.

"Where's your chef?" she asked as she glanced around the large commercial kitchen.

"You're looking at him," he said, smiling.

"You?" She sounded more than skeptical.

"What? You don't think cowboys can cook?"

"A can of beans over an open fire, maybe."

His smile broadened. "I hate to make you eat your words, but I can cook you under the table."

Her blue eyes sparkled. "We'll see about that, Duvall," she said, putting down her box of supplies and tying on her apron.

They cooked in a companionable silence, both lost in their work. He would catch whiffs of what she was making and turn to watch her. Her intensity surprised him. He had to reformulate his first impression of her from the wedding reception. All he'd seen was a blond airhead, more than a little flaky, upchucking her champagne.

He stepped closer to see what she was cooking up. An interesting aroma rose up from the pot, mingling with the rich, sweet scent of Laci Cavanaugh's perfume. It was more than he could stand.

"Are you trying to steal my secrets?" she asked, cutting her eyes to him.

"I have to have a bite."

She grinned and handed him a spoonful.

He couldn't believe the flavors. "It's amazing."

Her grin broadened into a blazing smile. He looked into those big blue eyes and did the worst possible thing he could do. He leaned over and kissed her. It was just a brush of their lips, a commingling of tastes and touch.

The bolt of shock that rocketed through him wasn't just from the spark of the kiss. The moment their lips touched, Bridger knew hiring Laci Cavanaugh was out of the question.

Was he crazy? He couldn't have this woman in his kitchen. She would be too distracting. Just watching her cook was a huge turn-on since she clearly loved cooking as much as he did—and she was damned good at it. He loved the way her brows knitted when she was concentrating on slicing vegetables. Or the way she gently bit her lower lip as she melted butter.

Who would have thought someone who looked like her could cook?

Not to mention the fact that he'd completely forgotten why he'd made a point of running into her again.

He hadn't even gotten around to asking her about the Whitehorse Sewing Circle and her grandmother.

Laci's cell phone rang in her purse, making them both jump back from the kiss.

"Can you get that for me?" she asked as she dusted flour off her hands, then scrutinized the buttermilk biscuits she'd made. She slid the pan into the oven and set the timer as if pretending the kiss had never happened. Or perhaps she was unaffected by it.

Her phone rang again. She shot him a look. "It's in my purse," she said, her hands white with flour.

He nodded numbly. He'd never known a woman who would let a man in her purse. Carefully he peeked into her shoulder bag, looking for the cell as it rang a third time.

The purse had several recipes torn from magazines with printed changes written in the margin. She'd already changed the recipes before she'd even tried them? The arrogance of the woman. He loved it.

He spotted the cell and snapped it open before the phone could ring again. "Hello?"

Silence.

"Hello?" he repeated.

"Who is it?" Laci called from the stove.

"Laci?" asked a female voice on the other end of the line.

"Just a minute." He handed Laci the phone. She had begun caramelizing onions on the stove as she said hello.

"Laney," she said, sounding pleased, and smiled over at him. "It's my sister." The sister must have asked who'd answered the phone, because Laci turned her back to him and said, "Bridger Duvall." Silence, then she said, "He's opening a restaurant in Whitehorse… Not sure…We're here cooking…It's a long story." She laughed, then asked how things were going in Hawaii.

Bridger turned back to his own cooking, shaken by his reactions not only to the kiss but also Laci's nonreaction, if that's what it had been. He wanted to snatch the phone from her and kiss her again, only this time *really* kiss her.

Behind him, he heard Laci gasp and turned as she dropped the phone to the floor. She'd gone white as her apron.

"What is it?" he cried.

"She's dead," Laci croaked out on a sob. "She'd dead."

Bridger lunged toward Laci, catching her just an instant before she hit the floor.

A few moments later, Laci blinked her eyes open and slowly focused on the face hovering above her. A very handsome, concerned face. She sat up with a start.

"What happened?" Bridger asked. "Talk to me."

Tears filled her eyes. "She's dead."

"Who's dead?"

"Alyson."

Bridger sat back on the floor. "Spencer's Alyson?"

She nodded through her tears. "Laney just saw it on the news in Hawaii. Aly was swimming." She choked on a sob. "She drowned." She burst into gut-wrenching sobs. "I knew it. I should have stopped her."

Bridger scooted closer and took her in his arms. She leaned into him and cried for her friend and for herself. She had let this happen. It was all her fault.

Bridger held her, letting her sob her heart out, offering his shoulder and an occasional paper towel.

Finally she took a shuddering breath and sat back.

He handed her another paper towel, his eyes dark with concern.

"I'm sorry about your friend," he said.

She nodded and dried her tears. She had to do something. She was one of the few people who knew the truth about Spencer Donovan.

Rising unsteadily to her feet, she looked around for her purse and car keys.

"Let me drive you home," Bridger said, joining her. "You're too upset."

"I'm not going home," she said, buoyed by growing anger and Cavanaugh determination. "I'm going to the sheriff. He needs to know the truth."

Bridger frowned. "The truth?"

"Spencer killed her."

BRIDGER STARED AT her as he watched her search for her keys and purse. "Laci, you can't really think that Spencer would—"

"He killed her. Oh, my God, he *killed* her." She was sobbing again, mumbling how she should have done something.

"I thought you said she drowned while swimming," he reminded her as she found what she was looking for in the supply box she'd brought and turned to leave.

"I don't know the specifics," she said, shaking her head at him as if he wasn't paying attention. "I just know that he killed her and if I don't do something he'll get away with murder." She charged toward the door.

He called after her, but there was no turning a wild bull when it was seeing red. Just as there was no turning Laci Cavanaugh when her mind was made up, apparently.

All he could hope was that the sheriff would set her straight and calm her down. He sighed and looked around the kitchen, still stunned that the pretty young bride was dead and Spencer was a widower after only a few days of marriage.

It brought home how brief life could be. He'd promised himself after his mother died that he would live his to the fullest. But, of course, he hadn't. Instead he'd gone on this quest to find his birth mother.

The timer went off on the oven. He took a hot pad and pulled out the biscuits Laci had made and turned off the burner heating the onions, too worried about her to even think about food right now.

He could understand wanting someone to blame when you lost a person you loved. He just hoped that Laci came to her senses before Spencer returned.

The last thing Spencer needed at a time like this was his bride's best friend trying to get him arrested for murder.

SHERIFF CARTER JACKSON motioned Laci into his office. She closed the door and took a seat, having pulled herself together as much as possible on the three blocks to the sheriff's department.

"I just heard about Alyson. I'm so sorry, Laci," Carter said, making her tear up again. "I know how close the two of you were growing up."

She nodded, fighting to keep from bawling again. "There is something you don't know." Her throat was so dry she had to swallow before she could continue. "Spencer killed her."

Laci had expected the sheriff to be surprised, but all he did was nod.

"Your sister called me when she lost the cell phone connection with you," he said.

"Then she told you?"

"She mentioned your suspicions," Carter said carefully. "I called the sheriff's department on the island and talked to the investigating officer. Apparently Alyson had been in the habit of going for a swim early in the morning. This day was no different. An eyewitness from the shore said it appeared she got a cramp. The witness tried to reach her, but she'd gone under by then."

Laci was shaking her head. "Where was Spencer during all this?"

"He'd gone to the room to get something," Carter said.

How convenient. She didn't believe it. "He must have given her something, drugged her or—"

"There will be an autopsy, so if there are drugs in her system, they'll find them."

She nodded, still afraid that Spencer would get away with this.

"We're all just sick about what happened."

She stood and picked up her purse. "Alyson was a strong swimmer. She was on the swim team in high school. She wouldn't have drowned unless he did something to her."

"Strong swimmers get cramps and drown, Laci."

She shook her head. "He killed her."

"Based on a look?" the sheriff said quietly.

So Laney had told him. "I know it doesn't seem like much, but his mask slipped for that instant and I saw his true feelings. I knew he was going to kill her. I should have tried harder to stop her—"

"Why would he marry her if he really had those kind of feelings toward her?"

It was the question Laci had been asking herself for two days. Alyson's family didn't have money. The ranch would be worth something but not enough to kill someone for, right?

"Laci, it was an accident," Carter said.

"I know it sounds crazy," she admitted. "But won't you please investigate Spencer Donovan?"

"The death occurred out of my jurisdiction, and as I said, it's being investigated."

She was close to tears again. "Please, at least check out his background?"

The sheriff nodded slowly. "If you'll do me a favor. Keep your suspicions to yourself?"

She nodded. "You'll let me know what you find out?"

"I promise."

BRIDGER CALLED A half dozen times and stopped by on his way home, but Laci's car wasn't in the drive, nor were any of the lights on inside the house.

He could imagine how it had gone with the sheriff and hoped she was all right.

Finally he called her grandfather. Titus Cavanaugh was a big, powerful man, both in stature and in his standing in this part of Montana. Bridger had butted heads with him only the one time over the adoption business and, more to the point, over his wife, Pearl, and her part in it.

Finally Titus had sworn on the Bible he used for his Sunday church services that he knew nothing about Bridger's birth or adoption. Bridger had believed him.

"I'm trying to find Laci," he said without preamble.

"And who might you be?" the older man asked.

"Bridger Duvall. I was with Laci today when she got the bad news about her friend Alyson. I'm worried about her."

Silence, then finally the man said, "You can reach her at her friend McKenna Bailey's."

"Thank you, I'll do that." He hung up, wondering if Titus would have given him the information if he knew Bridger hadn't given up on finding his birth mother. Far from it.

"Hello, you've reached the Baileys. Leave a message and we'll get back to you."

Bridger hesitated, then said, "McKenna? It's Bridger Duvall. I'm trying to find Laci. I'm worried—"

"Bridger?" Laci said as she came on the line.

He breathed a sigh of relief, surprised how good it was to hear her voice. "Laci, I was worried about you."

She made a small wounded sound. "I'm okay." She didn't sound okay. She sounded miserable.

"Listen, if there is anything I can do..."

"Thanks, but there isn't anything anyone can do now," she said. "Thanks for calling, though."

He felt so helpless. "You take care of yourself."

"THE POLICE HERE are convinced that it was an accident," her sister said when Laci called the next day.

"Based on what?"

"An *eyewitness*," Laney said.

"I want the name of that eyewitness," Laci said.

"You aren't serious."

Laci had never been more serious in her life. "If you can't get it for me, I'll get the sheriff to help me."

"All right," Laney said. "I'll see what I can do. Laci, you're starting to worry me."

"I know her death wasn't an accident. He killed her."

"Okay, but if you're right, why? What was his motive?"

"He's sick. Maybe he didn't want to marry her. Maybe he was forced to. Maybe Alyson was pregnant."

"Laci, even if she was pregnant, Spencer didn't have to marry her. There wasn't anyone holding a shotgun to his head at the wedding, was there?"

She knew her sister was right. Still, she made a note to check back with Sheriff Jackson about the autopsy and whether Aly had been pregnant. "What other motive could there have been? It wasn't like Alyson or her grandfather had a lot of money."

"That old ranch house and even the sizable land the Bannings owned can't be worth much in that part of Montana," Laney said. "Sweetie, I think you're wrong about this and I hate to see you accuse the man of something he didn't do based on—what?—a look? You realize that if he loved her as much as he seemed to—to everyone but you—then he is devastated right now. He just lost his wife, the woman he loved and swore the rest of his life to. And even worse, he probably feels responsible. If he hears that her best friend now suspects him of killing his wife, imagine what that would do to him. You can't go off half-cocked with this, Laci."

"I know." She had to admit those rational thoughts *had* crossed her mind in her more sane moments. "But what if *I'm* right and he's getting away with murder?"

Her sister sighed.

"I know what you're saying, but I'm not wrong about him," Laci said stubbornly. "And I'm going to prove it."

"Laci, I really don't like the sound of this," her sister said with both reproach and fear. "If you're right about him, then he's dangerous."

"I have to find out the truth. I owe Aly that much at least."

"You couldn't have stopped her from marrying him," Laney said adamantly. "I love Nick so much there isn't anything anyone could have said to keep me from marrying him. If Spencer is the man you think he is, then on some level Alyson knew but refused to believe the truth about him."

"You think she suspected something was wrong?"

"If you're right, then, yes, I do," Laney said. "But she wouldn't have wanted to believe it. You telling her would have only cost the two of you your friendship."

Laci knew her sister was right. "Still, I wish I had tried harder to warn her."

"By doing what? Throwing yourself in front of the car after the reception? Come on, Laci, you know that wouldn't have done any good. Stop beating yourself up over this. Nothing you can do now will bring Alyson back. Let it go."

She wished she could.

"At least let it go until I get back," Laney said. "Whatever plot you're hatching can wait until next week, can't it?"

Laci leaned back, pressing the phone to her mouth as she fought tears, remembering Alyson waving from the back window of the car as it sped away, remembering how she'd said she was having the time of her life in Hawaii.

"Promise me you won't do anything rash," Laney

said. "On second thought, I know you. I'm coming home early."

"No," Laci said, wiping at her tears. "You're on your honeymoon."

"I'm not unless you promise me you won't do anything until I get back."

What was a few more days? Laney was right. It could wait that long. Alyson was dead. Nothing could change that.

Just then she heard a car on the county road to the north. Out the kitchen window she saw Spencer Donovan's vehicle. She ducked back out of sight as the car seemed to slow as it passed.

Spencer was back in Old Town Whitehorse.

"Laci?" Laney asked on the other end of the line. "I want you to promise you won't do anything until I get back or I'm getting on the next plane home."

She hated fibbing to her sister, but she knew that if she didn't promise, Laney would cut her honeymoon short and do just what she was threatening.

Laci crossed her fingers and squeezed her eyes shut. "I promise."

CHAPTER FIVE

"I WAS JUST getting ready to call you," Sheriff Carter Jackson said when Laci got him on the line the next morning.

"You found something?" She couldn't help but sound hopeful. If the sheriff had discovered anything incriminating on Spencer Donovan, then there would be an investigation by professionals. Laci wasn't foolish enough to believe she could do a better job of investigating Spencer than law enforcement.

"Probably not what you were expecting," the sheriff said. "I talked to the detective on the case in Hawaii. The autopsy confirms that Alyson drowned. There were no drugs in her system. No sign of foul play."

"Was she pregnant?"

"No." He sounded surprised by the question. "Laci, Alyson's death has been ruled an accident. The case is closed."

"But what about Spencer? There has to be something in his background—"

"I ran him through our computers. Laci, the man hasn't even had a speeding ticket in years."

She couldn't believe this. "What about his business?"

Alyson had led her to believe that Spencer was wealthy. That had to be a lie. "Is he really rich?"

"Rich is a relative term, but he seems to have done very well with his investment business," the sheriff said. "You aren't thinking he was after Alyson's money?"

She wasn't sure what she was thinking. Maybe that was the problem. She wasn't thinking at all—just letting her heart rule, as she'd done all her life.

She took a deep breath and let it out slowly, trying to hold herself together.

"Other than the one look you thought he gave his bride, what is it about Donovan that has you so suspicious?"

She felt tears burn her eyes. Other than a feeling based on nothing more than a look, there wasn't anything he'd done or said that would prove him a killer. "There's really nothing you could find on him?"

"Nothing. I hope the information gives you some peace of mind," the sheriff said. He seemed to hesitate. "Spencer Donovan stopped by my office earlier. He'd heard I'd been asking about him and his business. I told him it was standard procedure in an accidental death. I'm not sure he believed me, but he was cordial enough about it. I didn't mention your name, of course."

"Thank you for running a check on him," she said, feeling even worse. Carter had to think she was a nutcase.

"Mr. Donovan told me that he's staying out at the Banning ranch down the road from you. Is that going to be a problem for you?"

"I guess not since apparently there is nothing to

worry about when it comes to him," she said. "Did he mention how long he would be staying?"

"Didn't say. I would assume at least until after the funeral. He said services are planned at the old Whitehorse Cemetery tomorrow, but I imagine you already knew that."

The moment she hung up, the phone rang. It was Laney. She told her sister what the sheriff had found out.

"What is it going to take for you to accept that this man isn't a killer?" Laney asked.

She wished she knew.

"I did get the name of the eyewitness who tried to save Alyson," her sister said.

"Maybe the eyewitness was in on it," Laci said as she scrambled to find a pen and paper. "Maybe Spencer hired this guy."

Laney groaned on the other end of the line. "The eyewitness was a woman. Her name is Joanna Clemmons from Atlanta, Georgia. She was visiting Hawaii on a church conference. Sound like a hired killer to you?"

Laci wrote down the woman's name, although her enthusiasm had waned. "I'm crazy, aren't I?"

"You're just not thinking straight, sweetie," Laney said comfortingly.

"I thought for sure she might have been drugged. Or maybe pregnant and he didn't want the baby."

"You know that if Alyson had been pregnant she would have told you," Laney assured her. "You two were best friends for too many years. She always told you everything."

Did she?

Laci wasn't so sure about that as she made another

promise to her sister she had no intention of keeping, fingers crossed, and got off the line.

"I NEED YOUR HELP," Bridger said when Laci answered the phone a few minutes later. He'd called her numerous times to see how she was doing.

She always told him the same thing: that she was okay. But he could tell by her voice that she was far from okay. He just hoped now that Spencer was back in town that she didn't still think he'd killed his bride on their honeymoon.

"I need a chef," Bridger said. "I'm having a small, invitation-only sampler just to test my proposed menu for the restaurant. The problem is that I'm in over my head. I need help. I'm *desperate*."

"As flattering as that is…"

"Laci, I need *you*. And I think it's time you got back to cooking." He could hear from her surprised intake of breath that she hadn't expected him to know that she'd been so upset she couldn't even cook.

"How did you—"

"I can't do this without you. I can drive down and pick you up—"

"No. What are you making?"

He smiled to himself, knowing once he told her, he'd have her. He rattled off his menu.

"You don't want to make that for dessert. Not with it supposed to rain this afternoon. I have a chocolate flourless torte that would be perfect." She sighed. "I'll be there in an hour. I'll stop by the store and pick up what I need to make it."

He breathed a silent sigh of relief. "I owe you."

"Yes, you do. Wait until you get my bill."

LACI STOPPED BY the grocery store to get what she needed to make her flourless chocolate torte, grateful to have something to do. But, in truth, also looking forward to spending time with Bridger.

The local grocery was small, the aisles narrow, but she found what she needed and pushed her cart into the checkout line.

"Excuse me."

Laci heard the male voice, recognizing it at the same moment a chill raced up her spine.

"Laci?" Spencer asked from directly behind her.

She turned, afraid of what she was going to say. She'd thought about coming face-to-face with him. All she could think about was clawing out his eyes, screaming obscenities at him.

But when she saw his face, she did neither. His dark eyes were sunken with dark circles under them. He looked horrible. She hadn't expected this, and even while she told herself this could be part of his act, she felt for him and the pain she saw in his face.

"I'm so sorry about Alyson." Her words surprised her. She sounded so civil.

He nodded. "Thank you."

She turned back as the cashier announced her total. Laci's hands were shaking as she pulled the money from her purse and paid for her groceries.

"If you wait, I can help you out with those," Spencer said behind her.

"That's all right. I can manage," she said, not looking at him.

"See you around, Laci."

She stumbled from the store, shaken. Was it possible she was wrong about Spencer Donovan?

Opening her car, she put the groceries inside and, unable to help herself, glanced back toward the store.

Through the large plate-glass window she saw him at the checkout. He was paying for his groceries, but as if feeling her gaze on him, he turned in her direction.

Their gazes locked and he smiled, but the smile never met his eyes.

ONE LOOK AT her and Bridger knew he'd done the right thing dragging Laci into town. He tossed her an apron, biting his tongue to keep from asking how she was holding up. The way her fingers trembled as she tied on the apron said it all.

Laci had left her recipes in the kitchen at his restaurant the other day. He'd tried her flourless chocolate torte, trying to read the changes she'd made in the margin.

It had turned out all right, but he really wanted to taste hers. Somehow he knew it would be better than what he'd made even following her recipe.

"What do you need me to do?" she asked, stepping to the sink to wash her hands.

"I tried your torte recipe," he confessed. "I would like to taste it after *you* make it."

She smiled over her shoulder at him, what he suspected was her first smile in days. "What makes you think mine will be better?"

"Just a feeling," he said with a laugh. Just like the feeling that he'd called her in the nick of time. He could see the grief on her face. She looked thinner, her eyes rimmed red, her face pale.

He went to work on one of the entrées and left her to it. They cooked in silence. He watched her come back to life slowly as the kitchen filled with the sweet scents of rich, creamy butter, chocolate and raspberry.

He relaxed into the pleasurable work, the only sounds that of pots and pans and wire whips and wooden spoons and the occasional ooh or aah as one of them tasted their work of art.

The kitchen was warm and safe, just as it had been when he was a child. His mother had taught him to cook. His father had taught him to ride a horse and fish.

Both of his adoptive parents were now gone. His father from a heart attack seven years ago. His mother finding peace six months ago after a long battle with cancer.

She'd given him one final gift: the truth. Since then, he'd often wondered why he hadn't known he was adopted. Or even suspected it. How was that possible?

A door opened and closed. A female voice called, "Hello?" as cowboy boot soles thumped across the wood floor of the restaurant into the kitchen at the back.

As if conjured up from his thoughts, his twin, Eve Bailey, stopped in the doorway.

"So you're really doing this," she said. Like her sisters and mother, Eve was all cowgirl. She wore jeans, boots and a Western shirt. But recently he'd noticed she was wearing makeup and fixing her hair differently. He suspected it was for the same reason Sheriff Carter Jackson was spending more time down in Old Town Whitehorse. There appeared to be some old-fashioned courting going on.

Bridger was glad to see it. He'd seen the way Eve's eyes lit when the sheriff was around.

"You got the invitation for tonight, didn't you?" Bridger asked. "I reserved a table for you." He didn't add that the sheriff had already called to reserve his best table. Wouldn't it be something if the sheriff popped the question tonight?

"Hi, Laci," Eve said.

Laci had been so involved in her cooking she hadn't seemed to have heard Eve come in.

"I assume you two know each other?" Bridger asked. He and Eve were older than Laci, but both women had grown up in Old Town Whitehorse, and as small as that community was, they probably knew each other's life histories.

"Of course," Laci said and laughed before saying hello to Eve, then going back to her cooking.

Bridger was just getting to know the town and the people. He felt as though he was thirty-two years behind even though it was the only reference spot he had in his search for his birth mother.

Eve talked for a few minutes about the weather, her new horse, the price of hay. She seemed to be avoiding mentioning Alyson's death, her eyes flicking to Laci's thin back as the younger woman continued to cook.

Bridger walked Eve out to her pickup.

"Is Laci all right?" Eve asked. "You know Alyson Banning was her best friend."

He nodded. "She'll be all right. It just takes time." He could feel Eve eyeing him.

"I'm glad you stayed around," she said as they reached her truck and she started to open the driver's-side door.

"Me, too." He wanted to apologize again for being such a jerk when he'd first come to town. He'd thought Eve Bailey was in on the cover-up involving his adoption. He hadn't realized how wrong he could be.

His mother had told him about the phone call in the middle of the night. His adoptive parents had driven all the way to Whitehorse and waited in the dark, wintry cold at the cemetery. They'd almost given up when an older woman had appeared out of the snowy darkness with a bundle.

Inside had been a baby and a new birth certificate that would make them the birth parents.

Only there'd been a mix-up. They'd been given the baby boy—but the wrong birth certificate. The birth certificate was for a little girl named Eve Bailey who'd been born the same night at the same time. His fraternal twin sister.

What he and his twin had in common was their quest to find their birth mother. But unlike him, Eve believed the answer was lost forever with Pearl Cavanaugh's stroke.

"You do realize that Laci is Pearl Cavanaugh's granddaughter, I assume," Eve said.

It was eerie the way she often knew what he was thinking.

"That isn't what this is about," he said.

She cocked a brow at him, no doubt remembering how driven he'd been to find out the truth just months ago. Not that things had changed. He was just going at it differently, he told himself.

He planned to charm them with his culinary craft. Seduce them with food cooked with his love and care. Show them he wasn't going anywhere until he got the truth. And eventually he would get what he was after. He hoped.

Eve was one of them, an Old Town Whitehorse resident, and she hadn't been able to get to the truth. Was he kidding himself that staying here was the answer?

"Laci loves to cook almost as much as I do, and I needed a cook. It's that simple." He wished.

Eve was still giving him the eagle eye. "So she's working for you?"

Was she? "I hope so." It was true. The kiss aside, he needed her expertise. She'd had some good suggestions about the menu, and the woman could cook. As long as he didn't let her distract him, everything would be fine.

"Do I say break a leg or what?" Eve asked.

"Good luck will do," he said and grinned at her. "You look nice. Date?"

"Uh-huh." Eve glanced away, shy when it came to Carter.

He smiled. "Carter's a good man."

She cut her eyes to him. "You'd better get back to your cooking."

"Eve…" he said, feeling a strange lump in his throat. So many times he'd regretted telling her he had no interest in getting to know her. His own twin sister. He'd been angry.

Since then, they'd made a pact to keep their relationship a secret. At least for the time being. There hadn't been enough evidence to expose the Whitehorse Sewing Circle, and telling everyone would only open up the whole sorry mess. "I'm glad you stopped by."

LACI BREATHED IN the scents of the kitchen, glancing around, grateful that Bridger had called her to help.

Not that she didn't know what he was up to. He was too smart to make anything for dessert that could be affected by damp weather. He just knew that she needed this and had come up with an excuse to get her down here.

Still, it surprised her that this man she'd only just met knew that the one thing she needed most right now was to be cooking.

Under normal circumstances she would have balked at such obvious manipulation. But the truth was she needed to lose herself for a few hours. She was beginning to question her own sanity since from all appearances Spencer Donovan was no more a killer than she was.

And yet her instincts told her she was right. Alyson had been murdered. And she was the only one who knew the truth.

She heard Bridger come back into the kitchen as she slid the tortes into the oven and set the oven timer.

"I couldn't have done this sampler without you," he said behind her. "Thank you. You saved my life."

She nodded without turning around as she put her recipes away. She was the one who'd been saved and they both knew it. Getting ready for his invitation-only sampler night had kept her so busy she hadn't had time to agonize over Alyson's death. Or what to do about Spencer Donovan. As if there was anything to do.

She just hoped her tortes turned out. She loved cooking here with Bridger, but she'd been too aware of him this time. She just hoped she hadn't left anything out of the recipe. One thing was for sure—she couldn't take the chef job he'd offered her, even if she was tempted. She couldn't work this close to the man. And just the thought made her a little sad.

BRIDGER HAD STOPPED just inside the kitchen door, watching Laci as she slid the tortes into the oven and set the timer, then began putting away her recipes.

She had a dab of flour on her cheek, her face a little

flushed from the heat of the kitchen, her eyes bright
and shiny. He'd never seen a more beautiful, desirable
woman.

For years he'd been busy running the ranch and taking care of his elderly parents. He'd told himself he
hadn't had time for relationships, but the truth was he
hadn't met a woman who'd interested him enough to
get involved.

Until now.

He had an idea what he was getting into with Laci.
She was without a doubt a walking bundle of contra-
dictions. Underneath all that sexy blond cuteness was
a talented, imaginative, intelligent woman who would
have to be reckoned with. She would be a challenge
for any man.

He watched her dust flour off her hands as he stepped
closer. She turned to him. Her smile was his undoing.
He reached to brush the dab of flour from her cheek.
Her skin was warm and silken. He felt a shaft of desire
shoot through him like nothing he'd ever experienced—
and knew he was lost.

"LACI." HE CUPPED her cheek with his hand, his eyes
locked with hers.

She didn't dare breathe, didn't dare move, as his
mouth dropped to hers. The kiss rocked her back on her
heels. His arms surrounded her and pulled her closer.

She let herself go, lost in his kiss, in the warm, sweet
taste of him, in the luscious feel of being enveloped by
him. A soft moan escaped her lips. There was no turning back, and she suspected Bridger knew it, as well.

"Laci?"

She wrapped her arms around Bridger's neck as he

swept her up in his arms. He drew back to look into her eyes. She saw the question and answered it with a kiss as he carried her upstairs to his apartment above the restaurant.

He kicked open the bedroom door and lowered her slowly to the bed. "You sure about this?"

She'd never been so sure of anything. She smiled up at him and pulled him down as she pushed aside her vow not to jump into anything. She needed this. She needed Bridger. All her emotions were so close to the skin. She needed to be nurtured, and this felt so right. It couldn't possibly be wrong.

Bridger lowered himself beside her. She felt shy and excited all at the same time. Her heart raced and her fingers trembled as she began to unsnap his Western shirt, averting her eyes from his.

He covered her hand with his, stopping her.

With one finger he lifted her chin so that their eyes met. Slowly, painstakingly, he leaned toward her and brushed a kiss across her lips.

She caught her breath as he slowly began to undress her. She ignored the little voice in her head that argued that this was too soon, that she didn't know this man, that she'd just leaped, that she would regret it... as Bridger drew her close and she melted into his arms.

A SOUND AROUSED LACI. It took her a moment, lying there in Bridger's arms, to realize what it was. The timer on the oven.

"My tortes!" she cried and jumped out of bed, throwing on her clothing as she rushed downstairs to the kitchen.

A few moments later, Bridger came down dressed in

jeans and a shirt, his feet bare. He came over to where she stood.

"Wow," he said, admiring her creation. "Wow," he repeated, only this time focusing on her.

She beamed under his gaze and stepped easily into his arms for a kiss. "Wow."

He smiled at her, making her recall too well their lovemaking. It had been a healing for her, a need that was tied up in her grief over her best friend's death, in her sense of loss.

"Your guests will be arriving in less than three hours," she said.

He nodded and sighed. "Laci—"

She touched a finger to his lips, afraid of what he might say. Her eyes locked with his and the kitchen suddenly felt much too hot. He was going to kiss her again, and she feared neither of them would remember dinner—or his guests—if he did.

"Congratulations!"

Bridger jerked back, swinging around.

Laci felt her heart plummet—not just from the disappointment of the almost kiss—but from the recognition of the male voice.

Spencer Donovan burst through the kitchen doors and froze. She pressed herself into the counter, trying to make herself invisible. Just the sound of the man's voice stole her breath and sent her heart pounding in her ears.

"You always said you were going to open a restaurant someday," Spencer was saying as the two men shook hands. "I just never imagined it would be in Whitehorse, Montana."

Spencer and Bridger knew each other? Had known each other before the wedding? The realization was an arrow to her heart. She'd just assumed Bridger had been at the wedding for the bride since he lived in Old Town Whitehorse—not there on groom's side.

She must have let out a gasp at Spencer's words. He peered around Bridger and saw her. His expression changed instantly. She saw something flicker in his gaze.

"Thanks," Bridger said, drawing Spencer's attention away from her. "I never thought my first restaurant would be in Whitehorse, either. Spence, I'm so sorry about Alyson."

Spencer only nodded, looking upset. "Well, I just had to stop in and congratulate you. I couldn't miss tonight—not when I know how much it must mean to you. Even when we were kids you always talked about opening your own restaurant."

Laci felt sick. All she wanted to do was flee. But she couldn't move, couldn't breathe.

Spencer should have been in mourning, but here he was out on the town. She knew she wasn't being fair. The man had a right to eat. But it ticked her off that he looked better than he had at the supermarket earlier. His tan seemed more prominent, and he was dressed up in jeans and a sports jacket over a button-up shirt. His gaze shifted to Laci. She looked into his dark eyes and felt as if she were drowning in a deep, dark, bottomless well.

"Well, I should go," Spencer said and shook Bridger's hand again, slapping him on the shoulder. He gave Laci a nod and was gone.

She gasped for air, grabbing hold of the counter for support. *"You two know each other?"* she demanded the moment Spencer was out of earshot.

Bridger looked at her as if worried about her sanity. "You saw me at the wedding."

"But I had no idea you were there as *his* guest."

"I thought you knew. Spencer and I are both from Roundup."

She hadn't known. But she should have. She'd just assumed because Bridger lived in Old Town Whitehorse that he'd been Alyson's guest. The entire community was always invited to every event, whether it was a wedding, a baby shower or a birthday.

"You should have told me he was your friend."

"We're not exactly friends," Bridger said. "I hadn't seen him in years."

She groaned. "He certainly sounded like your friend. Why did you let me go on about him being a killer without telling me about your friendship?"

"Laci, I knew you were in shock and upset. I didn't really take what you were saying seriously."

She couldn't believe the man was capable of actually making her more angry. *"You didn't take me seriously?"*

"What you were *saying* seriously."

She threw her hands up in the air, almost too exasperated to speak. "You saw him just now. Did he look like a man who is grieving?" she demanded.

"I know you're upset about the death of your friend, but you can't believe he purposefully killed his wife. Why would he do that?"

Admittedly that part didn't make any sense, especially given what the sheriff had told her. Spencer Donovan appeared to be an upstanding citizen. But appearances, as they say, could be deceiving.

"I don't know why he killed her, just that he did," she

said, her chin going up in determination. "But I'm going to find out." She took off her apron and tossed it down.

"Laci—"

"You should have told me you were *his* friend."

"I told you—we aren't—"

"Do not say you aren't friends again. You were at his wedding as *his* guest."

"Only because we ran into each other in Whitewater a few weeks before the wedding. Before that, I hadn't seen Spencer in years."

She waved that off, wondering why he was trying to hide the fact that they were friends. Probably just to get her to work for him. She tried not to think about their lovemaking. Was that also to get her to cook with him?

"Come on, Laci," Bridger said as she picked up her purse and keys to leave. "I'm sorry he upset you. I really was enjoying having you here."

She could see that he wished they could go back to where they'd been earlier. About to kiss—and probably make love again. What made it worse was that so did she. "I have to go."

He looked as if he was trying to think of something to say to get her stay. But maybe he realized there was nothing he could say at this point.

She wasn't sure what made her more angry: the fact that he'd failed to tell her he and Spencer Donovan were friends, or that he didn't trust her instincts about Spencer after what they'd shared.

She gave him one last look before stalking out. The look felt filled with regret as well as anger that she had to leave this kitchen and him and, maybe worse, that there wouldn't be an encore to the kiss. Or the lovemaking.

Outside, she opened her car door and started to get in when she saw it. A single long-stemmed yellow rose. She stared at the flower, uncomprehending. Bridger hadn't put it there. When would he have? But who else would give her a rose?

She looked around, seeing no one. It had to have been Bridger, but she liked to think he was too imaginative in the kitchen to resort to flowers, the oldest cliché in the world. That he would have given her a perfect petit four that he'd baked and decorated.

Unless, of course, she didn't know him as well as she thought she did. She sighed and tossed the rose onto the passenger seat, reminding herself that she hadn't seen his friendship with Spencer coming, so clearly she didn't know Bridger as well as she'd thought.

The car smelled sickeningly sweet. She glanced over at the rose as she started the engine, feeling guilty for her lack of gratitude. Someone had left her a rose, no doubt as a nice gesture. So why did the mere sight of it make her feel queasy?

A FEW MILES down the road, she rolled down her window and tossed the rose out, feeling terrible and yet relieved to have it gone.

She hated to think what her sister would say about her throwing away a gift. Fortunately Laney was in Hawaii and would never know. Otherwise, Laci feared that this might be seen as just more irrational behavior on her part.

Everyone else thought Spencer was just who he appeared to be. All the evidence backed it up. And surely no one would see a rose as a threat. Or Bridger's friendship with Spencer as a betrayal.

She knew she wasn't being fair to Bridger. But she couldn't help how she felt. She was so lost in her mix of emotions that it didn't even register that she was being followed until she was almost to Old Town.

She glanced in her rearview mirror and saw the headlights, belatedly aware that the car had been back there ever since she'd left Whitehorse.

Her heart began to pound as she drove through the near ghost town, past the school, the community center, the old Cherry house. There was no moon tonight, no stars peeking out of the low cloud cover. The sharp black lines of the house were etched against the dark sky. She felt a shiver as she thought of the note she'd been left about her mother. Had the same person left the rose?

Down the county road, she swung into her drive, anxious to get home, hoping there would be no more presents, no more surprises tonight. She'd been so happy earlier, so fulfilled in Bridger's big kitchen. And in his bed. She had loved working with him. The thought made her feel even worse since they wouldn't be working together again. Or making love again.

As she parked in front of the house, she realized she hadn't thought to leave a light on when she'd left. The place was cloaked in darkness. She cut the car lights and engine but didn't get out.

She waited, hoping she was wrong about the car following her. Bridger wouldn't have followed her. He couldn't have left the restaurant, not with guests coming.

The car's headlights came down the county road, the driver seeming to slow. She slid down a little in her seat, hunkering in the dark car and holding her breath, fearing the car would turn into her lane. But it went on past and took the next road—the one to the Banning ranch house.

Spencer!

She sat, gripping the steering wheel, her heart a bass drum in her chest as she fought to catch her breath. Rational thought argued that he hadn't followed her. That he'd just been going home himself.

But she knew. Just as she knew that he was responsible for Alyson's death. Spencer Donovan hadn't just followed her home, he wanted her to know that he'd followed her and was close by. And that there was nothing she could do about that any more than she could prove he was a killer.

She let out a cry of frustration as she opened her car door and raced up the porch steps. She stumbled and almost went down. Otherwise, she might not have heard the scuttling sound of something sliding across the porch floor as she caught herself.

She unlocked the front door, reached in and turned on the porch light, already knowing what she was going to find on her porch floor. A small white envelope. Exactly like the last one, right down to the two neatly hand-printed words: *Laci Cherry*.

CHAPTER SIX

THE WEATHER IN Old Town Whitehorse could—and did—change in a heartbeat. The next morning the air was cool and crisp, the sky a crystalline blue. Every day was a gift since it wouldn't be long before winter set in with below-zero freezing temperatures and snow often accompanied by howling winds.

The one thing that never changed was the speed and intensity of the gossip in the community.

The Old Town Whitehorse grapevine was as dependable as death and taxes. And this bright fall morning it hummed with the news du jour leaving everyone for miles shocked.

Word that Violet Evans might soon be released from the criminally insane unit of the Montana state mental hospital was the talk of the town.

The Whitehorse Sewing Circle was no exception.

"Why, that woman has always been crazy," whispered Muriel Brown, who probably knew crazy better than most. She took a few stitches before she added, "Do you remember when she was about eleven? That fire at the school?"

"There was no proof Violet was responsible for that," Alice Miller pointed out with a frown. Violet Evans was now being blamed for everything that had happened in Whitehorse from the time she could walk.

"How about the summer that all the cats in the neighborhood started disappearing," whispered Ella Cavanaugh. "I told you that Violet Evans was behind it. I saw her pulling her little red wagon up the road, just grinning like the cat that ate the canary. She had a dirty old blanket over whatever was inside that wagon. I should have stopped that girl right there." Ella shuddered. "She always gave me a bad feeling, that one."

"If Pearl was here, she wouldn't allow this kind of talk," Alice Miller said pointedly.

"Well, Pearl isn't here," Muriel snapped. "But Violet Evans will be soon." She lifted a brow. "She and her mother might both be back here sitting across from us. How do you feel about that?"

Alice pursed her lips but said nothing. Everyone had been quite pleased that Arlene Evans had announced she was too busy with her internet dating service to quilt for a while.

"I just think it's shameful the way her mother tried to marry her off," Corky Mathews said in an attempt to still the ruffled feathers. "All the humiliation that poor child went through, it's no wonder she had bad feelings toward her mother."

"Bad feelings?" snapped Muriel. "The *poor* child tried to kill her mother!"

"Who hasn't wanted to kill Arlene?" Shirley Keen shot back with a laugh.

No one could argue that Arlene wasn't a bone of contention in Whitehorse. Just as no one would have been one bit sorry if Arlene took that bunch of bad seeds of hers and left the state.

"Have you seen her *son* lately?" Shirley asked, glancing toward Helene Merchant, who had brought the news of Violet's imminent release.

"Now there is the scary one of that family," Helene said. "Bo Evans, mark my words, is a psycho killer in the making. Have you seen how long his hair is? And you know Floyd left Arlene. I heard she leased the land. What else could she do? It wasn't like that boy of hers was going to run the place."

"I saw him hanging out by the old Cherry house the other night," Corky said. "I've seen lights in that place again."

"Probably because the house is haunted," Helene said with a shiver.

"I saw Bo once trying to break out the rest of the upstairs windows in that house," Corky said.

"I know he's the one who threw that rock through my window two years ago," Helene said. "He's always been a bad seed."

"It's Charlotte Evans who scares me," piped up the small voice of the elderly Pamela Chambers.

"I heard Charlotte got fired from her nail job in town and hasn't even looked for another one," Muriel chimed in.

"So they're all going to be in that house again," Ella said. "You know it's just a matter of time before something tragic happens out there."

"Will probably end up killing each other," Helene said.

They all nodded as if that wouldn't be such a bad thing.

"Just so long as they never let that Violet out of the mental hospital," Muriel said.

The talk turned then to Alyson Banning Donovan's funeral later that morning and what a tragedy it was.

"That poor man," Alice said of Spencer Donovan.

"I wonder what he'll do now. Can't imagine him staying," Helene said.

The women stitched for a few moments in silence, then began to plan for the Old Town Whitehorse Christmas bazaar just weeks away and what crafts and food everyone was going to bring.

BRIDGER WAS IN the kitchen at the restaurant when Spencer stopped in. Last night, the test run had been a huge success. Especially Laci's torte. Bridger had called to tell her, even though it had been late. He'd had to leave a message on her machine, suspecting she was there but didn't want to take his call.

He'd thought about trying to explain how it was between him and Spencer, but the story was too long and involved to leave on an answering machine. Not to mention he knew he'd be wasting his breath. Laci had no reason to believe him. Especially with Spencer acting as if they were long-lost friends.

But, damn, Bridger felt she should have given him the benefit of the doubt. Hadn't what happened between them meant anything to her?

Damn it. Just his luck to fall for a woman who was impossible. Couldn't Laci see that? Why would Spencer kill his wife on their honeymoon? It made no sense.

Bridger glanced around the kitchen. He had a ton of work to do if he hoped to open before Christmas. But he couldn't get Laci out of his mind.

As Spencer walked into the restaurant kitchen, Bridger saw him look around as if expecting Laci would be there. Is that why he'd stopped by? It gave Bridger more than an uncomfortable feeling. Had Spencer heard about Laci's suspicions and her determination to prove him a killer?

"I'm sorry if I messed things up for you yesterday evening at your opening by stopping by like that," Spencer said.

"No, it was fine. It wasn't my opening. I just wanted to get a response from the community as to what I planned to serve, so I did a sampler night," Bridger said, realizing he sounded nervous. Realizing also that he hadn't invited Spencer. Did Spencer feel slighted?

Spencer was looking at him funny. Or was it his imagination? "I didn't mean about the restaurant. I meant about you and Laci Cavanaugh. I saw her leave not long after I did."

Spencer had hung around outside long enough to see Laci leave?

"You should have a bell on that kitchen door so you'll know if you're about to be interrupted."

"It wasn't like that. Laci's a chef. She's been helping me with some ideas for dishes for the restaurant." Why was he lying about his feelings for her to Spencer?

"Sure, whatever you say. You two looked good together. I hated interrupting your kiss."

Bridger just wished Spencer would get to why he'd come by. "How are you holding up?" Bridger asked pointedly, remembering what Laci had said about the man's apparent lack of grief last night. "I would have invited you to the sampler last night, but I thought you wouldn't be interested in socializing yet."

Spencer gave him a look as if to say he had been doing fine until Bridger had brought it up again. "I'll never get over Aly's death. I blame myself. I should never have let her swim alone like that. But she was such a strong swimmer and she enjoyed it so much…"

"I know how hard it must be," Bridger said, not knowing but feeling chastised. He told himself that every person grieved in his own way. Part of him still hadn't dealt with the past, and he knew it.

"I just take it a day at a time," Spencer said, moving around the kitchen, picking up utensils and putting them down as if nervous.

Not half as nervous as he was making Bridger. What was this visit about? *Something*. He knew Spencer well enough to know that the man hadn't just dropped in. Spencer always made him feel guilty. For not keeping in touch all these years. For not feeling close to Spencer. After everything that had happened during their childhood, shouldn't he feel something more than a resentful indebtedness?

"It's probably wise taking it a day at a time," Bridger said.

Spencer turned to look over his shoulder at him. "I try not to think about it," he said pointedly. "It's bad enough I'll have to live with the memory the rest of my life. Actually, that's why I'm here."

Finally, Bridger thought, remembering how he had wanted to turn down Spencer's wedding invitation but had felt trapped into going. Just as he felt on the spot now.

"I was hoping you'd go to the funeral with me this morning," Spencer said. "I don't know anyone else in town. I mean, I've met people, but you're the only person I really *know*."

Bridger felt the full weight of their past press down on him. He knew at that moment why he'd avoided

Spencer for years, resenting the bond between them, hating the guilt as well as the shame.

But Spencer was wrong about one thing. He *didn't* know Bridger, hadn't even when they were kids. Sure as hell didn't know him after all this time.

Nor could Bridger be sure he knew Spencer, he reminded himself, thinking of Laci's suspicions.

"I wouldn't ask, but I'm feeling a little desperate," Spencer said. "I guess it's the grief, but I feel like I'm never going to be allowed to be happy and that Alyson's death is all my fault because of my rotten luck."

"That's crazy."

Spencer nodded, avoiding his gaze. "Maybe."

Bridger tried to come up with an excuse not to go to the funeral with Spencer, but in the end he had no choice. He'd planned on attending the funeral anyway for Laci. He couldn't very well tell Spencer he couldn't make it and then show up.

"I really would appreciate it," Spencer said. "I'm having a tough time, but with you there, well, it will make things a little easier."

"Sure." What else could he say? He thought of Laci and groaned inwardly. She would just see this as more betrayal, but there was nothing he could do about that now.

"Great," Spencer said, giving him a slap on the shoulder. "I knew I could count on you, old buddy."

The *old buddy* grated and only made Bridger feel worse. They discussed where and when to meet and Spencer left. Bridger reminded himself that Spencer would be leaving town soon, probably right after the funeral, and it would be the last he might ever see of him. But he feared it would be too late to patch things up with Laci.

Laci woke with a terrible headache. She hadn't slept well last night. At three, she'd gotten up and taken something to help her sleep. And now she'd overslept and felt horrible.

Unfortunately she was also still spooked just knowing Spencer Donovan was only down the road from her. She didn't like being afraid. And knew she might not even have a reason—if she was wrong about him. That was why she had to find out the truth, she'd realized on waking. She wouldn't be able to rest until she did.

Doing something also kept her mind off Bridger. She felt sick as she realized she'd done exactly what she'd sworn not to. She'd leaped before she'd looked. She didn't know Bridger. Wouldn't have guessed that he was a friend of Spencer Donovan's. What else didn't she know about him?

She picked up the phone and dialed information in Atlanta for a Joanna Clemmons, telling herself that the woman probably wouldn't be listed or might still be in Hawaii.

The automated voice on the line gave her the number. Laci dialed, holding her breath.

A woman with a Southern accent answered on the second ring.

"Joanna Clemmons?" Laci asked, then rushed on before the woman thought it was a telemarketer calling. "I'm calling about the drowning of Alyson Donovan in Hawaii. I understand you were the only eyewitness?"

"Yes," the woman said cautiously.

"My name is Laci Cavanaugh. Alyson was my best friend."

"Oh, I'm so sorry," Joanna Clemmons said quickly.

"Can you tell me what happened?"

"Well, I already told the police, but I had seen your friend swimming in the morning while I was at the hotel. She apparently loved the water."

"Yes," Laci said, closing her eyes to fight back the tears.

"This particular morning the surf was rough. I just caught glimpses of her out there and then suddenly I realized she was in trouble. I heard her scream for help and then she went under as if struggling."

"Where was her husband?"

"He was in their cabana but came running out to the water after her scream for help."

"Did he try to save her?" Laci asked and held her breath.

"He did."

Laci heard the hesitation in the woman's voice. "But?"

"He seemed to hesitate. I got the impression he didn't swim."

"But he finally went in the water?"

"Yes. Apparently he isn't a very good swimmer. I was afraid he was going to drown before the hotel staff could get him to shore after... He was so devastated."

Sure he was. "There wasn't a lifeguard on duty at the hotel?"

"Not on the beach."

Laci wondered if that was another reason Spencer had chosen that particular hotel.

"I am so sorry for your loss," Joanna said.

"Thank you. I appreciate hearing what happened." Laci hung up, blinded by tears of pain and fury. She wasn't sure how Spencer had done it, but she was all the more convinced that Alyson's drowning was no accident.

As Laci got out of bed, she knocked the white envelope off her nightstand. It fluttered to the floor, landing faceup. The words *Laci Cherry* stared up at her.

She let out a curse at the sight of the envelope. She'd forgotten about it, she'd been so upset about Spencer. Had he really followed her home last night, as she suspected? He'd definitely driven by slowly, as if watching her from the darkness of his car.

She shivered at the memory. He frightened her much more than some stupid note, she told herself as she picked up the unopened envelope.

The sender made her angry. She was tempted to throw the stupid thing away without opening it. If someone had something to tell her, then she wished they'd just do it and get it over with. Why the games?

Was it possible Spencer was behind this? Alyson might have told him about Laci's family. How she and Aly were both raised by grandparents—and why. So Spencer would know about Laci's father and mother. And about her grandfather and grandmother Cherry.

She shook her head at her own paranoia. Spencer had been in Hawaii with Alyson when the first envelope was left on her porch. Even she was beginning to wonder if she wasn't making a case against him because she wanted someone to blame for her friend's death.

If only she hadn't seen that look he'd given Alyson at the reception.

Angrily she ripped open the envelope, pulled out the sheet of paper and braced herself for what she would find printed on the page.

But nothing could have prepared her for what was written there.

Your mother never left town.

CHAPTER SEVEN

"WHERE DID YOU get these?" Sheriff Carter Jackson asked, picking up the two small white envelopes Laci had put in separate plastic bags.

"They were left for me on the porch at the house," she told him.

He nodded and, after pulling on a pair of latex gloves at her insistence, opened the bag she'd marked "No. 1."

His gaze rose from the note to her.

Laci said nothing, waiting for him to read the second one.

"Any idea who might be sending these to you?" he asked after he'd read them.

She shook her head. "I've always been told that my mother left town because she couldn't live without my father. Is there something else I should know?"

Carter put the notes back in the envelopes. "That's what I've always heard, as well. After you called and said you were bringing in the notes, I did give Todd Hamilton a call. He was sheriff when your mother left. He's living over in Great Falls now with his daughter."

"So the sheriff was called in?" This was news.

"Apparently your mother left a note saying she needed some time alone, but when your grandparents didn't hear from her after a couple of weeks, they filed a missing-person's report with him."

Her mother had left a note? "She didn't say where she was going?"

"No. The fact that she took a few personal items with her indicated to the sheriff that she'd left of her own free will."

Laci didn't like the bad feeling she was getting. "Wasn't he concerned when she didn't turn up?"

"The missing-person's report went out across the country, but while there were some unconfirmed sightings, she was never located." The sheriff seemed to hesitate. "It was assumed she didn't want to be found."

"No one suspected foul play?"

"There was no reason to. Your mother was young, her husband had just died, she had two small children…" He shrugged. "That's a lot for anyone to face, let alone someone her age."

Laci shook her head, not wanting to believe her mother had just run out on them because she wasn't strong enough. How could the daughter of Pearl and Titus Cavanaugh have been a quitter? It went against the genes.

And yet Laci had considered quitting after all the evidence pointed to Spencer Donovan's innocence even though her instincts told her he was a murderer.

"Thank you for the information," she told the sheriff as she got up to leave.

He rose from his chair. "Let me know if you get any more notes. I'll run these for prints and get back to you. In the meantime, I wouldn't put much stock in them. If someone knew where your mother was, they would have come forward before this, don't you think?"

Unless for some reason they couldn't.

Laci was lost in thoughts of her mother and the person who was sending her the notes as she drove to the post office to pick up her mail. She said hello to several people she passed. The post office was where you eventually ran into everyone from the county since Whitehorse didn't have door-to-door mail service, and even with rural delivery out in Old Town Whitehorse, packages were often held at the P.O. to be picked up.

As she was coming out, she suddenly sensed someone watching her. She shivered as she looked up but saw no one. Walking to her car, though, she couldn't shake the feeling. It wasn't until she started to open her car door that she saw him.

Spencer Donovan. He was sitting in the coffee shop across from the post office. He acted as if he'd just noticed her and nodded brusquely before turning away.

Laci found herself shaking as she pulled open her door, convinced he'd been following her, would know she'd gone to the sheriff's office this morning. Only he wouldn't know that this time it had been about her mother and not him.

As she opened her car door, she caught the sweet-sick smell of the yellow rose before she saw it lying on her driver's-side seat.

MILK RIVER EXAMINER reporter Glen Whitaker walked past the new restaurant and peered in the window. He'd been trying to get an interview with Bridger Duvall since he'd moved to the area.

Other than a brief article about Duvall's business license to open the restaurant, he'd found out little about the man and had no luck in getting Duvall to talk to him.

Which Glen found as strange as Bridger Duvall himself. Most anyone who opened a business wanted the free publicity of a feature article in the newspaper.

But then, apparently Bridger Duvall wasn't most people. First he'd rented the old McAllister place in Old Town and now he was starting a business in Whitehorse. There was talk that he would be moving permanently into the apartment over the restaurant since the old McAllister place had sold to a former detective and her husband.

On top of that, no one knew anything about Bridger Duvall—where he'd come from or, maybe more important, why he was here.

But apparently he had some connection to that man who'd married Alyson Banning—Spencer Donovan. Glen had also been trying to get an interview with the widower, with about the same luck as he'd had with Duvall. He'd heard that the two men were friends. Interesting.

Also interesting was a brunette woman Glen had seen several times—right after he'd seen Spencer Donovan. The woman had clearly not wanted to be seen. Glen had gotten the impression that she was following Donovan. To meet up with him later?

Glen had a nose for news that he was glad to realize he hadn't lost. Since moving to Whitehorse he hadn't covered much of interest. But he sensed that there was definitely a story in either Spencer Donovan, his recently drowned wife or this brunette. Or at least in Bridger Duvall and what he was up to.

Both men were unknowns and new to the community. Glen felt it was his job to find out as much about both and let residents know who was living right next door to them. Not to mention the fact that he was nosier than hell.

He had to drive down to Old Town Whitehorse to do a story for the newspaper on Alice Miller's ninetieth birthday this afternoon and Alyson Banning's funeral this morning. He'd take a few photos and—who knew—maybe catch Spencer Donovan off guard and get an interview. He was very curious about the man's wife's death.

Glen hadn't been in Old Town Whitehorse in months, not since he'd been beaten and left beside the road. It had been a humiliating experience, one he tried not to think about. An Old Town Whitehorse teenager had been caught and was supposedly behind a series of men bashings, but Glen still felt strange whenever he had to do a story down that way.

As he was walking to his car, he saw Bridger Duvall pull up and go into the restaurant with a large box of supplies.

Glen watched him, thinking the man must be anxious to get his restaurant open since he'd been working day and night on the place. It gave Glen an idea. While he was down in Whitehorse maybe he'd stop by the old McAllister place and have a look around before Duvall moved out. What would it hurt?

THE WHITEHORSE CEMETERY perched on a small hill overlooking what was left of Old Town. Trees had been planted in and around the clusters of gravestones.

Bridger stood next to Spencer beside the open grave, his hat in his hand. A breeze sent what was left of the leaves showering down from the trees, scattering them around the weathered gravestones. The sun slanted down through the branches as Titus Cavanaugh, the patriarch of Whitehorse, stood next to Spencer, his Bible in both hands, and waited for everyone to gather around the coffin.

Where was Laci? He hadn't seen her, but there were too many mourners for him to find her in the crowd without being obvious. He knew she had to be there. He just wished he was with her, feeling awkward and conspicuous standing next to Spencer.

Like Spencer, he was an outsider. He hadn't even known Alyson. Hell, he couldn't even say he knew Spencer after all these years.

Bridger could feel eyes on him, feel the curiosity and the animosity. Old Town Whitehorse was a close-knit community. The members of the Whitehorse Sewing Circle had thrown up a silent barrier to keep him out.

"They protect their own," Eve had told him. "The Whitehorse Sewing Circle is impenetrable. They're worse than a secret society when it comes to keeping secrets. If they wouldn't tell me, there isn't a chance in hell they will tell you."

He was finding that out. Just as he was sure many of them knew he visited Pearl Cavanaugh and the other elderly former members of the sewing circle at the nursing home.

"It is on the saddest occasion that we are gathered here today," Titus began. "We come to say goodbye to Alyson Banning Donovan. Only days ago, we gathered in the community center to marry this couple and give our blessing to their marriage."

As Titus continued, Bridger scanned the crowd for Laci. No sign of her. He tried not to worry. One woman in the crowd caught his eye. She had dark hair and eyes…and was about the right age to have given birth to twins thirty-two years ago.

A lot of women in the county could have been his and Eve's birth mother. But more than likely he and Eve had been brought in from somewhere else. Did someone in this town know the truth? Was that person watching him now, worried that he would find out who they were?

He felt an intent gaze on him and looked up to see the reporter from the *Milk River Examiner*, Glen Whitaker, watching him with open speculation. Bridger knew exactly what the man wanted. He'd been dogging him ever since he'd moved to Whitehorse, but more so since the death of Dr. Holloway.

The man could be a problem. Bridger knew he had to watch his step. At one point, he thought about telling Glen Whitaker the whole story, but he knew enough about Old Town Whitehorse to know that exposing the Whitehorse Sewing Circle would only make the residents close ranks even tighter around their secrets. Add to that, there was no proof.

And if there were records on the babies somewhere— which Bridger prayed there were—then he didn't want to do anything that might make those involved destroy them to protect themselves and the adopted babies.

The wind moaned in the tops of the nearly bare branches of the trees and scuttled along on the ground, kicking up fallen leaves as Titus read a short passage from the Bible, then asked if anyone had something they wanted to say.

"Titus suggested a graveside ceremony," Spencer had told him when they'd met at the cemetery. "Too many people for the community center. Better this way. Short and sweet. It's what Alyson would have wanted."

Or what Spencer wanted, Bridger thought. How well had Spencer known his wife? Bridger couldn't imagine that the subject of funerals had ever come up when they were dating. And they hadn't dated long before they'd decided to get married, from what he'd gathered.

Such a big decision to be made so quickly. He believed, as his adopted parents had, that marriage was for life. Maybe that is why he'd never met anyone he wanted to spend the rest of his life with—even before he found out he wasn't who he'd thought for the last thirty-two years.

Several residents stepped forward to say how badly they felt for Spencer, how much they missed Alyson. Bridger glanced down the hillside and spotted Laci at the edge of the trees. She wore all black, including a black hat that hid most of her blond hair.

Even from a distance he could see that her blue eyes were rimmed in red from crying. He wished he could go to her. Wished she'd give him a chance to explain his relationship with Spencer along with why he'd been at the wedding, why he was standing here with him now.

Beside him, Spencer followed his gaze to Laci, then shifted his feet and began to cry quietly, his body jerking spasmodically as if fighting to hold back his tears.

Bridger saw Laci's expression. Her face was set in fury and disgust as she watched Spencer, clearly not believing his grief.

Titus closed his Bible and said, "Let us pray."

Bridger bowed his head in prayer, unable to shake the bad feeling he had.

"Amen." He looked up to find Laci gone. A sliver of worry burrowed under his skin. If he knew Laci—and he was beginning to—then she wouldn't stop until she exposed Spencer for the man she believed him to be. A cold-blooded killer. But what worried Bridger more was even the slightest chance that she could be right.

LACI WAS HALFWAY down the hillside when Bridger caught up with her.

"Hold up," he said, sounding out of breath. "Hey, you all right?" He must have realized how stupid his question was. "Of course you aren't all right. Sorry."

She watched him look down at his dress boots, then up at her as if at a loss for words.

"I've missed you," he said. "I was hoping you'd come back to the restaurant. I need you."

She felt her heart deflate. He just needed a *chef.* "I told you—I have my own catering business."

"Laci, please, can't we at least talk about this?"

"There's nothing to talk about," she said and glanced past him to where residents were offering their condolences. Spencer, as if sensing her gaze, glanced up and looked right at her.

"Come on, Laci, don't let Spencer come between us." Bridger pulled off his Stetson and raked a hand through his hair. "And don't even try to tell me there isn't anything more between us than cooking."

She couldn't, even if she wanted to. They'd been amazing together. How could she tell him that she'd broken her vow to herself and—worse—as hard as she'd tried, she didn't regret what she'd done. In fact, all she could think about was being in his arms again.

"I have to go." She met his gaze. "I just need to sort some things out."

"Tell me this doesn't have anything to do with Spencer Donovan," Bridger said.

She couldn't, so she didn't even try. Turning, she walked toward her car feeling Spencer's eyes boring into her back like a bullet.

"Laci." Bridger caught up to her. "We have to talk about this."

"He's watching us right now," she said. "He's worried that I'm going to make trouble."

"He's not the only one. You have to let me explain about Spencer. I hate to see you so upset and angry."

"You don't believe he killed my friend," she said, daring him to deny it.

"No, I'm sorry, but I don't."

She started to turn away from him, but his words stopped her.

"I'm worried about *you*."

"If he isn't dangerous, then what's to worry about?"

"What you're doing to yourself. This anger you have toward Spencer. You have no evidence that he had anything to do with his wife's death."

"Not yet."

He pulled off his Western hat and raked a hand through his hair again. His hair was dark and thick, a little long at the neck. His skin was lightly tanned. There were tiny crow's-feet around his dark eyes. It caught her off guard just how sexy this man was, she noted now with irritation.

"This is what I'm talking about," he said. "This vendetta you're on. I know what it's like to get on a quest and lose sight of everything else. What if you're wrong about Spencer?"

"And what if *you* are?" She shook her head, tears burning her eyes. Bridger was the one person she needed to understand, but he was blinded by his friendship with Spencer. "I can't let him get away with murdering Alyson." She stole a glance past Bridger. Spencer was talking to her grandfather, but his gaze kept returning to her and Bridger. "If he's innocent, then why doesn't he like me talking to you?"

"I don't give a damn what he likes," Bridger snapped, his anger surprising her.

"Then why do you keep defending him?" she demanded. "You said yourself you hadn't seen him in years. How could you possibly know what he's capable of anymore?" She shook her head. Why *was* he defending Spencer? "What aren't you telling me?" Something. She could feel it.

When he didn't answer, she turned to leave.

He grabbed her arm. "Spencer saved my life."

She turned to stare at him, stunned.

He let go of her and sighed. "I told you we grew up together in Roundup, Montana. What I didn't tell you was that we were crossing a frozen creek near town one day and I fell in and went under the ice. Spencer jumped in after me, managed to break through the ice downstream and save my life. It almost cost him his."

She finally understood his loyalty to Spencer. "You were kids. He's changed," she said quietly, seeing the weight of this debt on Bridger. "I talked to the eyewitness. Spencer stood on the beach and let Alyson drown. By the time he went into the water it was too late."

Bridger looked away for a moment. "There's something you have to understand. Spencer got caught under the ice after he saved me. I called for help, but by the time we got him out he was unresponsive. While the EMTs were able to revive him, from that day on he was terrified of water."

"Then why a honeymoon in Hawaii?"

"When I ran into Spencer and he told me he was getting married and invited me to the wedding, he told me that Alyson had her heart set on Hawaii—and you said yourself she loved to swim. He said he didn't have the heart to tell her Hawaii was the last place he wanted to go."

Laci couldn't believe the way Spencer had set it up even before the wedding. "I have to go."

"Laci—"

"Did you know he's been following me?"

"What?"

"Every time I turn around, he's there. And that's not all. He's been leaving me presents."

"Presents?"

She saw the disbelief in his expression. "You think you know Spencer. Well, so do I. I know he's hiding something and I'm going to prove that it's murder." Her eyes locked with his. She wanted desperately for him to believe her, needed desperately for him to believe her, but saw that he couldn't because of the past he shared with Spencer Donovan. "You and I don't have anything else to say to each other."

"Apparently not, since you seem to have your mind made up no matter what."

She turned and walked to her car, not looking back. He didn't follow her. When she reached her door, she turned. Bridger had gone to his pickup and stopped to look back at her. Their gazes met and held for an instant. Then he looked away as he climbed inside his truck, started the engine and pulled away.

As she opened her car door, she saw another yellow rose was lying on the driver's seat. Only this time there was no doubt in her mind that it was a warning. Or who had left it for her.

She shot a look toward the gravesite. Spencer stood alone on the hillside, his head bowed over Alyson's grave. His features were in shadow, but she knew he was watching her out of the corner of his eye. Watching her. And Bridger.

CHAPTER EIGHT

LACI WENT STRAIGHT home and got on the internet to see what she could find out about Spencer Donovan now that she knew Bridger and Spencer had grown up in Roundup, Montana. She had a place to start, at least.

As far as the sheriff and the authorities in Hawaii were concerned, the case was closed, but she couldn't let it go. Her instincts told her there was a lot more to the story.

As she worked, she tried not to think about Bridger. What did she know about the man, anyway? Hardly anything. He was still as much a mystery to her as he was to the rest of Old Town Whitehorse and the county.

So why did she feel that she knew him on an even more intimate level than lovemaking? She remembered cooking with him in his kitchen, that feeling of being home. Isn't that why his friendship with Spencer felt so much like a betrayal?

She could just imagine what her sister Laney would have to say about it. Laney would flip if she even knew that Laci had been hanging around with the Mystery Man of Old Town Whitehorse, let alone having been to bed with him.

Or possibly worse—that Laci had broken her promise and was now about to go after Spencer Donovan. She typed in *Roundup, Montana* and *Spencer Donovan*, then waited to see what came up on the screen. It felt good to be doing something about Alyson's death even if it turned out she was wrong about Spencer, wrong about Alyson's drowning being murder.

A high school alumni website came up on the screen, and her heart began to pound as she stared at the photos. Apparently Spencer had been one of the popular kids, so he showed up in a series of random shots.

There were photos of a younger Spencer in both basketball and football uniforms. His motto, according to the caption under one of his photos, was Take No Prisoners.

But it was a photograph with one of his teammates that caught her attention. Spencer and a boy named Tom Simpson had apparently been close friends. The two were photographed together, Spencer's arm resting on Tom's shoulders, both of them grinning at the camera.

It didn't take her long to find Tom Simpson. Tom had become an attorney and still lived and worked in Roundup.

Laci copied down the information, grabbed her purse and headed for the door. She could be in Roundup in less than two hours. Too bad Montana had done away with its no-speed-limit law, otherwise she could be there even sooner.

BRIDGER WAS STOCKING the pantry at the restaurant, cursing himself because he couldn't get Laci Cavanaugh out of his mind and yet knowing the best thing he could do was get as far away from that woman as possible, when he looked up and saw his sister, Eve Bailey, standing in the doorway.

It was the expression on her face that stopped him cold. He quickly climbed down and ushered her to a chair.

"What's wrong?" he asked, still surprised how easily he could read her—but, then again, they had shared the same womb and the same genes.

"They were razing what was left of Dr. Holloway's office building and the construction crew found something," Eve said. "A steel box. The sheriff has taken it to his office and is trying to find someone who can open it. The lid got too hot in the fire. It's going to take a welding torch to open it. They aren't even sure the contents will still be intact." She stopped, tears in her eyes. "But this could be what we've been looking for."

He'd thought this moment would complete him. He was finally going to know the truth. He should have been ecstatic, but instead all he felt was anxious and strangely afraid.

He reached for Eve's hand and squeezed it, seeing that she, too, was shaken. "You've been waiting for this for so long," he said. For him it had only been months and yet it seemed like a lifetime.

"I'm scared," his sister admitted, something he knew was hard for her. Eve had the exterior of a porcupine. She hated to show any vulnerability. They had that in common. "We may wish the truth had died with Doc."

"We have the right to know who our mother was and, if possible, the circumstances of our conception and birth."

Eve smiled ruefully. "Having the right is one thing,

actually facing that knowledge…" She shook her head. "Isn't it enough to know we were adopted?"

"Maybe for you," he said, knowing she'd been as desperate as he was to know the truth. Had her desire cooled, as his had recently? "I want to know who she was, the circumstances, no matter what I learn." Was that true? He hoped to hell it was.

She nodded. "I told Carter to call us when he gets the box open. He's promised he will." She hesitated. "He's worried about what's inside, what it will do to you and me and the others, the Whitehorse Sewing Circle babies—the ones who don't know they were adopted."

She didn't have to add that the sheriff would be most worried about what the contents would do to Eve. Bridger had seen the love in that man's eyes for Eve Bailey. According to local scuttlebutt, Carter Jackson had hurt Eve back in high school, dumped her for someone else who he'd married and later divorced. But Eve was having trouble forgiving him. It didn't help that Carter's ex had almost killed her.

He could understand her lack of forgiveness. He was still wrestling with that, angry at his adoptive parents even though both were now dead. It was hard to trust again.

That's why he knew he had to distance himself from Laci Cavanaugh. He reminded himself that his interest in her had originally only been to find out what she knew about her grandmother's underground adoption agency.

Right. So how did he explain that he'd never gotten around to asking Laci about the Whitehorse Sewing Circle?

Because he'd found out that she cooked and he'd gotten sidetracked.

He knew it was more than that. There was something about Laci Cavanaugh that was captivating. An innocence. A mule-headed stubbornness. An enthusiasm about life that was contagious.

He shook his head. The woman also saw killers where there were none. The only smart thing to do was to give her a wide berth and not give Laci Cavanaugh another thought.

If only he could.

"If the records are in that box, we'll need to decide what to do with them," Eve was saying. "We've kept the adoptions secret and our relationship secret—"

"We only did that because there was no evidence," Bridger said, angry that Laci had gotten back into his thoughts. "If that box does hold information about the babies, I wonder how many there will be." He and Eve knew they weren't the only babies adopted out by the sewing circle. In fact, Bridger suspected their adoptions were just the tip of the iceberg.

"Carter's afraid Glen Whitaker might hear about what was found at the site," Eve said. "You know he's been poking around ever since we found out the truth."

Bridger nodded. "I saw him out in Old Town this morning. Let's hope he's still out there. But you have to realize this isn't something we're going to be able to keep quiet if that box holds the adoption records. Don't we owe it to the others to let them know? And I know people are wondering about our relationship."

"I guess that's something we'll have to decide when the time comes. Don't you sometimes wish you'd never learned the truth?" she asked.

Part of him definitely did. This whole thing had thrown a monkey wrench into his life, leaving him feeling off-kilter, unsure about the future, unsure about himself. Except when he'd been with Laci.

"Sometimes I do," he admitted. "But then I would never have known I had a twin sister."

Eve smiled. "A sister you didn't want any part of, as I recall."

"I'm still sorry that was how I felt originally. I was angry and upset. I thought you were in on it."

She nodded. "All water under that particular bridge now, huh?" She glanced at her watch. "I'm going to go by the nursing home and see my grandmother while I wait for Carter's call. He promised not to open the box until we're there. I hope you're right about Glen Whitaker being down in Old Town. I'd hate to see this on the front page of the *Milk River Examiner*."

But as she left, Bridger knew that the story coming out might be the least of their worries.

AFTER PHOTOGRAPHING ALICE MILLER's birthday party and eating too much cake and ice cream, Glen Whitaker got into his SUV outside the Whitehorse Community Center and checked to make sure he'd got enough photographs of the old lady and her friends.

He clicked on the digital photos, quickly reviewing what he'd taken at the party but more interested in the ones he'd gotten at the funeral.

He'd managed to get some of Spencer Donovan and Bridger Duvall standing together over the casket. Given the turnout, maybe his editor would deem it worthy of the front page.

Unfortunately, he hadn't been able to get an interview with Spencer Donovan. Glen had waited until almost everyone had left but Donovan. He'd gotten a few good photos of the man standing alone with the casket. And then he'd seen the mysterious brunette who was never far away when Donovan was around.

Glen had spotted her and even gotten several photographs before she'd seen him snapping her photo and taken off. Donovan had also seen the woman and had taken off right after that as though the hounds of hell had been after him.

And Glen had been left with the feeling that he finally had some bargaining power to get that interview. He dialed Spencer Donovan's cell.

"I told you I wasn't interested in—" Donovan started in the moment the reporter announced who was calling, but Glen cut him off.

"I know about the other woman," Glen said, bluffing, but he was rewarded with Donovan's sharp intake of breath. "We should talk."

"Do you know where the Banning ranch is?" Donovan asked.

"Of course." He checked his watch. He wanted to stop by Bridger Duvall's first. "I could be there in, say, an hour?"

"Fine. I'll see you then." Donovan hung up and Glen grinned to himself. So his suspicions about the brunette and Spencer Donovan had been on the money. He loved it when he was right.

So had Donovan hooked up with the brunette quickly after his wife's death? Or had the woman been there the whole time, waiting in the wings?

It certainly cast a new light on Alyson Banning Donovan's drowning in Hawaii.

As Glen drove down to the old McAllister place, there was no sign of Bridger Duvall's pickup. But then, he'd seen Duvall head toward Whitehorse after the funeral, no doubt back to his restaurant. It amazed Glen that the man didn't even have a dog to keep an eye on the place. He got out of his rig and walked toward the house.

Duvall's big black car was parked in the barn. The man at least had the good sense to buy a four-wheel-drive truck. It was required if you were going to live in this part of Montana and drive mostly unpaved roads.

He wondered if Duvall had already moved out of here. The place definitely had an unlived-in look about it, Glen thought as he peered in the windows before he tried the front door.

Unlocked. Which would make a man think Duvall had nothing to hide. Or, like a lot of these old places, the lock didn't work. He'd started to enter when he heard a vehicle coming up the road.

"Damn." He rushed to his rig, started it up and pulled around behind the barn just an instant before he saw a pickup top the rise.

Getting out, he edged to the corner of the building as the truck came to a stop in front of the house. He'd been betting it wasn't Bridger Duvall, and his instincts had proven him right.

Spencer Donovan climbed out of the pickup and glanced around as if looking for someone—and Glen swore to himself. Donovan had followed him!

At the front door of the house, Donovan knocked, then stuck his head inside. He had to know that Bridger wasn't here. But then, Donovan wasn't looking for Bridger, was he?

Glen realized that this must have to do with the brunette. He glanced down at his camera hanging around his neck. Donovan must know that Glen had photographs of the woman.

Glancing around, Glen spotted a pile of hay stacked against the side of the barn. He took off the camera and stuffed it deep in the hay, then went back to his spot at the edge of the barn, not looking forward to a run-in with Donovan if it came to that since he was trespassing.

Glen didn't see Spencer Donovan and was wondering where he had gone when he heard a metal clang behind him. He was frowning, wondering what had made that sound, as he looked back toward his vehicle but saw nothing.

He turned to peer around the end of the barn again, looking toward the house, worried about where Donovan had gone. That's when he heard the soft scuff of a boot heel on dirt directly behind him.

Glen spun around and came face-to-face with the business end of a shovel. He didn't even have time to raise his arm to deflect the blow. The metal made a hollow clanging sound as it struck, the pain blinding as it ricocheted through his skull.

His knees buckled as the ground came rushing up at him, but before he reached it he heard the second blow of the shovel—not that he felt it.

Glen Whitaker was dead before he hit the ground.

LACI WAS JUST leaving her house when the pickup Spencer Donovan had been driving came roaring up in her yard.

Before she could retreat back into the house, he was out of the truck and stalking toward her.

"What are you doing here?" Laci demanded.

"I have to talk to you," he said. "Could I come in?"

"No." She clutched the edge of the door, ready to slam and lock it if he came any closer.

"I don't understand why you're acting as if you're afraid of me," he said from the porch, sounding hurt.

"I *know*." It was out before she could call it back. "I saw the way you looked at Alyson at the reception."

Spencer stared at her. "What are you talking about?"

"You were on the dance floor. Alyson was visiting with one of the guests, and I saw your expression suddenly change." She saw the flicker of recognition in his eyes.

He stepped back, looked away, ran a hand over his face.

"I saw your face. I knew you were going to hurt her. I—"

"You're wrong," he said, raising his voice. "I thought I saw someone I used to—never mind. You think I killed my wife because of some look you thought I gave her? That's *crazy*."

"That's what you want everyone to think. But Alyson is dead. And we both know she was a strong swimmer."

"A much stronger swimmer than me," Spencer said. "That's why I wasn't with her." He looked away. "The truth is… I'm afraid of water." His gaze came back to hers.

"How convenient." She started to close the door. "And stop leaving those stupid yellow roses in my car!"

He blanched and looked around as if afraid someone had heard her. *"What?"*

"You heard me. Just leave me alone and stop threatening me." She stepped back to close the door, but he moved fast for his size. He stuck his foot in between the door and the jamb and shoved the door open, knocking her back as he took a step toward her. A scream rose in her throat as he grabbed her wrist, his fingers digging into her flesh.

"Don't do this," he said, his voice breaking. "You really don't want to do this."

She jerked free, scrambling toward the kitchen and the phone, praying she could reach it before he caught her. She jerked up the phone and dialed 9-1-1. The line began to ring. She turned, expecting to find him standing before her, ready to stop her.

But the kitchen was empty.

"9-1-1 operator. How may I help you?" the dispatcher said on the other end of the line.

Laci couldn't speak—just as she hadn't been able to scream earlier. She stepped cautiously to the kitchen doorway. Her front door stood open. She moved toward it.

"9-1-1 operator. Please tell me your emergency."

She hadn't gone far when she saw Spencer. He was walking down her driveway to his truck. She rushed to the front door, closing, locking and leaning against it.

"Hello?" the dispatcher said, sounding worried.

"I'm sorry. It was a false alarm." Laci hung up, her heart a sledgehammer in her chest. Tears blurred her eyes. She couldn't remember ever being so frightened.

She moved to the window, afraid Spencer was still out there, but his truck was pulling away.

She was right about him. Was it possible he would turn himself in now? She could only hope.

But in the back of her mind she kept asking herself: if Spencer Donovan was a killer, then why hadn't he come after her in the kitchen? Or was he just biding his time? Waiting for an opportunity to make it look like an accident, the same why he had Alyson's death?

All she knew was that she had to find evidence against him to get the case reopened—before she was next.

ATTORNEY TOM SIMPSON had an office uptown in a two-story brick building in Roundup, Montana, that said he wasn't as successful as he would have liked.

Laci hadn't called ahead, having a feeling that Tom wasn't going to want to talk to her. There was no secretary behind the front desk. Still at lunch, although it was almost two? Or on an errand?

Through his open door she saw him sitting behind his desk. He'd taken off his suit jacket. It hung on the back of his chair. She noted the gold wedding band on his left hand and a photograph of a woman and two small children on the corner of his desk.

He had his feet propped up on the old radiator by the window and was eating what looked like a turkey-and-cheese sandwich on white that his wife must have made him that morning for lunch but that he hadn't got around to eating until now. He was eating and gazing out the window, and for a moment Laci regretted that she had to disturb him.

"Mr. Simpson?"

Startled, he swung around and put down his sandwich as he reached for his suit jacket to cover up the mayo stain on his white shirt.

"Please don't let me interrupt your late lunch," she said, taking a chair across from his desk.

"I'm sorry—did we have an appointment?" he asked, glancing at his watch. "My secretary is out."

She shook her head and took a chair across from his desk. "I just stopped by to talk to you about Spencer Donovan."

Tom frowned. "Who?"

"Oh, you must remember Spencer Donovan." She'd photocopied several of the pages from the internet class reunion site and now passed him the one of the two young teammates grinning at the camera.

He took the sheet of paper reluctantly, barely glancing at it before handing the photo back. "Actually, right now isn't—"

"I'll be quick," Laci said, giving him her best smile. "Of course, your comments will be kept confidential."

"What is this about?"

"Spencer recently married my best friend. She drowned while swimming on their honeymoon." She refused to call it an accident and had to bite her tongue not to tell Tom that she knew Spencer had killed Alyson. But she feared he would take her for a nutcase and call the cops to throw her out if she didn't go at this carefully.

After her run-in with Spencer, Laci was more determined than ever to find evidence that would get Alyson's case reopened. She felt as if Spencer were a ticking time bomb. She had to act quickly—before her time ran out.

Tom Simpson looked sick to hear the news about the honeymoon death. "Poor Spencer."

Yes, poor Spencer. "I'd like to help Spencer through this but I don't know him very well. You knew him. Tell me about him."

"Well, it was years ago—"

"That's what I'm interested in. What was he like in high school?" she said, drawing her chair closer to his desk. "I just get the impression this isn't the first tragedy he's had in his life."

Tom looked sick. He picked up his sandwich, dropped it into the container it had been packaged in and shoved it into a desk drawer. She gave him time, knowing he was making up his mind about talking to her. Did that mean there was something to tell?

"I don't know what to say. He suffered some football injuries." He shrugged. "Other than that..."

She saw the change in his expression as he remembered something. "What?"

"Well, there was this girl in high school..."

Of course there was, Laci thought. "Don't tell me. She died, right?"

BRIDGER COULDN'T CONCENTRATE on work. He kept thinking about the box that had been found in the ruins of Dr. Holloway's office and what might be inside it.

And he couldn't help worrying about Laci. He'd hoped that telling her about Spencer saving his life would make her understand not only why he owed the man but also why Spencer couldn't have killed anyone.

But as short a time as he'd known Laci, he knew she wouldn't rest until she— Until she what?

He felt a jolt. Until she found out everything there was to know about Spencer Donovan. So why did that scare him so much?

His heart was pounding as he picked up the phone and called her home number, praying she would be home and not off investigating Spencer. No answer. He didn't leave a message.

He tried her cell. A message came up on the screen. Caller out of area? He swore as he hung up. Where had she gone? Who was he kidding? She'd gone to Roundup. She'd find out everything about Spencer.

But there was nothing to find. Laci would eventually realize she was wrong. She *was* wrong, wasn't she? He didn't believe for a minute that Spencer could kill anyone, right?

As if he'd conjured him up, the back door of the restaurant opened and Spencer walked in.

"The place is looking great," Spencer said, glancing around the kitchen before stepping into the dining room.

All the tables had come, as well as the chairs. The building was starting to look like a real restaurant.

There was art on the walls and tablecloths and candles on each table. With luck, the restaurant would be open before Christmas.

But Spencer barely gave the place a look. He appeared nervous as he glanced around the kitchen. "So where is your junior chef?" he asked, the question leaving little doubt he'd come here looking for Laci.

"Working up some menu ideas for me," Bridger said, wondering why when it came to Laci he lied to Spencer.

"Really? I thought I saw her heading down the highway out of town earlier."

Bridger felt his heart lodge in his throat. He'd forgotten that Spencer was staying at the old Banning place just down the road from Laci's. He had no idea where she was at this very moment, but he'd wager it was somewhere on the road to trouble.

"Did you need her for something?" Bridger asked, a little unnerved by Spencer's interest in Laci.

He seemed to hesitate. "I would imagine you know that she thinks I had something to do with Alyson's death."

Bridger winced. He'd known this was going to happen. "She's just upset."

"I don't think so. Someone had been in my house while I was gone. They'd gone through my belongings."

"Laci wouldn't..." Bridger let the words die off. In the state she was in, maybe she would. "I'll talk to her."

"Thanks, but I'm not sure that will do any good."

He studied Spencer, seeing a state of anxiety that worried him. "Something else?"

Spencer looked uncomfortable. "That reporter—Glen Whitaker? He called me earlier. He's been trying to get an interview. I finally gave up and decided to talk to him, but he never showed."

"That's odd." Bridger couldn't help but wonder why Spencer had agreed to talk to the man.

"I would imagine he's just doing the same thing Laci Cavanaugh is—digging for dirt. I really wish she wouldn't do that."

Bridger didn't know what to say.

"Sometimes I feel as if I'm losing my mind. I keep seeing her..." Spencer shook his head as if shaking off the horrific memory.

"It was an accident. You can't blame yourself. Alyson wouldn't want that."

Spencer nodded after a moment. "I froze. I stood there on the beach. Just the thought of going into the water..."

Bridger felt that old familiar anvil of guilt on his

chest. He was responsible for Spencer's fear of water. And because of that, wasn't he at least partially responsible for Alyson's death, as well?

"Spencer, if you hadn't jumped into that creek that day to save me…"

"I didn't bring it up to make you feel bad. It's just that you're the only person who can understand why I hesitated to save my own wife. It just brought it all back—the nightmares, everything from the past." Spencer rubbed a trembling hand over his face. "I'm not sure how much more I can take, you know?"

Bridger shifted uncomfortably on his feet. He didn't know what to say, let alone what to do.

Spencer seemed to pull himself together after a moment. "I've decided to leave town. I think as long as I'm around, it will only make things worse. I've put the ranch up for sale. Before you hear it from someone else, I've also sold the drilling rights to a gas and oil company. Apparently the land is worth more than Alyson and I thought."

Motive. Bridger swore to himself. Spencer had just provided a motive for murdering his wife. He tried to hide his surprise—and worry that Spencer might have known about the gas and oil *before* he married Alyson.

"I can't stay here with Alyson's best friend thinking I'm a monster," Bridger was saying. "I wish you could get her to stop this."

Yeah, Bridger thought, so did he. As if he hadn't already tried that. "What does it matter what she thinks? With you leaving, you'll probably never see her again." At least he hoped to hell that would be the case.

Spencer shook his head. "Still, it hurts me to think

that Alyson's best friend hates me. I know it shouldn't be messing with my head the way it is, but I don't think I can live with her believing I'm a murderer."

CHAPTER NINE

THE STEEL BOX sat on Sheriff Carter Jackson's desk, unopened, when Bridger arrived only moments after the call. Bridger had said goodbye to Spencer, unable to hide his relief that the man was leaving town.

Eve Bailey stopped pacing, her eyes locking with Bridger's as he stepped in and closed the door. It was the moment they'd both been waiting for. If they were right, the name of at least their mother and possibly the circumstances of their adoptions were in that box.

The sheriff lifted the lid and stepped back.

Just as Bridger had hoped, the box was filled with file folders, yellowed with age. He reached in and drew one out, handing it to Eve, before he took one for himself, his hand shaking as he opened it.

"It's the babies," Eve cried.

He barely heard her over the thunder of his pulse.

Eve sat down as if her legs would no longer hold her up.

Bridger's hands were shaking as he scanned the contents of the file in his hand and frowned. He picked up another and did the same before he swore.

"It's not here," he said as he flipped through more files.

"What?" he heard Eve say behind him. *"No."* She was on her feet, scanning the file in her hand. She threw it down on the desk and looked over at Bridger, tears in her eyes.

"What is it?" Carter asked, stepping closer. "Aren't they the adoption files?"

"Oh, they're the files, all right," Bridger said. "The answers are even here. There's just one problem—there are no names, no dates, nothing to know which of these files is ours."

"That's not possible," Carter said, picking up the file Eve had dropped.

Bridger studied the one in his hand. "These are worthless without the key to the code."

"Code?" Carter asked.

"At the bottom of every record," Bridger said.

Eve pulled out a file, read it and let out a curse. "You can't be serious. Animals and colors?"

"And flowers," Carter said from the sidelines. "I see what you mean."

Each file had the name of an animal, a color or a flower neatly printed at the bottom. Leave it to a bunch of old ladies to come up with *this*!

"So we don't know any more than we did," Eve said.

Bridger grasped a ray of hope. "We *will* know, though, once we have the key to the code."

"But I thought this would end it. I thought we'd finally know and it would be over, that we could quit wondering and searching," Eve said, sounding close to bawling. Carter stepped to her, wrapping her in his arms.

"It's more than we had, Eve. We're in here somewhere," Bridger said, holding up a handful of the files.

"We should be relieved that Dr. Holloway kept any records at all."

She nodded, clearly fighting tears, and burrowed
her face into the sheriff's chest. Suddenly the office
seemed too small, too intimate. Bridger put the files
back into the box.

"You'll put these away somewhere safe until we can
find the codes?" he asked Carter.

The sheriff nodded. "Don't worry. I'll take care of it."

Bridger glanced at Eve still in the sheriff's arms.

"I'll take care of that, too," Carter said.

Bridger nodded and smiled, happy that Eve and
Carter had each other. He'd spent so much of his life
alone and thought he was completely content with his
own company. Until Laci. Now he felt empty without
her. Did any of this matter anymore? He'd thought finding out the truth about his birth would fill that empti-
ness, but it had been Laci who'd filled it.

Once outside the sheriff's department, he dialed Laci's cell phone number again. It rang four times before
her voice mail picked up.

"Hey," he said, trying to hide his disappointment and
instantly at a loss as to what to say. "I was just thinking
about you." So true. "Call me, okay?"

He felt like a fool as he hung up. What was he going
to say when she called him back? *I miss you?* It was
true. Or maybe he'd say *I'm worried about you.* Also
true.

But what about what Spencer had told him? Had Laci
gone into Spencer's house, gone through his things?
Bridger didn't want to believe it. But he'd seen how
determined she was. He hated to think of her reaction

when she heard about the money Spencer would make off the Banning ranch.

The more he thought about it, the more anxious he became. Spencer had been acting so oddly at the restaurant earlier. Acting…afraid. Afraid of what Laci would find out about him? Or what the reporter already knew?

Snapping off his phone, Bridger walked to his pickup, hoping Laci called back soon. Better yet, that she'd get back here. Was there any chance Spencer knew where Laci had gone—and had possibly gone after her?

Spencer had been acting like a man with his back to the wall earlier. A *guilty* man.

Which would make Laci right. And make Spencer Donovan a dangerous man.

LACI TOOK A breath as she stared across the desk at Tom Simpson. "Tell me about the girl."

"There isn't much to tell, really," Tom said. "It was our senior year in high school. Spencer was dating a freshman named Emma Shane. He broke up with her. It was high school—you know how that goes. But Emma flipped out. She tried to kill him by attacking him with a knife at school. Failing that, she ran home and set her house on fire, killing herself and her parents."

Laci shuddered. "No one was able to save her or her family?"

"There was a large propane tank next to the house, but by the time the firemen arrived… The tank blew, completely incinerating the house and everyone inside."

"Was there any chance Spencer set the fire?"

Tom recoiled in shock at the question. "No, of course not. Spencer was with me. When the fire broke out, we were at football practice. We went over to see what was going on when we heard the sirens. Why would you ask that?"

She changed the subject. "Were you friends with Bridger Duvall, as well?"

"Not really. Bridger was two years younger. He didn't play football. He rodeoed. He and Spencer were neighbors but didn't hang out together in high school. If you know about Bridger, then you probably know that Spencer saved his life when they were kids. Made the front page of the paper. Spencer was a hero in Roundup."

She didn't know what to say. She'd thought the moment she heard about the girl's death she would have found *something* incriminating in Spencer's past.

"Emma had some mental problems," Tom was saying. "No one blamed Spencer for what happened, but I think he blamed himself. He wasn't the same after that. He went away to college. His family moved. As far as I know, he never came back to Roundup."

"End of story," she said more to herself than him.

"I'm afraid that's all I can tell you."

Another death. But Spencer Donovan apparently had nothing to do with it. Except for breaking up with the girl, who apparently had been unstable.

Just an unfortunate accident. Like Alyson's drowning.

"You two didn't keep in touch during college, then?" she asked, thinking maybe it wasn't all that strange. She'd lost track of people she'd known from high school—just not her close friends.

"Spencer went to Montana State University in Bozeman," Tom said. "I went to school in Arizona. Our lives took different paths."

"Do you know of anyone else who might have kept in touch with him?" she asked.

Tom shook his head. "Wasn't there anyone from here at the wedding?"

"No," she said, frowning. As far as she knew, Bridger had been the only person there on the groom's side. "Not even his family was there."

Tom shrugged. "His parents are probably gone by now. He was an only child, and both of his parents were older than the rest of ours."

She couldn't believe she'd hit another dead end. "Thank you," she said, getting to her feet and seeing his relief. "I'll tell Spencer hello for you."

"That's not necessary. I mean, he probably wouldn't even remember me."

She heard something in Tom's voice. He hadn't just lost track of Spencer, he'd let the friendship go. Was there a reason? Something that had happened other than the girl's death? Clearly Tom wasn't interested in having Spencer Donovan back in his life.

But as he retrieved his sandwich and took a bite, she knew whatever the reason, Tom Simpson wasn't going to tell her.

On her way out Laci noticed that his secretary, an elderly gray-haired woman, had returned and was sitting at her desk. She seemed about to say something to Laci when Tom called her into his office. She hurried in and closed the door.

Outside the building, Laci checked her cell phone and saw that Bridger had called several times. She listened to his messages, hearing in his voice how worried he was about her.

Who could blame him since it seemed she was trying to condemn a man for murder who'd had his share of bad luck already. A man who had nothing to hide.

"Hi," she said when Bridger answered. She knew she must sound a little contrite. And for a good reason.

"Hi." He sounded relieved to hear her voice. "You all right?"

"Yeah."

"I was hoping you might want to have some dinner with me tonight."

She glanced at her watch. "It would have to be late. I'm in Roundup."

"I figured. Everything okay?"

No. She felt hot tears burn her eyes. She'd been so sure about Spencer. Everyone had tried to tell her she was wrong about him, but she'd refused to believe it.

"I've been better," she admitted, realizing she might have been on this quest to convict Spencer of murder so she didn't have to deal with her grief over Alyson's death.

"Then a nice dinner might help?"

"Yes, it might," she said, smiling into the phone.

"Good. Just come by the restaurant when you get back to Whitehorse."

"Thank you. For everything," she added, feeling guilty and full of gratitude that he was being so nice after she'd been so awful about Spencer. "I'll see you soon."

"Laci? Be careful."

"I always drive carefully."

It wasn't until she hung up that she realized he might not be talking about her driving. She couldn't wait to see him, she realized as she dropped her phone back into her purse.

Now maybe she could put all this foolishness about Spencer behind her. Alyson was dead. She'd drowned in a swimming accident. Laci couldn't bring her back. She just had to accept that her best friend was gone. And no one was to blame for her death.

Wiping at her tears, Laci dug out her keys to open her car when she heard a door swing wide behind her.

"Miss?"

Laci turned to see Tom's elderly secretary motion to her. Curious, Laci stepped back toward the building.

"I overheard you asking about Spencer Donovan," the woman said conspiratorially. "I knew his mother. Bless her soul." She looked behind her as if afraid her boss might have seen her come out of the building. "You should talk to Patty. She owns the Mint Bar downtown." The woman looked as if she wanted to say more but suddenly clamped her lips shut. "Just talk to Patty," she said and, turning around, disappeared back into the building.

BRIDGER TOOK A few moments to enjoy his relief before he started planning what to make Laci for dinner. She'd sounded good on the phone. Obviously she hadn't found out anything incriminating about Spencer. Maybe now she could start healing.

He planned what to cook, only a little surprised how excited he was about seeing her again. All his attempts to exorcise her from his thoughts had failed miserably. He'd only been kidding himself that he wouldn't see her again.

Mentally he made his list on the way to the market.

But as he started back toward the restaurant, telling himself not to worry about Laci, he thought of the files he and Eve had seen earlier. They'd come so close to learning the truth about their birth.

Impulsively he turned the pickup around and headed out to the nursing home as he recalled his last visit and the woman who'd stopped by Pearl's room—Bertie Cavanaugh. He hadn't had a chance to speak to the woman. But he had plenty of time now, he thought as he checked to make sure Titus wasn't here visiting before he swung into the parking lot.

Bertie Cavanaugh was a large-boned, gray-haired woman with a perpetual scowl. She turned that scowl on him as he tapped at her open door.

Eyes narrowing, she demanded, "What do you want?"

"I'm Bridger Duvall," he said, although from her tone he suspected she already knew that. He stepped into her room, leaving the door open.

She sat on the end of her bed, a doll in her lap. When he'd first looked into her room, she'd been whispering something to the doll as she'd brushed its hair.

He knew this was probably a waste of time, but he had nothing to lose at this point. "How are you today?"

"Same as I always am," she snapped.

He tried a different tack. "What is your doll's name?"

She looked down at the toy in her lap and seemed surprised to see it. "Baby," she said with a soft, almost loving tone.

"She's pretty," he said, sitting down in the chair near the bed.

Bertie lifted her gaze to his, suspicion in her eyes again. "What do you want?"

"I want to know about the Whitehorse Sewing Circle," he said, sensing that there was nothing wrong with Bertie Cavanaugh's mind. "Were you a member?"

"For almost fifty years." There was pride in her voice as her chin came up.

"That's a long time," he said, trying to hide his excitement. Bertie would have been a member when he was brought to the old Whitehorse Cemetery to be adopted. But he worried that not all of the members might have known about the adoptions given how long the secret had been kept.

"Whose idea was it to use colors and flowers and animals as codes on the files?"

"Pearl's," she said without hesitation.

His heart was pounding so hard he thought it might burst. For the second time today he felt so close to learning the truth he could almost taste it.

"Who kept track of which symbol went with each baby?" he asked and held his breath.

Bertie studied him. "You're one of them, aren't you?" she finally said.

He nodded. "Thirty-two years ago my parents picked me up from a woman in the Whitehorse Cemetery."

Bertie nodded. "I recall hearing about that." She began to brush the doll's hair again.

"I need to know who my mother was."

"You know who your mother was," she said without looking up. "The one who took care of you."

"My *birth* mother."

Bertie let out an annoyed sound. "I'm tired. You should go. I have to get Baby's hair done before dinner."

"Bertie—"

"Leave," she snapped and met his gaze. "Leave before I call the nurse and tell her you were bothering me."

He rose from the chair. "I'm sorry I bothered you."

"Me, too," she said and went back to fixing Baby's hair.

As Bridger came out of the nursing home, he spotted Spencer standing beside his pickup, obviously waiting for him, and felt his stomach roil. This couldn't be good. He'd thought Spencer had left town.

"Visiting the old folks, huh?" Spencer asked, sounding amused. "You really are something," he said with a shake of his head.

Whatever Bridger was, it didn't sound like a compliment, and he realized that Spencer had been drinking. Great. As if things couldn't get any worse.

But at least Spencer hadn't followed Laci to Roundup.

"I just wanted to let you know I'm sorry."

"Sorry?"

Spencer wagged his head, looking close to tears. "You have no idea what I've been through. No idea."

Bridger couldn't argue that and didn't try. He could see that Spencer was even drunker than he'd originally thought.

"I just had to tell you that I'm sorry before I left. I won't be back."

Bridger tried not to let his relief show. "I'm sorry things didn't work out for you here."

"Sure you are," Spencer said sarcastically. "But they're working out for you. Things always work out for you, don't they, Bridger?"

He was surprised by the animosity he heard in Spencer's voice. "You aren't leaving tonight, I hope."

"Why, you worried I might kill myself on the highway?" Spencer's laugh was bitter. "That might be the best thing that could happen to me."

This kind of self-pity always put Bridger off. "Well, I wish you the best of luck."

"I'll need more than luck," Spencer said, sounding as despondent as he looked.

"You take care," he said as Spencer turned and disappeared into the shadows. A moment later the engine on his pickup engine fired up and Spencer left the lot in a hail of gravel.

"He's going to kill someone." Bridger reached for his cell, hating what he was about to do. But it was the best thing for Spencer—and whoever else was on the road tonight, including Laci. Maybe a night in jail would be the best thing for Spencer.

Or maybe it would turn out to be the worst thing Bridger had ever done to the man who'd saved his life. But he had a feeling he'd already done the worst thing he could do. He hadn't helped Spencer. Instead he'd fallen for a woman who was bound and determined to see Spencer behind bars for more than a night.

"So you want the goods on Spencer Donovan?" The woman's eyes shone with malicious humor. And alcohol.

Patty Waring had dark, straight hair cut chin-length, almond-shaped brown eyes and two empty shot glasses in front of her when Laci arrived at the bar.

"I was afraid you were going to miss happy hour," Patty said as she motioned to the cocktail waitress. "What are you having?"

"A diet cola," Laci told the waitress, who slid another shot in front of Patty.

"Killjoy," Patty said with good humor and patted the circular booth seat next to her. "So what is it you're looking for? And why?"

Laci liked the woman's straightforward attitude and decided her best approach was some of the same. "Spencer Donovan married my best friend—and she died on their honeymoon."

Patty leaned back, eyes widening, and let out a "Well, hell." She picked up the shot glass and drained it without blinking an eye.

"It seems he's had bad luck in his relationships with women."

Patty laughed. "That's one way of putting it. I assume Tom told you about Emma."

Laci nodded. "Everyone thinks he's innocent, including the police. The same with this girl Emma. Spencer had an alibi. But I can't help but believe there's more, something in his past, some indication of the kind of man he really is."

"Anyone mention what happened at college?" Patty asked.

Laci shook her head, knowing what was coming. Her heart began to pound in her ears, all her old fears rising like the tide. "What happened?"

"More bad luck. One girl he was dating fell down the stairs in her dorm. She swore she was pushed. Another got trapped in the laundry room with a spilled bottle of ammonia."

"Spencer's doing?"

"Apparently the girls thought so. But Spencer had an alibi each time. There was a rumor that the girls had broken it off with him and he'd been furious." Patty shrugged. "You've got to understand, I never liked Spencer. He was stuck-up in high school—you know, the real jock type. He acted like he didn't know me at college. So I only heard stories about him. Who can say if they were true or not?"

"Like about the girls at the dorm?"

She nodded. "The fiancée was a whole different thing, though. It was in the newspapers."

"Fiancée?" Laci couldn't hide her surprise.

"You didn't know he was engaged to be married?" She let out a little laugh and motioned for another shot. "Tiffany Palmer. Pretty, rich, naïve. Spencer only dated girls with money."

"What happened to her?" Laci asked, her heart pounding.

"In a nutshell? Hit-and-run driver. Killed on impact. Never caught the guy." She smiled. "The kicker? The description of the car matched Spencer's. However," she added quickly, "Spencer had reported it stolen two days before the hit-and-run. Rumor—that sweet little Tiff had been having second thoughts about marrying him. Seems she wasn't wearing her engagement ring when she was killed." Patty sat back and shrugged.

"But Spencer was cleared again?"

Patty nodded. "Airtight alibi for the time of the hit-and-run."

The waitress set another shot in front of Patty, but she didn't reach for it.

Laci let out the breath she'd been holding. "He could have hidden his car for those two days before the hit-and-run," she said, thinking out loud. "He could have set up the whole thing. Got someone to lie for him." She saw Patty's expression. "You don't think he killed her. Why?"

"Personally? I don't think Spencer has it in him. Plus, he had an alibi."

"He always has an alibi," Laci said. Still no proof. But another woman dead. How many bodies would it take before someone realized that this man was either walking bad luck or a killer?

"That wasn't the end of it, though," Patty said as she picked up the shot glass and turned it slowly in her fingers. Her nails were long and painted bright red with tiny little martini glasses on each tip.

"The fiancée's cousin also attended MSU. Christy wasn't like her cuz. She lived on my floor, and we became friends when she heard I was also from Roundup. Christy was convinced that Spencer had been after her cousin's money and had killed Tiff. Christy was determined to prove it. She started asking a lot of questions on her own."

Laci realized she hadn't touched her diet cola and took a sip.

"Spencer got wind of it."

"He threatened her?"

Patty laughed. "He was too smart for that. One night Christy came back to the dorm and she was freaking. Seemed every time she turned around, Spencer was there."

Laci felt a jolt. Just as Spencer had been turning up a lot around her.

"Then he started leaving her little souvenirs, and she just couldn't take it anymore. She went to the cops, afraid for her life, but of course she couldn't prove that Spencer had done anything, including stalking her. She quit school and that was the last I heard of her."

Laci's heart hammered. *"Souvenirs?"*

"Get this—a single yellow rose."

CHAPTER TEN

NOT FOR THE first time, Sheriff Carter Jackson got a call from the owner of the *Milk River Examiner* reporting that Glen Whitaker was missing.

It came on the heels of a call from Bridger Duvall about his friend Spencer Donovan. Carter had one of his deputies pick up Donovan. He'd just hung up when Mark Sanders called.

The problem with being a sheriff in a small town was that more people knew his home number than his office number.

"I hate to bother you at home," Sanders said in an excited, worried voice. "But Glen went out to Old Town to do a story on Alice Miller's ninetieth birthday party and hasn't been seen since. He knew I needed those photographs for tomorrow's paper. This isn't like him."

The sheriff remembered another time Glen had gone missing. That time he'd turned up beside a county road, beaten, his vehicle crashed in a ditch and with no memory of what had happened.

"You're sure he doesn't hit the bottle on occasion and this isn't like last time?" he asked.

"Absolutely not," Sanders said. "Glen doesn't touch the stuff. Something has to have happened to him."

The sheriff groaned to himself. "I'll send a deputy out to look for him. Was he planning to do anything else besides cover Alice's birthday party?"

"Not that I know of," Sanders said. "He's been trying to get an interview with Spencer Donovan…"

Great. "Okay, I'll do some checking and get back to you. You'll call if you hear from him?"

"I really need the photographs in his camera," Sanders said.

"I'll tell the deputy to be on the lookout for his camera," Carter said and hung up. He got on the radio and asked one of the deputies to drive down to Old Town Whitehorse and see what he could find out. He hoped Charlotte Evans wasn't up to her old tricks of taking out her frustrations on unsuspecting men.

Glen, he figured, would turn up. He did last time. Eventually.

IN A FOG of anger and grief, Laci got into her car to drive home. Grief for the senseless death of her friend. Anger not only that Spencer was a killer, just as she'd suspected, but that she might never be able to prove it.

Even if she could prove he'd left her the roses, it didn't make him a killer. And proving stalking in Whitehorse would be impossible. The town was too small—of course they would run across each other.

She was so upset that at first she didn't notice. But as she started her car, she sensed she was being watched.

There were a half dozen cars parked on the street. She didn't see anyone. But she couldn't shake the feeling that she wasn't alone. Spencer? Was it possible he'd followed her to Roundup? Or was it merely her overactive imagination in full swing?

As she pulled out, she glanced in her rearview mirror but didn't see anyone following her.

Unnerved and anxious to get back to Whitehorse—and Bridger—she drove faster than she probably should have. She knew her fears were justified. Was it just a matter of time before Spencer stopping threatening her with roses and set her up for an "accident"?

She was in such a state that she didn't even remember driving the hours to Whitehorse.

As she pulled up in front of the restaurant, she saw that there was a light on inside. She could see a shadow moving around in the back. Bridger. He was waiting for her with a nice dinner. He'd probably been cooking ever since they'd talked.

Her first impulse was to rush in there and tell him how wrong he was about Spencer Donovan. But in her heart she knew this wasn't Bridger's fault. Bridger hadn't known Spencer since they were kids. It wasn't fair to blame him. She could understand how he felt indebted to Spencer. After all, the boy next door had saved his life.

But she knew that wasn't why she couldn't spoil this evening. She needed Bridger to hold her, to make her feel safe, if even for a little while.

She couldn't go in there and tell him about Spencer. Not at first, anyway. What did she really have on Spencer? Nothing. Just like the cousin—Christy. The police in Roundup hadn't taken a single yellow rose as a threat any more than Sheriff Jackson would here in Whitehorse.

Laci sat for a moment, trying to pull herself together. *Don't spoil tonight.* She couldn't bear the thought Spencer would always be between them.

She saw Bridger come toward the front of the building. He must have heard her drive up, seen her headlights.

Just the sight of him warmed her to her toes. She thought of being inside his restaurant, thrilled to be with him. She cut the car's engine and climbed out.

He opened the front door of the restaurant, his smile so broad there was no doubt that he'd missed her. Maybe even as much as she had him. He looked so handsome standing there. She felt a wave of desire as she stepped into his arms.

He held her close. "I've missed you," he breathed against her hair.

"Me, too." They stood like that for a long moment, holding each other, then moved apart, both seeming a little awkward, a little shy.

"I hope you're hungry," he said.

"Starved." For food, for him.

He ushered her inside. She took a deep breath, taking in the wonderful scents of the food, of the man next to her, and thought she could die at that moment and regret nothing.

"I made something special," Bridger was saying as he smiled and took her hand.

She let him lead her into the kitchen. He'd set a table at the back, complete with candles. She felt a wave of sentiment for this man. Not love. It couldn't be love, not this quickly, could it?

She felt a little guilty as she sat down, saw all the work he'd gone to, but mostly she realized that he believed she hadn't found out anything in Roundup, that she was through trying to prove Spencer Donovan was a killer.

She could see his relief and couldn't bear telling him differently. At least not yet.

LACI HADN'T SAID anything about her trip. That worried Bridger. But he wasn't about to ask. He didn't tell her that he'd called the sheriff about Spencer or that he was half-ashamed for doing it.

The last person he wanted to talk about was Spencer.

But he did need to talk to her. He studied her face in the flickering candlelight, feeling a pull stronger than gravity. There would be nothing standing in their way soon. Spencer would leave town and no longer be between them. He felt a twinge of guilt—not for having Spencer picked up and thrown in jail for the night but for wanting him out of their lives.

"You're amazing," Bridger said to Laci.

She smiled at him as she pushed back her plate. "Amazing?" She shook her head. "I'm stuffed, though. It was wonderful."

He grinned, pleased. "I'm glad you liked it."

"I loved it. I've never met anyone who understood the importance of cooking."

He held his breath as his eyes locked with hers. He'd promised himself they wouldn't fall right back into bed.

"Come on," he said. "I don't believe you've ever seen my rooftop."

"Rooftop?"

He took her hand and led her out back and up a flight of stairs to the roof.

"What do you think?" he asked as he walked her to the front edge. "From here you can see the northern lights on a clear night."

"It's breathtaking." She hugged herself against the

cold night air, wondering why he'd brought her up here. "It scares me a little," she said, not realizing she'd spoken her fear out loud.

"Are you afraid of heights?" he asked, sounding alarmed.

"No, this thing between us. It's happened so fast…"

"You're afraid it isn't real."

She nodded.

"There is one way to tell."

She looked over at him, eager to hear it.

"One foolproof test that's infallible." He leaned toward her. "This."

His kiss was sweeter than the richest confection. She tasted him, reveling in the feel of his lips, the teasing of his tongue, the warmth of being wrapped in his arms.

His mouth sparked a desire in her that curled her toes. She felt fifteen again and knew just how dangerous that could be. Her lips parted and she drank him in. A sweet, deadly elixir. She felt intoxicated, drunk on this feeling and this man.

That alone should have warned her.

"Are we clear now?" he asked, drawing back to hold her gaze hostage.

"Perfectly clear," she said as he pulled her down for another kiss. She really had to get the recipe for this.

Bridger slipped his arm around her and pulled her closer. She raised her face to his kiss, her arms coming around his neck as her body pressed into his.

He held her, his mouth taking hers. She tasted faintly of vanilla.

For the last year since his mother had died he'd been searching for who he was. But holding Laci, he knew what he'd needed and wanted. He felt as if he'd found it. Nothing mattered but getting to know this woman. They'd skipped some of the steps. Like her, he felt they were moving too fast. It scared him, as well, because they didn't know each other.

At least Laci didn't know him.

He drew back to look at her. "Laci, there's something I need to tell you. Why I came to Whitehorse. Why I've stayed."

He told her everything, from what his mother had confessed on her deathbed to his visits to the nursing home to why he'd originally decided to open the restaurant.

Laci frowned. "You planned our meeting the first time."

He nodded but quickly added, "I never even got around to asking you what you knew about the Whitehorse Sewing Circle. Once I met you…"

"No one else knows about this?" she asked.

"I asked your grandfather Titus about it but he swears he knows nothing about it. I believe him. I had to tell you."

"So Eve is your twin sister?"

He nodded. "Some files were found, but unfortunately they're coded. Until we have the code…"

"And you're sure my grandmother is behind these adoptions?" she asked.

"I can't prove it until your grandmother regains her ability to speak."

She stepped away from him, hugging herself against the cold.

"We should go back inside," he said. "I didn't mean to just drop this on you, but I wanted you to know. I just thought you might like the view, and downstairs was a little too intimate. I needed a clear head. I was afraid of how you'd take the news."

She didn't turn to look at him. "Aren't you going to ask me if I know anything about the adoptions?"

"I don't need to. I know you would tell me if you knew anything." He placed his hand on her shoulder.

She turned, shrugging his hand off. "I'm sorry but I need to go home now."

"Laci—"

"I'm tired. A lot has happened. Thank you for a wonderful dinner, but I need to be alone."

"I've upset you. I'm sorry, but I had to be honest with you."

Laci nodded. "And I need to be honest with you." She told him everything she'd learned about Spencer Donovan, including about the yellow roses.

But as she finished she saw that he hadn't taken the threat seriously.

"They're *roses*."

"With *thorns*."

"Has he threatened to hurt you?"

"No. But don't you see? The man is dangerous. Women around him die or get hurt." She could feel her frustration growing.

"And I don't want you to be one of them," he said. "Spencer is leaving town. He's spending tonight behind bars. He isn't a threat anymore."

Bridger's logic infuriated her. "Maybe not to me, but what about other women?"

Bridger raked a hand through his hair. "We just keep going around about Spencer. Did you find proof that he killed any of the women? No. Or proof that he left the other women yellow roses?"

"You can't think it's a coincidence," she snapped.

"I don't know what to think. Frankly I don't want to think about Spencer at all. I want him out of our lives. I want you. I don't want to argue about Spencer. I hate it."

"Then quit defending him!"

"I feel like you put me in this position where I *have* to defend him. Even you admit you have no evidence of any wrongdoing on his part. The police and the sheriff have found nothing. Even if Spencer is leaving you the roses, they don't seem like much of a threat. And now that he's leaving town and right this moment behind bars…"

She shook her head, amazed at how furious she could be with him. He was so damned…fair. But he was wrong. "I don't think we should discuss this anymore tonight."

Bridger relaxed. "Good."

"I have to go."

He groaned. "I wish you'd stay."

She shook her head. "It's best I go." She turned on her heel and headed down the stairs, through the restaurant and to her car. Her head was spinning. She had needed him to take her side against Spencer. She knew it wasn't fair, but she didn't care.

Worse, she couldn't help thinking about what he'd told her. Her grandmother and the rest of the Whitehorse Sewing Circle had been operating an illegal adoption agency?

It was too bizarre to be believable, and yet she knew Bridger wouldn't have made something like this up. Especially given that apparently the sheriff knew all about it since he was dating Eve.

Laci stopped by the rest home. It was late, but she

just needed to see her grandmother. Pearl Cavanaugh's room was dimly lit. Laci stepped in, tiptoeing to the bed. Her grandmother was sleeping peacefully.

Laci bent down to plant a kiss on her cool, dry cheek. As she straightened, she felt tears blur her eyes. If only her grandmother would get better. If only she would be able to talk to Laci again. Laci missed their long talks. If her grandmother really was involved in something before her stroke, Laci knew she would have had her reasons. Laci really needed to hear those reasons.

Once outside again, she climbed in her car and drove the five miles to pull into her lane. The house was dark, the night even blacker. A wind had come up. It whipped the trees around the house and rocked her car as she got out and started toward the porch wishing she'd left a light on.

A coyote howled, making her jump. She glanced toward the Banning ranch. No lights were on. Bridger had told her that Spencer was in jail. She had nothing to worry about.

This time the note was stuck in the door. It dropped to the floor as Laci unlocked the door. Angry, she pushed into the living room, slamming the door behind her as she snapped on a light and ripped open the envelope with *Laci Cherry* printed on the front.

The words written inside shouldn't have shocked her. But they did.

Your mother's body is in the old Cherry house.

Laci dropped the note. It fluttered to the floor to land in a pile of broken glass. She stumbled back in surprise, finally seeing the room in front of her.

It had been ransacked: books thrown to the floor,

the couch cushions cut and bleeding stuffing, the lamps upended.

What struck her was that the house hadn't been burglarized—but vandalized instead. This was the work of someone who'd been furious.

She dug her cell phone out of her purse and was making the call to the sheriff when the front door banged open on a gust of wind.

She swung around, dropping the cell phone to snatch up the base of a lamp from an end table where it had been knocked over. She raised it as the door filled with a dark shape. Belatedly she realized that she couldn't have heard anyone drive up over the roar of the wind.

"EASY, IT'S ME," Bridger called as Laci started to swing the lamp base, ready to coldcock him.

She dropped the lamp and ran into his arms.

He could feel her trembling and near tears as he took in the room beyond her. He knew it wasn't just the ransacked house that had her upset.

After she'd taken off, he'd gone after her, fearing that she might be right about a whole lot of things. It was his fault that he'd let Spencer come between them. His guilt had made him defend Spencer even when he'd had doubts. Worse, he hadn't wanted to believe it. Even about the roses.

But who had done this to her house? Not Spencer— he was in jail. Was it possible he'd done this before Bridger had seen him and called the cops?

Laci pulled back to look up at him, her eyes a liquid blue that threatened to drown him.

"Here, let me do that," he said, taking her cell phone from her. He told the dispatcher what had happened. She patched him through to the sheriff, who told him to sit tight, not touch anything, he was on his way.

Bridger watched Laci kneel down to carefully pick up a note and envelope from the floor.

"The sheriff said not to touch anything," he told her.

"Too late," she said. "This was stuck in the door."

"Let's go wait in my truck." He led her out to his pickup and started the engine to clear the windows.

"This is the third one I've received," she said, handing him the note.

He snapped on the overhead light and read the note twice. "I don't understand."

"Someone has been leaving them for me."

"Why didn't you tell me about this?" he demanded, but her expression made it too clear why. He snapped off the light, pitching them into darkness. The only sound was the engine and the whir of the heater fan. "I'm sorry. I haven't exactly inspired your trust in me, have I?"

The night was mild for November, but only a fool wouldn't know it could snow at any time. This was Montana. Wait ten minutes and the weather would change.

Bridger looked out into the semidarkness. It was too dark to see the outline of the Little Rockies along the horizon. At first he'd missed mountains, but something about the prairie appealed to him. Its terrain appeared flat but was in truth filled with rocky, juniper-thick gullies and ravines. At first it also appeared harsh, barren, but it was neither.

He saw the lights before he heard the wail of the siren. It was going to be a long night—and nothing like he'd planned when he'd asked Laci to dinner.

He drew her to him as they sat on the bench seat of his pickup and waited for the sheriff.

"I need to ask you something," he said as he watched the sheriff's car grow closer. "Did you go through Spencer's house looking for evidence?"

Her eyes widened with surprise. "No. You think *he* did that to my house in retaliation?"

Bridger shrugged. He no longer knew what to think.

"I suppose you know about my parents."

He'd already heard the story and seen the old Cherry house.

"Every kid in town thinks the house is haunted," she said as the wail of the siren grew.

He didn't blame kids for thinking that. The first time he'd seen the house, it had given him an eerie feeling. Finding out that there'd been a murder/suicide in the house had certainly added to that.

"So you don't remember your father's parents?" he asked.

She shook her head. "From what I can gather, we seldom saw them before the...tragedy." She chewed at her lower lip for a moment. "I was too young to remember them. I can't even remember my parents."

"You had your grandparents. I had my adoptive parents," he said. "But it still doesn't keep you from wondering about your real parents, does it?"

"I'm sorry I got so upset earlier," Laci said. "I'll do what I can to help you find your birth mother."

He smiled. "Thanks."

"I know what it's like not knowing your mother. In my case, both of my parents." She sat up straighter as Sheriff Jackson pulled into the yard and cut his lights and engine.

"What is this?" Laci asked as she picked up something from the floorboard.

He looked up to see that she was holding the photo album he'd found in the basement of Doc Holloway's house. He'd tossed it on the seat, but it must have fallen to the floor on the drive out here. Once he'd made up his mind to go after her, he'd been in a hurry, hating the way they'd left things.

Laci snapped on the overhead light and ran her fingers over the cover of the album. He'd pretty much forgotten about finding it, he'd been so busy with the restaurant. And Laci.

She flipped the album open to a page with photographs.

"It's just an old album I—" Her shocked expression stopped him. "You recognize the girls in the photographs?"

Her voice broke as she asked, "Where did you get this?"

"In an old house owned by Dr. Holloway." Was it possible the girls in the photographs were part of the adoption ring, just as he suspected?

He saw that Laci's hands were shaking as she clutched the photo album to her chest, her eyes filling with tears.

"This had to have belonged to my mother. She took the album with her when she left. The photos are of me and my sister Laney."

CHAPTER ELEVEN

"Okay, calm down," Sheriff Carter Jackson said as he and Laci and Bridger congregated in his office later that night. "I have forensics coming to go through your house to see what we can find, but I have to tell you, I doubt whoever did that to your house left any fingerprints."

"I'm more concerned about the notes about my mother, especially after discovering this album," Laci said.

Carter nodded. "How can you be so sure it's your mother's, the one she took with her?"

"I remember my grandfather saying it was blue, my mother's favorite color," Laci said. "I'd appreciate it if you wouldn't tell him about it at this point, though. I know how much it's going to upset him."

"I assume for that reason you also haven't mentioned the notes to him?" Carter asked.

She nodded and dropped into a chair across from his desk. "You think they're just a prank, don't you? But what if my mother never left town, just like the note says? What if she's buried in that house?"

"It doesn't explain how her photo album ended up in Dr. Holloway's house, either," Bridger pointed out.

"Especially given what we know about the doctor's connection to the adoption ring. I told Laci."

Sheriff Jackson didn't look happy to hear that. "Let's not jump to any conclusions."

"Unless Dr. Holloway had something to do with her death," Bridger said.

The sheriff shot Bridger a look. "Let's try to keep to the facts. I'll go out with some men and we'll see what we can find at the house. But let's keep in mind—it's been almost thirty years. If someone around here knew about this, why would they decide to tell you now?"

"I've wondered about that. Maybe the person is dying and has to get this off her conscience," Laci said. "Or maybe she's been gone all these years." She saw the look the sheriff gave her. "It doesn't mean the person doesn't know what she's talking about."

"She?" Carter asked.

"It feels like a woman is writing the notes to me," Laci said and shrugged.

"I did some checking," Carter said. "A friend of your grandmother Cherry's is in the nursing home. The nurses found her in your grandmother Pearl's room."

Laci sat up in alarm. "Is Gramma Pearl all right?"

"She's fine."

"Who is this woman who was a friend of Alma Cherry?"

"Nina Mae Cross."

"Eve Bailey's grandmother?"

Carter nodded. "Nina Mae has Alzheimer's so there's no way she sent you the notes. But there's a chance another woman at the nursing home took it upon herself to do it based on something Nina Mae had been saying."

"And this is the first time you mentioned this to Laci?" Bridger demanded.

Carter sighed. "Given Nina Mae's mental state, there was no reason to suspect that she knows anything about Geneva Cherry's whereabouts. Also, the notes Laci gave me had no fingerprints on them. It is doubtful that an elderly person living at the nursing home would make sure her fingerprints weren't on anything."

"Who was the woman who you think sent the notes?" Bridger asked.

"Bertie Cavanaugh."

"My great-aunt?" Laci said and saw Bridger's surprise.

"I found some stationery in her room that matches that of the notes," Carter said. "But it's a common brand sold at the drugstore in Whitehorse. Meanwhile, we'll search the old Cherry place."

"What are the chances there's something there to find after all these years?" Bridger said. "Laci said kids have played in that old house as far back as she can remember. You would have thought they'd have found anything of interest years ago."

"Unless…" The words caught in Laci's throat. "Unless the body is in the root cellar under the house."

Sheriff Carter shook his head. "Your grandfather had one of the local masons brick up the entrance years ago."

Rumor was that the root cellar was where her grandfather Cherry had taken his wife and killed her before taking his own life.

"Who does the house belong to?" Bridger asked, frowning.

"It was put up for auction for taxes after the incident," the sheriff said. "There were no offers on it. So I believe it belongs to the county."

"My grandfather had it bricked up after my mother left?" Laci asked, her voice sounding strange to her.

Carter nodded. "We'll reopen it tomorrow. If there is anything down there to find, we'll find it."

"Anyone ever figure out why Cherry did it?" Bridger asked.

"There was no note and no sign of a problem, according to the file I looked up about the deaths," the sheriff said.

Laci rose unsteadily from her chair. "When will you do it?"

"At first light—but I don't want you anywhere near there," Carter said.

She started to argue, but Bridger stepped in. "I'll go," he said more to her than the sheriff. "I'll be there and I'll call you as soon as we know something." He turned to face the sheriff. Laci could see the determined set of his jaw.

Carter looked as if he was going to object but must have seen it would be better than having Laci anywhere nearby. "Okay, Laci. Bridger comes as long as he stays out of the way—and you are nowhere near the place, agreed?"

Laci had no choice but to agree even though she knew she would go crazy until she heard. And she knew that Bridger knew it, as well.

He grabbed her hand and squeezed it as he pulled her to him and gave her a quick kiss, his gaze locking with hers. "Will you be all right alone in my apartment over the restaurant?"

"I'll be fine. Later I'll go down to the restaurant and

bake something," she said, holding up the key he'd given her earlier that night.

"Good thinking. Just keep the doors locked." He turned to the sheriff. "You picked up Spencer this evening for driving under the influence, right?"

Carter nodded.

So Spencer was under lock and key. Now all she had to worry about was what was in the old Cherry house.

The next morning she watched Bridger leave with the sheriff and the deputies in one of the patrol cars, headed for Old Town Whitehorse. It took all her self-control not to follow them, but she knew the sheriff well enough to know he'd meant what he'd said about her staying away.

Carter had allowed Bridger to come along only to keep her away. If she showed up, she was certain the sheriff would send Bridger away, as well.

She was too antsy to stay in the apartment—or even to cook. She decided to go see her grandmother.

AT THE NURSING HOME, her grandmother glanced toward her as she entered. Laci thought Gramma Pearl's eyes brightened, but it could have been just the light.

"Hi, Gramma," she said, taking the chair next to the bed. She was so anxious she feared her grandmother would sense it and it might cause the elderly woman more stress. She shifted her thoughts away from her mother and the old Cherry place and what was going to happen there and thought of Bridger.

Just the thought made her smile. "I think I'm in love." She grinned at her grandmother and thought she saw amusement in Pearl's gaze. "I know—you've heard it all before. Since first grade, huh? But this time, Gramma, I think it's the real thing."

She took her grandmother's hand. "It has me a little worried, though. I wish Laney was here so I'd have someone to talk to about it. Laney's still in Hawaii on her honeymoon."

Laci thought she felt her grandmother squeeze her hand. "Her husband Nick is really wonderful. He's a deputy here in town. They'll be home soon and we'll all be together again."

She just wished they'd be here for Christmas—and the restaurant opening.

"Oh, did I mention…I'm probably going to be working in a restaurant. My catering company didn't exactly take off. I think it was fate, my meeting the owner of a restaurant and a man who loves to cook as much as I do. Bridger Duvall is like no other man I've ever met."

There was no mistaking it: her grandmother's hand tensed. Laci looked into her grandmother's eyes and saw…what? Fear? Panic?

"It's okay, Gramma." Her grandmother's eyes had filled with tears and she seemed to be having trouble breathing.

Laci reached for the nurse's call button, alarmed by her grandmother's reaction.

A nurse came hurrying in. "What happened?"

"I don't know. I was just sitting here talking to her." Laci moved out of the way so the nurse could check her grandmother. "Is she all right?"

"Her pulse is up. She seems upset. Let's let her rest now. Maybe you could come back later."

Laci nodded, backing out of the room. Her grandmother's eyes followed her, the fear and panic still there.

IT WAS ONE of those gray days, the clouds low, the light dim like an early dusk.

Bridger stood outside the old, dilapidated Cherry house, huddling against the brisk wind. It was only weeks from Christmas. What snow had fallen in the middle of November had blown into deep drifts that had filled in the barrow pits and piled up like frozen waves beside buildings and fence lines, leaving the rest of the land clear.

One such sculpted drift ran along the lee side of the house and stood a good five feet tall.

He stared out across the wind-scoured land. He'd often wondered what he was doing here. More to the point, why he stayed. As the wind howled along the rotting eave of the house, he thought he knew the answer.

His adoptive mother had sent him here. He'd been lost. Lost and restless. True, he'd felt he didn't know himself and wouldn't until he found out who his birth parents had been.

Whitehorse had just been a stop-gap. He'd never dreamed of staying here when he'd rented the old McAllister place. Now he had a restaurant that would open in a matter of days, even ahead of schedule.

He smiled to himself. He'd never believed in fate. He'd always thought he made his own fate, just as he made his own luck. But if he hadn't come here, he would never have met Laci Cavanaugh.

Behind him, the deputies unloaded the equipment and the cadaver-sniffing dog from the vehicles.

"Just stay out of the way," the sheriff said to him not unkindly.

Bridger nodded and followed the men toward the front steps of the house, standing back as one of the men removed the sheet of plywood covering the door before breaking open the nailed-shut door to shine a light into the darkness inside, then motioning for them to follow.

LACI WAS SHAKEN as she drove to the restaurant and entered through the back. She couldn't imagine what had upset her grandmother. It wouldn't be like Gramma Pearl to get upset over Laci's change of career plans.

Not after Laci had changed her major at college a half dozen times.

She pulled out a pound of butter and cut it into the mixing bowl. Cookies. She would bake something rich and wonderful for Bridger. She was debating which of her favorite recipes to use when the back door opened and she realized she'd been so upset over her grandmother that she'd failed to lock it.

Spencer Donovan stepped into the kitchen, the door closing behind him. She stared at him in shock.

"I thought you were in jail," she cried, backing toward the knife rack. She grabbed a wide-bladed knife and brandished it front of her. "Stay away from me!"

"Laci, have you gone crazy?" Spencer asked, stopping just inside the kitchen doorway.

"Get out of here or I'm going to call the sheriff."

"The sheriff is down in Old Town and we both know it."

"How did you get out of jail?"

"It pays to have the best lawyer that money can buy," Spencer said, glancing around as if looking for Bridger.

"Bridger will be back any minute," she said.

"No, he won't," Spencer said with a sigh. "He went off with the sheriff down to Old Town." He stepped toward her. "You have everyone suspecting me now. Even Bridger, the one person who was on my side."

"Don't." She held the knife in front of her. "Don't come any closer."

He stopped and shook his head as if confused. "Why don't you listen to what I'm telling you? I didn't hurt them. I loved them. It wasn't me. If this doesn't stop…" His look appeared filled with worry. "It's not safe."

She stared at him, fear making her heart thunder in her chest. The knife in her hand began to shake as a tremor moved through her. Spencer was sick, just as she'd suspected. Why else would he hurt the women he'd supposedly loved? She gripped the knife tighter and stepped toward him. "Get out."

His gaze focused on the knife blade. He took a step back. "I never wanted anyone to get hurt. You have to believe me. I'm leaving town. I just wanted to see you and warn you to stop talking to people about me. If you don't, you're going to end up like the others." He mumbled the last words as he backed toward the door.

She waited until she heard the back door close before she rushed to lock it, shaking from her encounter and more convinced than ever that Spencer Donovan was a dangerous man.

THE POSTER ON the front door warned trespassers would be prosecuted. Bridger followed the others through the open door into the house.

The smell as he stepped inside wasn't just that of a closed-up house, that old, musty, vacant odor. This scent was one of decay.

Bridger glanced over at the sheriff and saw his face was tightened with dread.

There were piles of old clothes and broken pieces of furniture. The woodstove looked as if it had been used in the last thirty years, which meant a vagrant could have been staying here at one time. Or local kids had been using the place as a hideout.

"Watch for rattlesnakes," Carter said as they moved across once-sealed hardwood floors that were now grayed and buckled with age and water and ruin.

The smell of the house was bad enough. And while he wasn't afraid of rattlesnakes, Bridger also didn't much like surprising one, either.

His biggest fear was that they would find Laci's mother's body in this horrible old house. If a place could harbor evil, it was these four walls.

He didn't need anyone to tell him that something horrible had happened here. He could feel it. Just as he could imagine old man Cherry taking his wife down to the root cellar. She had to have known what he'd planned to do.

It didn't help either that Bridger had never liked small, dark places. His aversion stemmed from being accidentally locked in a trunk while playing with some neighbor kids when he was five.

They searched the upper floors of the house first, then one of the deputies opened the basement door. A wave of stale, freezing, putrid air wafted up. Bridger saw the deputy look to the sheriff.

"I'll go first," Sheriff Jackson said, and the rest of them followed him down the creaking wooden stairs, flashlights bobbing into the dark hole of the floorless basement and root cellar.

Bridger was only thankful that Laci would never have to come down here.

The basement was full of junk. He thought he heard something slither away into a dark corner. Mice?

To one side of the basement was an opening that he assumed had once led to the infamous root cellar. The opening had been bricked in.

"Let's open it up," the sheriff said, and two of the deputies removed sledgehammers from their gear and went to work.

The sound of steel against stone echoed like gunshots through the cold, still basement.

Bridger stood back, praying they wouldn't find anything but fearing they would. No one knew why the Cherrys had died down here. Not even the closest neighbors could know what went on behind closed doors.

Marriages were never as they appeared from the outside. He thought of his own parents. He'd never heard them raise their voices in anger toward each other. Their love for each other gave him strength but also set the bar so high he'd feared he would never have that kind of relationship. Until Laci.

Except he wasn't his father's son. He'd always feared he would never measure up to his father. He didn't have his adoptive mother's forgiving heart or his adoptive father's calm, cool disposition. And for a very good reason, as it turned out.

The pounding stopped. The bricks lay in rubble beneath a huge dark hole large enough to climb through.

Carter handed him a flashlight and ordered one of the men to remain there. The other deputies picked up shovels and stepped through the hole after the sheriff. Bridger followed the cadaver dog.

The first thing that hit him was the smell of something dead. He'd grown up on a ranch, and it was a smell he knew only too well.

He took shallow breaths as he moved along the wooden shelves filled with dozens of dusty quart jars, the contents murky and indiscernible. Bridger swore under his breath. What a horrible place to die.

Ahead, the sheriff and two deputies had stopped at a spot where the dirt floor rose in a hump like that of a grave. The dog was already there, leaving little doubt as to what they would find.

A deputy turned up a spade full of dirt. Bridger heard the shovel strike something on the second attempt and watched with dread as the blade turned up the first bone.

CHAPTER TWELVE

"THE REMAINS ARE that of a male, late twenties or early thirties, and they definitely haven't been there thirty years," Carter said when Laci arrived at the sheriff's office. "It's not your mother."

Laci dropped into a chair and closed her eyes, fighting tears. "Then why would someone send me those stupid notes?"

The sheriff shook his head. "I can only assume the person knew about the bones and thought they were your mother's. We found another entrance to the basement from the outside that has been used since the root cellar was bricked up."

"That would explain the lights people have said they've seen inside the house," Laci said.

Carter nodded. "Clearly there's been someone using the old house. From some of the paraphernalia we found, it appears to be drug users."

"If the bones aren't my mother's, then whose are they?" she asked, drawn back to what had been found in the old Cherry house.

"I'll know more after I get the results from the crime lab," Carter said. "I'm checking missing-persons reports now. The coroner says the remains have been in the root cellar for under ten years."

"What can we do if Spencer hasn't left town?" Bridger asked. "I don't want him threatening Laci again."

"Unfortunately, the way this works is unless he breaks the law, there isn't much we can do," Carter said. "Laci can get a restraining order against him—"

"A piece of paper isn't going to keep Spencer away from her," Bridger snapped.

The sheriff nodded. "If he contacts you again, Laci, I'll have him picked up. But you've seen how long I was able to hold him the last time. Unless he commits a crime…"

"What about the photo album Bridger found in Dr. Holloway's house?" she asked, thinking of her mother.

"We checked the house, Laci, but it's been thirty years. Any evidence that might have been there is long gone. We didn't find anything. I'm sorry."

"Why would the album be there?" She knew what she wanted him to tell her. She needed a good explanation for her mother leaving the album in an old house in Whitehorse—an explanation other than her mother leaving it behind because she never left town alive.

He shook his head. "Your guess is as good as mine, I'm afraid. I really think you should talk to your grandfather about it. There might be some simple explanation."

She got to her feet and Bridger followed suit. She wished she could go back to believing her mother was alive and living somewhere far from here.

"Well, thank you for letting me know about the bones you found." She wished she knew what to feel.

Bridger put his arm around her as they left. "I'm not

letting you out of my sight until Spencer is gone for good," he said once they were outside.

She rested her cheek against her chest. "Sounds good to me."

BRIDGER AND LACI spent the next few weeks getting the restaurant ready for its grand opening.

Bridger was relieved that there had been no sign of Spencer. At Laci's insistence, the sheriff was doing more digging into Spencer's past, talking to Patty Waring and others. Laci's biggest fear was that Spencer would trap another woman in his deadly snare.

Bridger convinced himself that Spencer would lay low for a while. He would know that he was being investigated even further. That alone worried Bridger, though. He'd seen how upset Spencer had been when he knew that Laci thought he was a killer. Why else had he stopped by yet another time to warn her off?

But the fear that the investigation would make Spencer return to Whitehorse waned as the days passed. Bridger was starting to believe they would never see Spencer again.

As the grand opening night of the restaurant drew near, the town of Whitehorse took on the look of the coming Christmas holiday. Bright colored lights adorned the town square, shops sported dancing Santas and snowmen and Christmas music played on the town's only radio station from morning until night.

Bridger found himself getting into the holiday spirit. He'd anguished over finding the perfect gift for Laci for weeks now. At his insistence, she'd moved into the apartment over the restaurant with him. That way she was always close by—usually right there in the large restaurant kitchen with him as they planned every detail for opening night.

Her grandfather Titus hadn't taken the news well—even after Laci had explained about Spencer. But Titus has been cordial enough since then, and Bridger had begun to think everything might work out yet.

Spencer was gone if not forgotten. Bridger's dream of a restaurant was about to come true. And then there was Laci... He smiled to himself at the thought of her.

They spent much of their time either cooking or upstairs in his bed, making love. Their lovemaking went beyond touch, beyond desire, beyond pleasure. They came together as if it had been destined long before they were born.

It seemed too good to be true.

He feared that someone would come along and take it away from him. Spencer Donovan, perhaps.

Just as his mother had taken away his idyllic memories of childhood when she'd told him he'd been lied to about who he was.

"You look worried."

He glanced up to see Laci standing across the kitchen, studying him.

"Is it about opening night?" she asked.

"No, it's nothing," he assured her as he stepped to her, taking her in his arms. "It's nothing, really."

LACI KNEW HE had to be nervous. All this work and finally here it was—opening night.

She wouldn't have given anything for the time they'd spent together getting the restaurant ready. The days had flown by as if in a dream. And now, finally, it was opening night. She was determined that nothing would spoil this for Bridger.

Laci had been baking cookies for several days now and freezing them for the holidays. She would miss her sister and Maddie. Christmas wouldn't be the same. But she would be spending the holidays with Bridger and she was crazy about him. So it would all be fine.

She realized as she leaned into Bridger that she hadn't thought of Spencer in a long time. She felt a stab of guilt. That also meant she hadn't thought about Alyson. She knew she'd done everything she could. Not that it had helped.

"Don't worry," she told Bridger. "Tonight will be a night you'll never forget."

He chuckled. "Let's hope that's because it's a success and not a disaster."

"Oh, don't be silly. With my desserts, how can it miss?" she joked.

He drew back to look at her. "I know I should wait until Christmas…"

She felt her heart kick up a beat.

"…but I have a little something for you." He reached into his pocket and pulled out a small red envelope.

Her fingers trembled as she took it.

"This is just the first part of your Christmas present."

She smiled uneasily as she ripped open the envelope and took out the single sheet of folded red paper. A check fluttered to the floor, dropping like her heart. "My paycheck?" She'd thought they were in this together. Now she realized he saw her as just an employee. And a lover.

"Read the note," he said as if sensing her disappointment.

She read the note. Twice. "You want me to be your partner in the restaurant?" Her voice broke.

"I do. The check is for all your work. I know you have your heart set on your own catering business, but I hope you'll take my offer."

She didn't know what to say. Or to feel. "I need to think this over." She couldn't help her surprise. Or her disappointment. What had she expected? A proposal of a different kind? It was way too soon. He was offering her half of his restaurant, Northern Lights.

But as the rest of the staff came in to get ready for the opening, she knew what she really wanted Bridger to offer her was his heart.

SHERIFF CARTER JACKSON got the call at home as he was getting ready to go pick up Eve for the grand opening of her brother's restaurant.

"Sheriff? It's Deputy Ryan. We just found Glen Whitaker."

Something in his deputy's voice warned Carter that the news wasn't good.

"It appears he was bludgeoned to death with a shovel," the deputy said, taking Carter by surprise. He'd expected a car accident. Or a heart attack. Anything but murder. And as the days had passed, he'd started thinking maybe Glen had just up and left town.

Carter swore under his breath. "Where?"

"Found him and his vehicle out behind a barn at the McAllister place. I'd say, from the looks of him, he's been here for a while. Also, we found his camera. It was stuffed into some hay bales behind the barn for some reason."

"Don't let anyone touch the camera. I'll call the coroner and meet you out there." Carter hung up, still shocked, and called Eve to tell her he was going to be more than late. And he'd been so looking forward to tonight. In fact, he'd planned to pop the question after dinner.

"It's fine," she said when he reached her. "McKenna is home. She'd love to go with me. Meet us there if you can."

As Carter drove toward Old Town Whitehorse, he wondered what Glen had been doing at the old McAllister place. And where had Bridger Duvall been at the time? For weeks Bridger had been living in the apartment over the restaurant with Laci Cavanaugh. And the hidden camera? None of it made any sense. But then, murder was often senseless.

He told himself that no way did Bridger have anything to do with this. Unfortunately, Glen had been killed on property being rented by Bridger. Still, why would Bridger want to kill Glen? Why would anyone want to kill Glen, for that matter?

Carter just hoped that Eve's brother had an airtight alibi.

LACI PEEKED THROUGH the swinging doors to see Bridger shaking hands with the patrons. She glowed with pride. Bridger had done it. Northern Lights was a huge success.

Bridger spotted her almost as if he'd sensed her there, almost as if he'd missed her. He smiled, a smile that was so brilliant it was blinding, and motioned for her to join him.

She nodded but didn't move as other departing guests called him over so they could congratulate him. Dinner had been over for some time, but many of the locals had hung around even after the help had cleared the dishes and cleaned the kitchen and left.

Laci loved seeing the way the town was supporting

the restaurant and Bridger. She felt as if she would bust with happiness, and the thought came pouring out of her as if from some deep well of emotion inside her.

She loved him.

She *loved* Bridger Duvall.

Not like the other times she'd been in love. This time was different.

The realization should have panicked her. Would have panicked her if she'd had more than an instant to think it.

An arm circled her waist, drawing her back from the door at the same instant a cloth was clamped over her mouth.

She drew a breath to scream but only managed to draw in the sickening smell of the chemical on the cloth.

The room began to swim. She tried to fight off her attacker, but it was useless. As she was being pulled toward the back door, she blindly grabbed at the counter for something to use as a weapon to defend herself.

She knocked over the pitcher of sweetened cream, felt the stickiness, and then her fingers were in one of the leftover tortes. She'd know that texture anywhere. Just as she knew who her attacker had to be. She frantically tried to write the first letter of his name in the surface of the torte as she was dragged backward.

She felt her body go limp from whatever drug she'd been given. The last she remembered was the dark alley and the slamming of a car door.

LIGHTS GLOWED BEHIND the old barn on the McAllister place as Sheriff Carter Jackson pulled up.

He'd seen a lot of crime scenes, but this one struck

him as more than a little unusual given that the killer had simply dropped the murder weapon beside the body.

"Wrap that shovel carefully," Carter ordered. "I want to check it right away for fingerprints." He glanced at the barn wall and Glen Whitaker's vehicle. There were footprints in the soft dirt—Glen's boots and a smaller shoe. The killer's? If so, the killer had very small feet—small enough to be a woman's.

Carter noted the uneven ground between the vehicle and the barn. On closer inspection he saw where someone had laid a hand on the outside of the car for balance. "Get the prints off here, as well. I'll take them in myself." He turned to see his deputy waiting with a small camera bag. "Let's see those photographs."

Carter took the digital camera back to his patrol car and turned it on. Instantly he saw that the camera was indeed Glen Whitaker's. There were numerous shots of Alice Miller's ninetieth birthday party and shots of Alyson Banning Donovan's funeral.

He flipped through them quickly, anxious to see the last photographs that Glen had taken, hoping there would be a clue as to who killed him. Like the camera, Glen's vehicle had been hidden behind the barn. Also, given where Glen's body had been found, it followed to reason Glen himself had been hiding back there. But why?

Carter was disappointed when he reached the end of the photographs. There was nothing before the funeral. He swore and went back through the photographs, stopping on an image of a woman in the background at the funeral.

There were several more photographs of the woman. Glen had zoomed in on her, snapping a shot as the woman made what appeared to be a hurried getaway. Why was that?

Carter had never seen the woman before.

So what was Glen's interest in her?

The last shot at the funeral was of Spencer. He seemed to be going after the mystery woman.

A deputy tapped on the window. "I have those prints ready for you to take."

Carter raced back to town with the prints and the photographs. While he ran the prints, he called Mark Sanders and asked him to stop by.

"I've never seen the woman before," Sanders said. "I have no idea why Glen would have taken shots of her."

"She and Spencer Donovan were the last people photographed before Glen Whitaker was murdered," he told the newspaperman.

BRIDGER GLANCED BACK toward the kitchen, disappointed Laci hadn't joined him. Darn the woman. It was just like her to think it would steal his thunder.

The night had been an unmitigated success. He couldn't believe it. He felt as if he were floating on air. His own restaurant.

But tonight would have meant nothing without Laci. And now that it was almost over, all he wanted to do was share the rest of the night with her.

Earlier, he'd seen the expression on her face when he'd offered her the partnership in Northern Lights. He'd thought she would be pleased. But she'd seemed disappointed. He hoped he could explain later, explain what he was really offering her.

Most of the guests were leaving. He said his goodbyes. As he pushed open the doors to the kitchen, he was shocked and disappointed to see that the room was empty. No Laci.

The back door was partially ajar. He went to it and looked out. The alley was also empty. Upstairs, he called for her, but she wasn't anywhere around.

Back in the kitchen, he started to worry. She'd left without saying goodbye? She must have been more hurt than he'd thought. Sometimes he was such a fool.

He turned and glanced back at the kitchen. One of her chocolate tortes was sitting on the edge of the counter. Something looked odd about it.

He stepped to the torte and let out a curse when he saw that someone had ruined the smooth surface.

Who would do such a thing? Laci? Had she left mad?

But as he stared down at the torte he saw that the marred surface was in the shape of a letter. An *S*.

His heart began to pound harder as he looked around and noticed that Laci had left her purse and her car keys in the cupboard where she'd put them earlier in case she had to run out and get any last-minute items.

She couldn't have left without them. Then where was she?

As he started to step toward the back door again, the sole of his shoe stuck to the floor. Something sticky had been spilled there.

He reached down and felt the white, sticky substance, then stood and checked the counter. There'd been some clotted cream in a container next to the last torte when he'd gone out to bid the guests a good-night.

The container was empty, the cream drying on one side where it had been spilled.

That's when he noticed that the cupboard by the back door was ajar. He stepped to it, fear rising in his chest as he pulled open the door. At first nothing looked out of place. Then he saw that the box of matches he kept next to the emergency candles was gone.

What the hell had happened back here after he'd left?

He looked back toward the spilled cream and saw the marks where something had been dragged across the cream-sticky floor.

The sight set his heart racing.

The drag marks led out the back door and into the dark alley.

Bridger was reaching for his cell phone to call the sheriff when he looked up and saw a figure silhouetted in the kitchen doorway. *"Spencer?"*

CHAPTER THIRTEEN

"WHERE'S LACI?" BRIDGER DEMANDED, snapping shut the phone to launch himself at Spencer. He grabbed him by the collar, driving him back into the wall. "Where the hell is she? If anything has happened to her—"

"I swear to you I haven't done anything to her," Spencer cried, his eyes wide, terrified. "You have to believe me."

"I'm through believing you. I should have listened to Laci. She tried to warn me. She told me about the damned roses you were leaving her." He tightened his grip on Spencer, seeing the fear in his eyes, a fear much deeper than what Bridger might do to him.

Bridger stepped back and looked at him, seeing how disheveled he was, how unnerved. "What the hell is going on?"

"I warned Laci," Spencer cried, his voice breaking. "I told her to quit snooping around in my past. I knew this was going to happen. That's why I came back."

Bridger stared at Spencer, his heart thundering in his chest, his blood roaring in his ears. "What are you talking about?"

"She's not dead."

The words rocked Bridger back on his heels. "She better not be dead."

"Not Laci. Emma."

"Emma?" Spencer was talking nonsense. Was he drunk again? "Emma Shane?"

"She's not dead," Spencer repeated.

"That's crazy. We saw her in the house right before it blew up."

Spencer was shaking his head, his face still chalky, beads of sweat breaking out on his forehead. "I'm telling you, she didn't die in the fire. I've *seen* her. I couldn't tell anyone because I knew they'd think I was crazy, but I saw her at the reception."

Bridger stared at him openmouthed. "Your *wedding* reception?"

"That had to be the look Laci said she saw. I just glanced up and there Emma was. But then I blinked and she wasn't there and I thought I just imagined her." Spencer put his face in his hands for a moment before looking up at Bridger again. "It wasn't the first time. I've seen her before. I thought it was just the nightmares. You remember the horrible nightmares I had after..." He rushed on, the words tumbling out. "She looks different. Her hair is long and sometimes it's dark brown and other times it's blond or red or—"

"You've lost your mind," Bridger said, grabbing him again. Spencer was crazy. It was the only explanation. "You're the one who took Laci. She left an *S* in the top of the torte as you were dragging her out. Now what the hell did you do with her?"

"It wasn't me," he managed to rasp. "I swear to you. It was Emma." His eyes locked with Bridger's. "She drowned

Alyson and killed the others. I know that now. When Laci told me about the yellow roses..." He broke down.

Bridger let go of him, remembering what Laci had told him about the other women in Spencer's life. Spencer was much sicker than Bridger could have imagined. "You need help."

"See?" Spencer said, his voice breaking. "This is why I didn't tell anyone about her." His face crumbled. "Don't you see, if she's been leaving Laci yellow roses, then Laci is next."

Bridger's blood ran cold. "What do you mean *next*?"

"Emma's going to kill her—just like the others."

LACI WOKE, HEAD ACHING, sick to her stomach. The car rocked on what felt like a gravel road. She tried to sit up and felt her head swoon.

Where was she? She couldn't remember anything.

Her eyes blinked open, then closed, her lids too heavy to keep open. She tried again and saw that she was in the back seat of a car that was speeding along a gravel road. Her hands and feet were bound with duct tape, and there was a French Canadian station on the radio.

She felt groggy as she pushed herself up until she could see that she was in a large SUV. A woman with long, dark hair was driving. Past her was nothing but darkness, the SUV's headlights cutting a golden swath into it.

"Oh, dear," said the driver, glancing in the rearview mirror. "She's awake."

Before Laci could react, the woman swiveled in the driver's seat and jabbed a syringe into her arm.

"You really need your rest, dear," Laci heard the

woman say as the car swerved and Laci tumbled to the floorboard behind the front seats.

In an instant she felt the drug coursing through her veins. The rear of the car blurred. She struggled to get up, but she no longer had control of her limbs. Her body seemed to website. She fought to try to keep her eyes open, but it was a losing battle—one she lost quickly.

BRIDGER TRIED NOT to panic. Laci couldn't have been gone long. If Spencer had taken her, then he couldn't have taken her far. And Bridger had to believe that was the case given that Emma Shane was dead—and Laci had left an *S* shape in the top of the torte as she was being dragged out of the kitchen.

"Where is your car?" Bridger demanded as he opened the safe he kept under the kitchen counter and took out the .357 Magnum along with a box of cartridges.

"Out front, but Laci isn't—" Spencer looked from the gun to Bridger, then lurched into the bathroom. Bridger heard him retching, then keening like a wounded animal. Bridger waited, then opened the door and dragged Spencer out, wondering what had happened to that older boy who, in an act of heroism, had saved Bridger's life that day in the creek.

"Come on, we're going to find her. You're going to take me to her."

"If you want to find Laci, if you want to save her, you have to believe me. Emma has her." He looked as if he might break down again. "I don't know what she plans to do with her. I swear."

Spencer looked terrified and confused. Dead or alive, Emma Shane had been haunting him for years. Bridger thought of the bad luck Spencer had experienced with women over the years. As Laci had said, no one had that much bad luck. Crazy or not, Spencer was Bridger's only hope of finding Laci and saving her. If it wasn't too late.

"Emma can't be caught. Or stopped," Spencer said in a small voice.

"Like hell," Bridger snapped. "Because you're going to help me find her." But even as he said it, he thought of the big open country of this part of Montana. Laci could be anywhere. Was he really starting to believe that Spencer might be telling the truth?

Bridger reached for Spencer, afraid of what he might do to him but stopped as he caught sight of the cupboard that he'd found open earlier. The only thing missing, he remembered, was a large box of matches.

His heart leaped to his throat. "Fire. Oh, God. I think I know where Laci is," he said as he grabbed hold of Spencer and shoved him toward the door.

THE COMPUTER SCREEN on Sheriff Carter Jackson's desk flashed. He stared at what came up, blinking in disbelief, then shock. The prints matched. He had his killer.

But this couldn't be right. According to the fingerprint analysis, the print taken from the side of Glen Whitaker's vehicle belonged to a woman who'd been dead for twenty years.

Maybe even stranger, the name sounded familiar.

Emma Shane.

It came to him in a rush. Emma Shane, the woman who'd killed herself and her family after Spencer Donovan had broken up with her in high school.

Emma Shane was *alive*?

He sat for a moment, trying to understand what this meant. Emma Shane must have seen Glen Whitaker taking her photograph at the cemetery and followed him out to the old McAllister place. Who knew what Glen might have been doing out there.

So she kills him—but doesn't find the camera with the photographs.

But what was she doing in Old Town Whitehorse to start with? Spencer. Spencer had gone after the woman in the photograph Glen had taken. Spencer knew she was alive.

Carter leaned back in his chair, trying to make sense of this. If Emma Shane was alive and she'd killed Glen to keep her secret—

Laci. Laci had been doing her own investigating. Who knew what she might have turned up by now? Was it possible she'd found out that Emma Shane was alive and doing…what?

Carter sucked in a breath as an answer came to him.

Killing people.

He grabbed his hat and keys and drove over to Duvall's restaurant, only to find the place empty. Laci's car was there, but no sign of Duvall's pickup—or Duvall.

What worried him was that the restaurant door was unlocked, the lights still on. It looked as if they'd left in a hurry.

As Carter was leaving, he noticed that something sticky had been spilled on the kitchen floor.

His concern increased measurably. Getting on his radio in his patrol car, he put out a call to all law enforcement to pull Duvall over if sighted. Also Laci Cavanaugh.

The radio squawked the moment he put it down.

"It's Bridger Duvall."

"Patch him through," the sheriff said, already fearing what he was going to hear.

"Laci's missing. I have Spencer and we're headed for Old Town. He swears he had nothing to do with this—"

"Bridger, we found Glen Whitaker murdered behind the barn on the old McAllister place. It looks as if Emma Shane killed him."

Bridger swore. "I'm on my way to Laci's house. I have a bad feeling—"

"I'm right behind you," the sheriff said as he turned on his siren and sped toward Old Town Whitehorse.

BRIDGER DROVE TOO fast, his mind racing, his heart lodged in his throat. He tried not to think about how much of a head start Emma had on them. Or that he might be wrong about where Laci had been taken. That Emma had another plan for Laci, something even more diabolical.

Spencer sat in the passenger seat of his pickup looking shell-shocked. He hadn't said a word since Bridger had told him what the sheriff had said.

Emma Shane was alive.

Outside the pickup, the night blew past. The road south ran through open country, the sky as starless as the land was treeless.

As he came over a hill, his headlights caught on the old Whitehorse city-limits sign. It was so weathered and worn he could barely make out the lettering. The sign listed to the right, its base surrounded by tumbleweeds.

Bridger blew through Old Town, taking the curve by the old Cherry house hard. Just a little farther. He raced toward the dark horizon and Laci's house just over the next few hills, praying he wouldn't be too late.

As he came over the last rise, he stared in the direction of Laci's house, holding his breath. No orange glow. No flames shooting upward in the sky. He felt weak with relief.

He remembered the day he'd followed the smell of the smoke to Emma's house. He'd been several blocks away when he'd heard the crackle of the flames devouring the dry wooden structure. He'd never forgotten that sound mingled with the shriek of sirens and, closer, the cries of neighbors.

Spencer said he'd seen Emma standing at a second-floor window, backlit by flames, when the propane tank next door had exploded and the house had disintegrated before their eyes.

"How is it possible Emma is alive?" Spencer said next to him.

Bridger glanced over at him, seeing the terror in his eyes. For twenty years Spencer had lived with Emma's ghost. He must have thought himself insane. Even now he didn't want to believe she was alive. Neither did Bridger, because he was certain she had Laci.

Bridger turned down the road to Laci's house, careening into the yard and jumping out of the pickup.

He ran up the steps of the porch, realizing that there was no car in the yard. No one was here. Behind him, he heard Spencer get out of the pickup.

There was a small light burning at the back of the house. As he ran into the living room, he noticed that nothing seemed out of place—not like the time he'd found Laci here and the place ransacked.

In fact, the house looked so normal his heart sank. He *had* guessed wrong about where Laci had been taken. It didn't appear that a criminally insane woman had kidnapped her and brought her here.

But as he raced into the kitchen, he caught the glint of chrome through the back window. There was a car parked out behind the house.

He turned and ran for the stairs, remembering what Spencer had said about seeing Emma standing in the upstairs window of her house just before the explosion.

He hadn't gone far up the stairs when he smelled the nostril-burning reek of gasoline and heard a sickening thud overhead.

LACI'S EYES FLUTTERED as she hit the floor and came to. She looked up, trying to focus not only her eyes but also her brain.

Where was she? Her bedroom? That made no sense. How had she gotten here? She couldn't remember anything but feeling sick.

Her eyes focused on a point over her. A woman's face came into view. The woman looked vaguely familiar.

But what was the woman doing here? And what was that smell? Laci wrinkled her nose and tried to sit up. The woman had a smile on her face, but something definitely wasn't right.

Laci couldn't remember anything for a moment except getting ready for opening night at the restaurant. But now she was home, in her bedroom?

Suddenly a chunk of memory dropped into place. Spencer! He'd grabbed her from behind at the restaurant and dragged her out.

"Where is he?" Laci asked, her voice scratchy. What had he covered her mouth with? Something that had left her tongue cottony. Her arm was sore. She had a vague memory of someone giving her a shot, but it was all jumbled in her aching head. "Where is Spencer?"

"Don't worry about Spencer," she said. "You don't have to concern yourself with him anymore."

Was it possible this woman had saved her? It's the only thing that made sense. "Have we met before?"

"We've seen each other around. We spoke at the wedding."

The brunette who'd been standing by the back door of the community center as Laci had run out. She remembered her now.

"How did I get here?" Laci asked, feeling as if her head was full of cobwebs. She remembered being grabbed at the restaurant, but everything else was a jumble.

"You don't remember the drive out?"

Laci shook her head and stopped at once, feeling nauseous.

"I brought you up here." The woman was looking at her strangely, studying her appraisingly. "I had to take care of you."

"After Spencer kidnapped me at the restaurant."

The woman smiled. "Yes, Spencer. It's a good thing I've been watching out for you."

A ripple of worry washed over Laci. "You've been watching me?" She remembered feeling as if she was being watched down in Roundup, but that couldn't be what the woman was talking about.

She reached up to rub her hand over her face and saw her wrists were chafed from being taped together. She frowned, trying to remember Spencer doing that.

"I always watch out for the women Spencer gets involved with," the woman said, making Laci look up in surprise.

"I'm not involved with Spencer," Laci said with a frown.

"Aren't you? Has a day gone by that you haven't thought about him? That you haven't tried to find out things about him?" The woman's voice became strident. "That you haven't kept digging and digging, even when he'd left town?"

Her chest constricted. "How do you know Spencer?"

"Spencer and I go way back." The brunette smiled as she picked up a red can from the floor that Laci hadn't noticed before. Laci caught the strong odor of gasoline. "I'm the woman he killed twenty years ago."

Laci stared at the woman, comprehension coming slowly.

"That's right," the woman said with a laugh as she read Laci's expression. "I'm Emma Shane." With that, she poured the contents of the can onto Laci.

Laci let out a shriek as the cold, foul-smelling fuel soaked her to the skin. She tried to get away but couldn't, her muscles refusing to work.

"Why are you doing this?" Laci cried as the gas fumes burned her eyes.

"Making sure Spencer suffers as much as I have," the woman said, putting down the fuel can and pulling a large box of wooden matches from her jacket pocket. She cocked her heard as she heard what Laci did. Footfalls on the stairs.

"Help!" Laci called. "Help!"

The woman smiled as she took out a cigarette and struck a match, the flame glowing brightly.

BRIDGER RACED UP the stairs, the .357 Magnum clutched in his hand, the stench of gasoline growing stronger and stronger.

He was almost to the top when he heard Laci call for help.

"We're up here. In Laci's room," a female voice said. "You're just in time."

Behind him, Bridger heard Spencer coming up the stairs.

At the end of the hallway, Bridger aimed the weapon into the room as he came around the open doorway.

He froze at the sight of Laci huddled on the floor, soaking wet, the room reeking of gasoline and a woman with long, dark hair standing over her, holding a lit match to the end of her cigarette.

He took in the scene, his heart in his throat.

Emma Shane. He could see that she'd had reconstructive surgery. But the eyes were the same, and enough of her facial features were intact that there was no doubt who he was looking at.

"Hello, Bridger," she said, smiling as she blew out the match and took a puff on her cigarette, sounding as if they were meeting over cocktails at a party. "It's been a long time."

Not nearly long enough, he thought.

He shifted his gaze to Laci, wanting desperately to tell her not to worry, everything was going to be all right.

But he knew better. All Emma had to do was drop that cigarette and this room would explode, going up in a flash of flames. Bridger knew he would never be able to get to Laci in time.

He looked into her wide blue eyes. "It's okay, Laci."

Her gaze said she knew better, but she wasn't going to argue the point. He saw her try to move her limbs and wondered what Emma had done to her.

"Emma."

Bridger turned at the sound of Spencer's voice next to him.

Spencer stepped past him and into the room. Bridger reached for him but couldn't stop him.

Emma's smile slipped at the sight of Spencer. "Don't come any closer," she said, holding the cigarette over Laci. "You wouldn't want another woman to suffer because of you, now would you, Spencer?"

Spencer stopped and Bridger stepped up beside him, afraid of what Spencer might do. He wasn't himself. But then, Bridger suspected he hadn't been for some time.

"What's going on, Emma?" Bridger tried to keep the panic out of his voice.

"It has to end here tonight," she said, sounding tired. "I can't do this anymore."

"Don't do it now," Bridger said. "Spencer isn't worth it."

Emma smiled ruefully. "So you finally figured that out. All these years he let you think he jumped into that creek to save you. But I saw the whole thing. Spencer fell in. He didn't mean to save you. He was only trying to save himself."

Bridger glanced over at Spencer. He looked like a sleepwalker, dazed, disconnected.

"Did he tell you that I was pregnant?" Emma asked. "That was why Spencer broke up with me. My father would have killed me if he'd found out, not to mention the disgrace in a small town like Roundup. Spencer used me, then discarded me. He ruined my life—and I've spent the last twenty years ruining his."

LACI SHIFTED ON the floor. She could feel her limbs again but feared her muscles would fail her if she tried anything. But she couldn't just sit here.

She could hear the desperation and desolation in Emma Shane's voice. This was where it would end—and end badly. She tried to move her body a little more, working not to draw attention to the movement. Emma was focused on Spencer and Bridger, but as the cigarette burned down, Laci knew time was also running out.

And if Bridger tried to get to her before Emma dropped the cigarette, he would be caught in the flames, as well.

"You should leave," Laci said from the floor. "Both of you just get out of here."

"No," Emma snapped. "They have to stay. I want them to see this. I planned this ending. That's why I took the matches and left the cupboard open. If you hadn't figured out where I'd taken Laci, I would have called to tell you. I want Spencer to suffer the way he made me suffer."

Spencer looked as if he was suffering. "You killed them."

Emma laughed. "Did you think you just had bad luck when it came to women? You always were a fool."

The words fell over Laci. Even with her mind still foggy, she understood. Emma had killed the women in Spencer's life. Emma had killed Alyson.

She felt a bolt of adrenaline shoot through her. She pressed her palms to the floor as she slipped her feet back. Her legs felt too weak, but in her fury she forced her feet under her. Emma must have heard her as Laci shoved herself to her feet. She slammed into Emma, driving her forward toward Spencer and Bridger.

Spencer seemed to come out of his trance as Laci suddenly shot to her feet. He lunged for the gun in

THE MYSTERY MAN OF WHITEHORSE

Bridger's hand. A shot boomed as Bridger shoved him aside and grabbed for Emma and the glowing cigarette.

It all happened in an instant. Bridger grabbed Emma's hand holding the cigarette and twisted cruelly. Emma screamed in pain as he ripped it from her fingers and shoved her aside to reach for Laci.

Everything seemed to stop as Bridger dragged Laci out, extinguishing the cigarette before wrapping her shivering body in his arms.

As he glanced back into the room, he saw Emma's face, the smile on her lips, as she struck a match. Spencer charged the woman in a rage. Just as he reached her, Emma dropped the lit match. It hit the floor just as Spencer barreled into her, driving her back into the gas-soaked corner of the room.

Emma's smile broadened as she wrapped her arms around Spencer, taking him down with her as the room exploded into a blaze of fire.

Bridger swept Laci, still soaked in gas, down the stairs and out into the cold December night. Behind them, the whole house went up, lighting the night as sirens wailed in the distance.

Laci stood under the hot spray of the shower. Bridger had stripped off her gas-soaked clothing and his own and climbed into the shower with her, holding her trembling body.

She thought she would never be warm again. The last thing she remembered before the ride into Whitehorse to his apartment over the restaurant was looking back to see the house in flames. She'd closed her eyes at the thought of Emma and Spencer in there, their arms wrapped around each other like lovers as flames devoured them.

"I'm so sorry," Bridger whispered as he gently soaped the gas from her skin. "If I'd just listened to you..."

She touched a finger to his lips and shook her head. "I was wrong about Spencer."

"We were both wrong about Spencer." She heard the bitterness in his voice, the pain. "He knew about Emma, but in his fear and his guilt he did nothing."

"Did he know? Or was he like the rest of us, hoping that he was wrong, hoping he could find happiness?" She shook her head. "We're all weak. We're all afraid."

Bridger smiled down at her. "Not you Cavanaugh women," he said. "You're the strongest woman I know."

Laci wrapped her arms around Bridger, pressing her cheek against his solid chest. She cried for Alyson, for Tiff. For any others who had suffered because of Emma's pain.

Bridger held her, smoothing her hair as the water beat down on them. Laci wondered if anything could wash away the stench of gasoline on her skin. Or the memory of Spencer and Emma engulfed in flames.

It would take time. The house was gone, completely destroyed. The flames had taken not just the house, but any memories of a life her mother and father had had there before her father was killed, her mother abandoning the house and her daughters.

Laci knew her grandfather Titus would take it the hardest. He must have thought that as long as the house stood waiting there was hope that his daughter Geneva would return to it.

Laci held out no such hope. She feared that whoever had sent the notes knew the truth: her mother had never left Whitehorse. Just as the photo album with Laci's and Laney's snapshots hadn't left. Would she ever know the truth? She doubted it. Some mysteries were never solved.

Gramma Pearl always said there was a little good hidden in the bad, something to ease the pain. Laci leaned into Bridger and let him ease the pain.

CHAPTER FOURTEEN

Laci looked up as a gust of wind and the sharp, sweet scent of pine filled the front door of the restaurant.

Bridger burst in with the biggest Christmas tree she'd ever seen. "Thank the lucky stars that the ceilings in this apartment are ten-footers," he said, laughing. "I saw this tree and knew it was The One."

She couldn't help but smile as he stood the huge tree. It was magnificent.

"I know what you're thinking," Bridger was saying. "How will we ever be able to decorate such a large tree, right?"

"It did cross my mind."

He grinned, and she heard voices coming through the kitchen. She gave Bridger a questioning look as he leaned toward her and gave her a quick kiss.

Her heart leaped and her eyes blurred with tears as she heard her sister's laugh just before Laney burst through the kitchen door into the restaurant, holding an armful of Christmas decorations. Behind her was Nick, her husband and Whitehorse's newest deputy, with more decorations. They'd changed their plans and come home for Christmas, inviting all his relatives to Montana for the holidays instead.

Their grandfather Titus came in pushing Gramma Pearl in a wheelchair. Pearl cradled a bottle of champagne in her lap and gave Laci a half smile, eyes twinkling.

Behind them were the Bailey girls—Eve, McKenna and Faith—and Sheriff Carter Jackson and his older brother Cade.

Laci was surprised to see Cade. She knew he usually spent the holidays out at his cabin near Sleeping Buffalo. Christmas had been hard on him since his wife was killed in a car accident on Christmas Eve six years ago.

They were all laughing and brushing snow from their coats as they put down the Christmas tree decorations they'd brought.

Laci hugged each and every one of them, kneeling down to take the champagne from her grandmother and plant a kiss on her cool, dry cheek. She was doing so much better, and Laci saw in her eyes happiness at being here.

"I have Christmas cookies!" Laci announced. She'd almost forgotten that she'd made the cookies before the grand opening of the restaurant.

While the men put up the tree, Laney came into the kitchen with Laci.

"How are you?" her sister asked, giving her a hug.

"I'm okay," Laci said. "I'm sick about the house, though. Is Gramps all right?"

Laney smiled and nodded. "I think he's relieved. He was talking on the way here about giving us each a piece of the ranch so we can build our own houses. Not too close but close enough our kids can play together."

"Our kids?" Laci laughed, then saw her sister's expression. "Oh, Laney, you're pregnant?"

Her sister nodded through her tears. "I just found out. Did I mention that twins run in Nick's family?"

Laci hugged her. "I'm going to be an aunt."

"So tell me about Bridger," Laney said.

And she did.

"You're in love with him," her sister said when she'd finished.

Laci nodded.

"And how does he feel about you?"

"Well…" How did he feel about her? "He gave me half of the restaurant as an early Christmas present."

Laney must have heard the disappointment in her voice. "Eve told me why he was here in Whitehorse. I asked Gramps about the sewing circle. I couldn't tell if he knew what Gramma had been up to or not. But he definitely doesn't know any details. I'm sorry."

"It's all right. I just wonder if Bridger will ever be happy until he finds out the truth about his birth," Laci said.

They took the cookies and glasses for the champagne out front and watched as the group finished decorating the tree.

"I saved the best part for you," Bridger said and handed her a beautiful glittering angel. He swept her up, lifting her so she could put the angel on top of the tree.

"Someone get the lights," Titus called. The room went dark.

Bridger's gaze locked with Laci's as he plugged in the tree. An array of colored lights flashed on, the tree glittering with ornaments. It was met with a chorus of oohs and aahs.

"It's beautiful," Laci sighed as she smiled at Bridger. "Thank you." She knew she was thanking him for more than the tree. He'd brought everyone together here today knowing how much she needed her family and friends.

"There's more," he said softly as he stepped to her. In the glow of the lights from the tree, he reached into his pocket and came out with a small jewelry box.

"The second part of your Christmas present," he said. "I can't wait until Christmas."

Her eyes widened in surprise as he opened the box to reveal a breathtaking diamond engagement ring.

She began to cry as he knelt down on one knee and said, "Laci Cavanaugh, I want you to be more than my partner in this restaurant. I want you to be my partner in life. Will you marry me?"

She couldn't breathe. For maybe the first time in her life she was speechless. She looked around the room at the faces of the people she loved. Christmas music played on the radio in the kitchen, and on Main Street she heard sleigh bells and children laughing.

She couldn't have envisioned a happier scene as she looked into Bridger's dark eyes and felt as if everything that had happened had been leading to this moment. Hadn't she always believed in destiny? Well, she did now.

"Yes," she finally managed to say, her voice cracking. "Oh, yes."

And then she was in his arms. Everyone was cheering and laughing. Her grandfather popped the champagne and someone turned up the radio.

"Silent Night" was playing. They stood, champagne glasses raised, Bridger's arm around Laci, and all sang as the lights on the Christmas tree glowed as warm as her heart.

"Merry Christmas," Bridger whispered.

"Merry Christmas."

EPILOGUE

As CHRISTMAS DAY APPROACHED, it continued to snow. Huge white flakes drifted lazily down from the heavens. The Christmas lights came on in the park. Everywhere there were people on the main street, shopping, and carols playing on the radio.

A new year was approaching. It would be a time of joy and sorrow.

Pearl Cavanaugh was doing much better, but while she attempted to speak, the words were unintelligible. But given her determination, Laci and Laney had no doubt that their grandmother would recover her speech.

Eve and Bridger held out hope that eventually they would know about their births and might even find their birth mother.

Carter was still waiting for an ID on the male body found at the old Cherry house. In the meantime, he'd set up a sting operation to find out who was selling drugs down in Old Town Whitehorse.

A kind of peace hung over Whitehorse as the snow fell and shoppers scurried along the street with brightly lit windows. A sense of hope that the future held promise, that all the bad times were behind the community.

At the state mental hospital, a patient on the criminally insane ward blinked and focused on the nurse's face in front of her.

"Doctor!" the nurse called.

"Where am I?" the female patient cried, looking around wildly, fear apparent in eyes that had been blank and unseeing for months.

"Easy," the doctor said, coming into the room and to her bedside. "Do you know your name?"

She nodded slowly. "Violet Evans."

The doctor smiled. "That's a place to start, Miss Evans."

"But what am I doing here?" Violet asked tearfully. "Have I been injured? Was I sick?"

"Let's just take it easy, all right. You've been sick. I'll tell you everything. All in good time."

Violet nodded and leaned back. He was right about one thing: it was just a matter of time. A matter of time before she got out of here.

Wouldn't everyone in Whitehorse and Old Town be surprised to see her back? she thought as she smiled weakly up at the doctor.

"Tell me I'm going to be all right," she whispered.

"I think you're going to be just fine, Violet Evans. You have the rest of your life ahead of you."

Unlike some of the residents of Whitehorse, she thought with a smile.

* * * * *

We hope you enjoyed reading

DARK HORSE & THE MYSTERY MAN OF WHITEHORSE

by *New York Times* bestselling author
B.J. DANIELS

HARLEQUIN®

INTRIGUE

EDGE-OF-YOUR-SEAT INTRIGUE,
FEARLESS ROMANCE.

"He's going to want to kill me—and you," she'd told
Ledger before he left. "I shouldn't have involved you in
this. I'm so sorry."

"Hey," he'd said, lifting her chin with his warm fingers
until their gazes met. "I've been involved since the day I
fell in love with you all those years ago. I couldn't let go.
I know I should have, but once I saw how he was treating
you..."

"That's why you need to be careful. Give him time to
cool down."

She had smiled at the man she'd loved for as far back
as she could remember. So many times she'd regretted
her hasty marriage to Wade. She knew now that Ledger
would never have cheated on her. But back then she'd
had her mother and Wade telling her different. She'd
been afraid that the reason Ledger had put off marriage
was because he didn't love her enough.

When she'd seen the photos of Ledger with some other woman at college…

She knew now that Ledger and the woman had just been friends. Her mother had wanted her with Wade for her own selfish reasons.

"I've made such a mess of things," she'd said, hating that she sounded near tears. She'd cried way too long over Wade and the mistake she'd made.

Ledger had cupped her cheek. "It's nothing that can't be rectified. I just want you to be sure of what you want to do now. I don't want to talk you into anything. Whatever you do, it has to be your decision. So maybe you should take this time to—"

"I've already filed papers to begin divorcing Wade. He knows it's over. I'd kicked him out of the house and I had packed up my things and moved them into the apartment in town. I guess I'd gone back to the house for something. I didn't expect him to be there…"

"That's all behind you, then." He'd leaned down and given her a gentle kiss. She'd wanted to pull him to her and kiss him the way she'd often dreamed—and felt guilty about. But it was too soon.

She'd jumped into a bad marriage. If she and Ledger had a future…

Don't miss
DEAD RINGER,
available September 2017 wherever
Harlequin® Intrigue books and ebooks are sold.

www.Harlequin.com

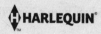
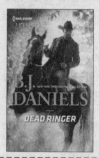

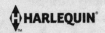
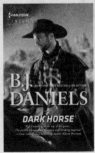  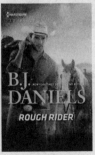

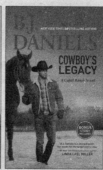

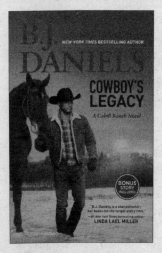

Reward the book lover in you!

Earn points from all your Harlequin book purchases from wherever you shop.

Turn your points into *FREE BOOKS* of your choice
OR
EXCLUSIVE GIFTS from your favorite authors or series.

Join for FREE today at
www.HarlequinMyRewards.com.

Harlequin My Rewards is a free program (no fees) without any commitments or obligations.

MYR17